HAVEN

A LOWTOWN NOVEL

Lindsay J. Pryor

piatkus

PIATKUS

First published in Great Britain in 2017 by Piatkus

1 3 5 7 9 10 8 6 4 2

A CIP catalogue record for this book
is available from the British Library.

ISBN 978-0-349-41697-7

Typeset in Goudy by M Rules
Printed and bound in Great Britain by
Clays Ltd, St Ives plc

Papers used by Piatkus are from well-managed forests
and other responsible sources.

MIX
Paper from
responsible sources
FSC® C104740

Piatkus
An imprint of
Little, Brown Book Group
Carmelite House
50 Victoria Embankment
London EC4Y 0DZ

An Hachette UK Company
www.hachette.co.uk

www.littlebrown.co.uk

For Moth

CHAPTER ONE

It was her chance to escape. Her one and only chance.

Ember stood on the far side of the room, its vastness exacerbated by the high ceiling. Thirty feet away, four panel members faced her from behind their lengthy table.

Whilst waiting outside, she'd convinced herself she'd look each of them in the eyes. Instead, her gaze fixated on the solitary, empty, plastic chair that was strategically placed ten feet away from them.

It had been less than ten minutes since the last applicant had been dragged out of there yelling and thrashing. Two security guards had come bounding up the polished corridor to join the two already forcing him out. Eventually they'd taken an arm and a leg each as his curses had continued to ricochet around the clinical, vacuous space, all the way to the exit.

'You have no right to judge me!' he'd yelled. 'This system is beyond contempt! It's the children that suffer. My children who are suffering. You're condemning them. You're condemning them all!'

To her shame, she'd lowered her head. The two other people who'd also been sat waiting for their turn outside had done exactly the same. There was no fighting the system. There was no escaping the societal prison that bound those who were bottom of the ladder, except by doing exactly what she was doing then: try to get out of Lowtown and start a better life across the border in Midtown.

'Our next applicant is Ember Challice,' one of the male panellists announced. Artificial light glinted off the delicate, silver-rimmed glasses that perched on the edge of his nose as he lowered his head to examine the paperwork neatly piled in front of him, paperwork he casually flicked through with his chubby fingers.

The other three panellists – two women and another man – remained silent, as Ember shifted under the weight of their unwavering scrutiny.

'Take a seat, Ms Challice,' the spectacled man said, indicating the empty chair without yet granting her the courtesy of eye contact.

Ember sat down, interlaced her fingers and rested her clasped hands in her lap. She kept her feet together and firmly on the floor, her thighs straining under the pressure of her attempt to stop them from trembling.

'Thirty-one years of age,' the spectacled man continued. 'Single. No dependants. No family. She has secured sufficient finances to fund her rent for basic premises in Midtown for the minimum requirement of the twelve-month trial period. This has been acquired through savings from her full-time work as a waitress and deputy manager at a café in Lowtown, wherein she has performed consistently for the past fifteen years. Five sick days have been registered showing good overall health.

'She will be actively seeking work in the service industry

on arrival in Midtown but has also secured a provisional place at Midtown College having passed all necessary entry examinations and aptitude tests. In fact, she *exceeded* all entry examinations and aptitude tests,' he added, his surprise evident in his tone. 'She will fund the first year of her studies through the sale of a small apartment she owns in Lowtown, which has been in the family name for a considerable length of time. Beyond those twelve months, she's planning to maintain part-time employment to continue to fund her studies.

'Ms Challice passed all three detailed medical examinations as well as the mental health evaluations. There is only one outstanding query, which we will come to shortly.'

Ember's heart skipped a beat. There was no way of them knowing. No way of anyone knowing her secret – and certainly not from any kind of medical examination. *Unless* there was something she didn't know.

'She has no criminal record or any marks against her regarding social disorder. She has no proven links to the third species community – vampire, lycan or any other kind of non-human.' He flipped through a few more pages. 'She was brought up by her aunt, the sole sister of her mother Rhona Challice, the latter having died from an accident when Ember was five years old.'

Ember clenched her interlaced hands at the use of the word 'accident'.

'Authority records report the accident occurred while Ms Challice senior was trying to prevent her son, Ember's twin brother, from being snatched from their home,' he continued. 'He was never found. Records show her father had absconded before she was born. Her aunt, her last remaining relative, died three years ago. Terminal illness. Ember lived with her and cared for her up until that point.'

Ember remained focused on retaining her composure as they

continued to clinically highlight the most personal aspects of her life as if she wasn't there. But this was the process. This is what had to be done. Any indication of protest or indignation would lead to what she had witnessed less than twenty minutes before.

'It is her aunt's apartment, Ms Challice's current home,' he continued. 'Which she'll be selling to fund the first year of her studies.'

The panellist removed his glasses and placed them neatly on the paperwork in front of him before finally making eye contact. 'Congratulations on getting this far in the process, Ms Challice. I'm sure you are aware that very few applicants make it to this point.'

She knew it only too well. It had taken her ten years. The first seven years had been about saving up enough money to meet the basic financial entry point. Most failed at that first hurdle.

Stage two had consisted of three years of aptitude tests, personality tests, morality tests, medical examinations, lie-detector tests, detailed explorations into both her work and social ethic and also her family background. If the conspiracy theories were to be believed, passing stage two was fraught with corruption. As such, many had either been rejected or had given up by now; the system was set up to make applicants fail. There was no appeal process.

For the very few who made it through, there was stage three. *This* stage.

'I am,' she said as calmly as she could, despite still balancing on a knife-edge as she awaited the query that could bring all her hopes crashing down around her. She couldn't fail now. She'd made a promise. The very last promise she'd made her aunt.

'You're aware that this meeting constitutes the final stage of the process?'

'Yes.'

'And should you pass this final stage, your admittance into Midtown will rest solely on one final medical examination on the day of entry?'

'Yes.'

He glanced at the other panel members, which was clearly their cue for questions.

'I hear your plan is to work at The Facility once you qualify,' one of the women said – a blonde woman with painfully invasive blue eyes.

'Yes,' Ember confirmed.

Based in Midtown, The Facility was the primary medical research centre globally. It had led pioneering research into the healing effects of vampire blood – more specifically, the purest of vampire blood, the blood of vampire royalty, or the Higher Order as they were known – on human conditions.

When the third species had outed themselves eighty years before, it had not been to instigate war but a symbiotic relationship: to offer their healing abilities in exchange for blood sharing.

The revelation had prevented an all-out war but, with the potential of tens of thousands of third species being revealed, global action had been taken. To safeguard humankind, society had been restructured and the divisions had begun – both physical and social. Cities, villages and towns no longer existed like they once had. Instead, areas were segregated into locales. Each locale had been sub-divided into four bordered districts expanding outwards from the core like ripples. With it, a new world order had begun.

What had been discovered during the ongoing research since, however, was that whilst Higher Order blood could indeed heal, the effects were temporary. Eight decades later, humans were still seeking a permanent cure in order to free themselves of the relationship that had necessitated their tolerance of the third species at all.

'You have a particular interest in molecular biology and are hoping to work in the research department focused on finding the permanent cure,' the woman added.

'Like many others,' Ember said, 'I believe there is a way to bind vampiric blood to human blood, which will grant us the same advantages natural to their genetics. I would love to be a part of the team trying to discover what that bond could be.'

'For what outcome?' the second woman asked.

'I would like to see the self-healing abilities, heightened immunity and prolonged life of the third species being used in a more widespread nature rather than being reserved only for the already fortunate.'

The blonde raised her eyebrows slightly. 'By fortunate you mean residents of outer districts such as Midtown and Summerton? Those who have *earned* their place for improved medical care as well as every other privilege? Do you have issue with the Global Council's system, Ms Challice?'

The system that had promised to be temporary but, instead, had been continually reinforced to benefit the elite. Subsequently, Midtown had increased in affluence like its neigbouring Summerton on the outskirts of the locale, whereas Lowtown – her district – had gradually become nothing more than an extension of Blackthorn: the impoverished core where the vast majority of the third species had been forced to reside.

Those third species were as much victims of the system as the humans who didn't tick enough social, intellectual and medical boxes to corroborate their worth. Humans like her aunt. Like the rest of her family.

As a gaze laden with challenge and curiosity stared back at

her, Ember refused to look anywhere but directly into the blonde woman's eyes.

'I fully understand that resources are limited,' Ember said as part of the learned spiel she had used on more than one occasion during the painstaking process. 'I fully appreciate that, currently, lines need to be drawn. There's simply not enough to go around and that means tough decisions need to be made. I am not challenging the system. On the contrary, I am supporting the Global Council's mission statement that they want to achieve equality one day. I want to be an active part of enabling that to happen.'

The woman's eyes narrowed pensively.

But nice try, Ember said to herself as silence descended.

'But we've already heard you lost your aunt to a terminal illness,' the second woman said, recapturing Ember's attention. 'Your mental health evaluation has identified *this* as highly likely to be the primary motivation behind your career choice rather than selfless motivations. This is our one concern, Ms Challice.'

Her heart skipped a beat. Nothing to do with what she was. Nothing to do with her heritage.

'An innate resentment of the system is inevitable considering your aunt may not have lost her life had she not been a Lowtown resident,' the woman continued.

And the authorities couldn't afford to have political unrest amongst the ranks in Midtown. Every resident's vote counted and that meant every voter needed to be biased to the current system. *That* was what mattered to them.

What mattered to her was that there was not an iota of remorse from any of them that her aunt *could* very well still be alive if she hadn't been born in Lowtown. Could have still been alive if she'd had a way out of the hopeless system that had not only existed but had been reinforced amidst the greed, selfishness and ignorance of those at the top.

Could have at least been spared some of the excruciating pain in those final months.

Her throat knotted but she held back her tears. She scrunched her hands together. 'I have made no secret of the fact I am aware that my aunt didn't get the treatment she needed because of her Lowtown residency. But I can choose to respond to that in anger and achieve nothing, or I can use it to fuel my determination to work for the Global Council and make the changes they want, improve the situation for all, and thus leave a more worthwhile legacy in the process. I know which of those would make my aunt proud.'

A lengthier silence descended as all four pairs of eyes scrutinised her.

'You specified in your application that it was your aunt who had first encouraged you to begin the application process,' the blonde finally interjected.

'That's right.'

'So you've intended to move out of Lowtown for a long time.'

'For as long as I can remember.'

'Hence your impeccable record. Your faultless record, some would say.'

'I have determination, focus and self-discipline. I would like to be able to prove to those who say this system is unfair and corrupt that it is possible to better yourself by having those skills. My success in this process would reinforce that. It would help diminish some of those rumours.'

It had been the response she'd been waiting for that very opportunity to give. She knew as well as they did that they had to let a certain number through. She knew her profile was flawless. She knew they'd be fools not to take a chance on her to fulfil their quota. She was entirely dependent on them not being fools.

In the few minutes that followed, conferring was executed behind shielded mouths.

'Any further questions?' the spectacled man finally asked out loud, readdressing the panel.

There was a shake of the head from each of the others.

It was over quicker than she'd anticipated.

Perspiration coated her palms, her breathing was shallow, the tightness in her chest intensifying as they scribbled on the paper in front of them.

The walls expanded and contracted around her. Black vignettes framed her vision as she awaited the decision these four strangers would make about her life from then on. The compulsion to further fight her corner became overwhelming as the spectacled man looked through each ballot paper, but he quickly tidied them into a neat pile.

'I propose we set a transition date of the twenty-fourth,' he said. 'Ten days from now.'

Her heart leapt. The thrum of blood flooded her ears.

He slammed a stamp down on her file.

'You will arrive here at the Midtown border at six a.m. on the twenty-fourth,' he said, closing her file. 'You will need to have all of your basic belongings with you. If you pass the final medical, your residency will be confirmed. During the trial twelve-month period, should you lose your job, your home, your college place, or run out of funds, you will be removed and no re-application will be permitted for a period of five years. Do you understand that?'

She could barely breathe, her throat constricting as she fought back tears of relief. 'I do.'

She'd done it.

Ten years, and she'd finally done it.

'Then the sincerest of congratulations, Ms Challice,' the

panellist said, as he removed his spectacles. He didn't quite manage a smile. 'We wish you luck with your transition.'

The other man and the second woman nodded, whilst the blonde sent her the sincerest wink of approval.

CHAPTER TWO

Ember tied her apron around her waist before knocking on the door.

'Yeah?' the gruff voice echoed from inside.

She stepped into the windowless office tucked at the back of the café.

Harry was drowning in paperwork under his lamp as he sat hunched over his desk, his thick-rimmed glasses masking his gaunt face, the magnification emphasising the bags under his eyes.

Ember closed the door behind herself in the cramped space before slipping sideways into the metal chair on the far side of his desk.

'So?' he asked, his eyes locked on hers.

'I passed,' she said, the first time she had uttered the words to another human being since she'd got back from the Lowtown–Midtown border two hours before.

His gaze dropped immediately. He tidied a few sheets of

paperwork on his desk. He nodded. 'Well done,' he said, before finally making eye contact again, albeit fleetingly. But even in that brief moment the minor glossing in his eyes was visible, despite the shadows cast on his face.

She tried to remind herself this was just a job. At least that was how it had started. Fifteen years later, it had become far more than that. Harry had become far more than that. Harry Winslow had become the father she'd never known. He might have been a man of few words, and irritable most of the time, forever carrying the world on his shoulders, but he was always there for her.

'You always were too good for this place, Ember.'

'Too good for an honest day's work?'

His smile was brief. 'So when are you leaving me in the lurch?'

'The twenty-fourth.'

'Next week?'

'I'll work right up to the final hour.'

Harry nodded again. 'Then you'd best go and tell Casey the news. That girl's been pacing the last few hours.'

Ember stood. There were so many things she wanted to say as he reverted his attention back to his paperwork. Maybe too many things for that moment. So instead of saying anything at all, she turned her back on him, resolving to save it for another time.

'She'll miss you, you know,' he said, just as she reached the handle.

Her grip tightened.

'We all will,' he added.

She wanted to look back over her shoulder. She wanted to meet his gaze. But she couldn't for fear of him seeing the tears that smeared her vision. She couldn't do it to him. And he'd understand that.

She stepped back out into the small passageway and closed

the door behind her. Clearing her clogging throat, she headed down past the staff toilets, the lockers, the utility door on her left, and then the kitchen, before taking a right into the café.

From behind the counter, Ember clocked Casey to her left, stood with her back to her as she served a customer. To her right, Yvonne looked straight over. As Ember promptly signalled with a thumb up, Yvonne responded with a wink and a smile before turning her attention back to serving.

Grabbing her order pad and pen from under the counter, Ember tucked them in her apron.

It was quieter than usual. Away from the hustle and bustle of the more central establishments in Lowtown, Harry's place was rarely overrun with customers. It was primarily used by those who liked to keep themselves to themselves, who liked to enjoy a quiet and uncomplicated drink or a simple meal without needing to constantly check over their shoulder. As such, it had never been a thriving business, barely keeping its head above water by relying mainly on the regulars. Regulars who, to the financial detriment of the place, never had money to burn.

The biggest profit limiter, though, was closing the doors at nine, shutting out the most lucrative hours. But it also kept his staff and his customers from having to contend with the night crowds.

Residents of Blackthorn – unless they were the tagged cons – were allowed to cross the border into Lowtown from dusk until an hour before sunrise. In the beginning, it had mostly been about acquiring produce or deals. Now one of the increasing reasons for Blackthorn residents to enter Lowtown was to gather feeders for vampire sires, offering humans locked in Lowtown's dead-end system a better way of life either there or back in Blackthorn. In truth, they were no better than the human gang members now notorious for offering the exact same lies.

It was why she maintained a watchful eye on Casey, the lull most likely the reason why she was allowing herself time to chat or, as quickly became apparent, flirt. Casey was never short of attention, pretty girl that she was. She had good survival instincts though, so knew how to deflect to the best of her ability. But now she was being remiss, no doubt influenced by how good-looking the young guy was. Because that was how vampire sires operated: sending their most appealing gatherers out, primarily human in order to distract from obvious intentions.

Ember scanned the café again. Jasper, sat in in his usual seat in the furthest corner to her right, looked up from his book, and Ember offered him a wave. The old guy had been coming there almost the entire time she had worked there. Two coffees twice a week were all his limited budget would allow, but he knew how to make them last an entire morning or afternoon – and Ember knew how to sneak him an extra fill-up or two on the colder days, or when he looked like he needed the company. She referred to it as the loyal customer bonus scheme. And more than once, Harry had removed the money she'd placed in the till and shoved it back in her pocket.

That was how Harry ran his business. He could have played it differently, but he chose not to. And, thus far, he was one of the few lucky ones who hadn't been involuntarily dragged into the seedy underworld by the human gangs whose tendrils had long been squeezing the lifeblood out of Lowtown. Instead, he refused to be sucked into the disillusionment and resentment of the system that had allowed the gangs to thrive, feeding off misfortune to better their own odds, dismissive of the irony of their oppression of those less powerful in their bid to rebel against the Global Council that did the exact same to them. A few – namely the Hordas clan and the Voys – dominated the various factions, the best jobs and opportunities reserved for those who were in with the right people as had become the norm.

Instead of working nineteen-hour days in that windowless cubbyhole to barely make ends meet, Harry could have earned more, but his life wouldn't have been his own any longer. His two daughters wouldn't have been his own. He'd forever be in debt, and could forever be called upon to repay by whatever means the debt collectors judged suitable.

Rather, he hoped his unblemished record would mean he'd one day be able to give his two girls the chance Ember was now taking – a chance she had now proved *was* possible. With Iona months away from becoming eighteen, she could have been the first, her sixteen-year-old sister only a couple of years behind.

Leaning back against the counter, Ember glanced back at Casey, who was still uncharacteristically oblivious to her presence, before turning her attention to the dusk-laden street beyond.

She'd tallied up five days since he'd last been in – the guy whose name she still didn't know. In the six months he'd been coming there, he'd never introduced himself. Every time she'd served him, he'd barely even made eye contact let alone shown any interest beyond that. It piled on the evidence as to why even attributing thinking time to him was irrational, him no doubt more firmly rooted in her head than she was in his.

Nonetheless, he'd become her guilty pleasure, the potential of his presence always something to look forward to. Beyond that, there was reassurance in seeing him; knowing he'd survived another day. It felt absurd that someone who she'd barely spoken to had become such a significant part of her life – had consumed so many of her thoughts – but he had.

Worrying whenever he didn't show up had taken her into new territory though. She knew she couldn't afford to feel attached to him; she'd worked hard not to feel attached to him. Because the only thing she did know about her nameless stranger was the very reason she shouldn't have been paying him any attention at all. Because despite not once ever having seen him smile, she *had* managed to catch a glimpse of those extra incisors characteristic of his kind. Incisors used to feed.

From the first time she'd seen them, she'd worked hard not to judge, especially as his frequenting the café as much during the day as early evening confirmed that he was a Lowtown resident and, as such, would have earned his place. For some people that was enough to lower their guard, but even if Ember hadn't been on the cusp of leaving, she'd never lower her guard around a vampire. Ever.

So whatever it was that he did, whatever business he conducted in that café, it remained a mystery. A different person met with him every time. There was never the laughter and smiles of a casual meeting, just the firm shaking of hands at the beginning and at the end. Sometimes the meeting would last a few minutes, other times as long as a couple of hours. And that was it. Mr Mysterious, as Casey had nicknamed him, would, it seemed, now remain forever that.

Casey who finally turned around and, in doing so, yanked Ember back to the present. She instantly realised she'd been twisting her engagement ring around her forefinger again which she regularly did, according to Casey, when she was thinking about her stranger. The engagement ring she'd replaced the moment she'd got back to her apartment to prepare for work.

'Well?' Casey mouthed, her lips remaining parted in anticipation.

As reality sank in for the second time that night, Ember sent her a small nod and a smile.

Casey beamed, her eyes glinting with elation. She turned

to say something to the customer she'd been flirting with and, seconds later, the friend she'd come to think of more as her little sister joined her behind the counter, her eyes wide with delight. 'It's a yes?'

'Date set for the twenty-fourth. If I pass the final medical at the border, I'm in.'

Casey let out a squeal before wrapping her arms unceremoniously around her. 'You did it! You actually did it!'

Glancing over Casey's shoulder mid-hug, Ember's stomach flipped, her gaze meeting *his* momentarily as he stepped through the door. Her heart pounded as he turned left towards one of the booths.

'Let me finish this order and you can tell me *all* about it,' Casey said, before pulling away towards the coffee machine.

As usual, her stranger flicked through his phone whilst waiting to be served, that permanent frown darkening his expression as he remained locked in concentration.

She removed her order pad, nervously but discreetly clicked the top of her pen a couple of times, hoping, being nearby, that Yvonne would get to him first. But Yvonne had only just started her next order.

With another couple of clicks of her pen, Ember conceded and forced herself away from the counter. As always, she was grateful he didn't look up to watch her approach, her excessive awareness of her every movement making her feel awkward enough.

'What can I get you?' she asked.

As if she didn't know: black coffee and a glass of tap water.

'Black coffee, please,' he said, meeting her gaze only fleetingly out of polite acknowledgement before reverting his attention back to his phone. 'And a glass of tap water.'

She glanced down at his thumb that swiped the screen; at

masculine hands with short, clean nails. No wedding ring. Nails that were as meticulously maintained as his stubble and closely cropped but full head of light-brown hair.

It was difficult to tell the age of vampires. They weren't immortal like stories of old dictated. Instead, as soon as vampires, as with all third species, reached their peak, their aging drastically slowed down. In human years, he looked to be in his mid-to-late thirties, given away only by the subtle evidence of lines at the corners of his eyes. She guessed that was why he wore the facial hair – maybe to age him a little because his features were otherwise youthful, exacerbated by his large, soulful eyes. Intense, dark brown eyes in a constant state of pensive observation. Because whenever he did manage to look her in the eye, even though only fleetingly, she felt it somewhere deep, as if he was withdrawing information from her with just a glance.

But despite his attractiveness, despite the care he took over his appearance, he never came across as overly bothered by his looks. His clothes were always understated as if to blend rather than attract attention: dark jeans, grey T-shirt or hoody, waist-length jacket that he buttoned up around his neck against the breeze.

She never once saw him smooth down his hair, or check himself in the glass, or readjust his clothes. His lack of vanity was a theory reinforced by his lack of indulgence in the female attention he got. He didn't even raise a smile when someone was clearly flirting with him. Instead, he had that same severe frown as if they were an imposition on his time, as if he were even questioning their presence near him. For that reason, approaching him always felt awkward.

'On its way,' she said, wishing she could come up with something more original, realising she'd become as predictable in her responses as he was in his requests.

Stepping back behind the counter, grabbing a mug and a glass, she glanced back over her shoulder to where Casey had resumed her position with the guy. Her stomach lurched as she saw Casey's left hand furtively brush his; tucked something in her apron pocket along with her notepad.

Leaving his full cup of coffee behind, the guy promptly left, but not before sending Casey a wink and a smile on his way out of the door.

And not before he met Ember's gaze briefly in the process.

'Yvonne, I'm going to need you to cover for a few minutes,' Ember said, backing up to her colleague who was already stood at the coffee machine. 'Usual on table six.'

'I'll yell if the stampede arrives,' Yvonne remarked, not needing to make eye contact to confirm her flippancy.

On her way back over, Casey's smile dropped the second her eyes met Ember's again; the second she took in her demeanour. The second she worked out she'd been spotted. Because five years of knowing Casey meant Ember recognised her panicked and guilty face.

Ember indicated the doorway to the corridor. And Casey knew better than to argue to the contrary.

'Ember . . .' Casey began, not yet having time to come up with an excuse.

'What did he give you?'

Casey rolled her eyes. 'Come on . . .'

'What did he give you, Casey?'

With a heavy sigh, Casey pulled the business card from her apron pocket.

Ember reached for it but Casey snatched it back.

'Are you going to convince me not to date now too?' Casey asked. 'On top of everything else I should and shouldn't be doing?'

'You know as well as I do how this works. He's working for a sire. It's written all over him.'

'Or maybe he's just a nice guy who has showed interest.' She folded her arms. 'If you must know, it's not the first time we've met. He's not been pushy or anything. We met in a bar.'

'Where?'

'Here in Lowtown.'

At least she didn't say Blackthorn. Nonetheless, Casey had never been that negligent. She was either at work or was at home looking after her mother.

'Since when have you been going to bars?' Ember asked, keeping her tone as calm as she could.

Casey held her gaze for a few moments as if deliberating her response.

'What has he offered you, Casey?'

Casey rubbed the back of her neck as she looked over her shoulder, wary of being overheard. 'Things haven't been good, OK?' she said, lowering her voice. 'With Mum. She's on the downward spiral again. She hasn't even been able to get out of bed the past two weeks.'

Her mother had developed depression ten years before when Casey had just turned eleven. Deemed as a blight on the system, they'd been evicted from their home in Midtown within a matter of a year. The last ten years had been a downward spiral for her mother ever since.

'Medication?' Ember asked. 'Is *that* what he's offered you? Casey, you know as well as I do that anything they ship out on the streets and in bars isn't the real thing. They're just money spinners, preying on people who are desperate.'

'Yeah, well, I don't have much choice, do I? I can't afford the prices the legitimate dealers are constantly upping, let alone cope with the increasingly sporadic supplies. Mum needs consistency. I can't afford to buy in bulk and she can't afford to miss a dose. The erratic supplies are screwing with her system.'

For the last few years in particular, the dealers were buying all the supplies the second they came in, then increasing the prices before selling them on. The Hordas clan were rumoured to be at the heart of it, treating Lowtown like a Monopoly board and using lives to gain one-upmanship against their only true rival: the Voys.

'You know what it's like better than anyone,' Casey reminded her. 'What with everything you went through.'

Ember didn't take the bait. Discussing her past right now would do neither of them any good. 'I'm out of here in just over a week. I will get you the money you need. I will get you the medication you need. The real stuff.'

'You'll barely be able to afford living there yourself for the first year, Ember. Besides, I'm not your responsibility and neither is Mum. You've helped us out enough. I need to stand on my own two feet. Now more than ever.'

Ember felt the second pang that night, the first over leaving Harry – and now her.

'Being a feeder is not going to make that happen, Casey. You know that's ultimately what this is about. He's reeling you in and using this to do so.'

'Then what else do I do? I'm not getting out of here. Ever. Even if I could one day raise enough money to get back into Midtown, I'm not smart like you are. I'd never pass half of their tests. Besides, there's not a hope in hell of Mum gaining residency again and I'm not leaving her behind. I need to focus on making a life for us here. Siring can work really well, even you have to admit that. And he reckons I can get myself a good one – someone who will really look after me *and* Mum.'

'For every one it works for, there are nine for whom it doesn't. Casey–'

Casey caught hold of both of Ember's forearms, her eyes resolute – eyes of desperation thinking they were seeing light at the end of the tunnel when Ember knew all it was was someone lighting a match to burn down the exit.

'Ember, we can't all do what you've done. And I've accepted that. My mum needs me now. *I* need this now. I need to make my own choices. I need to find my own way through.'

She squeezed Ember's hand before pulling away and making her way back out.

Ember raked her hands down over her face as she sighed with frustration before following behind her.

She stepped back behind the counter to see her stranger was already heading out of the door. He hadn't waited for his coffee, or his water.

Heart sinking, she watched him pass the window outside, lifting the collar on his jacket to fend off the cold evening breeze.

And she watched him not look back.

CHAPTER THREE

‹──●──›

Ember grabbed her change of clothes and trainers from her staff locker before heading into the toilets.

She slipped out of her uniform of black trousers, fitted pale pink shirt and ballet flats and swapped them for her shapeless jeans, sweater and trainers. She pulled on her puffer jacket and zipped it up to conceal her feminine form before tying up her long hair and tucking it beneath her baseball cap.

She'd always classed herself as fortunate not to have the kind of looks that instantly grabbed attention like Casey's did. It had certainly become a helpful survival tool in Lowtown. Being a woman alone on the streets of Lowtown was still a risk though, making blending and keeping a low profile essential.

Collar up and baseball cap down over her eyes – ears kept free to any prospect of being followed – Ember kept up a steady pace as she made her way home. It was less than a half an hour walk and primarily across the quieter parts of Lowtown near the Midtown border. She nevertheless always kept to the main streets and, as there were several routes back to her place, regularly interchanged between them so as not to create a discernible pattern.

Being in the quieter area also thankfully meant no one had ever really shown much interest in her apartment. Housing in Lowtown had become a serious issue after the Global Council had discovered that less people than they initially thought measured up to the rigorous screening process. As well as protection rackets now being rife, forced landlordship for extra profits had not become uncommon either.

She headed towards the narrow lane that ran down the side of her building, once a small hotel before it had been converted into apartments. Her entrance was around the back: left into the alley, then the next left around to the rear. The external door to her and her neighbour's place was adjacent to the dead-end.

They were the only two apartments accessed from the rear now: hers and Cam's. Or what *had* been Cam's. She hadn't seen or heard from him for almost two months now, leading her to believe he was one of many who left one night, never to return.

People regularly went missing in Lowtown and the authorities couldn't keep up. At the last count, less than twenty per cent of cases were solved, and even less than that were ever acted upon at all. Instead of the statistics encouraging increased funding to combat the problem, the authorities chose to finance the demands for higher protection at Midtown's border instead. As had become the norm – instead of tackling the issue or safeguarding those caught in the middle – they raised the walls and the division further.

So, despite knowing she should have reported him missing, it was obvious Cam's case would have been one they'd decide not to pursue. Once they'd got a glimpse of his standard behaviour, it would have been deemed a pointless use of resources.

Cam had been a nightmare those past four years: the late-night parties, the sound of his movies and other nocturnal activities oscillating against her bedroom wall on a regular basis. And, because they shared the same stairwell, the set-up had made avoiding him, or his mates, impossible. Both of their apartments were on the first floor, hers directly to the right at the top of the stairs, and Cam's to the left past the curve of the balustrade. The second floor had long been bricked off. Every night returning home from work, she'd never known who she'd bump into in the stairwell; or whether he'd have left the external door open again, leaving her to combat whatever fate had been awaiting her, as he'd stumbled home too inebriated or high to care.

The last thing Ember needed was any more trouble moving in so had opted to plead ignorant and not flag up to the authorities that the apartment opposite hers was potentially vacant – especially with her application so close to succeeding. What they discovered afterwards was up to them.

Less than fifty feet away from the alley, the tiny hairs on the back of her neck began to prickle, the base of her spine tingle. It had been a second sense since she was a youngster, and had become second nature for surviving there: knowing when she was being followed. She didn't need to look over her shoulder; every instinct told her that her reaction was far from paranoia – a belief confirmed when she heard the rare sound of footsteps at that point of her journey.

Her stomach knotted. She tried to swallow but saliva wasn't forthcoming in her arid mouth. This could be it. This could be the night she didn't make it home. Or, even if she did, the night all her hopes, everything she had worked for, were ruined. Ten years of struggling and this is what it would come to – the irony of being within reaching distance of both her front door *and* her way out of there and having both snatched away.

Having second thoughts about whether to lead them back to where she lived, she looked ahead to the empty street looming beyond. There were no public places left for her to enter without needing to turn around – and that would take her straight into her follower's, or followers', path. She had no choice but to continue. She loathed doing it. But knowing she might not even make it to the next day, she focused on what she needed to make happen now.

Ember slipped both hands into her coat pockets as she maintained a steady pace. She subtly removed her keys with one hand and debated between the pepper spray and her flick knife for the other. She opted for the pepper spray, knowing that would be most immediately disabling and thus buy her more time.

Her ears tuned into the silence. The temptation to check over her shoulder to see how close they were was overwhelming, but any indication that she knew she was being followed could prompt them to up the ante quicker. She needed to close the gap between herself and the outer door first. She needed to give herself a fighting chance.

Taking a left down the alley at the side of her building, she caught a glimpse of them in the corner of her eye: two of them and, from their stature, most likely male.

Her stomach vaulted.

Turning left again into the back alley, she cast a wary glance into the ten-foot square recess on her left that contained the large industrial bin – a recess she had always hated passing in the darkness.

She needed to get to the end of alley. If she got through the outer door and managed to lock it, she'd be safe. Failing that, she might at least be able to fend them off in the stairwell and get into her apartment.

As she continued to maintain her steady pace, the back alley narrowed in on itself, the darkness intensifying as her portal to safety seemed too far down the end of an ever-increasing corridor, the ground beneath her like a conveyer belt pulling her in the wrong direction. Her thighs felt sluggish, weakening by the second as her anxiety intensified. When she was less than twenty-five feet away from the door, she knew it was all or nothing. Ember sprinted with everything she had.

Her chest and thighs instantly burned from sudden exertion, despite having always kept herself fit for that very cause. She skidded to a standstill outside the door. She shoved her key in the lock.

Her stomach flipped as an arm locked around her neck, yanking her backwards. Her hand gripped the mace as she was spun away from the door. She instantly sprayed the canister in the face of her second attacker.

He cursed under his breath, clamping his forearm over his eyes as he stumbled away.

Shutting her eyes, she turned her head away and sprayed behind her to try and blind her restrainer too. But the mace was knocked from her hand. She was slammed face-first against the wall opposite.

But she was *not* being taken down that easily.

Shoving her hand back into her pocket, Ember withdrew her knife and stabbed it into his thigh. With gritted teeth, she twisted the blade as she simultaneously used the wall for leverage to shove him, and herself, backwards.

He lost balance, taking her down with him. She promptly scrabbled to her feet, brought her foot down hard between his splayed thighs without hesitation before bringing the heel of her trainer down onto his face.

Seeing her other attacker attempting to blink away the pain, she smacked her knuckles hard into the bridge of his nose, advantaged by his watery eyes still partially blinding him.

She reached the door again. She turned her keys still hanging in the lock. Stumbling across the threshold with haste, she fumbled to remove them. Succeeding, she slammed and locked the door from the inside just in time for a shoulder to reverberate against the other side.

Heart pounding, light-headed, she fell back against the wall beside the door, directly at the foot of the stone stairwell.

Lit only by the narrow, meshed opaque window above the door, the electrics having burnt out years before, it took her eyes a few moments to adjust. It was the one thing she hated about that space. More to the point, she hated the pitch-blackness of the utility area recess that lay out of sight under the stairwell itself.

Her heart pummelled her ribcage. All she could hear was her blood thrumming in her ears, her rapid, shallow breathing amidst the backdrop of curses and threats muffled by the thick metal door as if she were under water.

For now she was safe.

For now she . . .

Ember flinched. Her breathing snagged. She pressed her back tighter against the wall as she detected the mass half way up the stairs in front of her, less than ten feet away.

Despite the abuse beyond the door escalating, it suddenly felt like a gateway into a world of lesser risk. Because as she pieced together a human form, size and stature alone told her it was most definitely a male lying face down in front of her. Cam. Cam had returned – drunk and unconscious on the stairs like she'd found him countless times before. Because he was unconscious. He didn't stir or flinch even as her two furious attackers pounded the door outside.

As her vision adjusted further though, she could see this figure was more svelte than Cam's stocky frame. From what she could tell, he was taller too. Neither did this stranger dress like Cam; Cam always having opted for gregarious and oversized clothing – brightly coloured harem trousers and T-shirts mainly – whereas this guy was in darker, more fitted clothes.

Someone else had moved in. Someone who, up until then, she'd known nothing of. Because based on her having to unlock the door, whoever it was had entered by legitimate means. This was not a random break-in. This was not someone opportunistically taking shelter for the night.

Regardless, more significantly, she could no longer be sure they were even human.

Willing her attackers to go away and not wake him, Ember glanced up towards the security of her apartment. There she could safely call the authorities out of earshot. Because there was no way she could turn around and go back out, nor did she have anything left to defend herself with in there – trapped in the bottom of an isolated stairwell with a potential ticking time bomb.

As her attackers finally fell silent, the emptiness of the stairwell was exacerbated – not least because of how far she was from anyone capable of hearing her screams or cries for help.

Threading her two keys between her fingers as a makeshift knuckle-duster, breath held, Ember didn't dare take her gaze from him for a second as she took her first step up.

Pressing her back to the wall opposite the rusted metal balustrade that he laid closer to, trainers silent against stone, she ascended, her free palm brushing over concrete and flaking paint.

Finally in a position to see his profile though, she froze.

CHAPTER FOUR

———•———

Ember's defences dropped a fraction as she stared at *her* stranger, partially in relief, but primarily due to being bewildered as to what the hell he was doing there.

It was only when her eyes adjusted further, when she dared to take another step up for a closer look, that she saw it: dark liquid having spilt out from beneath his coat.

Blood.

Fuck.

She dropped back down a couple of steps. Injured vampires eventually self-healed. They self-healed even quicker if they fed. His instincts would *dictate* he fed.

Prospects of sabotage struck. A set-up. It was too much of a coincidence for it not to be – him being there in the café all that time and now on her stairwell. She thought back to the blonde woman's wink. How easy it had been to get through that final stage. How maybe she hadn't got through it at all. How maybe the conspiracy theories were right. How maybe the guys outside had been a part of it too.

Driven by *her* instincts for survival, she sprinted up the steps.

Despite her hand trembling, she eventually unlocked her door.

She glanced back down the stairs. He hadn't moved a fraction.

Inside, she slammed her door behind her, bolted it, and fell back against it.

But if the authorities had intended sabotage, they could have done so long before then. And if he *had* been placed in the café as some kind of test of her resolve, they surely would've done better than some guy who, despite being good-looking to the point of inevitable distraction, hadn't even been arsed to string a sentence together. Acknowledging her paranoia, she steadied her breathing. He was nothing to do with the authorities. And he'd be OK. He was a vampire – of course he'd be OK.

But there was also a chance he wouldn't be; that maybe the injuries had been too severe.

She reached into the inside pocket of her coat for her phone. Unlocking it, she keyed in the emergency number.

But held back from connecting.

Any calls would be registered. The second she got through, everything would be recorded – her report of a vampire on her stairs. A vampire she couldn't disprove a connection to. A vampire she couldn't prove hadn't come to visit her by pre-arrangement. Simply reporting his presence near her home would leave her implicated. It would throw open a whole raft of questions. Questions meant delaying her application – maybe even by months pending further investigation. It could destroy her chances altogether. One shadow of a doubt was all they needed. They didn't need proof to condemn her: *she* needed proof of her innocence. And, right then, she had nothing.

Besides, she couldn't call the emergency services anyway without knowing more. They were slow enough responding to human cries for help in Lowtown, let alone vampires.

As thoughts of her aunt's final hours filled her head, reminding her of the cruel negligence of the system she'd turned to for help, pleaded with for help, she pressed the heel of her hand to her forehead to block out the pending spiral of despair she always teetered on the edge of when revisiting those memories.

She yanked herself back to the present. At the very least, they'd want to know if he was still alive. Her stomach churned, her heart beating a little faster at the prospect she might already be too late.

Stepping into her kitchenette, Ember grabbed a paring knife from the drawer. Phone in one hand, keys swapped for the knife in the other, she tentatively opened the door and peered back outside.

The stairwell remained silent. Her stranger remained face down and unmoving.

Leaving her door open behind her, Ember warily descended the steps, ready to make a hasty retreat at any moment.

Placing her phone down within easy reach on one of the steps, knife still gripped in her hand, Ember crouched beside him to press the fingers of her free hand against the pulse point on his wrist. His flesh was ice cold. She'd heard the rumours, just like anyone else growing up in Lowtown, but she'd never touched a vampire before. Had never actually made physical contact with one of his kind. But all her medical research for her college application supported her concern that he was too cold even for one of his kind. A glimmer of unwarranted grief tightened her throat as she waited for any sign of his characteristically slow-beating heart.

Waited in the silence. In the stillness.

Eventually, she felt it. Relief consumed her. But as she retained her fingers over his pulse, it was definitely too slow – weak too. She leaned a little closer to hear his breathing. It was shallow, intermittent.

It didn't make any sense. Even if the injury had occurred a matter of minutes before her arrival, he should have been self-healing by now.

Something was wrong. Something was definitely wrong.

Knowing he was too far gone to wake up yet, or to have enough strength to do anything even if he did, she collapsed onto the step.

She *had* to make that call. Call and implicate herself in order to have any chance of saving his life. Unless . . .

He had a phone. He *always* had a phone with him. She'd seen him tuck it into the inside pocket of his coat enough times. She could call someone he knew. They could deal with it.

But then *they* could implicate her. Maybe use it against her.

She pressed the heel of her hand to her forehead again as she cursed under her breath. She had to at least try. She had to at least test the water.

She reached for his hand and eased it aside to free up access to the inside of his coat, and caught sight of a glint of metal.

Keys. No doubt the keys he'd used to get in prior to collapsing. If she had any doubt he lived there, it dissipated.

Bypassing them, she reached inside his coat; she heaved a sigh of relief as her fingers brushed plastic. Removing his phone, she withdrew back up to the top of the steps. She slid the bar across the screen. Of course it was locked.

'*Shit.*'

Knees to her chest, elbows resting on both, knuckles pressed to her temples, she stared down at him.

She couldn't leave him to die. Not only because she didn't

believe herself capable, but because he'd done nothing to deserve it. He'd done nothing to her. He'd never even shown the slightest indication of wanting to hurt her. He'd had more than enough opportunities if he'd meant her any harm. He could have been waiting in the stairwell for her at any point – *if* he knew she lived there.

She eased back down to rejoin him. Switching her phone light on, she peeled his jacket back – and recoiled at seeing his shirt sodden with blood.

He wasn't just injured, something was *badly* wrong. There was no way he should have been bleeding out that much. Vampire coagulation was more advanced even than that of the lycans. She knew enough about vampire physiology to know that. *Everyone* knew that.

Ember ran back up to her apartment and grabbed the nearest towel. Crouching beside him again, she abandoned her knife on the steps to bunch up the fabric and apply pressure to his wound.

Holding the pads of her fingers on his pulse point again, she counted. Easily fifteen seconds passed between beats. She counted nearer twenty seconds a couple of minutes later.

She knew exactly what was happening. It was all the confirmation she needed: he *was* dying.

'Shit, shit, shit,' she hissed under her breath as she continued to check her watch, her own pulse lifting as his slowed.

If his beats dropped to three a minute, he wasn't coming back. What he needed was human blood, and fast. He would self-heal then, unless he was at the point where he was already too weak.

Unless her continued delay meant she was already far too late.

Heart pounding, keeping pressure applied to his wound, Ember unlocked her phone and dialled the emergency number.

Out of the choice of human or third species related incidents, she picked third species. Out of the sub-categories of vampire, lycan, or other, she picked vampire. Out of crime related or medical related, she picked medical.

And she waited.

And she waited.

She checked her watch.

Ten minutes later, which felt more like twenty amidst his weakening pulse, she was still waiting.

'We will get to your call as soon as we can. All lines are busy. We will get to your call as soon as we can. All lines are busy. We will get–'

With a growl and a '*fuck!*', Ember conceded and disconnected.

She could call Harry. But that would only implicate him too. And there was no way she would risk him coming up that back alley with no idea if her attackers were still out there waiting.

But she couldn't sit there doing nothing, waiting for some miracle to happen.

Flapping his jacket back again, she lifted his T-shirt to examine the wound more closely under the light of her phone's torch. It was deep, most likely a stab wound. But as she wiped away the blood with the towel, the shape of the wound, the type of abrasion and the ring of dirt told her exactly what it was: a gunshot wound.

Only gangsters could afford guns in Lowtown. The guns themselves weren't the issue; it was the availability of bullets that had depleted over the decades. Yet someone had obviously deemed her stranger worthy of taking one. A hate crime maybe. Or he'd got himself embroiled with the wrong people.

She pressed the towel over the wound again. She stared back down at the keys under his hand. There was only one option left unless he was to die in front of her.

She knew it was insane, negligent, but the prospect of not helping him felt even more ludicrous. She couldn't let him die

in front of her. Couldn't let him die because she was more concerned about bettering herself.

She tugged off her coat and pulled off her sweater. She used
the latter to wrap around his waist to keep the towel pressed
over the wound. Laying her coat over him to offer some extra
warmth, she grabbed his keys. She ploughed up the stairs. She
shoved the key in the lock to Cam's apartment. She heaved a
sigh of relief when it turned.

The place was the exact mirror image of her own, so she knew
exactly where she was going.

She hurried into the kitchenette and yanked open drawers
and cupboards, searching for where he might keep his spare
syringes. Because all vampires had syringes. For a multitude of
reasons, connected feeds – or 'bites' – had long been outdated
in exchange for syringe feeds.

Finding none, she headed to the bathroom next to it. There
was only one cabinet and it was bare.

She pushed the bedroom door open. And halted at the
threshold as the sight in front of her confirmed her situation was
a hell of a lot worse than she'd first thought.

CHAPTER FIVE

—◦◦◦—

Ember stared down at the collection of guns spread across the bed or, more to the point, the components of what looked like dismantled guns lying amongst cleaning clothes and brushes.

Either he *did* work for the authorities after all, or he was neck-deep in something illegal.

She grabbed the doorframe for balance.

It couldn't change a thing. If anything, more than ever, she needed to make sure she kept him alive. If he worked for the authorities, they'd trace him back there. And if he didn't, the last thing she needed was the authorities finding all of that next door.

Heading over to the bedside drawers, she opened each in turn before finally coming to several syringes in the bottom one. Syringes *and* a pair of handcuffs. Handcuffs that further ignited her paranoia, but nonetheless could prove more than useful right then.

Grabbing them and a couple of the syringes still in their packets, Ember ran to the threshold. Skidding to a halt, she ran back into the bedroom to grab the blanket folded on the foot of the bed.

As loose bullets hit the bare floorboards, she froze.

She berated herself that the obvious answer hadn't struck her sooner.

Snatching a bottle of whisky she'd seen on his counter, Ember hurried back across to her own apartment.

She stood at her kitchen worktop. Despite her hands trembling, she managed to rip open the packaging on the two syringes. She'd have to make it look like a cooking accident. It was the only way. Reaching for another paring knife from the drawer and a mug from the cupboard, Ember cupped her hand over an apple.

'Come on, come on, come on,' she chanted, trying to convince herself to stop wasting time and get on with it.

And sliced the knife through the apex of flesh between her thumb and index finger.

She winced. Sickness rose from the pit of her gut and scorched the back of her throat. She blinked the tears of pain from her eyes.

Holding her hand over the mug, she gathered as much blood as she could in it. After rinsing her wound under the tap, she reached for her first-aid kit, cleaned her wound quickly and added a plaster.

She placed the tip of one syringe and then the other in the mug. Two *had* to be enough.

Grasping the filled syringes, the whisky, her first aid kit and the blanket, she hurried back down the stairs.

Falling to her knees beside him, she quickly checked his pulse again. It was barely there, telling her she may already be too late.

'Don't you dare die on me now,' she muttered.

She pulled the towel and her jumper away from his wound to

see he was still failing to coagulate – except now she'd worked out why.

She felt around the front of his abdomen, his body hard to the touch. As her fingers traced over the curves of his well-honed muscles, she failed to find an exit wound. Her suspicion was confirmed.

Knowing she couldn't waste another second, she headed down the steps to the other side of the balustrade. She attached the cuff to one of the rusted metal spindles before reaching through the bars to secure the other around his wrist nearest them. The risk was too great if she didn't.

Crouching back beside him, she pulled on her disposable gloves. She saturated some layers of lint with alcohol and smeared it over the wound. Grateful she had never been one to be queasy, not least because of all the care she had given her aunt, let alone her assessments to gain her college place, she opened the wound a little. She slowly and carefully plunged two fingers deep inside to try and to locate the bullet she now knew was lodged inside him. *That* was the problem. *That* was the issue. *That* was the answer as to why he wasn't healing.

Frustrated at failing to find it, she grabbed her phone torch again. Parting her fingers to open the wound as wide as she could, she peered inside. And saw it: the tiniest glint of metal.

Resting the phone on his back so she at least had some light even if misdirected, she reached for her medical scissors. Using her parted fingers as a guide, she pushed the scissors down between them until they tapped metal. Catching the edge of the bullet, she dragged it backwards until she was finally able to snag it between her middle and forefinger.

She promptly dropped the bullet and scissors onto the step and, as blood started to pool again, she pressed the towel back down over the wound. She reached for the syringes. With his circulation so weak, she opted to plough the contents directly into the wounded area.

Once she'd emptied both syringes into his system, she secured the towel back into position.

Having done all she could do, common sense told her to get back up to her apartment and lock the door. Instead, she collapsed down against the wall beside him. Instead, her gaze lingered on his thick, dark lashes before wandering down to his masculine lips.

'Who are you?' she whispered, her fingers back on his wrist as she waited anxiously for a lift in his pulse.

The thought of him dying and her question never being answered, the thought of losing him at all, filled her with an emptiness that felt so misplaced considering that was all he was, all he had ever been: an unknown.

Nonetheless, as fifteen minutes passed, to her immense relief, his pulse didn't wane. She leaned over him to check his breathing, which was no longer laboured. Her blood was working, giving his body enough strength and, subsequently, buying him some time to at least attempt to recover.

After another fifteen minutes, she eased the towel away to see that the first signs of coagulation had definitely set it. It was the best sign she could have hoped for. He was far from out of the woods but he was no longer guaranteed to die. The rest was down to how fit he was, how strong he was, how much damage she had done trying to remove the bullet. And how much damage the bullet had done in the first place.

Knowing there truly was nothing more she could do, she reached for her first-aid kit and proceeded to clean him up, wiping the wound area with alcohol once more before covering the wound with gauze and tape.

Returning to her apartment, Ember washed the blood from

her hands. Grabbing a bin bag, she made her way back down the steps. She gathered up everything she had used, from the syringes to the lint to her sweater and the towel, and dumped them all in the bag. Picking up their phones and his keys, she took everything back up to her apartment.

She stripped off and used the medical scissors to cut through the shirt of her uniform, removing the logo of the café and anything else that would trace it back to her on the rare chance her clothes would be found. Despite knowing no one was going to waste time riffling through bins, let alone run a costly DNA analysis on a patch of blood or investigate further when it was found to be vampire blood, she still knew that if a random search was done on her or her place and traces of vampire blood were found, that would be an entirely different story.

Once she'd separately bagged the logos from her other clothes, once she'd wiped every trace of evidence from the floor and from their phones, she headed into the bathroom.

Ember stepped into the bath under the shower and scrubbed and rinsed thoroughly, cleaning under her nails until her fingertips were red raw.

Once she was done, she cleaned the sink and the bath.

She perched on the edge of it, holding her towel at her chest with one hand, her other hand grasping the pendant on the chain around her neck.

She'd saved a vampire's life.

She'd actually saved a vampire's life.

The guilt weighed heavily, causing a knot in her stomach and trying to force tears to the surface. But she suppressed them. She'd saved a life. She needed to make the nature of what he was irrelevant.

She twirled her engagement ring around her finger a couple of times before finally forcing herself from the bath's edge.

Pulling on her dressing gown, she cleaned down the kitchen worktop before adding the bloodied apple and mug to the bag too. She rinsed off the paring knife to use in place of the flick knife she'd lost in the scuffle. It was hardly a thorough clean, but she knew that would work in her favour should her wound be discovered and questioned.

Once she was convinced there were no condemning traces left, she dressed into a clean uniform for work and grabbed her only other jacket – a light one she wore on warmer days, but which would have to suffice for now.

She wiped his phone and keys over again and placed them in her inside pocket.

Closing and locking her apartment behind her, she headed across to his. She wiped over everything she had touched, closing drawers and cupboards in the process. Finally, she wiped over the front door before closing and locking it behind her.

She hovered at the top of the steps for a few moments, one black bin bag containing the bulk of the evidence in one hand and the smaller bin bag in the other.

He still hadn't so much as flinched. Eventually, he would stir though and she needed to be out of reach and near the exit when that happened.

One step at a time, avoiding any traces of blood, she made her way down to the foot of the stairwell.

She removed her coat from his back and shoved it into the larger bin bag before throwing his blanket over him in place of it.

Placing the now-sealed bags in front of the door, she stepped around the far side of the balustrade and slid her hand through the metal spindles to feel his pulse. It was stronger, more regular as, thankfully, so was his breathing. He was going to pull through; that was now a given. What she did from there she had yet to work out. She could only hope he would be appreciative enough for her to be able to reason with him – because she knew exactly what she needed *him* to do.

She nestled down at the bottom of the stairwell and set her watch alarm for half five. Her two attackers might have now felt like a distant nightmare, but she knew they could be back. And, if they were determined, there was every possibility they could return later that morning. She needed to leave at the crack of dawn to throw them off the scent. As well as that, the Curfew Enforcement Officers would still be out at that hour, hopefully a deterrent to her attackers who wouldn't want to risk coming across them. As for her journey back home that afternoon, she'd deal with that when it came to it.

Head resting back against the wall, she gazed up at her still-unconscious stranger.

She needed him gone. That's what she had to tell him: she needed him as far away from there as possible, at least for the next few days. After that, it didn't matter what he did. After that, none of it would matter. As soon as he woke – whether that would be in a matter of minutes, an hour, or the rest of the night, maybe even when she got back from work – she'd ask him to go. Though false imprisonment was hardly the grounding for a reasonable discussion, she *had* saved his life and he needed to recognise that. She'd make sure he recognised that.

She toyed with her engagement ring again, spinning it round and round her ring finger as she watched him sleep. Exhaustion struck her hard as the early hours hit, only the adrenaline rush having kept her awake until then. But his melodic breathing, exacerbated by the echo of the stairwell, had become hypnotic, comforting almost.

She closed her eyes, convincing herself she was just going to rest them, but the residual effects of the day – the journey to and from the interview at the border, several hours in work, the events of that night – started to take over as her adrenaline finally waned.

CHAPTER SIX

It took Ember a while to realise the consistent, nagging beep wasn't related to the events of her dream. And when she finally did snap back to reality, she clamped her hand over her watch, muffling it from waking her stranger.

She half expected to see him sat on the steps, fully conscious, staring her down as she remained out of arm's reach. But he remained face down and unflinching. Ember switched off her watch. She listened in the silence. During those few minutes, not once did he swallow – even vampires unable to fake that basic physiological response to being asleep.

Her behind numb from the cold floor despite the additional blanket she'd brought down for herself, her legs and neck aching from the position she'd fallen asleep in, she unsteadily forced herself to her feet as she struggled to come to her senses.

She needed to get moving straight away. She was only on the morning shift that day which meant she could get back home by half two. There was every chance he'd still be in recovery and not have a clue what had happened. She'd been tempted to leave him a note just in case, but it would be something to incriminate her.

Unlocking the outer door as quietly as she could, she stepped out into the grey hues of the pending morning light. Placing the two bin bags on the floor outside, she cast one more glance over him before closing and locking the door behind her.

It was a cold day but dry, the breeze whipping the loose strands of her hair against her cheeks as she looked down at where her baseball cap lay wet and dirty on the ground, having been trampled on during the scuffle the night before. A scuffle that felt as though it had occurred days ago, not hours.

What she'd done since felt even more surreal – that she had jeopardised everything, a decision from which there was now no turning back. Like that first shove from the top of the slide, she'd made her choice and now had no option but to go with it.

She looked down to the end of the alleyway. Everything lay silent beyond. The paring knife now having replaced her flick knife in her pocket, Ember carried the two bin bags down to the recess.

She lifted the metal industrial bin lid to drop the bags inside – one up one end and one up the other. She closed it quietly before turning towards the exit.

And flinched.

The one still had blood on his jeans from where she had stabbed him in the thigh. The other's eyes looked red, swollen and irritated from the mace. Eyes that glowered at her; a face she then recognised from the café: the guy who had slipped Casey his number.

His companion was of a comparable age – maybe in his early twenties too. Any other details were a blur as her heart pummelled her ribcage, the rapid rush of blood from her head inciting a sense of disassociation from what was happening. Because it wasn't real. That was what she wanted to tell herself: none of it was real. She was still asleep in the stairwell. Her watch alarm was yet to go off. It was nothing more than a nightmare off the back of the trauma.

But it *was* real. It was as real as the three ten-foot high walls that surrounded her.

Her throat constricted as inevitability struck its blow.

They were waiting for her to speak. That's what made it even worse. That as well as the fact they'd laid in wait for that long. For them, this had become personal. The hatred in their eyes, as if somehow *she* had wronged *them*, emanated such, as if defending herself – and succeeding – had been a slight against them. And for succeeding, they intended to make her suffer – evident in their relishing in her panic, awaiting either her futile attempts to escape or to beg for her life.

Checking over their shoulders to confirm isolation, satisfied that she had been left to ponder her fate for long enough, they wasted no more time.

And neither did she.

Ember leapt up onto the industrial bin, the palms of her hands reaching the top of the wall five feet above. With the toe of her boot using the worn-away mortar between the brickwork for leverage, she hoisted herself up.

She knew the wall was narrow and most likely not safe enough to take her weight, but she also knew she was nimble and fast. Her only possible plan was to descend into the courtyard on the other side of the recess and make a break for it through the gate and out onto the street beyond. Her chances would be small before they figured out her plan, but it was the only chance she had.

But before she'd got her first foot up onto the top of the wall, she was dragged backwards off the bin and thrown onto the floor.

Seconds later, the blow to her head having left her too stunned to move, she felt herself leaving the ground. She was slammed over the industrial bin face-first, weight pressing down on her back to keep her there.

Her paring knife snagged in her jacket pocket as she tried to retrieve it, but her restrainer had predicted her that time. Her jacket was promptly tugged off her, wrenching her shoulders. Between them, her two attackers all but tore her sweater off too, nearly suffocating her in the process.

She tried to fight back but couldn't find the leverage, her restrainer's thighs lodged between hers, his one hand on the back of her neck to hold her down, the other clenching her right arm as he spread it out.

The removal of her sweater, the subsequent exposure of her short-sleeved tunic, then made sense as her second attacker took a hold of her wrist. He slammed a fist full of syringes on the top of the bin, no doubt not clean.

Her pulse turned frantic at the sight of the first needle in his hand.

She tried to wriggle but the strength of the men holding her down was too great. She hated herself for it, but the words slipped out regardless. 'No. *Please.*'

But her primary restrainer's breath was hot against her ear. 'It'll all be over soon enough. Sorry, sweetheart, but we can't have you putting the prized goods off.'

The prized goods no doubt meaning Casey.

It also meant they weren't going to let her walk away from it alive. Neither were they going to waste a profit. These were the worst kinds of gatherers. These were the ones who collected blood to sell it quick and cheap.

Her second attacker, the guy from the café, tapped the veins in the crook of her arm as if he'd done it countless times before.

As she saw her whole world, her entire future, any semblance of hope slipping away, she yelled out for help.

Her protests were instantly muffled by his hand over her mouth. They weren't listening. They weren't the remotest bit interested.

No one was interested.

She bit his hand as a last ditch attempt to break free.

The scuffle was brief though. Both her attackers resumed their position.

As the second one tightened his grip on her wrist, she gritted her teeth, watched the syringe approach her arm through blurry eyes.

Blood sprayed onto her face. Warm, wet blood that caused her to blink away the traces on her lashes.

Nate woke with his cheek resting on stone, his whole body aching.

With a groan and his 'fuck' muffled by the step, he tucked his right hand up under his jacket and T-shirt to reach the small of his back and the source of the pain.

His fingers brushed fabric; brushed what felt like gauze and tape.

He pressed his left palm down on the step to give him leverage to sit up but, finding his movement to be restricted, he turned his head to look at the metal cuff that clinked against the steel spindle. Instead of standing, he moved into a kneeling position.

Instantly detecting a feminine scent in the stairwell – *her* scent – he looked down over his right shoulder.

Ember.

She wasn't there now but she had been very recently from the subtleties of her fragrance lingering in the air.

The backdrop of dark grey hue beyond the grate above the door told him dawn was almost on the horizon. He checked his watch. He'd been unconscious for at least nine hours.

Twisting his torso, he peeled back the gauze to examine the wound. The scent of hemlock and garlic beneath the alcohol reinforced what the state of the wound already told him. Only garlic caused that kind of damage, and only hemlock paralysed a vampire and knocked them out cold the way he had been.

He checked for the exit wound but his abdomen was clear, meaning the bullet had been angled to remain embedded inside him. Whoever was responsible had clearly wanted a slow but guaranteed death whilst he was unconscious, further confirming what he'd already suspected: it hadn't been a random shooting – he'd been targeted.

He'd managed to tuck himself in a recess as he'd waited for the shooter to show up. A shot as good as that one had been meant it was a professional job – and professionals always checked their job was complete.

Nate had got an arm around his throat easily enough, but his shooter's thrashing had, in light of his wound, weakened him quickly. Having realised that he wasn't going to get information out of him soon enough and not willing to risk being the weaker of the two, he'd promptly tightened his chokehold as he'd fed to help give him the strength he'd needed to heal. After he'd finished, he'd tightened his chokehold even more until finally the shooter had stopped struggling. To be sure, Nate had snapped his neck.

But when his wound hadn't started to heal despite his feed, Nate had known something was wrong. With his apartment too far away on other side of Lowtown, he'd headed to his backup apartment. He'd got through the door and as far as the stairwell before he'd felt something pop inside him, confirming that the only thing that had saved him to that point was the mechanism malfunctioning initially. As was no doubt originally intended, he'd lost consciousness immediately.

Now the fact he was not only still alive but also healing told him that Ember – or someone she knew – had removed the bullet. And not only had she removed the bullet, he'd been given human blood to kick-start the healing process that his body would have been too damaged to implement for itself. Ember, seemingly, somehow, had saved his life – before handcuffing him to the stairwell. Handcuffed him with *his* cuffs.

He looked around for any sign of the bullet. Any sign of anything. But the stairwell was empty. The keys to his apartment were gone from beneath his hand. His phone had been taken from inside his jacket pocket.

He sank back on his haunches. He could tell from the state of his T-shirt and the step that there would have been a lot of blood. There was no way she would have risked even a trace of it being revealed on her clothing or any other belonging. She would have cleaned up, no doubt. Wanted to dispose of any evidence – the bullet with it.

The bullet he needed.

He glanced up at her closed door before he reached for the cuff and flicked the self-release mechanism he'd had installed in it, freeing his wrist. He clutched his still-aching side and used the balustrade to help him to his feet.

The fact she'd felt the need to cuff him proved she would have had more sense than to risk trying to make her way back down past him once he was conscious again, adding to his gut feeling that Ember was no longer there. And if Ember was no longer there, there was every chance the bullet was no longer there either.

Reaching her door, he knocked anyway.

He waited.

When there was no answer, he knocked again.

Cursing under his breath, he stepped over to his own apartment. He kicked the door once and then twice, it splintering and swinging open on the third kick.

He crossed into the bedroom and grabbed his spare set of keys from his jeans he'd discarded over the back of the chair. He tore off his bloodstained T-shirt and reached for a fresh one from the holdall by his bed. He'd shower when he got back.

And then he caught it on the breeze, echoing down the alley through his partially open bedroom window: voices.

A scuffle.

Male voices that were thirty feet away, yet as clear as if they were directly below the window. And amongst them was the brief plea of a woman's voice.

A voice he'd recognise anywhere.

CHAPTER SEVEN

———◆———

Arms freed, Ember wiped the blood from her eyes.

She snatched back a breath as she pushed herself upright from the bin, the dead weight behind her now gone. She stared down to her right at the syringe-holding guy now flat on his back on the floor, his smashed and bloodied jaw the result of having taken an almighty blow to it. The weird angle of his neck confirmed it had been broken in the impact.

She turned one eighty and leaned back against the bin as she looked to her new right, to where her primary attacker was struggling in a chokehold. Forearm around her attacker's neck, the guy responsible was squeezing the breath out of him.

A guy she instantly recognised.

Cold pins and needles spread over her body, her breathing the only thing she could hear.

Her primary attacker flayed in a futile attempt to free himself but her stranger's stance and chokehold were firm and uncompromising.

He was killing him. And she simply stood there watching.

She willed herself to say something, to do something. Instead she remained silently tentative as she tried to figure out how the hell she was going to avoid being next. She glanced to her jacket laying behind her stranger, her knife still in its pocket.

A moment later, a subtle crack ricocheted around the recess. In the subdued morning light, her primary attacker flopped to the floor.

Her gaze dropped to the dead body. To both dead bodies. To her attackers he had killed without hesitation and, from what she could see, without remorse.

As her stranger clutched his side, reminding her of his injury, she took what she knew could be her only chance.

But no sooner had she skimmed past him, Ember felt an arm across her waist, a hard body against her back as she was turned one-eighty to face the recess. Lifting her left arm, she reached behind her head and grabbed hold of the hair at the back of his. She yanked as she simultaneously elbowed his wound with her right arm.

He jolted with the pain of it, but he didn't let her go. Instead, his grip tightened as he lifted her from the ground and carried her back to the bin.

Cold metal pressing against her cheek again, Ember felt him kick her legs apart with his. He pinned her left arm down against the lid before wrenching her right arm up her back. Pressing the heel of his hand under her elbow, he pushed upwards, causing her to wince and freeze with the pain of it.

'Let's get something clear, Ember,' he said, his voice as impressively – or worryingly – controlled as his restraint. 'If I had any intention of killing you, abducting you, raping you or feeding on you, I've had more than my fair share of opportunities. So calm yourself down because that hurt like fuck and I *will* lose my patience if you attempt anything like that again.'

As he let her go a moment later, she spun to face him, her free hand clasping the shoulder he had wrenched, pain still shooting down her arm and making her fingers tingle.

He clutched his side, his scowl telling her his claim about the discomfort was true.

The glaring question became insuppressible. 'How? How did you get out?'

He rubbed the back of his head, her clearly having made an impact there too. 'What did you do with the bullet, Ember?'

Twice now he'd used her name. It threw her off kilter more the second time now she was able to process it. He needed information from her – maybe the only reason he had intervened. Maybe the only reason she was still alive. After all, she'd just witnessed him murder two people. Two humans.

And she'd saved a vampire capable of such. She wasn't just in it up to her neck: she was already drowning.

'Ember.' His tone was as firm and uncompromising as his sullen glare as he recaptured her attention.

So much for saving his life.

She remained silent as she swayed between whether giving him the information would be her worst or best decision.

'You saved my life,' he reminded her, 'and now I've saved yours. That means we're even. Tell me what you did with the bullet and then we're done.'

'So you say.'

He took a step towards her.

Ember instantly took a backwards step in response.

'I'm asking nicely,' he said.

And she knew as well as he did that he had other options if she chose not to comply.

She lifted the lid of the bin and threw the bin bag towards him. 'And just so *you're* clear, I'm not going to do anything stupid over what happened here. They got what was coming as far as I'm concerned.'

And not least because of what their intentions towards Casey had been.

'And you know where I live,' she added. 'You know where I work. You know who my friends are.'

'And you can't afford any of this to screw up your application. Not with only a few days to go.'

Her heart pounded. The fact that maybe she hadn't been paranoid about his reason for being there suddenly unraveled a whole new nightmare.

'How do you know about that?'

He crouched in front of the bag and split it open. He glanced up at her with a frown. 'Seriously?'

But she waited for his answer.

He reverted his attention to searching the bag. 'Not even whispers can escape a vampire's hearing. Not that your friend Casey knows the definition of that word. Certainly not earlier.'

He knew her predicament. He knew about her being on the cusp of leaving.

It was getting worse; his hold over her increasing. She needed out of there. She needed out of there now.

'In the towel,' she said.

He glanced up at her before unravelling the coiled fabric. His pensive gaze fixed on the bullet. He picked it up with a discarded piece of lint, obviously to avoid touching the silver encasement that she hadn't registered before.

Having received what he'd wanted, she took her opportunity to stride past him. All she could think about was getting as far away from there as possible. As far away from what she had done as possible. As far away from him as possible.

She snatched up her jacket along the way.

'Ember.'

Her heart skipped a beat. She turned to face him.

'My phone? My keys?' he asked, his hand outstretched.

She reached into her jacket pocket and removed them both. She stepped towards him to hand them over.

His cold fingers brushing hers as he took his belongings from her. But then he snagged her wrist. He glanced down at the plaster she had placed over her sliced hand. His hold remained firm but surprisingly gentle, and he met her gaze again.

'I told you: I'm not going to tell anyone, OK?' she reiterated. 'I don't know who you are or what you're involved in and I don't care. You're right: I'm not going to screw everything up. I just want to pretend none of this happened. I'm more than capable of pretending none of this happened. I saved your life, you saved mine, and now we're even,' she declared, reinforcing what he had said.

His hold remained unrelenting, his gaze entrancingly steady in the deathly silence, his handsome face still partially masked by the shadows of a dawn that had yet to encroach on the dark recess.

Discomfort coiled in her chest as fear mingled with a much more difficult feeling to swallow: the unforgiveable, disgust-inducing feeling of attraction as she gazed deep into his dark eyes. Attraction for a brutal killer – a brutal killer who still held her life in his hands. A brutal killer who may indeed only have let her live long enough to obtain what he wanted.

She tried to curb her heavy breathing but failed miserably. Flashbacks tilted the walls that closed in around them. Flashbacks that had always haunted her.

'There won't be any evidence,' he said, finally letting her wrist go. 'Of anything. I'll sort it.'

A part of her wanted to know exactly what 'sorting it' involved. A bigger part clung onto the seeming reprieve. A reprieve she opted to make the most of without jeopardising it with further questions.

She didn't remember her journey out of the recess, only the lingering sensation of his gaze burning into her back.

She didn't remember heading up the alley or making it back out onto the main street, nor the full extent of her journey to the café. The streets had been as much a blur as the people she may or may not have passed on them.

She had a vague recollection of stopping at one point. She couldn't recall where it had been or if it had garnered any attention. She just remembered falling against the nearest wall as the shock had set in, her legs unable to support her, her trembling hand clasped over her mouth. She'd sobbed until all the shock had released itself from her body. Her cry had been short and unsatisfying, her throat constricted and dry, and she'd taken a few deep and steady breaths to compensate. As she'd told herself over and over again: she was still alive. She had to focus on still being alive.

Nonetheless, the knot in the pit of her stomach at what she had witnessed remained. A crime she needed to report; that she was obligated to report – that her stranger would know she was obligated to report. Her stranger who, if he had any sense, would be long gone.

But that didn't change the fact he still knew where *she* lived. He'd let her go because he believed he had nothing to fear from doing so – arrogance or a truce? If he'd suspected to the contrary, she'd no doubt already be dead.

Instead, they now shared a dark little secret. A dark, dirty secret she had no idea what he intended to do about.

She made her way around to the back of the café, needing to access the staff entrance as the shutters were still down at that early hour.

Seeing light spill into the corridor from Harry's office, she called out, 'Only me, Harry,' so as not to startle him before making her way into the ladies.

'Ember?'

But she didn't hang around to respond, fearful of him seeing her shaken.

As recollections of the event set-in, as scenes played out in her head of worst-case scenarios, she grasped the edge of the sink.

'Ember?'

It was followed by a knock on the door.

'Ember, is everything OK?'

She always popped her head around the door when she was in early. The fact she hadn't would have already set off alarm bells.

'Everything's fine, Harry. I'll be out in a minute.'

She glanced at her reflection to see red raw eyes that would take ages to calm down. She quickly washed the dirt from her face from the scuffle, only then seeing the small graze on her cheek from where she recalled her skin scraping against concrete as she hit the floor.

'You decent?' Harry asked through the door.

'I told you: I'm fine,' she declared, splashing cold water onto her eyes.

He opened it regardless.

Ember met his concerned gaze in the mirror before distracting herself by washing her hands. Washing off the remains of the dirt. Her guilt. Washing under her ring which they no doubt would have stolen too if they'd been given a fraction longer.

He took a couple of steps in. 'Has something happened?'

She met his gaze fleetingly again. 'Why would it have?'

'Ember, you look dreadful.'

'I didn't get much sleep last night, that's all.'

He frowned as he closed in on her. 'What's that graze on your cheek?'

She instantly covered it with her hand. 'I fainted earlier.'

He raised his eyebrows. 'Fainted?'

'I told you: I didn't get much sleep last night. It's probably all the stress of the build-up to yesterday.'

His suspicion emanated from his frown. 'And your hand?'

Ember glanced down at the plaster. 'I cut myself by accident this morning. I wasn't concentrating.'

'I can say you hurt yourself in the kitchen here,' Harry said. 'That I witnessed it.'

'You don't need to do that.'

'We both know I do.'

She met his gaze, but looked away a split-second later. She nodded. 'Thank you.'

'Ember,' he said, closing the gap between them. 'Talk to me.'

She dried her hands. She looked back at him. Looked into eyes as laden with concern as if he were faced with one of his own daughters in trouble.

'A couple of guys jumped me last night,' she said, hoping her tone made it sound less of an issue. 'I got away. And I'm fine. Honestly. That's why I didn't get much sleep.'

His eyes widened in alarm. 'Did they hurt you?'

'No. I didn't give them the chance. Come on, Harry – you know me,' she tagged on, trying to raise a nonchalant smile.

It wasn't working.

'Why didn't you call me? I would have come to get you. You could have stayed at mine.'

'Because like I said, I'm fine. Harry, you know I've had my fair share of scrapes over the years. I know how to look after myself. I'm shaken up but nothing more. If it wasn't so close to my application, I would have already brushed it off by now.'

His brow remained furrowed. 'Did you know them? I mean, have you seen them before? Could you identify them?'

She refrained from mentioning one of them had been chatting up Casey – had been in that very café. She didn't want word getting back to her. She didn't need to know. If they had got away, she would have felt compelled to tell Harry – to have raised vigilance in the café, to have warned the others to keep a look out. But those responsible were gone. They were dead now. There was no need for anyone to know – not even Harry.

'I know that ring is a double-edged sword for you, Ember, but at least they didn't steal that.'

As his gaze remained weighted with concern, Ember discarded the towel she'd been clinging onto and turned to face him fully.

'Anyway, I don't look like the only one who hasn't slept.'

'Don't change the subject, Ember.'

'I'm not. So how about *you* talk to *me*, Harry?'

She folded her arms. She leaned against the counter. Because something was wrong. Now her shock was waning in the face of safety and familiarity, she could feel it.

'You're probably going to hear anyway,' he declared with reluctance lingering in his resolve. 'There are a few rumours on the circuit. Word of some gang interest building in the area.'

She stood upright, her arms dropping back to her sides. It was a rumour none of them needed to hear. 'Which gang?'

'The Hordas clan.'

'But this area is small fry. They've *never* shown an interest before.'

'Exactly. It's just a rumour. No one's confirmed anything.'

'Have you been asking around?'

'Yes. And we all agree it was probably something that started in a pub somewhere. You know what it's like. That's why I don't want you worrying about it. And I want you to come back to ours after work tonight. The girls won't mind bedding in together. You can have a room to yourself.'

'Harry—'

'Please, Ember. I know you're supposed to stay put at home in case the authorities call around to do one of their checks, but if by some coincidence it happens to be tonight, you can tell them you were assisting with paperwork – maybe even with preparing to hire a new assistant manager to take over from you,' he tagged on, his voice lifting as if surprising himself that he'd come up with a good excuse. 'That would be feasible.'

She held his gaze in the silence, tuned in to the dripping tap; the countdown of only a few days left to survive in that place. 'If you're sure.'

He gave one of his rare offerings: a smile. 'I'll cook something. The girls will want to say goodbye to you anyway. You may not get another chance over this next week.'

She knew she wasn't going to get the last word on it.

He pulled away.

'Harry . . .'

He turned to face her again.

'Thank you,' she said.

'Decide if you're still grateful after I've fed you,' he said as he headed to the threshold. 'After all, it's been a while since you've sampled my cooking.'

She laughed lightly. As he left, she reached up to her neck to find the reassurance of her pendant.

Her heart plummeted. She flattened her palm to her chest. She spun to face the mirror again. She yanked the collar of her shirt down.

It had gone.

All she had left of her, and it had gone.

CHAPTER EIGHT

———◆———

Located down a back alley, the doorway was invisible beyond steam clouds puffing out from the active kitchens.

It was an unassuming, paint-peeling black door, and one where you had to know to remove the loose third brick along on the wall to the right of it to access the latch that would open it.

Miller and Degard were sat in their usual places behind the door, playing cards at the table. Without an appointment, Nate knew he wasn't going to get in via any other means. Neither had time to reach for their guns that had rested on the table before Nate tranquillised each in the chest, knocking them both out cold before taking the keys from the table and unlocking the next door directly ahead.

At the end of the corridor, the guy instantly rose from playing on his phone. He removed his gun in preparation, making it even more important that Nate kept his strides casual and calm in order to keep his guard down until he got close enough.

And the closer he got, the more he could hear the music blaring from within. A genre of music that assured him the one he wanted was in.

He took the last obstacle out of the way in one more accurate tranquillising shot to his chest before opening the door.

Thrash metal echoed around the recesses, a tinging sound resonating in the air as it bounced around the plethora of pipe-work that dominated the space.

It had once been a maintenance room. Now nothing flowed through the pipes and nothing sparked on the switchboards. Now it was her office: a room as dark and grimy as her profession: one of the best and most skilled bullet creators in the locale. She was an artist as much as she was an engineer. And she worked for whoever paid the right price which meant, like him, she had no loyalty to anyone but herself. She called herself an entrepreneur. He'd called her worse things during sex – and she him.

She was sitting on a stool at her workstation, her back to him, her feet flat on the floor in her calf-length black boots that kept rhythm with the music. Her legs were spread as she worked, giving him full sight of her dusky thighs, her khaki shorts cling-ing temptingly into the curves of her full, rounded arse that he'd been up close and personal with in many an illegal way.

Her mass of dark hair was bunched up on top of her head, per-spiration trickling down the back of her neck from the humidity of the room and escaping into the back of her vest top.

He grabbed a stool from under one of the pipes and placed it directly behind her as she continued to hum to herself, pouring the liquid she had just finished melting into the line of bullet shells.

Spreading his thighs either side of hers as he sat behind her, he knotted his fingers in her hair as he simultaneously placed his blade to her throat.

Daisy was always quick to act and it would have taken her a split-second to smash her head back into his nose if the blade hadn't been there.

'Visor off and hands flat on the table,' he instructed against her ear. 'Fingers spread.'

'Nate?' Her head twitched to the side slightly as if needing to see him to confirm it.

'Hey, flower.'

She carefully removed the visor and dropped it in front of her before placing her palms flat on the table and spreading her fingers as he'd instructed. She knew better than to do anything to the contrary.

'Being as creative as always, I see,' he said.

'What do you want, Nate? And how the fuck did you get in here?'

'I knocked politely. As always.' He let go of her hair to hold the bullet shell, now in a plastic bag, up in front of her. He gave her a moment for her vision to focus. 'Your handiwork?'

She frowned. 'I'll need to take a closer look.'

'No distinguishing marks,' he said. 'No ownership stamp. So you can deny it's yours if you want to but this is quite the skilled engineering and I only know one who can pull something this sophisticated off. From what I can work out, it enters the body like any normal bullet, except this one's silver, of course. On impact, the front disengages inside the body. An unpleasant dose of hemlock, garlic and grains of silver get into the system. The victim blacks out from the hemlock dose, the garlic ensures they can't heal. They stand no chance of regaining consciousness. They lose too much blood. The silver grains gradually disperse. Vampire's dead a couple of hours later. It was designed to kill a vampire irrevocably and indefinitely – and it ended up in my blood stream.'

She subtly licked her dry lips. 'How the fuck are you still alive then?'

'I got lucky.'

'Luckiest bastard I know surviving this.'

'And don't I know it. Which is why I want to know who put it there.'

Her pulse picked up a notch. A trickle of perspiration crept down her temple.

'You know how it works. Like you, I don't ask questions, Nate.'

'But unlike me, *you* fucked up. And when you screw up, the job bites you on the arse. And you know *how* hard I can bite, Daisy. I want to know who hired you to make it. I want to know who you sold it to.'

'You know I can't reveal that. I'll be finished.'

'I have a six-inch blade to your throat. So, rather than worry about the future, I'd focus on the here-and-now if I were you. Tell me who you sold it to before I put this six inch blade right through the centre of your hand. You have eight fingers and two thumbs after that, all of which would be a shame to lose, not least because I've never had any complaints about how you use them. Who did you sell it to, Daisy? And how many?'

Her jaw clenched. She kept her eyes fixed ahead.

Catching hold of her hair again, Nate stood from his stool before kicking away hers. He slammed her face first onto the table, jammed the knife blade down between her middle and forefinger, causing her to flinch and her eyes to widen.

'Last warning. You know what the sight of blood does to me and you don't want me summoning what nature gave me, do you?'

She gritted her teeth before exhaling tersely.

He slammed the knife down between her little finger and forefinger.

She flinched. 'The Voys,' she all but spat out. 'The fucking Voys, OK? The Voys hired me to make it. I just sold them the one.'

He removed the blade, backed up a couple of steps and let her spin around to face him.

'The Voys? What's their issue with me?' he asked.

'I don't know. I didn't ask questions. You know my rules are the same as yours.'

'I wonder how they'll feel about knowing I'm still walking because of your dodgy craftwork.'

Her brown eyes narrowed. 'Oh, come on, Nate. Look, I didn't know it was intended for you, all right? I swear.'

'So you say.'

He turned away.

'Nate, we don't need to fall out over this.'

'One of your bullets nearly killed me, Daisy. I don't know what else would constitute a break-up.'

'OK, so I heard them saying the Hordas clan weren't getting any favours. I'm guessing they've hired you again, huh?'

Nate stopped. He turned to face her again.

'Whatever the clan want you for,' she added, 'the Voys didn't want to risk you succeeding.'

'You definitely heard them say that?'

'You know me, Nate. I don't repeat what I haven't heard with my own ears.'

That much was more than true.

'And what else have you heard?'

She tongued the outside of her teeth. She sighed before folding her arms. 'Look, I'm sorry they came after you, OK? Honestly, I had no idea.' She paused. 'Shit's getting bad out there. We all know the Hordas clan are taking over Lowtown chunk by chunk. The Voys are trying to sustain their territory but they're losing ground. They're forming a back-up plan. They want to spread their wings to Blackthorn.'

'They're thinking of taking on Blackthorn? The vampires there? Do they not realise the likes of Kane Malloy and Caleb Dehain will fucking eat them for breakfast if they get word of this, let alone if they step foot in either of their territories?'

'Which is why I think they're being left to their own devices. Between you and me, I'm hearing the Third Species Control Division are leaving this be for their own ends. They know the war is brewing between the two gangs. They know that if they let the Hordas clan get too big, it'll force the Voys to get into Blackthorn to gain new ground. And if Malloy in particular does go for them, the authorities have got a valid reason to bring him in. We all know how badly they want him. You want to do us all a favour? Make the biggest collection of your life, Nate. Take them Malloy, let them tick him off their most-wanted list, and then maybe the TSCD will do what they're paid to do and keep order in this district rather than letting it go to hell at the hands of the likes of the Hordas clan and the Voys.'

'You're suggesting I take on Malloy? And hand him over?'

'If anyone can, you can.'

'I'll forget that crossed your lips.'

Her eyes glimmered with uncertainty. With regret. 'I'm guessing maybe you should.'

'Which I will, *if* you make it up to me by putting those skilled fingers of yours to some good use before I leave.'

She raised her eyebrows expectantly. He reached into the back of his jeans and pulled out the necklace that he'd found under the dead bodies of one of Ember's attackers. He knew he should have left it there. He should have discarded it with them. It was just a cheap piece of costume jewellery. There must have been a load of them in circulation. But his gut knew better than that. What he'd seen with his own eyes two months before knew better than that. That nagging feeling that there had always been something familiar about her knew better than that.

'And *then* we can both agree we never had this conversation.' She exhaled curtly. 'Just as we always do, Nate.'

CHAPTER NINE

———◆———

Ember had spent all morning on tenterhooks, expecting him to enter the café. Every time the door had opened, she'd cast a startled glance in the customer's direction only to see anyone but him entering.

She still didn't even know his name. Hadn't asked his name. But he clearly knew hers – something else he had over her.

'You're edgy this morning,' Casey had said as she'd stepped alongside her at the coffee machine. 'Is everything OK?'

She'd continued to refrain from telling her about the attack the night before. She'd asked Harry to keep his mouth shut too, even though he still only knew part of the story.

'I guess the reality of knowing there aren't many days to go now is setting in,' Ember had said in a vain attempt at giving a valid reason.

Despite her own anxiety, Ember hadn't failed to notice that Casey had been casting her fair share of glances at the door every time it opened too. No doubt she had been expecting a visitor of her own – a visitor who had died at the hands of *her* visitor.

'Uh-huh.' Casey had placed her customer's cup next to Ember's as she too had waited for it to fill. There'd been a lengthy pause that was unnatural for Casey. 'I've heard the rumours, Ember.'

Her heart had skipped a beat. Her gaze had snapped to Casey's. 'Rumours about what?'

'I overheard someone in here talking about it only a couple of hours ago. You and Harry don't need to hide it from us.'

Ember's chest had tightened. 'Hide what?'

'About the Hordas clan paying a visit to Duke's place over on Monroe Street.'

Ember's stomach had flipped. She'd turned to face Casey fully. She'd lowered her voice. 'When?'

'A couple of days ago apparently.'

'Are you *sure*?'

Casey had shrugged. 'That's what I heard. It would make sense as to why Harry's been so bad tempered the last couple of days. Working until all hours, you know. If he can work any more hours, that is. So is it true?'

'I didn't know anything about this.'

And Harry had denied it. He had denied it that very morning, playing it down into nothing more than hearsay.

Casey had frowned. A moment later, her eyes had flared. 'Shit,' she'd hissed. She'd cupped her hand over her mouth as if in an attempt to take back the words. 'I bet he didn't want you to know. Not with you leaving.'

'Finish serving my customer for me, will you, please?' Ember had said, instantly pulling away from her.

She'd marched down to Harry's office. She'd only knocked once. She hadn't waited to be invited in. She'd closed the door behind her.

Harry had looked up at her. He'd disconnected from whatever call he'd been in the middle of with a quick, 'I'll call you back'.

'Is it true?' Ember had asked. 'About the Hordas clan hitting Duke's?'

His contrite expression had been confirmation enough.

'Why didn't you say anything to me?' she'd asked, taking the seat opposite him. 'Why didn't you mention anything?'

'What would have been the point?'

'The point is I'm the deputy manager here.'

'For only a handful of days more.'

Ember had folded her arms, leaned back in the chair, and shook her head as she'd stared him down. 'You should have told me. If not as deputy manager then at least as friends.'

'And because we're friends, I didn't want to worry you without good reason. It's a rumour, Ember. Nothing has been confirmed.'

'Nothing ever is with them until it's too late. Have you spoken to Duke?'

'I've tried.'

She'd leaned forward and rested her arms on the table. 'What does that mean?'

'He hasn't responded to my messages. And before you say anything, it might be a coincidence, that's all.'

Ember had frowned. 'You don't believe that any more than I do.' She'd paused. 'Is this why you've been quieter than usual? Grouchier than usual. Have you known about this for a while?'

Harry had known better than to believe she'd let it go. 'I first heard the rumour a few days ago.'

'And you kept me out of the loop because of my application.'

'I didn't want anything affecting it on the day, Ember.'

'Instead the Hordas clan could walk in here off the street at any point and you decided to keep that to yourself.'

'There are bigger businesses in this area, Ember. More popular and more profitable businesses. We're too small for them to take notice. We don't make enough for them to take notice. So to me that meant it wasn't worth worrying you at this stage with things that might never happen.'

'Or might not happen until after I've already left, right?' She'd glanced down at his busy desk. 'That's what all this extra pouring over paperwork is about. Is that why you asked me to get all of the accounts together?' She'd pressed her finger onto the pile of papers between them. 'If those bullies come here, we're *not* paying them a penny, Harry. You are not handing over *everything* you've worked for to some low-life protection racket.'

'You're getting ahead of yourself, Ember.'

'No. I know preparations when I see them.'

'And it's *my* business, Ember. I want you to remember that.'

'And *my* hard work too. And I care about this place, Harry. I care about you too.' She'd leaned back in her chair again. 'You'd thought they were the ones responsible for me getting jumped last night, didn't you? I saw the look on your face. I saw the worry in your eyes. Now it makes sense.'

'I want you to take the rest of the week off, Ember. I want this to be your last shift.'

She'd shaken her head. 'No.'

'I was planning to bring it up with you yesterday, but I didn't want to spoil your good news. Now that you know you're definitely going, it's more important than ever that you're not around.'

'From trying to convince me it's nothing but a rumour to kicking me out now?'

'I'm looking out for you.'

'And it sounds to me like you need me around more than ever. I'm not leaving you in the lurch. Not over this.'

'We can manage. Yvonne will step into the breach for now, I'm sure.'

'And she's got a young child at home. Should *she* be here? And what about Casey? How much attention is she going to garner from the likes of them?'

Had maybe done so already. That maybe Harry's assumptions about their involvement in the attack hadn't been wrong. Maybe they *had* come for the staff – Casey, her . . .

Her heart had pounded. If it were true, her stranger had taken on a couple of guys who worked for the Hordas clan.

'You can't rule me out unless you're going to rule them all out,' she'd said, trying to force herself to focus on the here and now. 'I'm staying, Harry. I'm staying until my time is up.'

Guys who were now dead.

Dead because of her.

Now, down on her hands and knees in the recess, she didn't need that playing on her mind amidst already rife recollections of that morning as she searched every dark nook for her necklace. They'd torn her jumper over her head. The possibilities that the loose chain had been caught up in it were high.

But nothing.

Ember sank back on her haunches, the sick sensation in her stomach intensifying.

Despite having accepted Harry's offer to go back to his for the night, and more than ever in light of their conversation, the second she'd found her necklace gone, she'd known she'd have to go back to try and find it.

Equally, she'd known she'd needed to confront what she'd done. She couldn't spend the next few days flinching every time the café door opened. She couldn't spend every minute worrying when her stranger was going to turn up, or what he might want from her. She needed closure. She needed to know what had happened was over.

Ember pulled herself to her feet and headed out of the recess.

It was pointless delaying. She needed to confront him – *if* he was still around. If he hadn't already thought better of it and had left while he could.

She headed down to the outer door, unlocked it, stepped into the shadows, and quietly closed the door behind herself.

She tentatively scanned the stairwell before feeling reassured enough to lock the door behind her.

He wasn't kidding when he'd said there'd be no traces left. Under the subtle glow of the afternoon light that pushed through the mesh window, she could already see that the blood on the stairs had completely vanished. Just like back in the recess, there wasn't so much as a stain.

Front door key ready in her hand, she ascended the steps one at a time.

The door to his apartment was shut but the splintering along the jamb, as well as the new lock, told her how he'd managed to get out to her that morning: he'd clearly had a spare set of keys in his apartment. But as for how he'd got out of his cuffs in the first place, that remained a mystery.

Despite the usual silence emanating from within his apartment, Ember maintained a watchful eye.

Until she detected the glint of metal dangling from the handle of her door.

She froze. Her gaze darted back to his door. She looked back at hers. She hurried up the last few steps. She removed the necklace.

She unlocked her door. She flicked on her lounge light. The fake, glass sapphire had the familiar dents and scratches she had come to love. Some of the links on the chain were new though. Not only had he given it back, he'd fixed it too.

She closed the door behind her. She drew all three bolts

across. She leaned back against it. Using the knuckle of her forefinger, she wiped away the tears that instantly gathered at the corners of her eyes as she crushed the pendant in her right hand, letting metal and glass dig into the backs of her fingers.

Her immediate instinct was to thank him.

But suspicion instantly set in: that maybe it had been a means for her to feel indebted to him further. Scepticism fuelled by the fact that, even more than twenty years later, it still felt like a betrayal to even consider one of his kind capable of decency – least of all with that very necklace a reminder.

Above all else, he was *still* there. Despite his witness living right opposite, he'd been arrogant enough to remain there.

She pulled herself away from the door and headed into the bathroom. She placed her necklace on the shelf above the sink before stripping off.

Having long passed her routine swift ten-minute wash-down, she sat down in the bathtub and let the shower spray rain down on her as she continued to put off the inevitable.

Because she *still* needed to know the truth. She still needed to challenge him. And if there was a fraction of a possibility that he'd done what he'd done out of decency, then more than ever she needed to revert back to her original plan.

Eventually, she dried herself off. She put on fresh underwear, her jeans, chunky socks, a vest top and her shapeless grey sweater over the top. She heated some leftover pasta in the microwave before taking it to eat on her lap in front of the TV.

Another hour had passed before she'd realised her food had turned cold and that she was no longer aware of the silent screen images that had become nothing but peripheral in front of her.

She headed into the bathroom to brush her teeth. She rubbed away the traces of perspiration gathering at the back of her neck at the knowledge she couldn't put it off any longer. She clutched the sink for a few moments to support her trembling thighs.

She checked her reflection as she tied her hair up in a scruffy bun knot. But she couldn't put her necklace back on. She couldn't go to him wearing that.

Before she gave herself time to rethink, she crossed her lounge. She slid the bolts back on her door.

She hovered at the threshold and stared ahead at his still-closed door, her pulse kicking up to an uncomfortable rate. As a vampire, he'd sense it. He'd know. So, taking steady breaths, she focused on calming her pounding heart.

Leaving her door ajar behind her, she crossed the top of the stairwell and knocked.

When there was no answer, she felt a paradox of relief and disappointment. But the silence granted her the confidence to knock once more – a little louder the second time.

When there was still no answer, she turned away. She'd almost reached her own threshold when his door clicked open behind her.

She spun one-eighty to face him.

Subtly backlit by the dim lighting of his apartment, he rested his forearm loosely against the doorjamb, a fraction above his head.

She couldn't tell at first if the sheen to his bare chest was sweat or water, but the undercurrent of a not-unpleasant masculine scent told her the former was most likely. That and his black sweatpants, sweatpants that rested low enough on his flat, toned stomach to reveal the subtlest hint of intimate hair beneath his belly button.

He'd been working out.

Or had company that she'd interrupted.

She instantly felt herself blush at the prospect of him not being alone; she didn't know why she'd assumed he would be.

'You returned my necklace.' It came out more bluntly than she had hoped, the drawback of not having planned what she was going to say. 'And you fixed it. Thank you.'

He folded his arms, further bulking out his biceps and his toned forearms as he leaned his shoulder against the doorjamb this time.

He was physically perfect. That was all she could think. There was nothing about him that could be faulted. And she hated herself for that being her focus in that moment. She hated that she allowed her gaze to wander over him to further reinforce his appeal. And her unease at the intimacy of his semi-nakedness wasn't helped by his unflinching gaze or his frown of curiosity.

'You're welcome,' he said.

She glanced to his exposed side, the dressing now removed. From what she could see from the angle, it was badly bruised but the wound already looked a few days old just from the past sixteen hours or so. The wonders of the third species – and the very reason the Global Council had spent decades trying to merge vampire blood with their own for the same effects.

She had to come straight out with it. 'I also wanted to check that everything was sorted this morning as you said it would be.'

'Not a trace,' he confirmed. His gaze remained unflinching. 'Is that it?'

For someone with so much leverage, his aloof dismissal threw her off guard.

'What do you want from me?' she asked.

He frowned pensively. 'Why would I want anything from you, Ember?'

Too many reasons trampled over each other in her head – none of them smart to vocalise as she stood alone with the vampire in the isolated stairwell.

'I need you to leave,' she said in another blunt statement.

He raised his eyebrows a fraction. 'I'm sorry?'

'I can't afford to have you around here. It's only for the next few days. I'll pay for the inconvenience if needs be.'

His frown deepened. 'You're asking me to leave the apartment?'

'For a few days, that's all. You know why I'm asking. Whoever shot you . . .'

'Has no idea where I am. I wasn't shot here.'

'But clearly you're involved with something I could do without. I don't want any trouble here.'

'You won't have.'

'And I don't need a . . .'

'A?'

'I don't need a vampire living next door.'

He unfolded his arms to rest one above his head again. This time he rested his other hand on his hip, drawing her attention to those low-slung sweatpants again. She had no idea if it was intentional on his part.

'I'm not trying to insult you,' she said. 'I'm not trying to be confrontational. I'm just stating the facts.'

'Uh-huh,' he said, annoyingly not giving anything away.

'Like I said, it's only for the time being. Until I leave next week. A vampire living opposite could raise questions. If you have feeders here, friends who come around . . .'

'No one comes around.'

'All the same, I need as few risks as possible. Someone who turns up shot and left for dead with guns in his apartment is someone I can't afford to have next door. I saved your life. All I'm asking you is to stay away until next week in return.'

'I saved *your* life. *That* was the return.'

'You could have died last night.'

'I could have died a lot of times. The novelty wears off soon enough.'

Ember felt her belligerence escalate at his stubbornness. 'I put myself on the line to save you.'

'Why?'

'Why what?'

She understood the question, she just wasn't sure of her answer.

'Why did you do it?' he asked. 'Why put yourself in that precarious position? Why not let me die?'

'I didn't have a choice.'

'Yes, you did,' he corrected her.

Seemingly he could be as blunt as her.

'OK,' she said, 'if you want to talk about this, tell me why you're here? You clearly knew my name which means you recognised me from the café. You certainly didn't look surprised to see me in that recess. You knew I lived here, didn't you? So how long have *you* lived here?'

'A little while.'

'Yet you've never said anything.'

'Why would I?'

'You've been visiting the café for weeks. Most people would say something.'

'And then what? We chat? Get to know each other? Walk each other home? That would have looked great on your application.'

'You've been eavesdropping on my private conversations.'

'Like I told you, your friends talk too loudly.'

'Why are you still here, despite what I witnessed?'

'Because you're not going to report it. Because you're too smart to report it.'

She stared him down in the shadows, his nonchalance amidst his frankness as unnerving as his being so utterly unperturbed by her challenge.

'Killing two humans would have you instantly ousted from Lowtown into Blackthorn, no matter how you've earned your residency here,' she reminded him.

She instantly regretted her rashness amidst her frustration.

He cocked his head to the side ever so slightly, but enough to make her stomach churn. 'Is that a threat?'

'We're both up to our necks in it. So why are you risking still being here? And why did you bother to return my necklace? Why did you go to the effort to have it fixed?'

'Because I could.' He stood upright, drawing her attention back to his body, back to the physical reality of her opposition. 'Listen, Ember. You don't want complications and neither do I. Let's continue that way. You need this place and, for now, so do I. It hasn't caused any problems this past week and it doesn't need to cause any problems for the next few days either. You stick to your routine and I'll stick to mine.'

She remained rooted to the spot, the prospect of his leaving having completely diminished in those passing minutes. That meant she was stuck with him – for the next few days at least. She needed to formulate a new argument, but one continued to elude her.

'Does it mean something to you?' he asked, breaking her train of thought.

'What?'

'The necklace. I'm guessing it's important to you for you to make the effort to thank me. I'm guessing it's more than a piece of tat.'

She fisted her hands at his choice of terminology. She held his gaze in the passing moments. 'It's *far* more than a piece of tat.'

'So from someone you cared about? I say cared in the past tense because I never see you with anyone.'

She didn't know why she did it. Why she chose to answer

him when she didn't have to. Why she allowed herself to feel vulnerable in front of him by doing so. But she had no doubt her frustration had been the biggest part of it, the hope maybe that would convince him to go, let alone the relief to finally be able to say the words to him.

'That's because they were murdered,' she said, the words clogging in her throat. 'By one of *your* kind.'

CHAPTER TEN

———◦◦◦———

Ember closed the door. Nate heard her slide the three bolts into place as she did every time she was locking down for the night.

He rubbed his thumb back and forth across his forehead. It was the final confirmation he'd needed. It was unmistakably her. His memory wasn't playing tricks. Nor was it some coincidence or twist of fate: it was the sheer logistics of Lowtown dictating it was inevitable their paths would cross again one day.

Though, reassuringly, even when he'd challenged her, she'd seemingly remained clueless of the connection.

He closed his own door, shutting her out as much as she'd shut him out. He stepped over to the kitchen. Spreading his arms, he rested his palms on the countertop and lowered his head.

More than ever, he needed to be thankful that the night before had finally marked the beginning of the end, the celebratory hug in the café having told him all he needed to know.

Taking the place across the hall from her *had* been a good choice, despite the risks. Risks born out of what was clearly mutual attraction, just as he had long suspected. Risks that had intensified as she'd stood in front of him in that stairwell, maintaining eye contact with him for longer than either of them had ever dared.

He'd seen her gaze wander over him. He'd heard her pulse increase. He'd detected the more anxious pace of her breathing. Despite her sternness, her coldness, something in her had reacted to him in a way she wasn't comfortable with – maybe hadn't been willing to acknowledge to herself. And she had confirmed why.

And because of that, it had taken balls to confront him like she had, now more than ever with her being so close to leaving. But he couldn't be gone like she wanted. That was the bottom line. His necessitated intervention the night before had proven that.

And her intervention in saving him, though at first having escalated his suspicion that she might know more than she had let on, had instead left him feeling she was simply what he suspected all along: just kind.

He made his way into the bedroom. He removed the contents from his holdall he'd left on the chair. He took out the compartment at the bottom. He grabbed a couple of the pre-filled syringes and headed over to the bed.

If she'd found them, she would never have had to put herself on the line.

He twirled them in his fingers before casting them aside. Tonight he needed more.

He stripped off his workout clothes and rinsed off in the shower. He pulled on his T-shirt and jeans, grabbed his keys and headed out.

He didn't care that he slammed the door this time. If anything, she might sleep easier knowing he wasn't there.

He locked and secured the outer door and made his way down the dark alley.

He headed to The Hive, nicknamed as such as it spanned a tunnel of cellars. Situated near the Midtown border, it had remained one of Lowtown's best-kept secrets, particularly as it wasn't in anyone's best interest for it to be disclosed – and especially for the sake of its frequenters from Midtown and Summerton.

That was exactly why the place had been set up: for the privileged to get their fixes with Lowtown and Blackthorn residents whilst maintaining the relative safety of being close to the Midtown border. The Hive was a carefully controlled operation, equally beneficial to both parties. It was also one of the rare establishments, aside from those owned by Caleb Dehain, one of the most powerful vampires in Blackthorn, where everyone who was there was guaranteed to be there voluntarily.

The alternatives were in abundance: places where participants were victims of the system, or were there out of sheer naivety. He'd come across more than his fair share of feeders in pretty bad ways in those types of places – feeders who had got mixed up with the wrong sires or vice versa. Because there was a dark and violent side to feeding for those who got their kicks that way, resulting in the feeder–sire relationship – though not illegal – remaining a frowned-upon system. Rumours rarely focused on those who managed to get in with the right sires doing well out of it, especially those who stood no chance of getting into Midtown anyway. The Hive was one such place.

It was, in essence, a playground for the wealthy. It was the ultimate high, the most extreme role-play for those bored with their low-risk, privileged lives, those having grown up schooled in the dangers of Blackthorn, of Lowtown and the third species who inhabited both. Visiting The Hive was the ultimate abandon and escape from reality and responsibility. It was a place where women and men faced their fears and embraced them, owned them even.

Vampires, in particular, had always been the main attraction – offering the blurred line between fear and arousal that was a potent high for many. Sex with one of his kind was the ultimate aphrodisiac and the wealthy paid the establishment healthily for the opportunity. Because it was only the wealthy and the powerful who could get away with it. Who could talk or bribe their way back across their respective borders. Who could afford a legal team to fight their corner if complications arose.

And that meant The Hive presented an abundance of opportunities for his business. He'd started getting involved with the place when he'd needed items that could only be acquired from across the borders, a session with him his mule's reward for successful delivery.

Business aside, there was only one he consistently met with for his own personal needs. Cordy had lived in Lowtown all her life and had been well looked after by The Hive. Feeding with her was uncomplicated. Few could give themselves up for regular feeds without the hitches of feelings getting in the way. Most of all, she never asked questions. He arrived, and she made herself available. If she needed him for anything in turn, he was there. He'd killed for her in the past and, during times when he'd needed it, she'd trusted him enough to allow him the ultimate high of taking her as close to the edge of death in a feed as either of them could survive. Most of the time, he merely came to collect pre-prepared syringes from her. More often than not, it didn't involve sex. But sometimes it did. This was one of those times. Not least because he needed a reminder of what he was. In light of his encounter with Ember, he needed a reminder of *exactly* what he was.

He stepped into the dim subterranean room, lit only by a lamp in the far right hand corner that was draped in clichéd red gossamer. The clients liked that kind of blatancy. There was only one small vent in the brickwork and no windows, so the walls were constantly coated in the lingering aroma of sweat and sex.

He closed the door behind himself. The door that had concealed the small recess for showering in after whatever act had been performed.

Tonight that act was simple. Tonight he needed to feel his extra incisors bite into warm flesh. He needed to feel and taste hot blood in his mouth. He needed to feel his feeder gasp and wince. Tonight he was there to bite *and* fuck – and get both over as quickly as possible.

He took off his jacket and draped it on the nearby chair before stripping completely – to prevent having to find clean clothing for the rest of the night than anything else.

Cordy, having received his text message, and for the same reasons, was already naked. She turned away from him, just as he preferred, and knelt on her haunches on the edge of the bed.

They rarely talked. There was nothing to discuss.

Tearing open the foil packet, he slid on the protection. Cross-contamination was never an issue between the species. Vampires didn't carry infections, their antibodies killing anything within minutes, which meant they couldn't transmit disease either. And the chances of a human falling pregnant by a vampire, let alone it going any length of term, was minimal too. But it was still possible which is why Nate didn't take risks. Not ever. And especially not with Cordy.

With both his feet firmly on the floor, he took hold of Cordy's hips. He tugged her back towards him so her parted knees were on the edge of the bed.

He entered her fully on the first attempt, forcing himself

inside her just as she preferred, Cordy groaning not with pain as she should have, but with pleasure as she always did.

Her breathing was instantly heavy, more so as he looped her long, dark hair around his fist several times before tugging her upright. His free hand clutched her between her legs to where he was buried deep inside her, applied an expert amount of pressure to her clit, making her flinch, her nails clawing at the hair at the back of his head.

She closed her eyes, relaxing into the sensation, trusting him completely. And the more she relaxed, the more she lost herself. And the more she lost herself, the less she cared that his lips were on her neck, that his incisors were sliding along the sensitive, vulnerable flesh. As was their routine, he didn't anaesthetise her with his saliva first. As always, she'd want to feel everything. It had always been the same for the past fifteen years he'd been visiting her.

As he felt her climax build, he plunged his incisors deep into her neck. She struggled a little as she inevitably always did, as her instincts for survival dictated she did, necessitating him to tighten his grip on her hair, to wrap his arm across her breasts to prevent her struggles from causing herself an injury.

As his incisors took hold as deep as they could go, his erection buried inside her, he fed.

The metallic taste filling his mouth had him coming moments later. And, during those few minutes, he lost himself in the euphoria, the release, the escape. He forgot about everything except for the simplest of pleasures; absorbed himself in the ecstasy that helped temporarily ease the emptiness inside.

Because she was going.

Ember was finally leaving.

It was all going to be over.

Finished, Nate withdrew. He gently clasped Cordy's jaw as he tilted her head back a little to check the severity of the wound he had created. Her pulse and breathing, though still rapid from her waning arousal, would return to normal soon enough. There was no permanent damage. He kissed her on the temple before pulling away.

Under the cool spray of the shower, he stared down at the tiled floor, watching the bloodied water trickle away.

He dried off. He got dressed. Glanced across to where Cordy was treating his bite mark in front of the mirror.

'You want to talk about it?' she asked.

'About what?'

'About whatever's on your mind?'

It was a first; his mask was clearly slipping.

But he didn't need to answer, and she wouldn't push it.

He dropped the money onto the chair. 'Let me know if you need any more.'

And headed back out of the door.

CHAPTER ELEVEN

For the third day running, he didn't show up in the café, and there had been no sign of him back home either. The building evidence that he hadn't any intention of holding anything over her, just as he'd claimed, should have felt like a relief. For some inexplicable reason though, it didn't. Instead, she felt only an underlying sense of loss.

Three days to go.

And the wrench she was feeling was a further reminder of why the sooner she left, the better.

'Ten minutes,' Harry called out, sticking his head around the corner as she finished wiping down the tables.

Ember turned the sign to 'closed' on the door, but didn't yet lock it.

She pulled down the blinds on the far side of the café. 'You hear that, Jasper? Ten minutes. Time to kick you out.'

Their last remaining customer hurriedly swallowed back the dregs of his cold coffee. 'On my way, little 'un.'

She headed over to the counter before joining him at the booth. She placed the paper bag in front of him. 'Take this off my hands when you go, will you? You know how much I hate throwing food out. But don't get too excited. There's a good healthy chunk of vegetable lasagne in there as opposed to the doughnuts I know you're hoping for.'

He laughed. 'You know me too well.'

She slid into the seat on the far side of his table. 'Have you got food in the house at the moment, Jasper? I mean real food. The weather's due to turn.'

'You need to stop worrying about me, missy. I've got plenty. I promise.'

It had been a regular question ever since the time he hadn't shown up there for a week. Worried, she'd taken herself around to his place after work: a small flat ten storeys up in a block near the centre of Lowtown.

She'd found him ill. Too ill to leave home. His cupboards had been empty for what looked like quite some time. He hadn't even been able to make himself a hot drink. Instead, he had survived on water from the tap. With no one to call and no one to check in on him, he'd deteriorated fast.

Ember had spent the next two weeks visiting him every day until he'd shifted the infection and got his strength back, taking food around from the café and having scraped enough together to get him the antibiotics he had needed.

'As if I have time to worry about you, Jasper, what with all the parties I have to attend and all my dates that keep stacking up . . .'

He smiled, his wrinkled eyes sparkling, but then he frowned. 'I've been watching you today. You don't look your mighty fine self. Doesn't look like you've been sleeping lately,' he said, glancing at the bags under her eyes.

She hesitated, uncertain how she would tell him. She'd dreaded it almost as much as telling Harry and Casey. 'I have some news.'

'Good I hope?'

'I'm going to be moving away from here.'

His eyes widened. She could see the edge of sadness and panic cross them despite him working hard to conceal both. 'Going where?'

'To Midtown. Believe it or not.'

He exhaled sharply. 'You made it?'

She nodded. 'I got through the final stage. I'm due to leave in the next few days.'

His sallow eyes flared again. 'So soon?'

She reached across and squeezed his hand. 'But I'm coming back for visits.'

He squeezed back. 'Good on you, girl. You've done well. Real well.'

'I need you to promise to keep an eye on this place for me though, OK?'

'You can rely on me, little 'un.'

Feeling the breeze of the door opening behind her, she glanced over her shoulder. 'I'm afraid we're closed.'

But Ember found herself standing from the booth; turned to face the three men who entered regardless.

The last of them, the larger and stockier of the three, a grey-haired guy with painfully cold eyes, closed and flicked down the latch on the door before tugging the blind down over it. The younger of the three, a slender guy with a mop of curly brown hair, dismissed her presence completely as he sauntered around the tables like some kind of premises inspector.

Then there was the third guy, maybe in his late forties or early fifties, with thick, greying blond hair. He took his stance centrally in the room, his hands deep in the pockets of his long, taupe trench coat.

Ember remained as a barrier between them and Jasper, having already warned him with her hand concealed behind her back for him to stay in his seat. 'Can I help you?'

The blond guy didn't even look at her as he continued to scan the café. 'Where's the boss?'

'I'm the assistant manager,' she said, taking a step forward.

But Harry appeared a moment later.

'Harry,' the blond man said as he removed his hand from his pocket to hold it out. 'Jonah Hordas. I'd like to think you've heard of me.'

Hordas.

Ember's pulse picked up a notch, not helped by Harry's complexion turning ashen as he froze to the spot behind the counter.

'I'd like a few minutes of your time. Let's take a seat,' Jonah said, indicating the booth to his left. The booth a few feet from where she stood. 'Mine's a coffee,' he said, finally addressing her. 'Black. Plenty of sugar. And you, Harry?'

It had begun: Jonah offering Harry a drink in his own establishment the onset of power play that was further reinforced by him sitting first, his claiming ownership of the space strengthened by him stretching his arms along the back of the seat.

Harry sent her a glance of concern, but Ember remained tactfully and sensibly silent.

'Usual?' she asked Harry, urging him to play along.

They had no other option.

He nodded. 'Please.'

She locked gazes with him briefly as they passed each other, trying to give him her look of reassurance that they could handle it.

'We're in midst of a very exciting business expansion,' she heard Jonah exclaim as she stepped behind the counter.

Having shut down and cleaned the coffee machine, she opted to heat up the percolator.

'We already have several thriving businesses in the centre of the district and now we're looking to branch out further, somewhere closer to the Midtown border to make life easier for some of our clientele.'

The very thing Harry had spent his entire working life trying to avoid.

'I'm afraid the place isn't for sale,' Harry said, doing his utmost, she could tell, to sound as resolute as possible.

'Harry.' Jonah's light-hearted drawl echoed around the café. 'I think you misunderstand. I don't want to buy your place from you: I just want to own it. Let me put my cards on the table to save us both time. *This* is the place I'm interested in. And I'm sure we can come to an agreement over how we can make that happen.'

As she turned to grab the milk from the fridge, the grey-haired guy's icy eyes gave her a purposeful once-over from across the counter, the slight sideways cocking of his head no doubt intending to be intimidating as he lingered on her breasts.

This was *not* happening.

She turned her back on him again, her heart pounding painfully as she finished making the two coffees.

Reluctant to expose her anxiety, she opted for a tray to take the cups over rather than carry them by hand and have them clatter on saucers.

'I run a clean establishment,' Harry declared. 'For the sake of my staff and my clients, I'd like it to remain that way.'

'And I'd like to work *with* you on this, Harry, not *against* you. I find working against people to be so time-consuming: the constant monitoring let alone coming up with creative and effective ways to ensure they take the hint that compromise simply isn't an option.' There was a dramatic pause. 'I don't want to have to go down that route with you. I'm here to help you; help this business turn over a really good profit. That's ultimately what I want. I'm sure it's what you want too. This place could be a gold mine situated where it is – for both of us. The arrangement is simple: I give you advice on how to run it, I send clientele your way, you reward me with your profits and, that way, you get to keep working here. All of your staff do.'

Ember placed the tray down between them.

'Though I must say,' Jonah added, snagging her forearm before she had a chance to step away. 'That might have to be the first thing we take a look at.' He looked up at Ember. 'Sit here, sugar,' he said, releasing his firm, cold grip to tap the seat beside him.

Ember knew, for all their sakes, not to argue.

'Take this uniform, for example: it's not what people want to see. They want to see legs. A bit of belly. Some topless action in certain quarters. My clients want to be able to relax; to enjoy themselves.' Every part of Ember recoiled in repulsion as he rested his arm across the back of the booth seat behind her. 'I'm sure your staff know how to be hospitable; accommodating of any extra needs.'

She kept her gaze lowered. She gritted her teeth in disgust.

'Because it all starts with creating the right atmosphere,' Jonah added. 'The right atmosphere breeds the right deals. And the right deals breed money. Look at you both: how tense you are. This is what I'm talking about. And yet it's so easily resolved.' She felt his eyes burn into her. 'Unbutton your shirt for me, sugar.'

Ember met his gaze. Jaw clenched, her stomach somersaulting

as her mind raced ahead for a way out, she fought to keep her fists firmly on the booth seat either side of her.

His eyes narrowed pensively. 'Hang on a second. Do I know you?'

'I doubt it,' she said.

'No?' He frowned. 'There's definitely something familiar about you.' He smiled; a smile that chilled her almost as much as his soulless eyes. He reached for her top button. 'Maybe it'll come back to me when I get a look at your better attributes.'

'Leave her alone,' Harry said, his palms flattening against the table.

Jonah smirked. 'Don't tell me you've never been there, Harry. All those dark hours after closing time? She isn't as pretty as that cute little brunette that works here, granted. What's her name?'

'Casey,' the grey-eyed guy said.

'Yeah, that's right. Thanks, Stirling,' Jonah said. 'Casey. I *like* Casey. Now there's a pretty little thing in desperate need of some attention.'

Ember's pulse raced enough to flat-line, not just from repugnance at the way Jonah had said Casey's name, or the smirk that had accompanied it, but the confirmation that they *had* been watching.

'But still,' Jonah said, reaching for her top button again. 'Waste not, want not.'

As she used every ounce of willpower not to smash her fist into his nose, Harry stood at the same time as she saw Jasper step into view in the corner of her eye.

'You heard him! You leave her alone!' Jasper said. 'Picking on a young girl. You should be ashamed of yourself.'

Ember snapped her head towards Jasper to warn him to keep out of it, only to see Stirling had already closed in. A split-second later, he ploughed his fist straight into the side of Jasper's head.

The thunk of him landing against the table and then the floor chilled her blood, Jasper's elderly hands reaching up to protect himself from Stirling's fist coming at him again.

Fury blazing, Ember lunged out of the booth to intervene, but Jonah grabbed her hair and yanked her back against him.

She looked left at Harry only to see the bead of sweat rolling down his temple. His jaw had slackened, his face was ashen again, his eyes bulging in horror as the curly-haired guy held a gun to the back of his head.

A gun Ember knew they would use. A gun they would use if she so much as flinched.

A tear trickled involuntarily down her cheek as Stirling's fist and then his foot slammed into Jasper until, moments later, everything fell silent. Deathly silent. Ember could hear only the echo of her ragged breaths, the sound of the storm beating against the windows.

Fucking cowards, was all she could hear her inner voice saying. *Fucking, fucking cowards.*

She knew Jasper was dead. She knew he was gone. Another tear involuntarily streaked down her face, as much as she hated his murderers seeing them.

Jonah smacked her face-first down on the table.

'See,' Jonah said, clearly addressing Harry. '*This* is how you manage your place. You take no shit from your clients and no shit from your staff. And that's what I'm going to help you with. You don't want customers who sit over the same coffee all day, every day – you want *real* customers. Those willing to pay above and beyond for what you can offer them. *Clients*, Harry. *Real* clients. Get rid of him, will you, Stirling? He's bringing down the tone.'

Ember stared through her mask of hair, her nails digging into the edge of the seat as she saw the jeans of Jasper's murderer pass by, Jasper's shoes hanging off his limp feet as the former carried him over his shoulder.

She heard the door being opened; she felt the breeze against her legs and feet. And then it was closed again.

'Now,' Jonah said, his breath hot against her ear. 'While me and your boss close this deal, you're going to clean up after the mess you started by not doing as you were asked. And I don't want to see as much as a trace left, do you understand? If there is, *you*'ll be next. And then we'll see if Harry here can do a better job cleaning *you* up.'

Jonah released his vice-like grip on her neck.

Ember got up out of the booth seat. In a glaze of shock, of grief, she made her way back behind the counter, into the corridor and through to the utility area.

She scanned the bottles of disinfectant, of bleach – of all the things she could throw in their faces. But it would achieve nothing. Nothing at all. And she sure as hell wouldn't be quick enough to stop them pulling the trigger. And they *would* pull that trigger. All Harry was – just as they all were – was nothing more than expendable cheap labour.

She placed the bucket in the utility sink and turned the tap on. She squeezed in the disinfectant before grabbing the mop. Shoving the cleaning cloths in her apron, she glanced across her shoulder to see Stirling filling the doorway.

Her stomach lurched. She clutched the mop handle as she faced the sink again, watching, urging, the bucket to fill quickly. When it was midway, unable to stand feeling him watching her any longer, she turned off the tap and lifted the bucket out of the sink.

She tentatively headed over to the door, hoping he would move out of the way in the process.

He didn't.

She met his gaze. Her grip tightened on the mop handle that she could so easily ram up under his jaw if she was feeling stupid enough to do so.

He looked back down at her chest. 'Ember,' he said, running the very tip of his forefinger over the name badge resting above her breast.

He dragged his finger across to her cleavage, ran it down her buttons, his gaze following its path.

He looked into her eyes again, his glinting with unwarranted triumph as she waited on a knife-edge. But, to her immense relief, he retreated.

Brushing past him, she hurried back through to the café.

Her breathing snagged again at the sight of Jasper's blood on the booth seat, on the table, on the floor.

Barely holding back her tears, her rage, she placed the bucket on the floor. She wiped down the seat and the table. She mopped the floor; mopped up the last traces of him. She made two trips back to the utility area to refill her bucket as, all the while, Jonah reclined in the booth seat, sipping on the coffee she'd made him.

Her gut wrenched with every wring of the cloth, her throat clogging with held back tears of betrayal as she finished the job as quickly and effectively as she could – cleaning away every trace of evidence. Every last trace of her friend.

'Now *polish* the floor,' Jonah said to her. 'And if I'm not satisfied, you'll polish it again.'

She got down on her hands and knees, her cheeks burning with the humiliation under the weight of all eyes being upon her.

'I don't know about you, Harry,' Jonah said, 'but I love seeing a woman down on all fours. There's nothing sexier.'

There was a tense pause.

Ember's hand fisted around the cloth. She polished the floor hard enough to remove the pattern on the tiles.

'Anyway. Let's cut to the chase and say the deal is done, shall we, Harry?' Jonah finally said. 'I expect everyone in work as normal tomorrow and the day after that and the day after that until the new arrangements begin.

'We already have a list of your staff, so if anyone doesn't turn up for work, I will find them and I will redeploy them. I don't know if you've heard but there's a very lucrative little earner doing the rounds lately. Vampire Russian roulette, they're calling it – the new ultimate high for risk takers. Competitors take one syringe after another until someone draws the unlucky straw of dying blood. It's all about how close they can get before that lethal final syringe kills one of them – and, of course, how long they can keep the subject alive in order to get there. I don't want to be looking to make up my profits that way, not that those two lovely daughters of yours wouldn't make me a very decent profit indeed.'

Ember glanced up to see any resolve Harry had left dissipate in front of her eyes.

It was over. This was it.

She pulled herself to her feet.

'What kind of profits are you expecting?' Harry asked, his voice wavering.

'Either eighty per cent or two thousand a week, whichever is greater.'

'We don't even make two thousand a fortnight.'

'Then eighty per cent it is.'

'But out of that money, I have salaries to pay, I have the upkeep. I barely take home enough to–'

'Based on how your business is run *now*, Harry. But that *will* change.' Jonah moved out of the booth. 'I'll make sure someone drops in tomorrow to check everything is as it should be. And, remember, if any of your staff think about going walkabout, I'll hold you liable for not keeping control. I'll be back soon to discuss arrangements further. Until then . . . ' He held out his hand. He smirked. 'Come on now, Harry. Don't leave me hanging.'

As Harry held out his hand, Jonah took control in being the one to shake.

Before he stepped away, he looked down at the floor to examine her handiwork. 'Cracking job. I knew you'd get there, Ember,' he declared, with a smack on her behind. He looked back at Harry. 'See, all they need is a little bit of motivation and inspiration. You're going to do great, Harry. Real great. We're going to make one hell of a team. I can just feel it.'

CHAPTER TWELVE

Nate headed down the back alley to take the rear exit to the bar.

He hoisted himself up over the wall before silently descending the other side.

Crossing the concrete courtyard, he picked the padlock that opened the door into the storeroom.

He headed through the darkness, through the beer and whisky barrels, before picking the door-lock on the far side.

He made his way down the corridor. He removed his gun from the back of his jeans. He listened against each closed door for voices as he passed.

It had taken three days to determine where they would be. Three days of patience.

Nate opened the door. Three out of five of the Voy boys were there. They all simultaneously looked up at him from the midst of their card game.

Their eyes flared in alarm, in shock at the sight of him, let alone of him still being alive. Two of them drew their guns, but not quickly enough.

Without hesitation, Nate finished all three of them in swift succession, a fatal bullet to each of their foreheads before they'd had time to think, taking down their two bodyguards in the process too.

Without so much as another glance in their direction, he headed back out the way he'd entered.

CHAPTER THIRTEEN

———◆———

Ember sat in the booth she had scrubbed clean, in the exact same seat she'd been in whilst talking to Jasper.

Rain lashing against the blackened pavements outside, she stared at the empty space where her friend had been alive and well some two, maybe even three, hours before. She'd sat in the silence for so long she'd lost count.

She remembered the muffled sound of Harry's voice as he'd called his daughters to tell them he was on his way home, insisting they lock everything up until he got there; and that they let no one in in the interim. But, as yet, he'd said nothing to her. Instead, he too now sat in silence in the same seat he'd been in the entire time.

Her mind was on a constant loop of the events, of what she could have done differently. It had poured with rain the first night she'd met Jasper too – the night she'd lost Liam. It had been Jasper who'd called her having found Liam's phone, having chosen the most frequently used number.

The second she'd got the call, she'd pounded through the streets, her clothes sodden from the downpour, her hair plastered to her face.

The crowd around him in the alley had been small as they'd awaited the emergency services. Jasper had been the one to spot her and cross the street to meet her half way – a stranger who, in that moment, felt like the only person she knew in the world.

At first she'd felt nothing as she'd elbowed her way through the few bystanders to fall to her knees beside Liam. Like a wax-work, he'd lain cold and pale and lifeless on the alley floor, the bite wounds to his throat looking like make-up from some kind of macabre special effects horror film. Because none of it felt real as she'd waited for him to blink, waited for him to move, waited for him to respond as she'd shaken his body, as she'd pleaded with him to wake up.

Jasper had assured her the emergency services were on their way but, as he was already dead, it would be quite some time. In the meantime, the bystanders had been trying to protect his dignity from passers-by, and from bodysnatchers who would find other uses for him.

It had taken six hours for the authorities to finally come to collect his body. And when they had, they were a disposal ser-vice only. With no witnesses, there was nothing more they could do. She'd had to sign to say she was the next of kin, had seen him being removed, and to agree to cover any costs for his cremation if she chose to reserve a memorial place for him.

Then he'd been taken away.

Barely able to stand from the cold and the pins and needles in her legs, Jasper had escorted her to her aunt. When he'd built up to doing so, he'd handed her the small cardboard box with the engagement ring in it that he'd found in Liam's inside coat pocket alongside his phone. And Jasper had waited with her and her aunt until she'd cried out every tear to the point of passing out with exhaustion.

'I'm sorry, Ember,' Harry finally said, breaking the silence that had dominated the space between them. 'I'm so sorry.'

'They're cowards, Harry. Bullies and cowards.' She stared over her shoulder at him. 'Who else beats a seventy-two year old to death?'

Harry dropped his gaze.

'We're going to the authorities,' she said. 'We're going to the authorities *now*.'

His eyes flared with alarm. 'We can't. You know we can't.'

'So we do what? Roll over? Agree to this? We can't, Harry.'

'What choice do we have? The authorities aren't interested in us and the Hordas clan know it.'

'But that's exactly how they operate: their power is based on fear. People don't report it *because* they think it's pointless.'

'No, people don't report it because others have tried and those they care about have paid the price for it.'

'Or that's nothing more than rumours – yet another scare tactic. We can't be taken in by it. That's how they win.'

'So you're going to call their bluff? Is that it? With *my* family on the line? It's OK for you, you're out of here soon. You don't have anyone to care about.' His gaze was instantly fiercely apologetic. 'Ember . . .'

She shook her head. She stared back at the empty space where Jasper had been sitting. 'They murdered Jasper right in front of us. I'm not going to pretend that didn't happen.'

'You think they're going to come rushing here with forensics? With the body already gone? And you having cleaned up? How will that implicate you, Ember? You know reporting this could jeopardise your chances.'

'I don't care about that right now.'

'But Jasper would. You know he would. Ember, it would achieve nothing. All it would do is bring a whole heap of worse trouble. I can't risk them coming for my daughters. I can't risk them coming for all of you. We've been lucky to avoid it for this long. We can't win this, Ember. I know too many people over the years who have tried and failed. The Hordas clan are untouchable.'

'No one's untouchable. At least let me try. Maybe get some advice.'

Harry moved over into Jasper's seat to sit in front of her. 'How many of these cases do you think they get a month? You know how many places are under protection rackets around here. All that will happen is we'll go onto some list, being pushed further and further down in priority. Even if they did pursue, it's our word against theirs now. And in the interim, we'll be right in the Hordas clan's grasp with them knowing we grassed.'

She shook her head. She stared back out into the darkness, bypassing her own reflection.

'The authorities don't give a shit,' Harry continued. 'You think they don't get a few backhanders from the Hordas clan and vice versa? You know the conspiracy theories – that the authorities are using the gangs to keep order so they can focus their resources on Blackthorn, and in turn the authorities turn a blind eye.'

'But what if that's all they are, Harry: conspiracy theories? Created by those who want you to believe it. People like the Hordas clan whose power thrives on people believing things like that because it stops us doing anything. But we *can't* just sit back. We have to try and fight this. If they've come here, they're coming into this area. We can't hand it over to them. Our decision is setting the marker. We *can't* give in to them.'

Harry shook his head wearily. He clutched it in his hands for a moment before looking back at her, his eyes grave. 'I have two daughters and nowhere to go. Nowhere to hide. I say we put up and shut up. In days you'll be gone. I won't be. You report this and all you're doing is leaving me with the aftermath of your decisions. Do this one thing for me: let me deal with this *my* way. You want to help? Get yourself out of here so I have one less to worry about. Don't ruin it now because, believe me, it'll change nothing for the better. All it'll do is make everything worse.'

CHAPTER FOURTEEN

The train trundled along on its track, rocking as it went around corners, the carriages in front intermittently feeling completely disjointed from hers in the process. It wasn't high-speed, and it certainly wasn't the smoothest of journeys, but it got her across Lowtown the quickest.

As it came to a halt, Ember stepped off onto the platform, the wind whipping through her hair as the stationary train opposite set off.

She headed up the steps and out onto the street.

The Third Species Control Division was to her right, the windows glinting in the diminishing late-afternoon sun. The TSCD, as it was better known, was home of the Vampire Control Unit and the Lycan Control Unit, along with housing the Intervention Units as well as the Curfew Enforcement department. The building she needed was next door: the only place to go if you wanted to report a crime in person as opposed to wading through the telephone system.

She hadn't slept the night before, after the incident with Jasper. Harry had insisted on her going back to his but after her continued refusal, he'd switched to insisting on at least dropping her off at home.

The stairwell had been deathly quiet, *his* apartment still the same. In many ways, she'd wanted to feel that her stranger was around.

She'd kept herself busy until the early hours, packing the last of her belongings, the TV a low hum in the background to give her some semblance of company.

In the end, she'd taken her duvet to the sofa so she could fall asleep in front of it, her mind still playing the horrors over and over again. Even when she'd managed to grab a few minutes of sleep, she'd woken in a cold sweat, her hands clasping the sofa as if she was on a slide down into a burning pit.

By five a.m. she'd been in the shower.

By half five, she'd been sat on her sofa watching the ticking clock, waiting to return to work, to the scene of the crime.

The walk there had felt like she'd waded through wet concrete, every step one of dread.

Once there, she'd prepped the front of the café as Harry had gathered the staff in the kitchen to explain what was happening. He didn't mention Jasper's beating. They'd both agreed no one needed to know about that.

From that point on, there had been no laughter and no banter as they'd gone about their usual practice; each of them flinching every time the door had opened, continually casting wary glances at any unfamiliar customers, wondering if one of them was the spy.

But when Stirling had arrived, despite her resolution to respect Harry's wishes, the clincher had come.

Stirling's attention had been firmly fixed on Casey from the outset. Ember had tried to intervene and deal with his order, but Stirling had been having none of it.

'I didn't place my order with you,' he'd said as she'd placed his coffee in front of him.

Ember had taken a calming breath. 'We interchange. It keeps the flow speedier.'

'No. My waitress disappeared into the kitchen when she should have made my drink straight away. Is she always this incompetent?'

'She's incredibly good at what she does,' Ember had said in Casey's defence, not least at having been the one to send her away. 'She was checking on another order by my request before coming back to you.'

'And that should have been dealt with by now,' he'd said, sliding the steaming, fresh cup of coffee back in her direction. 'So I'd like *her* to serve me my drink. Now.'

Her pulse had raced as she'd stared down into uncompromising grey eyes that had stared back into hers. Images of him beating Jasper to death the night before had weighed heavily on her decision. So despite being sickened at the prospect of Casey being treated like a worm on a hook, Ember had known she'd had no choice but to comply.

Ember had laid her hand over Casey's trembling one in the kitchen, squeezed to give her whatever reassurance she could. Casey had tried to force a smile, but her eyes had remained glazed.

'I'll figure something out,' Ember had assured her.

Despite the defeat already prevalent in her eyes, Casey had nodded.

Returning to her position behind the counter, Ember had watched the guy who was at least twenty years older than Casey, slide his middle finger up and down her outer thigh, a couple of inches further up her skirt each time.

She could see Casey recoiling in repulsion but she was too smart to retaliate. She too knew how to play the game.

But Ember also knew Casey had her breaking point. She knew there was every chance Casey would run. Run to a potential sire to save herself the indignity of it all. Run because of *them*.

Ember had clenched the knife she'd been cutting the cake with and withdrew it to rest at her side.

'Ember,' Yvonne had said, placing her hand gently over the top of Ember's knife-holding hand. 'Don't do anything stupid.'

Ember had torn her attention away from the scene in front of her to meet Yvonne's insistent and pleading gaze.

And, behind Yvonne, Harry had torn his eyes from the scene too. Their gazes instantly locking, he'd given Ember a silent nod. They'd both known what it had meant.

It was Ember's first visit to the response room. It had been blistering with activity from the moment she'd arrived, those waiting toying with the numbered tickets in their hands. Chairs filled the room, people waiting in haphazard queues to be called to the booths that spanned the wall ahead.

Behind the reinforced glass sat the people responsible for processing the reports – those who categorised whatever was reported into a triage system of response.

Three hours later, her number finally flashed up above the first booth in the far left-hand corner.

Ember perched on the edge of the fixed plastic seat.

'Please can you categorise the incident,' the woman asked.

'My place of work is being targeted by a protection racket.'

The woman barely met her gaze before entering the information on the computer, as if she'd heard the same story a hundred times that day.

'And your name?'

'Ember Challice.'

'The name of your establishment?' she asked as she typed.

'It's called Harry's. It's not owned by me.'

The woman looked at her over her glasses. 'You're not the permit holder?'

'I work there. I'm the deputy manager.'

The woman retreated from the computer to rest her folded arms on the desk between them. 'I'm afraid only permit holders can make a report such as this.'

'The owner didn't want to be away from the place for this long. He knew it could take a while. He's scared it'll raise questions and lead to repercussions if they turn up while he's not there. That's why I've come instead. It's the Hordas clan. They're the ones who are running the racket.'

'I'm sorry, Miss Challice, but I can't proceed without the owner being the one to report it,' she declared, despite the glint of empathy in her eyes.

She returned her attention to the computer and clicked her mouse several times.

'Can you at least give me some advice? That's why I'm here. We don't know what to do. We don't know who can help us.'

Withdrawing from the computer screen again, the woman removed her glasses.

'Miss Challice, I'll be honest with you,' she said, lowering her voice. 'There's a file piled this high on the Hordas clan.' She held her hand to her neck to emphasise her point. 'And a backlog like you wouldn't believe.'

'If there's a file that big, why is nothing happening? Why are they still active?'

'Prosecution requires proof. Proof requires investigation time. Even if the authorities did take on your case, it'll be weeks before it's processed, weeks more while it's investigated and months more before it goes to trial – *if* it gets that far. Even then, there's still no guarantee of conviction.'

'No doubt helped by backhanders.'

The woman's gaze didn't flinch. No denial escaped from her lips. 'I see from inputting your name that you've applied for Midtown residency and have made it through. So I'm going to give you the best advice I can: let your boss deal with this. Don't blow your chances by getting embroiled.'

She put her glasses back on again.

'They killed someone last night,' Ember said. 'Right in front of me. His name was Jasper Thekes. He was seventy-two years old. He died as an example to keep the rest of us in check.'

The woman frowned. 'Is the body available for investigation?'

'No. They saw to that. They even made us clean up after them.'

The woman sighed. She offered a small shrug of condolence.

Ember glanced at the woman's badge before meeting her gaze again. 'He was a real person, Janine. Not a number on a database. Not nothing more than a depletion in the population count to save resources.'

'And I'll record Jasper's death, but this is what I'm going to do. I'm going to leave who reported it blank. As I said, take some advice,' Janine said. 'If you were stuck in Lowtown and wanted to be a martyr to the cause, I'd say go ahead. But with a life in Midtown only days away, do the smart thing. Clearly this Jasper meant something to you and my guess is he wouldn't want you to throw your chance away now that he's gone. It won't bring him back. It won't change a thing. Certainly not where the Hordas clan are concerned.'

CHAPTER FIFTEEN

———◉———

Ember made her way up the exterior stone steps to the fourth floor of the graffiti-strewn tower block, music blaring from the weathered windows she passed floor by floor.

Having managed to get a spare key from him after that time she found him ill, she unlocked Jasper's apartment.

The place was cold. It stank of damp, the ceiling and parts of the walls blackened with mildew. It had deteriorated even since she'd last been there a year before.

Despite the mould on the ceiling and walls, everything was clean, cared-for, everything in its rightful place. His flat might have been small, it might have been modestly furnished, it might have been run down, but it was loved.

It was like many other homes in Lowtown: consisting primarily of the bare essentials. And as with most places in Lowtown, the mesh over the windows reflected the added need to protect what little you had from those who always wanted more.

She wandered over to the small side unit to pick up the photograph of Jasper with his wife and son.

You didn't live, just simply 'existed' in Lowtown – there was no progression, no hope – and it was getting worse. It felt like sitting on a ticking time bomb.

But, as had been the case with Jasper, there were nonetheless those like Harry and his late wife who had tried to. Who wanted only to live as normal a life as they could. To hope for the best. To hope that, one day, their children would make a better life for themselves across the border and achieve what they couldn't. All Harry had ever wanted was a family and a business to earn enough to get by with a few added luxuries on top. Now, after thirty-five years of working solidly towards the latter goal, it was all being stolen from him overnight by those who already had more than all of the people they suppressed put together.

Just like everything had been stolen from Jasper: first his son, then his wife, and now his own life.

She headed over to the kitchenette and opened the fridge to find nothing but an empty shell.

He'd lied to her.

Fridge wide open, she pulled out the chair at the kitchen table.

She leaned back and folded her arms. She'd had enough of crying. She knew what she needed to do.

CHAPTER SIXTEEN

———◦———

Ember ascended the stairwell to her apartment.

She poised on the top step, her gaze fixed on the stranger's door. Quick, clean, brutal, efficient: he was exactly what she needed. After more than three days since she'd last seen him, she could only hope he was still around.

She stepped up to his door and knocked, the sound of it painfully invasive as it echoed in the hollow of the empty stairwell.

She waited.

And then knocked again.

When there was still no answer, she made her way to her apartment. She grabbed her blanket from the sofa. Partially sitting on it, partially wrapping it around her back to keep the chill out, she perched on the top step.

He could be hours. He might even not come back that night at all. But, for now, she'd sit there and she'd wait. Anything was better than doing nothing. Anything was better than sitting alone in the silence of her apartment. Anything was better than risking him returning and her not knowing he was back, potentially missing him again and losing valuable time.

In the two hours that passed, her extremities turned numb despite the warmth of the blanket. Her mind slipped into slumber mode as she rested her forehead on her knees, so much so that she flinched at the eventual sound of the key in the lock.

As her stranger glanced up at her, her stomach flipped with a concoction of nerves and relief.

He closed and locked the door behind himself before standing at the foot of the stairwell. Thankfully, he was alone.

'I need to talk to you,' she said.

Without a word, he ascended with one slow and steady step at a time.

Ember dropped her blanket as she stood ready to greet him.

He stopped at eye level with her. 'I thought you wanted nothing to do with me.'

His unflinching gaze was laden with detachment, causing her resolution to waver for a moment.

'I need five minutes of your time, that's all,' she said.

She moved aside as he passed her, leaving her in the trail of his silence. But instead of slamming his apartment door behind him, he left it open.

Ember took her cue to follow.

He slipped his jacket off and cast it aside over the nearby chair before leaning against the side of the sofa. Arms firmly folded, his direct stare did little to ease her awkwardness. 'What do you want, Ember?'

'I want to hire you.'

His dark eyebrows lifted just a touch. 'Is that before or after I fuck off and keep well away from you?'

'I didn't say it like that.'

His eyes were laced with challenge. 'What makes you think I'm available for hire?'

'I've seen what you're capable of. I've seen the guns in this apartment. I've seen your meetings in the café. You're a professional of some sort – or could be. I need help and I think you're the one who can give it to me.'

He frowned as he studied her. 'Help with *what* exactly?'

'The café's in trouble. It's being hit by a protection racket. The authorities won't help me.'

'The café that you're going to be shot of in a couple of days. What does it matter to you?'

She maintained her calm. She had no choice but to maintain her calm. 'The people who work there are my friends.'

'Friends you're leaving.'

Her stomach knotted at his accusation. She had to bite back her retort. 'The racket want more money than the business can afford. They want the staff to work under the equivalent terms of slavery, and have already placed threats on those who don't conform and comply.'

'That tends to be how protection rackets work around here.'

'And that part of Lowtown has been free of them up to now, too small fry. It still is. This is about nothing more than gaining ground. If they own that part of Lowtown too, they'll own nearly everything. Harry's will be the first place of many more to come. If the Hordas clan succeed with Harry's–'

He raised his eyebrows again. 'The *Hordas* clan? You expect me to do something about the Hordas clan?'

'I want you to kill them. I want to hire you to kill them.'

His gaze was steady, almost cold in its analysis. He exhaled tersely before biting into his bottom lip as he looked away. A moment later, his gaze snapped back to hers. He stood. 'You need to leave.'

Her heart skipped a beat as he stepped away. He sauntered across to what she knew was the bedroom, pulling his T-shirt off as he did so and revealing his toned, heavily tattooed back.

As he disappeared from sight, she clasped the nape of her neck.

She couldn't give up that easily.

She dropped her hands back to her side. 'I don't expect you to do it for nothing. When I said "hire" you, that's what I meant,' she said, following him but stopping at the threshold to his bedroom. 'I'm willing to pay you.'

Side-on to her, he sat on the edge of his bed to remove his boots and socks before standing to drop his jeans. 'Even if you could afford me, even if I was willing, you most definitely couldn't afford me for this.'

'But I'm right,' she said, crossing the threshold. 'You *can* be hired. This *is* the kind of thing you do. Not just anyone has guns in Lowtown.'

'First saving a vampire's life, then being witness to the murder of two humans. Now trying to hire a contract killer.' He glanced across at her. 'You're having quite the week of it, aren't you, Ember?'

'Name your price.'

'You're a smart girl. Draw a line. Take no for an answer.' He pulled on a pair of black sweatpants that had been discarded over a near-by chair. He indicated towards the exit. 'Door's that way. And we'll pretend we never had this conversation.'

'I'm not giving up that easily.'

He closed the gap between them, Ember backing up across the threshold as he did so.

Reaching for the bar bolted above the doorframe, he lifted himself in one easy move, his eyes not leaving hers as he did so. 'So stand there. Watch me all night.'

'They killed Jasper. He's an old guy that used to visit us. Seventy-two and one of them beat him to a pulp. Stirling, his name is. He's the one who did it.'

'So now you're telling me you're hiring me for revenge?'

'Revenge *and* business. I know you can do this. I saw what you did out in that alley. Your responses were calculated. I saw how calm you were. The way you took those guys out—'

'Was about clearing a debt,' he said, releasing his grip from the bar, his bare feet silently hitting the floor. 'I thought I'd made that perfectly clear. We're done. Something *you* made *more* than clear.'

'Is that why you won't listen to what I have to say? Because I asked you to leave?'

'No, Ember, it's because I'm not suicidal. Take my advice: stay out of it. Focus on getting out of here. In five days, it won't be your problem any more.'

His exactness with her number of days left threw her off kilter for a moment. 'I might not even *have* five days with them in charge.'

'And that's the chance we all take,' he declared before resuming his workout again. 'Shit happens.'

'So that's it? You won't help me?'

'Finally, she gets it.'

She removed the wad of cash from her jacket.

'How much is that?' he asked, barely glancing at it. 'Two hundred? You think two hundred is anywhere near enough?'

'There are plenty who will work for that. I came to you first but you're not my only option. I've lived here a long time. I overhear a lot of conversations in that café. I know where I can go.'

'And anyone who accepts two hundred to go after the Hordas clan will be just as likely to kill you, rape you or sell you to a sire because they'll either be playing you or be fucking psychotic. The only people who would even hold this conversation with you will already be working for them. They'll double-cross you no sooner than look at you.'

'Then call it a down payment. If you want more, I'll get more.'

A curt laugh escaped his lips. 'You're not this naïve, Ember.'

'But I do need help. I could be talking a *lot* of money here. If I talk to all the businesses in the local area, we can gather enough to pay you well. I know they'll do it. I know they'll want to bring an end to this. If everyone works together, is proactive . . . '

His feet were back on the floor a split-second later. The speed with which he closed the gap between them took her breath away. Shadows consumed him, his outline ignited only by the streetlights.

'And what about you, Ember? What's your contribution to this cause? Those funds you put away to move to Midtown? Your home: your deposit for your college course? Maybe that would go *some* way towards my price. Are you willing to do that, Ember? Are you willing to give up your life in Midtown for this? Are you willing to put *your*self on the line for this cause like you're asking *me* to?'

Her pulse raced as his eyes gazed down into hers, Ember wavering as to whether it was a rhetorical question or a demand.

'Nothing you can do will be enough,' he added, confirming it was the former. 'You can't prevent this. You're out of your depth even asking. If they get one sniff of this, they'll burn the place down rather than make a profit on it, just to get you back. The people you're going up against, they see and know everything. I know what I'm talking about. You going after them will not save your friends; it's signing their death sentence – and yours. Quit. That's advice I'm giving for free.'

He backed up. He lifted himself up by the bar again, every muscle in his abdomen and arms tensing.

'I'm not going to do nothing,' she said firmly. 'This has to stop or they're only going to grow stronger. They are destroying lives and they're just going to keep wanting more. And the longer it goes on, the less chance we have of fighting back. That café is a droplet in an ocean to them but to Harry that droplet is his whole world. I can't let them take that from him.'

'And this is the last time I'm going to say it,' he said, letting go of the bar once more, his hands then resting on his hips. 'Goodnight, Ember. This conversation is over.'

CHAPTER SEVENTEEN

———◆———

'Not only is Stirling here again, but now I think another one of them has come in,' Casey said, her face ashen as she joined Ember in the kitchen. 'Table six.'

Ember lost her grip on her pan for a moment, her attempt to catch it again nearly causing her to burn her hand in the flames.

'Shit,' Ember hissed, Casey instantly turning on the cold water tap in time for Ember to run her hand under it.

She was never that clumsy – ever. Her concentration was shot.

'I'm so sorry!' Casey said, dampening a towel to wrap around it.

'I'm fine,' Ember said, taking her hand from under the flow of the tap to prove it. 'No damage done. I must have missed the flames.'

'If all this blows your chances of leaving . . .'

'It won't,' Ember reassured her, drying her hand off. She squeezed Casey's hand. 'Finish these eggs for me and I'll see to table six.'

The café had been sombre all morning. The customers were already picking up on it.

It had been bad enough that Stirling had been back, his full attention on Casey again. Now there was the prospect of an additional one too.

Taking a calming breath, she headed back out behind the counter. She glanced over at table six to see the guy sat looking out of the window. His hands were interlaced on the table, his back straight, his long face tight and stern. Tall and thin, he was in a smart shirt and trousers, making him seem almost alien in that place. His glasses were small and round and perched high on the bridge of his nose.

But he wasn't sat with Stirling.

And then it clicked: they said they could check up on her at any point.

As his eyes immediately met hers, it was as if he'd been waiting for her attention specifically, further confirming her suspicion. She sent him a polite smile of acknowledgement before removing her order pad from her apron on her way over.

She tried to stop her hand from trembling as she took his order, her wary attention equally on Stirling as he summoned Casey again.

Stirling on one side and now someone from the authorities on the other. It couldn't get any worse.

She registered the breeze from the door opening, but it took her a couple of seconds to finish with the spectacled guy before she glanced over her shoulder.

Her stomach somersaulted.

Avoiding her gaze as if she wasn't even there, her stranger instead looked immediately to the table where Casey had since been tugged onto Stirling's lap.

He'd come. That was all she could keep telling herself in the passing seconds: he'd changed his mind and he'd come. He'd thought better of her offer. For the first time since she'd received her news, she felt a glimmer of hope.

But rather than veering to an empty booth as he always did, he headed straight over to Stirling.

Her pulse picked up a notch. She wanted to tell him now was not the time – not with someone from the authorities sat right there.

He slipped into the same booth as Stirling, taking the seat opposite. And did what she rarely saw him do: her stranger smiled at him.

It was fleeting, a greeting, but the message behind it was clear: her stranger already *knew* Stirling. Not only did he know him but, from the way they ploughed straight into conversation, he was on friendly terms with him.

Her world closed in on her, faded black for a moment. Only when her chest ached did she realise she had stopped breathing.

'Miss?' she heard a distant voice say.

That's why he'd been visiting there all that time: *he*'d been the one scouting the place. He'd been working for *them*. It might have been the very reason he'd gone to her apartment that night. Until she'd thrown him a curveball by saving him.

And now they were even – something he'd made abundantly clear more than once now. He owed her nothing. Owed nothing to the woman whose plan he now knew. Knew she wanted to put a contract out on his employers. Had gone against the Hordas clan's instructions.

Bile formed at the back of her throat.

He had said nothing. He hadn't even given her the slightest indication when she'd gone to him.

But he *had* warned her to drop it. He'd instructed her to forget she'd even asked.

'Miss, a tea, please? Milk. No sugar.'

She glanced back down at the customer who now felt secondary to everything.

'Sure,' she managed to somehow say.

She headed over to the hot water machine. She started to fill the teapot.

Her throat constricted, she couldn't consume enough oxygen. Her thighs turned weak and heavy. Perspiration coated her palms and the back of her neck. She pulled away. She used both hands against the wall to prevent her from falling over as she headed down the corridor to the toilets.

She shoved open the cubicle door and fell to her knees over the bowl. She vomited what little food she had consumed those last couple of days, until a hand on her back made her flinch.

'Ember?'

She flushed the toilet as she struggled to her feet.

Not yet ready to meet Casey's concerned gaze, she stepped over to the sink. She washed her hands and her face. She thoroughly rinsed her mouth out.

'Yvonne said you went as white as a sheet. Are you OK?'

Ember raked her hands down her face as she fell back against the wall. 'I think I've fucked up, Casey. I think I've fucked up really bad.'

'What's happened? What have you done?' Her friend's eyes were wide with worry. 'Is it because of him? That guy who comes in here? He's sat with Stirling. He knows him. Is that why he's been coming here all this time? Has he been watching us for them?'

'What were they saying?'

'I don't know. Stirling sent me away. All I know is that his name is Nate. That's what Stirling called him.'

Nate.

'I spoke to him last night. To Nate,' Ember said. 'I asked him to help with the Hordas clan.'

Casey frowned. 'Help how?'

'I tried to put a contract on their heads. I tried to pay him to do it.'

Casey's eyes flared. Her jaw dropped. 'You tried to pay him to *kill* them?'

'I had no idea he's involved with them.'

Casey cupped her hand over her mouth. 'Oh, *fuck*.'

'I know.'

'And he didn't tell you?'

'No. But why would he? He's got me over a barrel. I can't believe I've been so stupid, Case. I can't believe I went to him.'

Casey grabbed hold of her upper arms. 'We have to warn Harry.'

'No. No, I need to talk to Nate first. I need to know what he's planning. Harry's got enough to worry about. And you mustn't say anything, Casey. Promise me. Not until I know more. I'll see if I can get him alone. I'll see if I can find out what he's playing at.'

'I'm not sure, Ember. This is not good.'

'I got us into this. I'll get us out of it.'

But by the time she'd made it out to the counter again, Stirling and Nate had gone.

And so had her spectacled visitor.

CHAPTER EIGHTEEN

On the whole, the Hordas clan handled their business in-house in order to keep their cards close to their chest. If it was something they couldn't handle themselves, they called in outsiders. For them to call him, for them to have been so specific about wanting him, it was a very particular job they wanted doing. A job with a guaranteed success rate. He knew that much from the contracts he'd fulfilled for them in the past.

Nate hadn't worked for them in a long time. It was a luxury he could afford himself. He couldn't exactly tell them to fuck themselves but he could proclaim himself to be too busy to take on more work, just as he had this time. Except, this time, they'd been persistent. They'd had word on the street for almost two weeks that they wanted to see him – something he had since learned from Daisy had evoked interest from the Voys; and had nearly led to him being killed.

And, finally, he had no choice but to be there – for his skin as much as the café's.

Nate ascended the broad, stone steps up to the double front doors of the large Edwardian house. The Hordas clan had the plushest residence in Lowtown, ironically less than a couple of miles from the Third Species Control Division Headquarters.

Knowing the routine, Nate waited in the generous foyer. In the twenty-plus years since he'd last been there, nothing much had changed other than a fresh coat of paint, the walls now pale blue instead of sage green.

Two armed guys marked the double-doors to his right, their attention not flinching from him as he waited. He chose to stroll as he did so, liking that it put them on edge, that it knocked their pulse rate up a little. Despite the fact there were two of them and one of him, both of them armed, he knew he still made them nervous. Vampires triggered that survival aspect of the reptilian brain still present in all humans since the dawn of evolution. The part of their brain that instinctively knew humans to be a notch down the food chain. They also knew of his reputation – something equally helpful in keeping them on their toes and earning their keep.

After only having to wait a few minutes, the doors were opened from the inside, Nate's cue to enter.

Antonia Hordas sat in the middle of the three-seater sofa, her long, slender legs crossed, her hands daintily clasped around her knee.

She'd been in her late-twenties the last time he'd seen her. The years had been kind to her. Her angular, defined features remained impressive. But her eyes were as cold and uncompromising as ever. Antonia was intelligent, competent and brutal – all traits that added to her appeal if the dominatrix vibe worked for you. He also liked to be in charge too much for them to ever see eye-to-eye. As a result, sex always had and always would be off the cards. It was an understanding they had that meant they could always get swiftly down to business without pointless games. The business she and her brother had run since their father's death ten years before.

'You've certainly kept me waiting this time, Nate,' she said as he took the seat opposite.

A glass of water was placed in front of him. A sherry was placed in front of her.

'I take it it's going to be worth both our whiles,' he said.

'I can assure you it will be. I have a job that requires a specialist. A specialist that doesn't ask questions. Who can guarantee to get the job done. A job that cannot risk being lost by even a single mistake.'

'What is it you want me to collect?'

It was the only question he ever asked. It was why he was top of his game. He never asked for the finer details. His rules were simple: don't ask questions, don't hesitate, and feel no guilt.

'It's not a what but a who.'

It was the last thing he wanted to hear.

'I only collect objects now, Antonia. You know that.'

'For this instance alone, I would like you to reconsider.'

This was not the way it was supposed to go, but he knew he needed to hear her out before he made his move.

She placed a device on the table that would fit in the palm of his hand – a flat and rectangular clear plastic casing containing red fluid. On the outside, a compass lay central.

'It's a locator,' she said. 'You follow where the hand is pointing. Once you're close, it'll spin wildly. Once you're within a few feet of your target, it will cease. That's where this comes in.' She placed a silver tube on the table and pulled out a clear glass vial within it. She unscrewed the pipette and placed a tiny amount of blood on the table. He knew it was blood. He could have smelt it from thirty feet away.

A cold chill rushed over him. Anything that involved blood was never good news. It screamed of dark magic. And dark magic usually involved witches. And he *never* fucked with witches.

This was anything but the scenario he wanted.

He should have walked out. He should have cut the deal dead there and then.

But he couldn't. This was no ordinary job that would have had him saying thank you but no thank you. This was a deal that needed to be done. This was why he had gone to the café in the first place that afternoon: to absolve Ember of any association by 'stumbling' on the situation for himself.

'Place this on the floor and follow its trail. It'll lead you straight to them.'

He met her gaze. The question burned inside him. *Lead to who?*

But he wasn't about to get into that conversation with her; he wasn't about to break his rules.

'Looks to me like you could have had someone else working on this, Antonia. Why wait around for me?'

'I need the best on this, Nate. And everyone knows you're the best collector there is. I need this done right first time. I need it done swiftly and effectively. I need *you*.'

He sank back into the sofa, his gaze steady on hers. 'Then maybe we need to discuss payment.'

'I will pay you generously.'

With money she had blackmailed, forced and stolen from others without compassion, remorse or hesitation.

'I have other ideas,' he said. 'Did Stirling tell you I met him at a little café over on Carlisle Street? A place called Harry's?'

'What of it?'

'I hear you're thinking of expanding there.'

'And?'

'You're not going to be expanding to that one.'

Her eyes flared at his directive. 'I'm sorry?'

'I'll make a deal with you, Antonia. You accepting or not accepting my terms will dictate whether I agree to take on this job or not.'

She exhaled curtly off the back of a laugh. '*That*'s why you're here?'

'I want you to pull out of the place.'

'You want me to pull out of some little backstreet café. *Why*?'

'Because I conduct business from there, and I don't want your kind of trouble attracting itself to where I do *my* deals. You'll complicate things for me. And you know I don't like things complicated.'

She slid her tongue along her lower lip as she pensively studied him.

'It seems we have very similar tastes for where we like to conduct our more private deals,' she said.

'It seems we do. Except I found it first.'

She laughed lightly – a dismissive laugh that made him loathe her arrogance even more. She stood from the sofa and wandered over to the window. She knocked back a sip of sherry. 'You know, if anyone else tried to make this deal with me, they'd already be dead.'

Antonia Hordas didn't bluff. Antonia Hordas didn't tolerate anyone who didn't do exactly what she instructed them to do. Antonia had ordered the slaying of entire families if one member had even just dared to look at her in the wrong way.

'And do *you* know that because of your persistent call out for me, the Voys got word and nearly killed me a couple of days ago?'

She looked across at him. Her surprise was clear in her eyes. 'Is that so?'

'It's your choice, Antonia. As you well know, I *can* get this job done. But it depends if it's more important to you than some backstreet café.'

She turned to face him. 'But I have an issue here though, Nate. We've laid down our cards. If we retract them, that could damage our reputation.'

'They're not stupid. They'll keep their mouths shut. Tell them you got a better offer.'

'I'll tell you what, Nate,' she said, wandering back over. She resumed her seat. She rested an outstretched, slender arm across the back of the sofa. 'I'll pull back for now. If you succeed in this job, I'll pull out for good. We'll call it a special arrangement – just between us. How's that for a deal? It's the best I'm going to offer.'

CHAPTER NINETEEN

———◦◉◦———

Nate only entered Blackthorn when he had to, especially at this time of night. Getting into Blackthorn wasn't the issue, but he knew he'd be cutting it fine getting back across the border into Lowtown.

With all legitimate third species Lowtown residents being chipped, he couldn't afford to be stopped and checked by the Curfew Enforcement Officers: those responsible for making sure residents of Blackthorn returned there before dawn. No illegal third species wanted to be caught by them. The CEOs had a reputation for being hardened, brutal and uncompromising when it came to those who didn't toe the line. They also didn't ask questions before hauling in anyone not tagged – and for him that wasn't worth the risk. Illegal resident he may be, but Lowtown was his domain and always would be. After all, he had no choice. Lowtown had been his home for a long time. Lowtown was the *only* place he could live.

He had a window of a few hours until it became unsafe. For

now, the border was advantageous, the security there nothing more than watchful eyes due to the ongoing depletion of resources.

Once successfully through, having moved with the tide of the crowds, Nate headed east, to the far side of the hub of Blackthorn, to where the streets were quieter.

Nate entered the store, the bell tinging above him as he did so. He passed through the shelves laden with herbs, crystals and other artifacts on his way to the counter at the back.

She was the only witch he dealt with. The only witch he semi-trusted. Tamara was a reliable source of information and, of equal importance, she was discreet. There were rumours that Kane Malloy himself used her. And if she passed Kane's approval, his trust was not a mistake.

Besides, she still owed him.

She was stood behind the counter with a young, kohl-eyed girl, the latter maybe eighteen or nineteen. Tamara's blue eyes instantly met his; eyes that were stark and vibrant against her black hair.

'My next payment isn't due for another two weeks,' she said as she pulled herself upright, placing her hand on her curvy hip in a defensive move.

'That's not why I'm here. Can we go to the back?' he asked, not wanting the young girl to be witness to the conversation.

Tamara gave him a contemplative and swift once-over before indicating for him to follow.

The aroma of the narrow corridor was intense – dominated by cinnamon and cloves – as he followed her through the heavy, velvet curtain to the back room and through to her home.

He took his seat on the sunken sofa in front of the fire before placing the locator on the low coffee table between them. 'Have you ever seen one of these before?'

She picked it up to examine it. She tilted it to the side to take a closer look at the compass component.

'Should I have?' she asked, her frown deep as she met his gaze over the top of it, her blue eyes laced with curiosity.

'There's blood in the compass – and blood in here.' He placed the vial on the table. 'Apparently, together they're some kind of tracking device. But we both know that every time blood's used, dark magic could be involved. I want to know what I'm getting myself into.'

'So this is for a job?'

'Yes.'

'And you're asking questions? Breaking your own rules. That's unheard of, Nate.'

'My first rule is self-preservation. That's why I'm making an exception this once.'

'And my services don't come for free any more than yours do.'

He'd collected an object for her only last week. It had taken him three months to track it down: a small, leather-bound book that could temporarily hold a human soul. He didn't ask her what she wanted it for. Like with all his collections, it was none of his business. He'd charged her significantly for it though and she was still in debt to him as a result.

As well as his rule of never asking questions, one of his others was to get paid in full – a rule he'd introduced a decade before. He'd only agreed to instalments because she'd agreed free access to her store for the next few months. With Tamara being one of the best underground sources of goods in Blackthorn, it had been a mutually beneficial arrangement.

'Tell me what you know and I'll waive half of the instalments,' he said.

Her eyes widened a little at the offer. 'If this *is* magic related, you know my kind's rules. I can't be disclosing things to you.'

'A human gave it to me. I think the secret's already disclosed.'

She held his gaze for a moment longer before heading out the back.

She returned some time later with a heavy book. She placed it on the table. She unlaced the string that bound it before flicking through the pages, using the various index tabs as she flipped back and forth between sections with the swift expertise of a lexicographer with a dictionary.

Finding the right page, she read through it before closing it again.

'What?' he asked.

'I can't talk to you about this,' she said. 'I'm sorry.'

'Be smart, Tamara.'

'*You* be smart, Nate. That better not have been a threat. Who gave this to you?'

'I can't tell you that.'

'Then we have a stalemate.'

'So this *is* witch related? Because that's the only reason why you wouldn't want to tell me. Right now, I'm going to follow that compass to wherever it leads and take whoever I find to the one who wants them. My guess is you have an obligation to do what you can to prevent that which can't happen without you telling me more.'

'But I'm not going to be preventing it, am I?'

'That depends.' He pulled out the only thing he knew would work. 'You don't want word getting back to Kane about who helped you with that book, do you? Not with how he feels about me.'

Her eyes narrowed. A few moments later, she reopened the book. She relocated the section before laying the book open in front of him.

'It's a witch finder,' she said, resentment emanating in her tone. 'What you have operating this is dead witch blood. It's designed to find family members from this specific bloodline.'

'So this is going to take me to a particular witch?'

'Yes.'

'What kind of witch?'

'I don't know. But the design of that device is archaic. It was said to have been devised centuries ago when a father's daughter was stolen. She was his only child. He sacrificed himself so she could be found and brought home. The compass helped locate her. The vial of blood pinpointed her. Witches have a stronger survival instinct than any other race; it's why we bind with nature so powerfully. That need to survive is what drives that droplet to find a familiar host. Nate, I don't know who wants this witch or why, but I can't be seen to advocate this as you well know.'

'Could it be serryn blood?'

Serryns – the rarest and most powerful of witches. Like sirens, they were the ultimate seductresses for vampires, but serryn blood was poisonous. No vampire in their right mind got within half a mile of a serryn. And it made sense that the Hordas clan would want one. He knew how valuable a caught one would be – or even one located.

'It's tough to say,' she said. 'Aside from the fact they've been rumoured extinct.'

'But it's possible.'

'Highly unlikely, but possible. If it was a serryn they were after though, it would make no sense to send a vampire after them. Not even you.'

Nate stepped back out onto the street.

He needed to pull out. He needed to back out.

But he knew exactly what Antonia would do if he did. Now he'd shown an interest in Harry's, she'd burn that café down and kill everyone in it as punishment. And then she'd put a price on *his* head.

He'd be finished.

CHAPTER TWENTY

Ember waited with her door wide-open so she wouldn't miss his return. *If* he returned.

Lounge light on, TV off so she could hear every creak, she sat on the edge of her sofa facing the door. Aside from her light spilling into the hallway, the stairwell remained in shadows; it had remained shrouded in silence for the three hours she'd been sat there. She hadn't even got around to changing or showering, despite wanting to get the grime of the day from her skin, fearful of him returning then leaving again in the interim without her having a chance to speak to him – or of him refusing to answer his door.

She needed to know what was going on. She needed to know if that was why he had been there all along. She needed to know if her friends were in danger. She needed to know if her chances of getting across the border were already gone.

When she eventually heard a click at the bottom of the stairwell, her heart skipped a beat. Her back straightened. She held her breath. For a moment she convinced herself it had been a figment of her imagination caused by longing, like seeing a mirage. Because there was no sound on the stairs to reinforce it. No giveaway clues in the echo chamber. So much so that when Nate eventually appeared outside her door, her heart leapt with the shock of it.

She wanted to stand but her legs wouldn't move.

He met her gaze, albeit fleetingly, before turning and heading across to his apartment.

'Wait!' Ember forced herself from the sofa to the threshold. She grabbed hold of the doorjamb for support.

His back remained to her as he slid his key in the lock.

'You didn't tell me,' she said. 'You should have told me.'

He turned casually to face her. 'Told you what?' he asked, his voice as steady as his gaze.

'That you know them. That you know the Hordas clan.'

'I know a lot of people.'

'OK, that you *work* for them,' she said, adding the specifics. 'You work for the Hordas clan.'

'I've done work for them. There's a difference.'

She *had* to know. 'Have you told them? Do they know what I asked you to do? This was *my* idea, no one else's. They can't hold my friends accountable for what *I* did. This isn't their fault.'

Because she was going to clear them of the responsibility of this. She was not going to let them suffer because of what she had done.

'No,' he said. 'I haven't told them.'

His answer was definitive.

Despite relief pooling through her, she needed to be convinced. 'Why not?'

He frowned. 'Why would I?'

His attention returned to his door.

'Why *wouldn't* you?' she asked.

He turned to face her again, his brow furrowed.

'Is that all this was about?' she asked. 'Did I complicate things by saving your life?' She crossed her threshold. 'You let me beg you for help and you said *nothing*. "The only people who would engage in the conversation already work for them." How did I not read between the lines with that one? Is *this* is what you do, Nate? That is your name, right? Do you bully innocent people? Advocate murder?'

'Unlike you?'

'That's not fair.'

He took a step towards her. 'You asked me to kill for you. Exactly how is that different? Does the morality behind killing someone vary according to the reason?'

'In this case, yes. When there is an aggressor, it's called self-defence. When there's no other way to prevent attack, it's justifiable to protect the non-instigators in the best way you can.' She took a step closer to him. 'Even after I told you it was the Hordas clan I was after, you let me continue.'

'I never disclose who my contacts are.'

'Then why did you come in the café earlier if not because you wanted me to know? If not because you wanted me to know you now have even more over me?'

His frown deepened. 'You think I plan to blackmail you?'

'Do you? Because if you do want something, Nate, just say. If you're going to use it against me, make it clear now. Is this why you moved next door? Is it because you knew I was getting into Midtown? Are you hoping to turn that to your advantage?'

'Like for money? A feed? A fuck? This might surprise you but I don't need to rely on blackmail to get any of those. I went to the café because I needed an excuse to go and meet with them off my own back without implicating you or any of the others.'

Her heart pounded as she stared at him in the shadows. 'Meet with them about what?'

'I've sorted it, Ember, just like you asked.'

'Sorted?' She shuddered at the prospect that her wishes had been met. 'Sorted how?'

'My way. They'll leave Harry's alone. That's all you need to know. And all *you* need to do now is keep your mouth shut and go about the next few days as if none of it happened.'

Her pulse raced as she waited for the punchline. None came. 'You helped?'

'If you want to see it that way.'

He turned his back on her again, the enigma of his words wrapping itself around her like an ethereal mist as she wracked her brains for clarity.

'Why?' she asked, her heart pounding to the point it made her light-headed. 'Why did you do it? Yesterday I couldn't afford you. What's changed?'

His sideways gaze met hers as he stepped across his threshold. 'Have you ever heard the cliché about not looking a gift horse in the mouth?'

He moved to close the door but she lunged forward, pressed her palm to the door.

'You don't owe me anything,' she said. 'You told me that yourself. This doesn't make any sense.'

'And I don't owe you. I didn't do it for you: I did it for me. All you did was give me the heads-up what was happening.'

'For *you*?'

'It's my place of business too, remember? So I got them to back off.'

'No one tells the Hordas clan what to do.'

'My work for them is freelance. They needed a job done so I did it in exchange for them backing off.'

'What kind of a job?'

As he moved to close the door, she pushed her foot across the threshold, her hand still pressed to the door.

'You saved my life when it would have been easier to let them kill me,' she said. 'You fixed and returned my necklace when you could have chucked it away. You're back here when you could be anywhere else. What's this *really* about? Who *are* you? What do you want from me?'

'I keep telling you: I don't want anything from you.'

'I don't believe you. There's more to this.'

He held her gaze for a moment longer before breaking first. When he looked back at her, he did so with sullen resolve in his eyes. 'I saved your life because you saved mine and because I hate owing anyone – whether they're alive or dead. I got the Hordas clan to back off so I can keep running my business from there without complications. And I gave you your necklace back because I felt sorry for you.'

'You felt *sorry* for me?' She exhaled tersely. 'There's nothing to pity about me.'

'No?'

'No,' she said firmly, hearing the indignation evident in her tone.

'Still wearing your dead fiancé's ring ten years later? I'd say there's a lot to pity.'

Her stomach lurched. She recoiled. 'How do you know about that?'

'Twenty-second of November, right? I saw you that night. I saw you breaking your heart over Liam's dead body in the alley, just as I saw Jasper give you that ring,' he said, indicating the one on her engagement finger.

She instinctively clasped her hand over it. 'What has my ring got to do with anything?'

'I was the one who got it for Liam. It's what I do. I'm a collector. I get my hands on whatever people want me to get my hands on. It's worth a lot of money. More than he could afford. When he stopped paying the instalments, I tracked him down only to find someone else had got there first. Apparently a sire wasn't too happy to hear your boyfriend had been up close and personal with his favourite feeder. He'd been screwing some girl for months. He was wrapped around her little finger – and that ring was what she demanded in order for him to prove his love to her. *That*'s why I felt sorry for you. That ring wasn't meant for you, Ember. It was meant for her.'

She felt as though she was staring at him down the length of a dark tunnel. As though she was in a backwards freefall.

'You're wearing the ring of a guy who's been dead ten years and didn't even love you. So like I said, quit looking a gift horse in the mouth. Get yourself out of Lowtown. Start your new life. Move on. Fuck knows you deserve it.'

CHAPTER TWENTY-ONE

———◆———

Nate slammed the door on her.

He'd already compromised himself enough – *more* than enough. He was even doing one more job for the fucking Hordas clan because of her. Collecting someone because of her. Something he swore he'd never do again – because of *her*.

And collecting a *witch* at that.

Hopefully her knowing he'd done what she'd asked, let alone him having mentioned Liam, had brought an end to her questions. If nothing else, he hoped he'd embarrassed her enough to not want to approach him again. That she'd keep a safe distance now until her time there was up, so he could continue to do what he needed to do until her time was up.

They'd given him a little over two days to get the job done, which almost coincided with her leaving. Somehow he was going to have to balance both. If not, he knew which one would have to give. Self-preservation would dictate which one had to give.

Nate stepped over to the kitchen window. He cupped the back of his head, his fingers interlaced as he gazed out at the slight change of light on the brick wall that signalled the impending dawn being a couple of hours away.

Three days to go. Soon, thankfully, she'd be gone and then he could abandon that apartment and move back to his own.

Wandering through to the bedroom, he opened the sash window for some much-needed air. He sat on the edge of the bed and opened his drawer for the full syringes he'd taken from his holdall earlier. Pumping the contents into his arm would help curb things, and it would make his much-needed climax even more satisfying as the new blood kick-started the flow of his own. Because he needed a release. More than anything then, he needed to lose himself for a short while.

He lay down on the sheets. Steadying his breathing as the added human blood coursed through his veins, he relaxed into the moment, into the sensation. Unfastening his jeans, he took hold of himself. Letting the night breeze caress his body, he worked his already straining erection from his and Ember's altercation, gritting his teeth as he closed his eyes.

He placed his fingertips on the wall behind him, knowing she was just beyond it.

Soon she would be gone from his routine, from the café, from his life.

As he tightened his grip on himself, the thoughts of sex with her weren't tender amidst his frustration and resentment – of what her life was going to be after that, of how someone else would eventually have her, of how empty his life would feel again. Sex with her in his head was impatient and hard and rough and all consuming. And he wanted his climax to linger so he could relish in the pain of it. But, instead, he came quickly, the orgasm powerful and lingering, trickling down his hand as he gripped and squeezed and silently groaned at the satisfaction of it.

And when it abated, when he removed his hand from the wall, the connection was again lost, just as she would soon be lost to him.

He lay in the quiet for a while, one hand behind his head, the other on his bare abdomen.

He could hear her through the wall: moving around, her shower door sliding, the distant whirr of her hairdryer. Another sleepless night for her.

Another sleepless night for them both.

Finally, he stepped into his own shower to rinse off quickly before towel drying his hair and body. Casting his towel aside, he wandered into his lounge to make a coffee when he heard her door close.

He paused in the renewed silence, half expecting to hear her knock on the door.

He'd ignore her. Whatever she wanted, whatever things she wanted to discuss further, he was not opening that door.

But the knock didn't come.

The slamming of the outer door did though.

It was four in the morning. Ember *never* went out at four in the morning. He headed over to the kitchen window.

He couldn't see her because of the bars being in the way, he couldn't hear her.

Nor could he go out – not so close to dawn, not with the CEOs already out on the streets.

'*Fuck*,' he hissed.

She was calling his bluff – she had to be. He knew exactly what game she was playing. Or at least he hoped he did. But she was still out there. She was still out during the dangerous couple of hours before dawn. CEOs had a reputation for playing hard with their own kind too – especially those they found out on the street, making their jobs harder.

He was *not* going to play the game. Ember was anything but stupid. She was not going to throw everything away when she was right on the cusp of leaving – not to prove a point.

Unless what he'd said about Liam had hit her harder than he'd anticipated. Unless he'd underestimated the impact. She'd worn his ring for years. He couldn't dismiss what that meant nor the impact of his revelation in light of that. Ember, even Ember, was capable of moments of irrational behaviour during times of anger, or grief, or confusion.

She was human. Just human.

And maybe moments from being out of sight.

Nate tugged on his sweatpants and grabbed his T-shirt. With no time to pull on and tie up his boots, he opted to stay barefooted as he hurried out of the apartment. Using the balustrade for leverage, he bypassed several steps before heading out of the door.

He stepped out into the alleyway, hoping for her sake that he didn't get a shard of glass through his foot.

And, to his right, saw her leaning back against the wall just a few feet away.

Ember turned ninety degrees to face him fully. Resting her shoulder against the wall, she folded her arms. She raised her eyebrows slightly as she glanced down at his bare feet; up at his still wet hair.

She didn't need to say anything.

Irritation coursed through him that she'd proved her point, that she'd given him no choice but to have gone along with it.

That, in fact, she knew he *did* have a choice. And she had forced him to show his hand.

Her point made, she brushed past him back into the safety of the stairwell.

He bit into his bottom lip. He shook his head a little, his hands on his hips. Stepping back inside behind her, he slammed and locked the door.

Ember was already at the top of the stairs. She was already making her way into the apartment he had left open. *His* apartment.

She stood in the centre of the lounge, her arms folded. 'Is someone paying you to look out for me, Nate? To keep me safe.'

'Like who?'

'I don't know. Harry can't afford to pay you. Casey couldn't. I don't know anyone who could. But you're *not* here by accident. I don't care what you claim, there's no way any of this is coincidence.'

'Coincidences happen all the time.'

'Like Cam going missing and you turning up? Did you kill him too?'

As her eyes narrowed in unrelenting suspicion, he wasn't sure if he was amused or offended by the ease of her conclusion. 'Maybe if I was gaining the penthouse.'

Dismissing his humour, she took a step towards him. 'Am I being groomed for something? *Because* I'm going to Midtown? It's almost as though you want to make sure I get there.'

His slow pulse picked up a notch at being cornered. Picked up a notch at the intensity of her stare.

'Are you protecting me?' she asked. 'Has someone hired you to ensure it happens for their own ends?'

'Protection isn't my thing, Ember.'

'Though it sounds to me like it could be if it's protecting *your* investment. Do you have your *own* plans in this? Is that why you got the Hordas clan out of there? Could you not afford to lose me to them? Because now you tell me about my ring too? About you knowing about my past. You've been watching me for months, haven't you? Something is going on here or none of this makes any sense.'

He needed to throw her off the scent. That was the most important thing.

'I didn't kill Cam. I won the place off him in a card game. I followed you home from the café that night I saw you still wearing the ring. I was going to take it back. Cam and his mates were all hanging around this doorway and I saw that they wouldn't let you pass. It might have been a game to them, and you handled it pretty well, but I knew next time, a different crowd, and it might not have been the same story. I followed him for a few days. I sussed out his haunts. I found out he was a keen poker player. Not as keen as me though.'

'You said you've only been here for a couple of weeks. He left two months ago.'

'I didn't win it to live here. It's an investment. I've had a job in this part of Lowtown recently. It's made it more convenient.'

Her eyes narrowed with intrigue. 'If you wanted the ring back, you could have taken it the night you saw Jasper give it to me.'

'Steal a ring from a lone woman, a grieving widow? And an old man? I wasn't that desperate. And neither was I when I saw what you were up against here. So I let it go.'

The way she looked at him made him uneasy – as if she was seeing him differently. Seeing him in a way neither of them could afford.

'And won this place to further keep me safe,' she stated.

'I've compromised myself out of pity.'

'Because you don't compromise yourself, do you, Nate?'

'No.'

'Why not?'

'Because I work for whoever gives me the highest price. I do whatever needs to be done without question, without guilt and without remorse. *Whatever* needs to be done.'

'Like killing people?'

'Like killing people.'

'And saving people's lives. And returning precious keepsakes. And helping people when you don't need to.'

'If you knew who I was, the things I've done, you'd hate me with every part of your being.'

'And would it make a difference if I hated you? Would it matter to you?'

'No, Ember, it wouldn't matter. Because I don't care. I can't afford to care. I will never care because my very instincts are fuelled by the *opposite* of caring.'

Ember stood her ground, her eyes narrow and questioning as she stared into his. 'What was it you said to me: "Fuck knows you deserve it"? Why? *Why* do I deserve it? Why are you so desperate to see me leave this district?'

She was getting too close. Far too close.

'Is there something more to this?' she persisted. 'Something more personal?'

'Is getting answers from me really more important than you seeing your plans through? Take a good look around, Ember. Look at where you are. Who you're with. Check what you're doing.'

'Exactly. You've had six months of opportunities, not least the last couple of weeks. I'm such easy prey for you. For someone who claims to be incapable of caring, you have incredible self-restraint. So enough is enough. Tell me the truth, Nate. What the fuck is really going on here?'

As Nate turned his back on her, as he stepped away towards the bedroom, she pulled the sleeves of her sweater down over her hands and folded her arms.

She couldn't let it lie. He could avoid answers all he wanted, but it only gave further weight to the fact there was definitely something more going on. She couldn't force it out of him though. She couldn't make him tell her what he didn't want her to know.

But it was there: that nagging doubt that he had been hired by someone. He had some kind of arrangement with someone. Someone who wanted her – just like they'd wanted her brother.

Or someone who cared about her.

She glanced at the open door to her apartment beyond, past the chill of the stairwell, the grey light emphasising what now felt even more like a vacuous space – the grey light reflecting what her life had become. And she knew if she left then, the opportunity would be gone. An opportunity she may never get back.

Light flickered from inside his bedroom, images casting their intermittent light on the floor, Ember working out that he had put the TV on, albeit mute. It was also the cue that he was planning to stay in there – that she would have to go into his bedroom if she wanted to persist.

He was expecting her to back down. He was expecting her to back off.

He had a lot to learn.

Ember stepped up to the threshold. The window in the bottom left-hand corner was open, letting in the night breeze and freshening the room as well as Lowtown air could.

In the shadows of the room, Nate reclined under the sheet on the left side of the bed, his chest now bare as he semi-sat up, his arm behind his head. He knocked the tip of his remote against his lower lip with his other hand, his gaze fixed on the TV screen that was beside her head to her left.

Her heart rate picked up a notch, his acting as if she wasn't even there making her feel like even more the voyeur, his nonchalance to her presence fuelling her discomfort.

So when his gaze eventually met hers, her stomach flipped. He was making it perfectly clear the ball was in her court. He'd laid down his warning, one that, amidst his continuing nonchalance, made her next move tougher.

The threshold became a line she wasn't sure she was ready to cross but, as he lay there looking at her, waiting for her to make *her* move, she knew she wasn't going to turn around and go back out.

'I knew about Liam,' she said. 'As in I knew there was someone else.'

It was the truth. She *had* known. For weeks before his death, she had known. She had waited for him to man up and tell her himself. Had been on the cusp of finally confronting him and then that call had come through.

'Then why still wear the ring?'

If he was interested enough to ask, she would answer him honestly.

'A reminder,' she said. 'That nothing is ever as it seems. That even those closest to you can betray you. And yet, like with Jasper, it can be a stranger who steps in to pick up the pieces.'

She slipped the ring off her finger. She approached his side of the bed. Placed the ring on the bedside table.

'Take it,' she said. 'Recoup the money Liam owed you. Then you have closure, right?'

He didn't confirm or deny the latter.

She held his gaze, the night breeze circling the room.

Nor did he ask her to leave.

As if someone else was controlling her, ignoring her better judgement, she perched on the side of the bed next to him.

The only alternative was to head to her own bed. A bed

that she knew would feel more isolated and cold than ever. As such, she knew she was staying for all the wrong reasons. She was there because she was lonely. She knew it was the worst hour of the night to make those choices, that the visceral was overriding cerebral. That hour was the darkest hour in any human psyche – the time when the deepest despair took over. It was the reflective hour and hers often shone the darkness of loss more than anything back at her. And to clamber from the abyss sometimes meant crawling towards the slightest glimmer of light, even if further darkness lay beyond. She needed a blast of heat, even if the chill was even more consuming afterwards.

Right then, she needed the company. She wanted *his* company. And it was more than apparent from his silence that he wasn't adverse to hers.

She knew the fool she was potentially making of herself, but never before had she not cared what happened next. The liberation of it gave as much an unfamiliar sense of euphoria as an adrenaline rush. For the first time, she understood why people took the risks they did.

Her heart pounded to the point she could hear her blood pumping in her ears. Goosebumps prickled her bare skin, the chill sweeping around her legs.

She reached for the sheet that covered him and dragged it down a little further so she could see the bruising on his side – the injury she had tended to. His skin was flawless again, as if it had never happened.

When Nate did nothing to stop her, she traced her fingertips over his hard, flat stomach, skimming the smattering of short, dark hair not far below his belly button.

She met his gaze again but only fleetingly. He made no attempts to touch her back – the remote remaining held to his lips, his other arm still resting behind his head. In many ways his lack of reciprocation made it easier, as if she was still merely admiring him from afar, as if she was playing on fantasies he remained unaware of.

She slid the pads of her fingers up his abs, the grooves hard beneath her fingers, his toned strength making her abdomen knot. He was cool to the touch due to his slower circulation – not cold, not waxy, instead pleasant like he'd been out in fresh air.

She flattened her hand over his right pec before sliding her hand across to his left, passing some kind of scarring over his heart along the way. The skin was raised like a branding and paler than the rest of his skin. She met his gaze ready to ask what it was but she knew he wouldn't tell her.

She reached up to touch his jaw, wanted to rub her thumb across his lips, but he gently caught her wrist as if wanting to refrain from the intimacy of such an affectionate move. Because this wasn't about affection to him. This wasn't about anything to do with intimacy.

And neither could it afford to be for her. This needed to be about the expulsion of months of frustration of being so close to someone she felt such an intense attraction to. This was about trying to move on; proving to herself that she *could* move on. This was about gratitude to someone who hadn't had to do what he had, whatever he claimed. This was about taking the only chance she might have. This was about her needing to see beyond her own fears and paranoia and prejudices; seeing beyond the extra incisors.

Seeing beyond her past.

She reverted her attention back to sliding her hand down his side. He was sculpted perfection. Everything about him was perfection, enabling her to convince herself that lust was her driving force.

And the perfection continued as he placed the remote aside,

as he used his free hand to ease the sheet down to his upper thighs confirming that he was naked beneath. More than naked, he was already hard.

Her left hand clutched the sheet on the far side of her thigh as she dropped her right hand to the side of his hip, uncertain what he was hoping she would do next. If he had any expectations at all.

Nonetheless, the temptation to touch every part of him was compelling enough that she didn't feel the need to wait for confirmation. She glided her fingers gently up his full, hard length, from deep at the base of his shaft to the very tip, where she circled her middle finger with a featherlike touch. His erection jolted instantly, lifting from his abdomen further, reassuring her that it hadn't been a bad move.

Wrapping her hand around his girth, her fingers unable to circle him fully, she slid her hand gently back down before gliding up again, pressing her palm lightly against his tip every few strokes.

Though his gaze had dropped to watch her, his eyes lifted the same time hers did; eyes so intense, so dark as to make the depths of her abdomen clench.

The light from the TV ignited wisps of her hair but left her face partially in shadow. But he could still see her scraping her teeth over her lower lip as she sometimes did when she was contemplating, wearing that small frown, the vertical fine lines above her nose defined as a result.

To anyone else she would have looked perfectly composed, well practised as she was at looking calm and in control. She'd had years of practice of looking calm and in control.

But he could hear her pulse racing. He could smell the feminine aroma of the light sheen to her skin. Because nothing got past him, from the subtlest increase in her breathing to that pacey human heart. Most of it was unintentional, but the human body had a way of giving away clues that the vampire body could keep well under control. It's what kept humans a notch down on the food chain – because humans were transparent when it came to basic physiological responses.

And Ember most definitely had the anticipation of someone who hadn't been intimate for a long time. In the six months he'd been at the café, he'd never seen anyone drop her off or come to collect her. He'd never seen anyone accompany her home. He'd never heard voices in her apartment. He was willing to bet that if she'd had relationships since Liam, they hadn't lasted. He was willing to bet, based on what she had said, that there had been no one since. More so because Ember had been biding her time to leave and wouldn't have wanted the complication of relationships – the hurt of leaving someone behind. Yet she was willing to put her escape on the line right then.

She was risking her convictions by feeling safe with him, by feeling grateful for what he'd done, by the attraction that continued to be betrayed in the way she touched him. And he was no doubt a novelty to her. She was curious, explorative. She'd never been with a vampire – that much was clear.

But ultimately, she was lonely. Whether she wanted to face it or not, the cocoon she had created around herself in preparation for leaving had left her disconnected. And she wanted that connection again. She wouldn't have dared risk it otherwise.

And that was why three a.m. was no time for her to be making decisions and no time for him either. It was the weak point for humans and vampires alike. A time when humans were at their most vulnerable and vampires more inclined to take whatever they wanted.

And he wanted *her*. He needed her irrational choices. He

needed to be her mistake. He needed her to hate him for it when it was over. *If* they got that far.

The right thing was to decline, but with her he wanted to do anything but the right thing. He wanted her in his bed. There was no two ways about it. And her tentative and gentle touch didn't ease his desire. But she *would* back out. At some point, she would pull away. She'd come to her senses – something he needed to speed up before he lost his.

He unbuttoned her blouse one-handed, heard her breath snag as he reached in and cupped her left breast. As he felt the warmth of her soft, firm flesh beneath the thin fabric of her bra, he knew he could bruise her in all the right places to raise questions at her final medical. Scratch her flawless skin. Nip her and graze her. Leave finger marks. He could come inside her without protection so they'd find traces of his sperm days after. She'd have no choice but to take a pill he could give her, another trace they would find in her body. And one bite would secure it – one deep, hard, scaring bite deep into her flesh and it would all be over.

She would be his.

But he could never have her. He could never be with her. And as her eyes warily met his, he hoped she sensed just that.

He thought she would back off then, but it seemed Ember was a little hardier than he had anticipated.

As he thumbed the cup of her bra down to expose her breast to him, Ember shuddered, and no more so than as he rubbed his thumb across her nipple, already hard from arousal, from the chill in the room.

And as he lowered his head, his cool breath teasing for just a moment before he licked, her whole body shuddered as a tingle shot to every nerve ending. Her stomach flipped, her abdomen clenched, a rush of heat pooled between her legs as his mouth encompassed as much of her as it could, his tongue sliding back over her nipple in the process.

She released his erection to press her hand to his chest as he sucked harder, a haze consuming her, Ember having almost forgotten up to that point that he wasn't human – that those incisors could do irreparable damage.

She tensed and pushed her hand against his chest as she recoiled.

'I'm not going to bite you, Ember,' he said, his gaze locking on hers again in the shadows. 'If I wanted to bite you, I would have.'

And he was right. It was the reason she'd allowed herself to sit there in the first place.

Despite his reassurance, as he pushed the sheet away, as he guided her back against him, the change of position unnerved her: not being able to see him, the added power it gave him being behind her, her limited movement compared to his, the feel of his ready arousal pressing against her back.

He gently held her throat as he rested her head back against his shoulder, before guiding her right hand behind her to wrap around his erection again. And she did, liking the way he throbbed in her hand.

He unbuttoned and opened her work shirt fully, her front-fastening bra next, exposing both breasts to the night air that circulated in the room. He ran his fingers beneath them before caressing and then squeezing both breasts simultaneously.

As he gently tweaked her nipples, she flinched and lost her grip. Nate tightened his on her throat to keep her against him though, coiled his hand around hers again, slid himself up and down in her hand to encourage her not to let go again.

Once seemingly satisfied she was going nowhere, he reached for the button on her trousers. He slid them down over her behind before wrapping his fingers around the hipband of her knickers.

She held her breath as he slid both down over her knees, leaving her to free them from her shins and feet. Legs bent at the knees like hers, he looped his ankles around hers, the draught caressing her inner thighs, cooling her sex as he spread her legs towards the open doorway.

His lips, despite being cold, displayed warmth in the tenderness with which he brushed them along the shell of her ear before taking her lobe deep into his mouth, nipping lightly with his teeth.

Through hooded eyes, she glanced out anxiously into the darkness beyond, his fingers and palms cool against her skin as he glided his hands down the tops of her thighs; did so three times before swapping to her inner thighs on the way back up. And as the flat of his fingers finally pressed against her sex, she gasped and arched her back, her fingers loosening on his erection again.

This time he allowed her to release him, clasped her breast in response to her bucking, his arm firmly across her, trapping her right hand at the small of her back where she had held him.

He spread her thighs further, his knees then locked on the inside of hers; her thighs that would have otherwise trembled had he not held them apart so securely. And not least as he brushed his thumb over her clit.

Being as tense as she was, he knew it was going to take a while longer to make her wet enough to slide his fingers inside her without causing too much discomfort. Despite no protests leaving her mouth, the position of him behind her was no doubt adding to her tension.

He could have opted to face her, to get her to sit astride him, to lay her on her back, but the intimacy would have been wrong – misleading.

Besides, he liked the upper hand it gave him. He liked to watch her mouth as she gasped, her breasts shuddering from her rapid breaths, her thighs trembling. It was a position that kept her perfectly accessible, that gave him total control. Just the way he liked it.

The position he held her in would make it harder for her to come anyway, prolonging the build up, making the end result all the more powerful. He continued to slide his fingers over her sex until he knew she was ready, exploring the delicate folds, intermittently brushing her clit with his thumb.

Because she *would* come.

He'd see to that.

Relax.

She kept saying it over and over in her head.

Relax.

And soon she started to lose sense of time and place to the point she could feel only his fingers against her sex, fingers that were as cool and hard as his chest that pressed against her back. Fingers that were as strong and as masculine as every other inch of his body.

She stared back at the open door ahead and the shadows beyond. She glanced to the flickering images on the TV – some action movie – a car racing through the streets in some kind of adrenaline-fuelled chase. It became almost hypnotic to the point she finally relaxed fully against him, let her head rest back against his shoulder, her body sinking against his, her legs no longer tense under his restraint. She registered that he'd parted her thighs further. She registered that his thumb strokes were firmer.

She didn't know if he'd make her climax. It had been so long, she could barely remember what it was like. She'd attempted it herself a few times but whenever she'd succeeded, it had been unsatisfying.

Since then, she'd barely bothered. She'd try some nights when she felt lonely. When the shadows fell on the apartment. When she could hear nothing but the ticking of the clock. Ticking away her life. She'd resolved on more than one occasion that if her application failed she'd try to forge a relationship there in Lowtown. That she'd move on. That she'd try and make some kind of life for herself. She'd thought about meeting people just for sex. No complications – just to ease the frustration and the loneliness some nights. But it was hard to find people to trust. It was hard to meet the right people. But the biggest issue of all – the risk it posed – was too great. Until *that* night. Until she now lay in bed with a vampire she barely knew other than him having saved her life – potentially twice now.

As she lay back against him, watching those flickering images, listening to the gentle patter of rain and the sound of her own breathing against the backdrop of his, the scent of his perspiration and pre-come mingling with hers, she didn't want to be anywhere else.

At that moment, she didn't even want to be in Midtown. She just wanted to be in that dark, shadowy room, cut off from the world, nothing to think about than the pleasure surging through her body. Because despite being restrained by him, she'd never felt more liberated. Like when her mind wandered to thoughts of him: of the day he might be outside the café after work; might offer to walk her home. Or he'd already be there waiting outside her apartment.

Now she *finally* had him. And his touch was every bit as exquisite as she'd imagined. His expertise was intoxicating. And when his finger finally entered her, she clamped her eyes shut, having him inside her even more fulfilling than she'd imagined in her most intimate dreams about him.

His erection throbbed in her hand at the feel of her tight heat, her arousal. He wasn't convinced she was even aware she was holding him again, her eyes glazed as they fixed on the flickering images of the TV screen.

But despite her arousal, deeper penetration was still restricted; her occasional wince and gasp confirming it *had* been a long time. But it only fuelled his need for her more.

He withdrew to push his middle finger inside her again, building a gentle rhythm, finger fucking her a little deeper each time, his attention fixed on the mounds of her breasts forced upwards by the grip of his forearm beneath them, the tautness of her fully erect nipples, the smattering of goosebumps over her skin beneath the perspiration. What was out of view, he could imagine: her legs spread apart by his, her sex fully exposed, his finger sliding in and out of her, the sheen of her escalating excitement coating his hand.

As her sex became accustomed to his penetration, as her breathing turned terse with arousal instead of tension, he slipped his forefinger in alongside his middle finger with his next push.

She jolted and gasped. Her breathing shallow and rapid again, her eyes now locked shut. He picked up pace, his two fingers fucking her harder as he intermittently brushed her clit with his thumb until her body finally relaxed, allowing him deep and free penetration. There was new tension in her legs. A different kind of tension taken from how her body trembled. Her nipples were as taut as her breathing, her pulse picking up another notch – short, ragged little gasps. She tightened her grip on his erection to the point of causing him pain, but he worked with it, her grasp allowing him to pump firmer into her hand, to feel her warm, soft skin restricting his movement, creating enough friction to be pleasurable.

He was losing her. His fingers were soaking. She whimpered. She squeezed him hard.

And he couldn't hold back any longer.

The room was a haze, her sex aching and throbbing.

She heard the drawer open beside her. She heard the tearing of foil. She felt his hand at the small of her back as he slid the protection down over himself.

Her stomach clenched. She was about to have sex with him. Full-on sex. The prospect seemed surreal, even after what they had done.

She was on her back a moment later, gazing up into his eyes, her thighs parted around his hips.

He interlaced her fingers with his, their hands palm to palm as he pressed hers down either side of her head.

She coiled her toes in the sheets. She clenched her hands in his as she held his gaze. Her pulse ratcheted up to a painful rate as he pressed the head of his erection against her sex, the anticipation making her hold her breath.

'Don't bite,' she said breathily. 'Please.'

He didn't respond as he slid his lips down her neck, down over her breast, his mouth closing over her sensitive flesh again – but this time with more fervour and less tenderness.

Arousal shot to her sex as he licked from her left nipple up behind her ear; released one hand to lift her a little, to arch her back slightly, and pushed inside her just an inch.

It was enough to cause her to flex her fingers but he tightened his grip, pinning both hands to the mattress either side of her shoulders again.

And as he met her gaze with a slightly playful edge to his eyes, she felt a pang she couldn't afford to feel, that she felt guilty for feeling; that had her wondering if this was far from simple lust as it should have been – at least on her part.

As Nate pushed an inch inside her, she snatched back another breath, her thought patterns lost in an ethereal haze, like a moment of remembering she had to do something but not being able to remember what – and then no longer caring what it was in the first place.

Because he was delaying. He was savouring the moment. He was torturing her in the moment, leaving her on the cusp of waiting.

She searched his eyes. She opened her mouth to speak.

And he thrust.

Ember gasped. Her whole body arched beneath his. She groaned as he pushed both hard and deep, not giving her time to adjust. A cold perspiration encompassed her. Goosebumps lined her flesh. Her toes curled tighter into the sheet. Her hands clenched his.

His jaw was tight, his lips sealed. He withdrew just a little but only to push even harder on the second penetration. Or fuck, as seemed more appropriate. That was the first word that appeared in her head. It was always a word she hated – a cold, callous, unemotional word for such an intimate act. But now it didn't feel cold at all. It was the only word she could find to define what he was doing. He pushed hard, harder than she had anticipated. Harder than she had experienced in love-making. But he wasn't making love to her. He was taking the upper hand. He was taking her. This was nothing to do with feelings. This was different to anything she had experienced.

At first it was uncomfortable, painful, the tightness of her body struggling to take him despite her previous arousal, her renewed tension no doubt not helping. But it quickly became something else entirely. The sensations screaming through her body were soon telling her it was nothing but good – physically at least. She knew her response was purely sexual. And she knew that was for the best. As his lips hovered inches from hers, as their breath mingled, as he avoided kissing her, she knew it was all it could be. And she wanted nothing more. She didn't want to forge a connection that would cause a greater wrench. She didn't want . . .

His wince startled her. His jolt unnerved her. At first she wondered if he was climaxing, but his scowl, his clenched teeth, the way he stilled, indicated it was as if something had caused him pain.

She stared deep into his eyes. Deeper and closer than she had ever dared, trying to work out what was wrong.

And then she saw something that distracted her, something ignited subtly by the momentary increased light from the TV screen: the subtle dark rim around his irises.

As unease cascaded through her, her body had other ideas. And seemingly, so did his. As she was tipped over the edge, she groaned as she came; the sensation made her whole body tremble and lose any sense of any world beyond his body against hers, within hers.

She heard him come too. She felt it in the tensing of his body, in the heavy breathing against her ear, his ejaculation seemingly powerful from the way he crushed her hands.

A tiny involuntary tear escaped the corner of her eye, dampening the sheet beneath her cheek as her orgasm peaked.

But within seconds of coming he withdrew, instantly pulling away from her.

CHAPTER TWENTY-TWO

———◆———

Easing to the edge of the bed, her body still trembling, Ember had difficulty standing at first.

She pulled her shirt over her chest, clumsily buttoning it up, missing a couple but she knew it didn't matter. She was only going across the hall. It wasn't like anyone would see her. She stood, surprised by how weak and shaky her legs felt, how sore she felt, how tender. She found her knickers and trousers and pulled them on.

She needed to be covered. She needed to feel back in control.

She heard the toilet flush and she heard the spray of the shower followed by a sliding door and the smacking of water against the plastic tray. He was washing her off; washing their experience away. He hadn't stopped to check she was OK. He hadn't even let her know what he was doing. He may even have been hoping she'd go away whilst he was busy.

As she heard the shower switch off, she sat back down and stared at the doorway in anticipation.

Because she had to ask him.

She felt sick her to her core in anticipation of her question, in anticipation of his response.

He didn't meet her gaze as he joined her in the bedroom again. He got dressed in silence, pulling on his shorts and jeans and a fresh T-shirt before throwing everything he could find into the holdall on the chair.

Her hands clenched into the duvet either side of her. 'You're leaving?'

'I've got a new job to do, remember?'

'This is what you do? Move from place to place?'

He didn't answer as he stepped around to the bedside table to remove his guns and add them to the holdall.

'As part of your collecting? Apart from rings, what else do you collect, Nate?'

'Whatever needs collecting,' he said, still avoiding her gaze. 'People want things they can't find and I find what they can't.'

A tidal wave of dread washed over her. The longer she stared at him, now with a sense of context, the familiarity became all too apparent. Like the re-emergence of a dream, memories started to gather. The puzzle laying in front of her started to come together section by section, and all the horrors with it.

And the word 'pity' took on a whole new meaning.

Why he'd hung around took on a whole new meaning.

But he wouldn't remember. Surely. There was no way he would recognise her as a grown adult: she'd only been five years old back then.

Unless there was a chance he'd recognised her necklace.

There was every chance the necklace was the key.

'*Does it mean something?*' he'd asked when he'd given it back to her.

'Nate, I need to ask you something before you go.'

He didn't respond.

'Third species have perfect vision. So why do you wear contact lenses?'

He stilled over his bag.

'I saw them,' she said. 'The outlines around your irises. I've never looked close enough before. I've never seen them in enough light before.'

He zipped his holdall shut. He turned to face her.

Her heart pounded as she waited on a knife-edge for his response.

'I have distinctive irises,' he said. 'It makes it hard in my line of work when I want to stay below the radar.'

The blood rushed from her head so fast that she felt herself sway.

'Can I see them?' she asked.

'No.'

'Why not?'

'Because I don't want you to.' His gaze was steady, his frown intense, before he pulled away. 'I need to get going.'

Her hands trembled. Her throat clogged. He was not walking away from her. Not yet. 'Do you regret it?'

He stopped at the threshold to the bedroom. He looked back at her. 'Regret what?'

'Murdering my mother.'

CHAPTER TWENTY-THREE

———◆———

Ember's gaze didn't flinch from his, her eyes narrowed, focused and uncompromising.

Mother.

It was like a punch in the gut.

The other woman had claimed Ember to be hers that night. He'd chosen to believe her. But if what just slipped from Ember's lips were true, it explained why the family resemblance was so strong, especially now that she was roughly the same age as her mother would have been back then.

He'd only laid eyes on her mother for that brief time, but it was a moment he would never forget. A moment that had never stopped haunting him. Her image forever engrained in his memory.

'And don't you dare try and tell me you don't know what I'm talking about,' Ember said, her tone impressively calm. 'I look like her. I know I do. And she was wearing that necklace the night she died. You saw it back then, didn't you? You recognised it when you returned it to me. That's why you asked me about it.'

He had no place feeling guilty. That's what he'd told himself over and over again for years until, in the end, he'd stopped thinking about it at all, pushing it deeper and deeper into his psyche.

It was probably why, out of context, he hadn't recognised her when he'd first seen her again that night in the alley, rain-soaked and sobbing with grief over Liam's dead body.

He should have taken the ring back that night. Instead, he'd been grateful to her – grateful for having seen the depths of her despair, reminding him why he was better off as he was, free of the pain like she felt then. She had reminded him why he'd opted to embrace the existence that had been forced upon him. She'd reminded him why he was better off that way. And *that* was why he hadn't taken the ring from her: his *second* mistake involving her.

Because if he had, he probably wouldn't have recognised her the next time he saw her ten years later – that day he'd walked into the café six months ago and she'd been the one to serve him. Served by the girl who still wore the ring of her dead fiancé.

He'd instantly been laden with curiosity: his *third* mistake involving her.

He should have walked away. Instead, he'd taken in every inch of her from her flat, black ballet shoes, up over her slender ankles and toned calves, to where her summer work dress had teasingly skimmed her knees. And sometimes when the light caught it, he'd indulged in a silhouette of her slender and shapely thighs. He'd linger on her small waist that helped emphasise the feminine curve of her hips, hips that involuntarily swayed seductively as she walked. And, as she stood behind the counter, he'd linger where the buttons of the front of her dress strained and gaped slightly over her breasts as she stretched and moved.

At first he'd kidded himself it was purely sexual until, in time, he'd found himself studying her face as much as her body – examining her delicate features, that occasional smile that was as warm and enchanting as her laugh. What had started as nothing more than a quiet, out-of-the-way place for his business meetings had become about, sometimes, finding himself going there just to be close to her.

Recognising she was attracted to him too had been torturous. The masochist in him revelling in the pain of knowing he couldn't touch her. Whenever she served him, the sparkle in her eyes had been impossible to hide. But so had the sadness within their depths. It was that which held him back – even when he detected her shallower breaths in his presence, the slight flush to her bare face, the way she struggled to maintain eye contact with him; the way her hand trembled slightly when she took his order. Then there was the way she subconsciously jutted one hip a little higher than the other as she stood in front of him, emphasising her curves as if subconsciously wanting to make herself more appealing to him. How it always snagged her attention when he had company in the café; her wary and inquisitive glances in their direction. The way she'd suddenly seemed uncomfortable in her own clothes, even her own body whenever he was around.

And then there were her pupils, dilating like crazy whenever their eyes fleetingly met; something she couldn't hide even amidst her downturned gaze.

So many times he wanted to push all those strands of hair back from her face to make her look him squarely in the eyes, to see how long she could sustain it, how close he could get his lips to hers before she broke. Before she relented to him.

But as well as her sadness, he'd picked up on the tension in her attraction. How she'd hated herself for it. She couldn't mask the sullen anger that crossed her expression at times. Anger that seemed directed more at herself than at him – the way she slid her nail back and forth across her forearm enough to cause indentations, her arm wrapped defensively across her body to form whatever barrier she could between them.

Because, still wearing her dead fiancé's ring, she had to feel guilty for that attraction. Attraction to the species that had murdered him.

So that was how it had remained between them for those first three months: he would watch her from afar, and she would watch him. Because, fortunately, when it came to self-restraint, they appeared to be equals in that arena. And his had intensified when he'd gut-wrenchingly overheard about her leaving. Because one bite, just one bite from him, one single mistake of being lost in the moment, would leave her entire future ruined. He wasn't willing to do that to her. Not for one night, or maybe a few nights, of nothing more than sex. Because he couldn't afford to connect with her on anything more than that. And Ember needed, *deserved*, so much more than that.

Never had his desire to make sure she left been stronger than the night he'd first got a glimpse of her necklace. From then on, it became his responsibility to make sure she escaped. She'd opened the door for herself and he'd make sure she got through it.

Except now she knew. Now she had pieced it together. Or, at least, she had pieced *some* of it together.

And that meant he'd now made his fourth mistake involving her. The last mistake he was ever going to make involving her.

He dropped his gaze and rubbed his thumb along the side of his jaw. He heard her heart rate knock up a notch at his hesitation. More so, no doubt, at his lack of denial.

He dragged his gaze up to meet hers again. 'You really didn't know?'

From the shock on her face, at the way her breath snagged at the confirmation of what she suspected, he guessed so. He knew her well enough to know she wouldn't have shared his bed if she had known, but he was always prepared for a surprise.

Her eyes glossed but he couldn't tell if they were tears of anger, relief or fear. 'I knew there was something before then but I just couldn't place it. There's always been something so familiar about you. I can't believe it has taken me this long to piece it together. Everything makes so much sense now.'

Her lack of recognition was excusable. She couldn't have been more than five years old at the time. She'd seen him for a matter of minutes.

'I *knew* none of this was random,' she said. 'That none of it was by accident. You being here, you hanging around, you helping me: *none* of it is coincidence.'

'The woman who defended you that night said you were hers.'

'My aunt. My mother's sister.' Her eyes narrowed. 'When did *you* know, Nate? How long have you known who I am? Is that why you didn't take the ring that night? Some kind of guilt?'

He dropped his holdall to the floor. Walking away right then was too easy an option, and Ember deserved more than him taking the easy way out. She deserved some kind of peace, especially about what happened that night, before he disappeared from her life – visibly, at least.

'For the first three months I went to that cafe, you were just that girl who still wore the ring of some guy she once loved. I hung around because I was curious about what kind of person still clings to that ten years on. And when I started overhearing about your plans to move on, I wanted to be around to make sure you saw it through.'

'How very noble.'

'Then I saw you toying with your necklace one night, a couple of months ago. You were stood behind the counter. You'd removed it from inside your tunic whilst staring into the distance with that glazed look on your eyes that you have when you're deep in thought. The blue glass caught the light and ...' He paused. 'I saw the resemblance in your profile.'

The profile he had stared down at from the top of the external stairs. The woman lying still and twisted at the bottom. That same blue stone glinting in the moonlight around her neck.

'I should have left at that point,' he said. 'I should have walked away.'

'Instead you hung around. Out of guilt. Not pity. Or maybe both. *That*'s what all of this has been about. You turned my life upside down, Nate. I guess seeing I'd done OK eased that guilt, huh? Made you feel a little bit better? So you became what: some kind of guardian angel until I left? Hoped it would take away the guilt completely?'

'I have nothing to feel guilty for. What happened to your mother was an accident.'

'An *accident*? Is that how you see it? Because what I see is a consequence of what you did.' She closed the gap between them a little. 'You broke into my home and snatched my brother. Why?'

'Because I was paid to be there, Ember.'

'To *collect* him? He was a *job*? A child? Why *him*?'

'I never ask for reasons.'

'You took him no questions asked? You just tore a child from his mother? What kind of person does it take to do that?'

'I warned you, Ember. I warned you I'd done things you wouldn't like.'

'Yes. Yes, you did. And I chose to ignore it. But I *never*

imagined this.' She shook her head. 'An accident and a job,' she repeated, incredulousness dominating her tone. 'My family: nothing more than an accident and a job.' Her eyes glared into his. 'Show me your eyes, Nate. Unless you're too much of a coward to look at me with your true ones.'

Before he walked away, he would leave her with that if that was what she wanted. If that was her choice.

She backed up at his approach. So as to be at eye-level with her, he sat on the chair under the window, directly opposite where she'd resumed her seat on the edge of the bed. Her breathing was rapid and shallow, her whole body tense, her knuckles pale as she gripped the duvet either side of her.

He lowered his head. He pressed his forefinger to each eyeball to remove the dark brown lenses before looking at the floor for a moment.

Finally, he looked back up at her, ready to face the child whose life he had ruined that night.

The child who had turned his life upside down too, even though she didn't know it.

The child, now a woman, who could still change everything if *they* found out she existed.

Her breathing snagged. She slammed the back of her hand against her mouth as she stared back at him.

Tears instantly filled her eyes. She pulled herself from the bed. She hurried out of the bedroom into the lounge.

He interlaced his hands as he cupped the nape of his neck, his gaze meeting the floor.

He could still hear her breathing so he knew she hadn't bolted completely. He should have known she wasn't going to. She had too many questions. She wasn't going to risk losing him without having asked them. Without having asked the only person she knew of who had the answers.

He pulled himself from the chair and made his way out behind her.

She was perched on the arm of the sofa facing the door. Using the flats of her fingers, she wiped the tears from her cheeks.

'You let me sleep with you knowing all of this,' she said.

'I told you you'd hate me.'

She looked across her shoulder at him, her eyes glowing with indignation. 'The fucking truth would have been less cryptic! Where did you take him?' she demanded, standing again.

'Ember, it was twenty-six years ago.'

'Not in my head! You might have been able to move on from your "job" but I haven't. Have you any idea what you did to me? For years I didn't sleep for fear of someone knocking down our door and taking me or my aunt away. I have three bolts on my door even to this day. I still can't sleep in the dark, listening out for every sound. I can't have the TV above a certain volume. I'm always looking over my shoulder. I struggle to trust anyone because I don't know if they have an ulterior motive. *You* did that to me. You and whoever it was with you that night.'

She stepped away, her hands clenched at her sides as if she was barely containing her rage. She spun to face him again.

'*Every* day I've wondered what happened to him. For years, I've tortured myself playing scenarios over and over in my head. Have you any idea what it's like to spend every day of your life imagining the worst horrors happening to someone you love? He wasn't just my brother, Nate. He was my twin. And those horrors don't ease with age and experience – they worsen it. Because I know what happens to snatched children around here, to the point I've never even been able to consider having kids of my own for fear that same thing might happen to them.'

Stray tears trickled down her cheeks that she swiftly wiped away again.

'Part of the reason I'm leaving this district, leaving behind all I know and love, is because I cannot live with that fear any more. Because I want to be normal. *You* stole my peace of mind, Nate. You didn't only steal my brother and murder my mother, you stole who I might have been.'

She closed the gap between them, her eyes blazing.

'You drove away and left my mother lying dead on the floor like she was nothing,' she added. 'So you're right: I don't think I'm capable of hating anyone more than I hate you right now.'

He should have grabbed his holdall. He should have left. He had no reason to stay there. He had no reason to stand around and take it. But he couldn't move from the spot.

He wanted to hear it. He wanted to face it. He wanted to face what he had done to her.

'Tell me *where* you took him and what happened to him,' she demanded. 'Was it some underground ring in Blackthorn? Did he suffer?'

But he couldn't tell her. He couldn't risk telling her. For her sake. Because he knew exactly what she would do if she knew everything.

'I didn't see him again,' Nate said. 'But it's not what you imagine.'

'It was twenty-six years ago, Nate. Whoever paid you probably doesn't even care about what happened any more, but I *do*. I need to know where he ended up. I need to know if he's still alive. What if he's still here in Lowtown? What if I have already bumped into him in the street?'

'I've never crossed paths with him again.'

Her eyes flared with resolve. 'Then maybe it's time you tried. You're going to help me find him, Nate. You owe me that much.'

'I owe you fuck all, Ember. I have done *more* than enough for you, including working for the Hordas clan again when I wanted nothing more to do with them – and that's for *you*.'

'You said that was for *your* benefit.'

Nate exhaled curtly. He shook his head as he walked away. He shouldn't have said it. It had escaped his lips before he'd given himself a chance to analyse the consequence. He needed out of there before he risked saying any more. He couldn't risk revealing any more.

But Ember followed him. 'Don't you dare walk away from me, Nate!'

He ignored her.

'You know more than you're telling me, I know you do,' she said. 'You say you don't ask questions, but this job was different, wasn't it? Otherwise why any of this?'

She was getting close, too close, her inquisitive mind working overtime. He needed to say something. He needed to throw her off the scent.

He turned to face her. 'If your brother's still alive, why hasn't he come to find you, Ember?'

'He might not remember me.'

'Like you don't remember him?'

'I had my aunt to remind me. Who knows what he's been told. Nate, I deserve the truth. You know more, so tell me. *Please.*'

'You want to know the truth? I wasn't with another vampire that night, Ember, but you wouldn't have seen that. By the time you looked out of the window he was already in the car with your brother.'

'*Who* was?'

He hesitated for a moment. 'Your father. I didn't hand your brother over to a random stranger, Ember. I came with your father. *He* hired me for the job. It was your father who took your brother away.'

CHAPTER TWENTY-FOUR

———◈———

Ember took a few steps back before collapsing onto the edge of the sofa.

Like how switching on a light could chase the shadows of a nightmare away, she'd succeeded with one. Eyes that had once haunted her dream were so less terrifying now: one grey, one blue. As a child she'd never seen anyone with different coloured irises before. It had been her first time seeing a vampire too. She'd learned everything she needed to know about vampires that night. She'd learned everything she needed to know about fear.

But now, even with those shadows gone, the horror had worsened.

'My *father*?'

He took to the sofa opposite hers. Bent forward at the waist, he rested his hands between his spread thighs.

'He found out about your brother's existence by accident. He caught a glimpse of your mother with him one day but she got away. He hired me to track her down.'

'Which one of you killed my mother, Nate?'

'It was an accident.'

'*Which* one of you?' she demanded.

'When I left you and your aunt, your parents were wrangling at the top of the steps outside. She was trying to grab your brother. She lost her footing. Your father didn't have a free hand to grab her unless he dropped your brother. He couldn't have stopped it even if he'd wanted to. It happened too quickly.'

'*Why?* Why was she trying to get away from him?'

'I keep telling you: I don't ask questions, Ember.'

'Why didn't he take me too? If he came for his children, why leave me behind?'

'I don't think he knew about you.'

'But *you* did.'

'Your aunt told me you were hers.'

'And you believed her? Just like that?' Because there was more to it. He was too efficient for there not to be. 'You never told anyone you'd seen me there?'

'I did the job I was paid to do and that was to collect your brother.'

'Paid.' She exhaled tersely. 'How much? How much was ripping my family apart without question worth in monetary value to you?'

'I'm not on trial, Ember.'

'Sounds to me like you're not comfortable with what you did otherwise why tell me any of this at all?'

'Because I don't want you living with that agony any more; it's not like what you've been imagining. I want you to know that.'

'That my father snatched my brother? That he killed my mother in the process? Aidan wasn't mistreated. My mother loved him. *I* loved him. And yet my father ripped him out of our lives. Ripped both him and my mother out of mine.'

Nate stood and headed into the bedroom, no doubt the last time he intended to do so.

Ember followed behind him.

'He has to be somewhere around here – or maybe in Blackthorn,' she said. 'He could never have got a child through to Midtown. Or did he?'

'I can't tell you anything more, Ember.'

'So that's it? My brother and father might be out there somewhere and you're saying nothing more? They're all the family I have left. There's every chance they're still alive. How old was my father? Even if he was in his forties, he'd only be in his seventies now.'

She clamped her hand over her mouth, her head in a spin. 'Not Jasper. Tell me it wasn't Jasper. Tell me that wasn't why he helped me that night Liam died.'

'It's not Jasper.'

'Then who?' She swallowed back her tears. 'You're the only one I know who's met him. You're the only one who knows what he looks like. Do I look like him? What's his name? At least tell me his name.'

'*This* is why I didn't tell you the truth. I knew what you'd want to do. I knew you'd want to waste time here trying to find them, putting yourself at risk when you should be focusing on leaving. Do yourself a favour: stick with your plan. Keep your head down for the next couple of days and then get the fuck out of here. Anything else would be a mistake, and your mother would have died for nothing.'

She watched him head over to the door and cross the threshold into the stairwell.

She hurried behind him; stopped at the top of the stairs as he descended.

'Nate, please.'

But he ignored her as he unlocked the outer door.

He closed the door behind himself. She heard the key turn –
and was left alone in the solitary shadows of the now-empty
stairwell.

CHAPTER TWENTY-FIVE

—◆—

'Ember, you look terrible,' Casey said. 'Did you not sleep at all last night?'

'Not much,' she said.

She didn't know how long she'd sat on the steps after he'd left. She hadn't registered anything at all until she'd felt the pain in her one foot as pins and needles set in from being locked in the same position for too long. Until she realised she was shivering. Until she felt how icy cold and numb her hands were to the touch.

She'd looked across at his apartment laying open, silence emanating from within.

Forcing herself to her feet, she'd stepped inside to scan the empty space, absorbing the hollowness.

In the bedroom, she'd perched on the side of the bed where she'd been with him only hours before, glanced at the now-blank TV screen. The room had looked so stark in the approaching dawn. So cold. So defunct.

She'd curled into a foetal position amongst the ruffled sheets and pulled his pillow down against her chest to hold it, the scent of him still lingering on it.

She didn't know when she'd fallen asleep. She hadn't intended to. Nor did she know what had woken her.

She'd returned to her own apartment to take a shower before perching on the edge of her own bed, still wrapped in her towel.

She'd clutched her pendant, just as she'd done that night as a child. As the authorities had come and gone, bagging up her mother and loading her into the back of a non-descript van, she'd clutched the pendant in bed as she'd sobbed.

She'd been kept away from the mumbles of her aunt and the officer, the latter not having stayed long. Her aunt had remained at the kitchen table for a long time after that, the heel of her hand against her forehead, her elbow on the table.

So as not to be a burden, Ember had washed her face and brushed her teeth and put on her nightclothes without being asked to.

The morning after had been worse than the night before. Then had come the worst feeling of all. A feeling she would never forget as she'd found her aunt asleep at the table. The apartment had felt so quiet without her mother and brother. Even at five years old, she'd known things had changed irrevocably. She'd made her aunt a bowl of porridge and a hot drink and left them on the table. She'd grabbed herself a book, taken herself back to bed, and had waited until her aunt had eventually woken.

Memories that had haunted her for over twenty years.

And Nate had freed her from them. For a short while, in his bed, in *that* bed, she'd finally felt liberated from her past, only to now have discovered he was a bigger part of it than she could have believed possible.

A part that had now left her too. Abandoned her.

Casey grabbed her arm and led her into the toilets before Ember had even had a chance to take her coat off.

'Harry's been trying to get hold of you for the past hour,' Casey said.

Ember had followed every step of her usual routine that morning except for oversleeping and forgetting to charge her phone.

'And so have I,' Casey added. 'The Hordas clan have backed out. They didn't give much of an explanation apparently other than saying they'd had a better opportunity.' She lowered her voice. 'But after what you said to me . . .'

'You didn't tell Harry about that, did you?'

'Of course I didn't. But he knows something isn't right. Ember, what have you got yourself into?'

'It's not down to me.'

'Everyone knows the Hordas clan don't back down.'

Casey grabbed Ember's arms and pushed up her sleeves until Ember yanked them free.

'What are you doing?'

'Tell me you haven't made some kind of deal with him,' Casey said. 'With Nate. Tell me you haven't blown your chances in Midtown for us.'

'No. No, I haven't,' Ember insisted, pulling her arms free. 'I told you: it's nothing to do with me. Nate turned down my offer. I confronted him about his involvement last night but all he said was that he was getting them to back off because it's his place of business. He doesn't work for them as in work *for* them. He's done some freelance work for them, that's all.'

'Like being hired to kill people?'

'I don't know what he does, and I don't care. It doesn't matter now. I'm having nothing more to do with him. It looks like we just need to be grateful he chose this place to conduct his business.'

Casey scrutinised her under the bright toilet light.

'Casey, I haven't jeopardised anything, I promise. And you have to stay quiet about this. For all our sakes. Promise me.'

Casey nodded.

'What about Harry?' Ember asked. 'What has he said about the change of plan?'

'He's given us all the same talk this morning. You'd better go and see him.'

Ember knocked on his door before entering his office.

'You look awful,' was the first thing he said.

'Thanks, Harry.' She took her seat. 'You don't look much better yourself. Casey just told me the news. I can't believe they've backed off.'

'Neither can I.' He tossed his pen onto the desk and sank back in his seat.

'When did you hear?'

'They came in mid-morning: the bastard that had killed Jasper. He ordered a coffee and sat there in silence for an hour before finally breaking the news to me.'

'What reason did they give?'

'They've found a more lucrative opportunity.'

'They're definitely leaving the place alone?'

Seemingly Nate had been true to his word; had stayed true to his word even after it had ended the way it had between them. Ended on the cusp of her, at last, finding out what had happened in her past. What had happened to her family. Her family who might still be alive.

'I don't trust them, Ember. So I'm not celebrating just yet. Not now we're on their radar.'

'What are you going to do?'

'I don't know. Sell up. Move before they come back.'

'You can't give up your life for them.'

'As opposed to having them take it as soon as they decide to walk back in here? It's not going to get any better. Sometimes you have to know when to cut your losses and quit.'

'And then what?'

He shrugged. 'I don't know. But at least I've been bought some thinking time. I've been talking to everyone this morning so you need to know this too. They've set a rule: we're not to tell anyone about the change of plan. They said if any of us talk, they'll go ahead with the takeover. So everyone needs to keep their mouths shut.'

Ember nodded. But Harry searched her gaze to the point she felt forced to break it before meeting his again.

'What?' she asked.

'You haven't got yourself into anything you can't handle, have you, Ember?'

'Like what?'

'I know you like I know my own daughters. And you don't seem surprised or shocked by this news.'

'I'm just tired. It's been a tough couple of days.'

'Which I haven't forgotten. I also haven't forgotten about that vampire who has been coming in here regularly for six months before this. He shows up again yesterday and suddenly the threat is off. I hope you haven't committed yourself to something to save this place.'

It could have so easily gone that way if that was what Nate had chosen, but he'd walked away. And despite the worry that maybe it would change now that she'd confronted him over his past, her gut feeling overruled it, telling her that, if nothing else, despite him denying his guilt, his actions right up to that point had been a contradiction.

'You know me better than that, Harry.'

Harry studied her for a moment, his eyes laced with suspicion. 'I've also seen the way you two have been glancing at each other for weeks. I've seen the way he's looked at you and how you've looked at him. I was worried he was a sire, so I kept a close eye.' He paused. 'I also know what a headstrong little madam you can be, especially when it comes to protecting those you care about. If you've got yourself into trouble, I want you to know you can come to me. And if it's over this place, I most definitely want you to come to me. I know you sometimes feel like you're on your own. I know you've felt like that for a long time. But you're not on your own. I'm here for you and I will always be here for you.'

The urge to tell him overwhelmed her. The desire to tell Harry what Nate had disclosed: that she was maybe far from alone. But Nate had been right: if either of them had wanted to find her, they could have. It was either confirmation that she had indeed lost them, or it was a devastating rejection. And if it was the latter, then that made what Harry had said about being there for her even more significant.

Wiping a couple of stray tears from her eyes, she squeezed around the side of the desk. She leaned over and she hugged him.

At first, Harry didn't seem quite sure what to do, neither of them accustomed to physical affection between them. But, after the shock subsided, he hugged her back.

'I'm not in trouble, Harry, I promise. Just as I promise you'll be rid of me as soon as possible.'

Because in that very moment, she realised what had failed to cross her mind whilst trying to get her head around the fact she still had family out there: her father might have come for her brother because he knew what Aidan was. If she went searching for them, she could walk into a life she'd spent all of hers trying to escape. A life she had promised her aunt she would escape.

A life her mother had died to enable them to escape. A life that would keep her imprisoned in Lowtown forever.

'Good,' Harry said as he gently eased her away. 'Until then, get back to work. I want those fingers worked to the bone these next couple of days.'

She reached the door. She turned to face him. 'Oh, and Harry ...'

He looked up at her.

'I know you often feel like you fall short for your daughters, but they're lucky to have you. They're blessed to have you. I want you to know that.' She paused. 'Even if you are a grouchy git most of the time.'

She could feel his smile as she exited.

She closed the door behind her. She stood in the corridor for a moment, the rain of relief palpable as it descended.

She had less than two days left. All she had to do now was focus on getting through them.

CHAPTER TWENTY-SIX

Nate sat in an armchair in the shadowed corner of The Hive's bar, a black coffee in one hand, the locator in the other. The dial told him his collection was to the south-west. It should take him less than a few hours to narrow it down, even if his target kept moving.

He never delayed a job. Efficiency was crucial. But even now, even decades on, the prospect of what he was pursuing chilled him. The prospect of the unknown that always went hand-in-hand with them. The prospect that this might be the collection he didn't succeed in; that he didn't make it out of.

'Looks like you need something stronger,' Cordy said as she placed the glass of whisky in front of him.

She nestled back in the armchair opposite.

He flashed her a fleeting smile as he tucked the locator out of sight in his pocket. 'You think so?'

'I know you don't like to talk, Nate, but I'm a good listener. A discreet listener.' She knocked back a mouthful of her own whisky. 'Something's been on your mind for a long time.'

'Just a few demons from the past, Cordy.' He knocked a mouthful back for himself. 'And not in the literal sense, before you ask.'

'And you're debating what to do about them?'

'One I've solved. Now it's time to deal with the second.'

'You *are* heavy laden.'

'It keeps my feet on the ground,' he remarked, casting her another fleeting smile.

'And your heart encased,' she retorted.

Her gaze lingered as she awaited his response. A response that he knew as well as she did wouldn't come.

'So why are you facing them?' she asked. 'And why now?'

'Because someone needs me to.'

'Someone?'

'Someone I owe a debt to.'

'And then you'll be clear?'

'I don't think I'll ever be clear of this one, Cordy.'

'Then why face your demons at all?'

'Because it means they'll be free of theirs.'

Her eyes studied his for a few moments. 'Yet you sit there looking like you've lost something precious. Something irretrievable.'

'I guess that's because I have.'

He knocked back the remains of the whisky and slipped money for it across the table.

She slid it back. 'Not this time. That one was on me.'

Leaving the bar, he wandered back out through The Hive.

He pulled his collar up against the rain and removed the locator from his pocket.

He'd walked the streets for three hours, drenched by the rain, when the dial finally began to spin. Vibrating subtly in his hand, it told him he was finally within reaching distance of his target.

He looked down the length of the quiet street on the far

south-west of Lowtown; a street he knew only too well. Primarily residential, his collection could be in any number of the various apartments. Could have any number of other witches with him or her.

He glanced left to the café, the light spilling out onto the glistening pavement outside. It had never looked warmer or more like home. And within that warmth, he found himself instinctively searching for her.

Ember finally moved into view as she served one of the window tables. The table he often chose. Her smile was polite. Functional. Professional. He knew the difference by now.

As if sensing him out in the darkness, she glanced up.

Masked by the shadows across the street, he knew she wouldn't be able to see him like he could see her. Her lingering gaze could nonetheless have convinced him otherwise.

As she reverted her attention back to her customers, even as she turned away to head over to the counter, she glanced once more over her shoulder, her frown telling him that sensing his presence had unsettled her on some subconscious level.

He looked back down at the locator as he strolled onwards, watching for the subtlest increase in its spinning that would tell him he was closing in.

But the further he ventured down the street, the slower the dial spun, reverting back to pointing north again. He turned one-eighty and back again before turning the full three-sixty. Each time, the hand always pointed in the same direction: the café.

He turned back the way he'd come. He'd only been walking for a matter of minutes before the dial picked up pace again.

He crossed the road to stand in the middle of the street opposite the café. The locator buzzed wildly in his palm. He closed in on the periphery of the café's front. The locator stopped. The hand fell to neutral – the first time it had done so.

His characteristic slow-beating heart picked up a notch.

Nate discreetly tucked the locator in his pocket as he entered the last place he needed to be. Ember's assumptions would be rife. It almost felt cruel to show up again. Walking out of that apartment had been hard enough. Hearing her plea for his help had been tough enough. Now to potentially raise her hopes – or her fears – was worse.

The warmth of the café, the scent of coffee and sugar-laden food, instantly encased him as he headed left to where a booth in the far corner by the window was free, where the table next to him was equally vacant.

He did his usual trick of scrolling through the phone, something he often did in-between casting surreptitious glances at Ember. Except now he was doing it in-between assessing the twelve customers. His target could be any one of them.

She re-emerged from out the back carrying a couple of bowls of soup. She stopped in her tracks, but somehow managed to retain her grip on the crockery.

She dropped her gaze from his instantly. The subtle lick of her lips betrayed her anxiety, her smile even more forced as she headed over to the table she was in the process serving.

He tugged his attention away from her to continue studying the rest of the customers, particularly to watch that no one left.

He removed the vial from his pocket and twisted it over and over between the fingers of his left hand under the cover of the table as he scrutinised each of them in turn. But he knew better than anyone that witches were impossible to detect them from any other human.

In the interim, he expected one of the others to come and serve him. He saw Casey move forward to do just that, but Ember caught her arm and said something in her ear – something undetectable even to him. Whatever it was, Casey squeezed her friend's arm and pulled away.

The girl had guts – something he had long admired in her more than anything. But he needed to remain as impassive to her as always. Give her as little attention as always. Do something to let her know as quickly as possible that his being there was nothing to do with her. And, above all else, was closed to further questions if that's what her approach had been about. This was not the time or the place – now more than ever.

'Usual?' Ember asked, her pen poised on her notepad.

It took a moment, but she finally made eye contact. Despite her attempt to give him an icy glare, the strength of the hurt behind her eyes dissipated it. The truth of both their pasts aside, what had happened between them that night before had meant something to her. In amongst everything else, it had been easy for him to forget that. And deny it all he wanted, what he had felt in the latter moments of having sex with her, the pain he had literally felt, was evidence that it had meant something to him too. She had got to him. On a level that had long been inaccessible, Ember had someone found a way in – further reason that the sooner she was as far away from him as possible, the better.

Out of all the things he could have uttered, he simply said, 'Please.'

She held his gaze for a moment longer, as if waiting on the cusp of something more, before pulling away. He half expected her to spin back around, to demand what he was playing at being there but, instead, she walked away in silence.

He closed his eyes for a split-second, trying to block out the way she'd looked at him, his grip simultaneously tightening on the vial. He couldn't relent. For her sake as much as his, he had to leave it be. But the draw was immense. The desire to take her aside and explain he was trying to protect her, that the risks to her if he told her the complete truth, was overwhelming

The sooner he was out of her life, the better.

He unscrewed the lid and subtly dropped the vial out into his palm. Checking no one was paying him any attention, he leaned forward as if tightening his laces and dropped a loaded pipette of blood onto the tiled floor.

He placed the pipette back in the tube and the tube back in the vial before tucking it away in his pocket again.

Discreetly, he watched the floor, waiting for something to happen.

What should have dispersed instead defied physics as the droplet rolled into a ball, solidified like a marble, and began its journey. It rolled away as if on a slant, passing all three tables in front of him.

He exhaled tersely, reassured that it did work.

Breaking the laws of physics again, it took a sharp right to veer out of Yvonne's way as she served a couple of tables away, before it got back on track again.

As Casey stepped out from behind the counter, it veered towards her, drawing closer and closer, Nate's frown deepening as it did so.

Casey.

One hell of a complication.

But then it took a sharp left past her towards the counter.

As Ember appeared from behind the counter to bring him his coffee, his heart rate picked up to an almost human pace.

Eyes downturned again, he watched the bead, not her, as she headed towards him.

Watched the bead stop as she passed it. Watched it trail back over its own path as it followed behind her.

She placed the coffee in front of him, the aromas bringing him into a sharp state of reality that he didn't want to be in.

He glanced up at her as if he'd never seen her before, as if he'd never really known who she was.

She hovered awkwardly as if needing to speak yet not being able to find the words. Until a customer called her away.

Nate stared back down at the floor as he watched the bead turn back on itself again to follow her path.

As she stopped, talked to the customer, it climbed her shoe, it climbed up under her trouser leg. Mid-conversation, she brushed it away mindlessly as if it was nothing more than an itch.

Nate rose from his seat. He brushed past her. He headed out into the cold night air.

He should have known. He should have linked both together. Suddenly it made sense. It all made perfect sense.

He marched down the street and veered left into the first alley he came across.

And punched his fist hard into the wall.

CHAPTER TWENTY-SEVEN

———◆———

Twenty-six years earlier

The rain acted like a metronome against the car roof, the dark alley their mask.

The subtle glow beyond the thin curtains of the apartment ahead told them someone was home. He'd detected two adult outlines. From their stature, composure, stance and movement, Nate ascertained them both to be female. And one of them, for just a short while, had carried a small child in their arms.

'This is it,' Nate said.

'Definitely?' Frank asked. 'I can't have any mistakes. This might be our only shot.'

'Then try and remember that.'

Nate looked back up at the windows. He'd never had anyone accompany him on a job. It made it trickier, more risky. Successful team work required years of working together, getting to know each other, unless there was that rare spark of connection that made it seamless. And he had neither with Frank. He didn't even like the guy. But the Hordas clan paid well – lucratively well. And they were willing to pay a ridiculous amount for this job. It was technically easy: a woman and her kid. It was the kid he'd been told they were there for. Frank's kid. She'd stolen him and Frank wanted him back. And Frank had wanted to be there to make sure it was his kid.

Nate wasn't social services. He wasn't judge and jury. He didn't ask questions. He didn't want to know. In fact, on this case, he felt the less he knew, the better. He'd spent years developing that tact and it was the reason his reputation was infallible enough for the Hordas clan to hire him whenever they wanted the best on a job. Whenever they had an important enough job to pay for the best. And his lack of concerns as to the whys when it came to their business made him their top preference. Off the back of that, he'd become top preference for many more cases and many more clients. His business had thrived as a result.

'You'd better be light on your feet,' Nate said, looking back at him.

Frank was a big guy – in height and girth, the latter of which was the result of being overindulged by the Hordas clan. He wasn't part of the family, Nate knew that much. But he may as well have been. The Hordas clan let few in, but Frank had been one of them.

'What are you fucking trying to say, Nate?'

'You know what I'm trying to say. And remember the rules: I'm not touching the kid. I'll kick the door in, I'll scan for company, I'll prevent any trouble, I'll have your back. The rest of it is down to you. And neither of us touch the women, understood? Or any other kids that might be in there. We keep it quick. We keep it efficient. We stay on task.'

'Trust me, I don't want to be in there a second longer than

I need to be,' Frank said. He reached for the car door. 'Let's do this.'

Nate took the lead. He ascended the metal outer steps, rain dripping from the handrail. It only took one direct blow to the lock from the sole of his foot to send the door ricocheting open.

He stepped inside, Frank close behind him.

The child jolted in his chair, the woman feeding him knocking back hers as she leapt to her feet.

The pang from the fear in her eyes was instant, but he swallowed it and kept his focus.

He was not there to wield his moral compass. He was there to get the job done.

He kicked open the bedroom door directly ahead, revealing it to be empty.

Catching a glimpse in the corner of his left eye, he looked down the corridor to where the tail of a long skirt fled back into the room.

The door slammed.

He glanced across his shoulder to the raucous in the kitchen-diner between Frank and the woman, the child already crying and screaming in his arms, the woman pleading with him to give him back.

'Fuck,' he hissed under his breath before heading down the corridor.

He kicked open the door to his left first to reveal a vacant bathroom before he kicked open the door to his right. It took two blows, it having been bolted. But it broke in the end.

The woman stood in the middle of the room, the knife in her out-held hand trembling in her grasp, her eyes wide with panic.

It wasn't a sight he liked to see. It wasn't a sight that gave him any pleasure. It was a sight that sickened him to his core that he had created it.

But it was a job.

Just a job.

No questions. No guilt. No hesitation.

Knife in hand, she should have been out there trying to help her friend, help the child. It made no sense that she was stood there. No sense unless she was protecting something.

Something he picked up the subtle scent of. A scent coming from the slatted wardrobe behind her.

He stepped forward.

'You stay the hell back!' she demanded, her voice shaking as much as her hand.

He snatched the knife from her a split-second later, as easy as snapping a branch from a rotten tree. He had her arms pinned to her chest a second after that, her back against him as he restrained her so he could open the wardrobe door.

From her nestled position amongst the shoes and jumpers, a small girl looked up at him, her large dark eyes crested by her heavy mousy-brown fringe.

Her startled gaze shot to the woman. Her grip tightened on the soft toy she was holding. She stared back at him.

Eyes that bore right into him.

No tears. No protest. Nothing but silence.

'Don't touch her!' the woman demanded. 'You leave my daughter alone!'

As she squirmed in his arms, he reached for the child regardless so he could take a closer look.

The little girl's teeth clamped down on his hand, a bite that made him flinch, before she withdrew deeper into the wardrobe, her eyes blazing with defiance.

He let the woman go. As he sucked the blood from the bite mark on his hand, he stared back at the woman, giving her the once-over: the same dark eyes, the same colour hair as the child.

The raucous out in the kitchen-diner had distanced, telling him Frank was already making his way back outside.

They'd already been there long enough. They'd got what they came for.

And no one had said anything about a girl. A girl was not on his list.

'*Please*,' the woman said, tears of frustration, of anger, of helplessness pouring down her cheeks.

The boy: that's all he'd been instructed to collect. Just the boy.

With one more glance at the little girl, he turned on his heels, the pit of his stomach telling him he was making a bad mistake.

He entered the kitchen-diner to see the full-on scuffle on top of the steps.

He reached the door.

He saw the woman trying to block Frank's descent. He saw her lose her footing, the wet handrail giving her no grip as she fell. His heart leapt as he saw her stumble backwards.

There was no way of getting to her past Frank. No way of breaking her fall.

He heard the other woman cry out behind him.

He watched Frank head on down the steps.

The other woman pushed past him.

Nate descended behind her, one step at a time.

'Rhona!' The other woman's voice trembled with panic as she fell down beside her. 'Rhona, can you hear me?'

But Rhona didn't respond, the angle of her neck making it clear it had broken in the fall.

'Fuck,' Frank hissed, reaching for his gun and raising it to the back of the other woman's head, but Nate grabbed his arm.

'You've done enough damage,' he said. 'You came for what you wanted.'

'And the bitch has seen too much.'

'Like she can do anything about it.'

Frank reluctantly pulled away, splashing through puddles on the way back to the car, the child screaming in his arms, his out-held to where his mother lay dead on the ground.

Nate knew what he should do. As he gazed down at the dead woman, the blue stone around her neck catching the light as Frank switched the car engine on and flashed his lights, he knew he should have put the other one out of her misery too. He should have returned upstairs for the girl. The girl who then looked down from the window, at the body directly below her.

Instead he walked away.

As he got into the car, the child had reduced to sniffles in Frank's arms, the small sound of, 'Mummy' escaping his lips.

Nate slammed the heel of his hand hard onto the steering wheel before reversing out of the alley. 'Fuck,' he hissed under his breath.

'It was an accident. She shouldn't have got in the way.'

'She's fucking dead, Frank,' Nate said, glowering across at him, Frank's nonchalance adding to the sickening feeling in his gut. 'No one was supposed to die.'

He glanced at the child, his red-rimmed brown eyes now wide and startled again, reminding him to watch his temper.

Eyes that reminded him of the girl he'd left behind.

He looked back at Frank. There was no way he was telling him. There was no way he was telling anyone.

And he was done with the Hordas clan. That was his last job for them. This was the last time he was involved in collecting people. Right then, he felt like it being the last job for anyone.

'Don't you worry, son,' Frank said, addressing the boy as Nate pulled out onto the main street. 'I'm going to take real good care of you. You're going to have the best of the best. You're one special kid. One very special kid.' He leaned closer to his ear. 'Because you're going to make my friends *very* powerful indeed.'

CHAPTER TWENTY-EIGHT

Ember knew the empty feeling in the pit of her gut was nothing to do with hunger. The ache in her chest was nothing to do with neither an exerted nor tense walk back home. If anything, she had plodded home less vigilantly than usual.

With just over two days to go until she was free of that district, her excitement should have been simmering. Instead, more than ever, it felt dampened by the question of what she was gaining in exchange for what she was leaving behind.

Amongst it was Nate. It shouldn't have hurt so much. Seeing him in that café again shouldn't have been as painful as it was. Watching him leave no sooner than he had arrived had been exactly what had left her with that ache. And she despised herself for it.

But she *had* to move on or lose the chance forever. She needed to get settled in Midtown first and *then* decide what she did from there. Because even if her father and brother were both still alive, they were the clichéd needle in a haystack. It would take money to find them. A lot of money.

But there was still that sense of betrayal even considering it. It was the one thing her aunt had pleaded with her to do when she'd finally told her that her brother hadn't been taken by chance: that she was not to go after him; that she could tell no one what she had learned about herself.

Witches were the pariahs of human society as much as the third species were. Classed as rare 'second' species because of being human but with additional skills, they didn't fit in anywhere except with their own. Humans viewed them with suspicion, coupled with them having a reputation amongst the third species for being untrustworthy. Neither attitude was helped by the fact they were impossible to detect. It was how so many witches remained undisclosed, even after the regulations had come into being. Those who had been approved for Midtown or Summerton, and who did choose to disclose their heritage, were forced not to practise. One hint of being a practising witch and you were banished, whatever your background. But a witch born to Lowtown was born condemned. Any disclosure would mean an instant dismissal of her application, practising or not. A witch born to Lowtown was instantly judged a risk: prejudiced, biased, dangerous.

And now it made sense why her aunt had never told her it was her father who'd taken her brother that night. Her aunt would have known she'd be more tempted than ever to find them. *If* her aunt had even known that's who'd come.

What she now knew couldn't change anything. She couldn't let it change anything. Not for now.

She turned the corner and headed down the alley. Taking a left and passing the recess, she stopped abruptly.

In all the years she'd been there, she'd never seen a car in the alley, let alone one parked a few feet away from her door. Expensive-looking ones like that certainly weren't a frequent occurrence around Lowtown.

Her thoughts flicked back to the spectacled guy in the café. The guy she had long forgotten about. His visit had been disastrous – her disappearing into the toilets and not returning until he had gone. She could only conclude that, if he had been a part of the authorities as she'd suspected, they'd now come to follow it up – a random drop-in, exactly as they had warned could happen. Either that, or they'd come to tell her that their offer had subsequently been withdrawn.

Her pulse picked up a notch further at what they might find – at what they might have already found.

As the breeze whipped behind her, as if edging her onwards, Ember glanced over her shoulder before taking a few wary steps towards the car. It was soon apparent it was empty, a fact that further exacerbated her unease. If it *was* the authorities, they should have been around to greet her.

She cast a tentative glance over her shoulder again before closing the gap between her and the car. There was no other option unless she was planning to stand there all night. Ember rubbed her hand down her arm as she stepped closer to the wall and out of the car's path. She checked out the back seat as she passed and found it equally empty.

Removing her keys from her jacket, she placed them in the lock to the outer door, all the while keeping a watchful eye on the car and the alley beyond. She turned her key, but it didn't budge. Frowning, she gave her full attention to what she was doing. She tried once again before removing her key and trying for a third time, her palm flat to the door. And then it gave way. It gave way without her needing to turn the key at all because it was already unlocked.

Ember's instincts screamed for her to hightail it back down the alley but, as the door crept open, she saw him sat waiting on the stairs.

Relief flooded over her, accompanied instantly by despair at her instinctive reaction to him.

She stepped inside and closed the door behind her. 'I thought you'd gone.'

'I had,' Nate said.

Her pulse picked up a notch at the prospect of all the possibilities as to why he could have returned. She knew there was only one reason she wanted to hear – and it was the reason she could do with least of all. 'So what are you doing here?'

Because whatever the reason, he'd been waiting for her return.

'I have information for you,' he said.

'About what?'

'Your family.'

Her heart skipped a beat. 'You said you didn't know anything more.'

'I lied.'

She clenched her keys in the palm of her hand. She folded her arms. She didn't dare take her eyes off him.

'You said you wanted to know everything that happened that night,' he said. 'I'll tell you what I know.'

She crushed the keys. 'At a cost?'

Because it was still there just as she was sure it would always be there – that distrust. Because why *wouldn't* he turn it to his advantage? Especially now.

He stood up. He sauntered down the stairs as if he had nowhere to be by any particular time. 'My car's outside,' he said as he made his way past her. 'You'll need to come with me.'

'To go where?'

'To my place.'

'You can say whatever you've got to say here.'

He turned to face her from the doorway. 'Ember, I'm offering to give you the answers you want. It's up to you whether you take me up on that. But I'm only offering once.'

Offering because she knew as well as he did that he didn't need to ask her permission if he had any intention of dragging her into the car outside.

She could only conclude that was why he'd come to the café earlier. But, for some reason, he'd lost his nerve to say what he was saying then. For some reason, instead, he'd left without a word.

'I can't risk being seen out there with you,' she reminded him, despite still not being convinced she cared enough about the consequences not to chance it.

'You won't be.'

He stepped outside. He got into the driver's side.

She didn't have to go: that's all she kept telling herself over and over again. She could close the door. She could walk away. She could never know. She could remain forever in ignorance; never really know what had happened and why. Never know the chances of them still being alive. Close the door on the last link to her past.

Close the door on Nate.

Instead, after a couple more minutes of hesitation, she followed the only lead she had.

CHAPTER TWENTY-NINE

———◆———

Despite having spent her entire life in Lowtown, Ember had never ventured to that quarter of the district, only ever having got as far as the TSCD Headquarters. Rumours were that, back before the regulations had been put into place, it had been an affluent area on the outskirts of what once used to be the city. It was still seen by many to be the same now, not least because it was occupied by the likes of the Hordas clan and the Voys and all those associated with them.

The first pang of regret and unease struck hard that she'd made a big mistake. That maybe her suspicions had been right: that her pending links to Midtown were of interest to someone.

Being there suddenly felt like an impetuous decision; needing to know the truth like leaping from a pier into a lake before realising, too late, that it was no longer there. Either way, she'd made her choice. She'd work out what she'd do from there a step at a time.

'What are we doing here?' she asked.

It had been the first time she'd spoken to him since she'd got in the car.

It hadn't taken them long to get there, less than forty minutes in fact, but they'd still made the journey in silence.

'This is where I live.'

She shouldn't have been surprised with his response. Especially not now she knew what he did for a living. From what she'd learned, he was no better than half of the people around there living off the back of others' misery.

Passing through a couple of low, stone pillars where gates would have once hung, Nate pulled up onto a section of dried turf, loose shale rebounding off the underside of the car.

Switching off the engine, he stepped out of the car immediately, slamming the door behind him as Ember craned her neck to look up at the partially derelict, imposing Georgian house shrouded in darkness both inside as well as out.

Taking her cue to follow, she stepped out into the chill of the night air as he removed a stuffed holdall from the boot of the car.

Ember wrapped her arms around herself as she followed him, stones crunching beneath her feet.

Nate unlocked the front door and led her across the entrance hall, the oppressive silence in the empty space far from appeasing her unease.

'Is *all* of this yours?'

'No,' he said, leading her right towards the broad, curved staircase.

She followed him up the first flight of stairs, the hum of a TV seeping out from behind one of the closed doors off the square landing to her left. It was impossible to tell which one.

Nate led the way up the next flight of stairs and the next before stopping in front of the wood-panelled wall. He pushed on one of the panels and the insert opened. He indicated for her to enter first.

Needing to bend over to peer inside, Ember glanced into the dark vestibule before taking a step back. 'Where does it go?'

'My home.'

Laden with apprehension, Ember glanced over her shoulder back down the empty stairwell before looking back at him. 'You first.'

He offered her a rare hint of a smile before ducking and heading through the narrow, low opening.

Within the darkness, she heard metal grind against metal: the sound of a key turning in a lock in an enclosed but vacuous space.

The vestibule switched from pitch-blackness to grey, Nate then visibly standing beside a regular open door three feet beyond.

After only a moment of hesitation, she stepped into the vestibule alongside him. His body brushed against hers as he reached behind her to close the panel, contact that was a painful reminder of the intimacy they had shared.

'After you this time,' he said, indicating the open doorway.

Ember stepped out into a vast room, muted moonlight glowing against the opaque glass of the two floor-to-ceiling tripartite arched windows to her left. Rough-hewn A-frame beams dominated the vaulted ceiling of the open-plan loft apartment, the walls consisting primarily exposed brickwork. Drawn-back curtains hung from the beams, seemingly the only way to subdivide sections of the room – or maybe to provide a barrier from the light that would have free access through the dominating windows.

This was the wing on the far side of the building. A wing that was accessed through a secret doorway to make it look to anyone who followed that he lived on one side as opposed to the other. She knew she shouldn't have expected anything less.

So far he hadn't put a light on, despite the dim corners of the room, giving the place an even snugger ambience. Despite the vacuous, minimalistic space, there was something very lived-in and homely about it, something warm and inviting, aided by the dominating scent of rough-hewn wood that was far from unappealing. And beneath it all was the scent of him.

A double bed was tucked away in a recess over her left shoulder. To her right, a snug area had been created in front of an inglenook fireplace that had been blackened by use, and was no doubt responsible for the subtle lingering scent of burnt wood in the air. The double sofa in front of it was doused in blankets, books stacked in various towers along the walls either side of it as well as on the small coffee table in front of it. Logs filled a basket beside it, telling her the fireplace was potentially still very much functional.

A small, open-plan kitchen was positioned directly ahead, and what looked like a bathroom through an archway that flanked it. From the quality of the former, quality that had no longer been available to Lowtown for some considerable decades, she could only assume that, in the area's heyday, this had once been a trendy and exclusive apartment.

'How old are you, Nate?'

She hadn't meant it to fall out so abruptly.

'Old enough to remember the regulations coming into being,' he said on his way across to the kitchen. 'And some considerable time before that.'

'More than a century?' she asked, adding on twenty years.

'More than a century,' he confirmed as he stepped behind the counter.

'Have you been here the entire time?'

'Lowtown?'

As he removed two mugs from one of the cabinets, she momentarily captured his gaze and nodded to confirm that was what she meant.

'Yes,' he responded.

Her next question fell out as unintentionally abruptly. 'Alone?' She didn't know why it should matter to her, but it did.

His gaze met hers fleetingly as he filled the coffee pot from the tap. 'Yes.'

She glanced over her shoulder at the bed again, and folded her arms as she looked back at him. 'How's that possible?'

'How is what possible?'

'For someone like you not to have anyone?'

He raised his eyebrows slightly. 'Someone like me?'

She nodded but he turned away, reverted his attention to activating the coffee machine without offering any explanation.

As coffee mingled with the aroma of wood, as Nate's response remained elusive, Ember tightened her folded arms on her stroll around the room's periphery. Aside from a couple of oil-painted woodland landscapes, the walls were bare. Bare except for the markings that were more prolific in the apartment than she had first noticed: on the walls, the floor, the ceiling, the beams; even one next to the fireplace. Symbols that gave her a peculiar and uncomfortable feeling.

She stepped up to the windowsill to take a closer look at the one engraved in the wood – a symbol that looked like it had been *burnt* into the wood.

She glanced back around at the symbols that she noticed were reminiscent in style of the one she had seen over his heart.

Suddenly the need to know about him was more overwhelming than needing to know about her own past.

'What are these?' she asked as he joined her to hand her a coffee.

'Protection,' he said.

She accepted the coffee from him even though she had no intention of drinking it, not until she knew exactly what he intended by bringing her there.

'From what?' she asked.

'From my past.' He took a mouthful from his mug. 'From dark magic.'

Her pulse picked up a notch as she held his gaze. Reality shifted slightly. Despite an inexplicable, overwhelming need to run, she was grounded to the spot instead. But there was no way he could know. Unless her father had told him. Unless Nate had known all along. That *that* was why he'd hung around her. That *that* was why he'd been protecting her. That *that* was why he'd made a quick exit when she'd put two and two together. That maybe those symbols might have been how he'd come to meet her father in the first place.

'Wards,' she said, determined to say nothing about her suspicions. Determined to wait for him to make the first move. Wards were renowned for protecting against spells – everyone knew that. And she wasn't sure she wanted the answer, but she asked anyway. 'You've had a run-in with witches.'

'One particular witch. A long time ago.' He stepped away and sauntered over to the sofa.

Not her father. That was all she could keep saying to herself. He hadn't had a run-in with her father. Or had he?

'It's how I started collecting,' Nate added. 'Trying, first, to undo the curse she put on me and, when I discovered I couldn't, finding a way to protect myself.'

The 'she' offered momentary respite from her peak in anxiety.

'It took me twenty years to track down the symbols and find out how to use them. Each forms part of an incantation that, as a whole, forms a protective barrier that can't be penetrated. When I'm in here, her curse doesn't apply. No magic applies.'

'So this is like your fortress. Your haven?'

'Something like that. Witches and their spells and curses are all rendered defunct within these walls.'

The discomfort squeezed to the point of restricting her breathing as his gaze met hers again, but she tentatively headed over to join him anyway.

She perched side-saddle on the end of the sofa, her body facing his, her mug clenched in both hands in her lap. 'Then why leave its safety to stay at the apartment opposite mine?'

'Because I refuse to let it be my prison.' His gaze lingered on hers. 'Not when I created it to give me freedom.' He paused. 'Within its walls, at least.'

'You said a curse. What did you do to evoke it?'

'It's more what I didn't do. She wanted me and I didn't want her.'

It was one of the aspects that made witches so vehemently unpopular with both humans and the third species. They were powerful and unpredictable when skilled and experienced, each family cluster with their own set of skills. But all witches were elementals: having the innate ability to manipulate nature as well as drawing their strength from it. It was one of the reasons for locking them away in Lowtown or Blackthorn to reduce their abilities, to create damage limitation, both districts as far away as possible from the abundance of nature reserved exclusively for residents of Summerton and, to some extent, Midtown.

'What kind of curse?' she asked.

'One that bears no consequence to any of this. That's not why we're here.'

Which meant maybe he didn't know. Maybe he had no idea what she was. Maybe her father had kept the truth concealed – needing a vampire's help but not being willing to disclose why.

Nate placed some kind of device on the sofa seat between them. A device that resembled a compass. A device that was clearly an intentional conversation changer.

'What's that?' she asked.

'It's for my current job. The job I agreed to do for the Hordas clan in exchange for them leaving the café alone. It's a locator for my next collection.'

The pause was almost painful.

'A witch,' he said.

Her heart thudded under the intensity of his unflinching gaze. His gaze *chillingly* unflinching amidst his silence. The walls closed in on her, the intensity of the aromas around her suddenly oppressive, reminding her of the enclosed space.

'*You*, Ember.'

CHAPTER THIRTY

———◆———

He had tricked her.

He had lied to her.

It had all been a set-up to gain her trust, to get her there – a place that would render her powerless. From what he had told her, he knew witches were something to be feared. He couldn't risk her losing her temper back at the apartment. He'd known all along he was going to come back for her. He might even have planned to lure her there from the outset. He had left to rethink and had returned with a plan, with the means to lower her defences to get her there.

But she had no initiated powers anyway. She wouldn't know what to do with them even if she did have. She didn't even know what kind of witch she was. Had no means of discovering what kind of witch she was without exposing what she was to the very community she so desperately needed to avoid.

'Why are you telling me this now?' she'd asked her aunt

amidst the shock and confusion of the revelation that felt years too late.

It had been impossible to be angry with her though, her aunt gaunt and exhausted in her deathbed.

'Because you have the right to know about your heritage, Ember. You have the right to know what you are, even if you choose to never act on it. I couldn't tell you before. It was always a dream of your mother's that one day you and your brother would get out of this district. If you'd known, you might not have got through the phases that you needed to get through. Ember, witches don't get into Midtown. I didn't want it to hold you back. The last thing your mother wanted was for what you are to take your opportunities away. And curiosity can be a terrible thing, especially when you're young.'

'So I'm a *witch*? Was Aidan? Was he one too?'

Her aunt's nod had been brief.

'Is this why he was taken?' Ember had asked. 'Because of what he was?'

'I don't know. I don't know why he was taken, Ember. All your mother ever told me was that she had been involved with a witch. That she never wanted him to know about either of you.'

'My father? This heritage has come from him?'

'Yes. From his bloodline.'

'Who he is? Where is he? Is he still in Lowtown?'

'I don't know. I don't even know if he was from Lowtown. I don't know if he's still alive. And you can't get embroiled in trying to find him. The witch community is close-knit, Ember. Once you're in, you can't get out. It's why your mother never wanted to be a part of it. It's why your father doesn't know you exist. She wanted nothing to do with him and wanted you to have nothing to do with him. All these opportunities would have been stolen from you.'

'What if it was him who came for Aidan? What if he found us somehow?'

'You saw the same thing I did that night, Ember. Vampires came for Aidan, not witches. Besides, it's impossible. He didn't even know your mother was pregnant. That's why I can't tell you how important it is that you keep this to yourself. No one need ever know. Ever.'

Except for Nate.

Nate who she now knew had helped collect her brother for her father – her father who *did* know where they were. Or at least where her brother was.

And just like Nate had collected her brother for her father, seemingly now he was collecting *her* for the Hordas clan.

She pulled away from him. She marched over to the door and reached for the key beside it. But her hand got nowhere near it. As if smacking into glass, her hand rebounded.

And it was obvious why.

She scanned the room. She hurried to the windows. Her hand failed to reach the glass, an invisible barrier preventing her from doing so. She had no doubt every potential exit was the same.

'You only got in here because I gave you permission,' Nate said. 'You can't leave again without it either.'

Because it kept danger in, if he so chose, as much as kept danger out.

'So this is why I'm here?' she said, turning to face him. 'Nothing to do with telling me about my family at all.'

'I need to know why the Hordas clan want you, Ember. *That's* why you're here.'

'Why they want me? Firstly, how the hell am I supposed to know what they want with a witch? And secondly, why does it matter to *you* why they want me? In fact, why am I here at all instead of already with them?'

The windows her backdrop, she stared him down. Ember stared at him with the same scared but defiant brown eyes he'd seen staring back at him from her place of hiding in the wardrobe that night.

Her composure was faultless though. More than that, her general reference to the Hordas clan wanting a witch as opposed to specifically wanting her indicated she was yet to put all the pieces together – to see that the two were inter-related. Either that or, as he'd initially suspected when he'd realised what she was, she was ingeniously deceitful.

But it *was* possible that she didn't know. That she truly had no idea at all of her father's involvement with the Hordas clan. And even if she genuinely didn't have a clue, there had been no shock in her expression when he'd exposed what she was. That meant she had to know something about her abilities, and that was what he needed, that was why she was there: he needed something to work with. He would gain nothing by alienating her any more than he already had by deceiving her into coming there. He needed her trust, not her defiance.

'Let me make it clear, Ember: you're here because I'm not entirely convinced that locator is the only one they have. You're here because the same rules apply to that locator as to you. The magic that drives it is defunct in here. That means for as long as you're in here, you can't be traced and that buys me some time because I have a decision to make. You're due to be delivered Saturday night. I never fail on a delivery. My entire reputation is reliant on me not failing to make a delivery. And the Hordas clan do not accept failure. Failing on this job could finish me here in Lowtown. Though that in itself may be of little consequence to you, my failure would also means the reversion of the deal I made with them regarding the café and your friends. So I need you to be honest with me. For the sake of your friends, you need to be honest with me. I'll ask you again: what kind of witch are you, Ember?'

'The non-practising kind and therefore the irrelevant kind. If they want a witch, I suggest you find one that might actually be of some use to them.'

He searched her eyes as they glared unwaveringly back into his. If she *was* deceiving him, if she was maintaining an act, she was painfully convincing.

'What kind of witch are you, Ember? What are your abilities?'

'I don't know.'

'A witch that doesn't know what she can do. Do you expect me to believe that?'

'Whether you believe it or not, it's the truth.'

'What are your abilities, Ember?' he persisted as he remained in his seat, his tone calm.

'I *don't* know, Nate. I have never practised. I have never wanted to practise. I will never practise. I have not been told, so I haven't got a clue,' she said, adamancy rife in her tone. 'What the hell does it matter to you? *Why* do you need to know?'

'Because as I said, I need to know why they want you.'

She frowned. 'You're making it sound like they're looking for me in particular.'

Still confusion reigned in her eyes. He needed to tell her more. He needed to test her more. He didn't have time to play games. He certainly didn't have time to buffer her any more.

'That device doesn't just locate any witch. It uses the blood of a dead relative,' he said. 'It *is* you they're looking for.'

She turned ashen. 'Dead relative? One of *my* relatives? Who are you talking about?' Her lips parted as she waited in painful anticipation. 'Not Aidan. Tell me you're not talking about Aidan.'

'No.'

'Then who?'

But moments later she stumbled back against the windowsill, leaned against it for support as if she'd answered the question for herself. Her gaze dropped to the floor. She looked back at him.

'My father? Have they killed my father, Nate? Have the Hordas clan killed my father to get to me? Why? Is that why he came for my brother that night? Was my father trying to protect him? From *them*?' She took a step forward. 'Is that why my mother was hiding us in the first place? Was she hiding us from the Hordas clan? Have they found Aidan? And now they're coming for me? This doesn't make any sense. I met Jonah that night. He even said there was something familiar about me.' Her frown deepened. 'But does he not know who I am?'

No, because he'd chosen to believe her aunt was telling the truth. And because even if she wasn't, Ember had already lost enough that night. And because when he got back in the car, when he was still hesitating, her father's words had sealed his decision. A decision he had revealed to no one since – especially not to the Hordas clan.

'There was no reason why he would. And they didn't kill your father, Ember. Not from what I heard. He died of natural causes. Five years ago.'

Her eyes flared a little, no doubt at the fact he had previously withheld that information.

'And your father wasn't hiding Aidan from them, Ember. He was working for them.'

Silence shrouded the room. He could see her piecing it together in front of his eyes. This was no lie: she genuinely was clueless.

'My father was working for the *Hordas clan?*'

'More than that, Ember: he was friends with them.'

She raised her eyebrows. Her eyes glossed in horror. 'My mother *was* hiding us,' she said, primarily to herself, as if she needed to say it out loud to process it, to believe it. 'From *him*.'

She dropped her gaze for a few moments before her eyes lifted to meet his again.

'But you were with him that night,' she added. '*You* were working for the Hordas clan that night.' She stared back down at the device. She looked back at him. '*That*'s why I'm here. *Fuck*,' she muttered. 'You let me go. I'm your dirty little secret. I'm your failure.' She took a step towards him. 'I'm here where they can't find me because you're scared they might know you fucked up by letting me go.

'This is why you've been staying so close to me. It's nothing to do with pity: you're protecting yourself, your reputation. Maybe even your life. You want me gone. Somewhere they won't find me. Somewhere where they'll not stand a chance of finding out you screwed up. That's why you wanted me out of Lowtown. You weren't protecting me: you were saving your own arse from them finding out you hadn't done your job properly.'

'As far as they're concerned, I didn't fuck up on anything. You weren't there that night.'

'And your laurels could have rested on that until I recognised you last night. I could tell them everything, couldn't I? Including how you made that deal with them because I asked you to. How you compromised yourself and why. That you conspired with me against them. I should be dead already. Instead you want answers. Why? Why does it matter what kind of witch I am?'

He could hear her heart pounding. He could hear her blood coursing through her veins like a distant river.

'Because your father said something that night. He said that handing Aidan over would make the Hordas clan very power-ful. Ever since that night, they have done nothing but grow in power.'

'You think the two are correlated?'

'I think their power is something to do with whatever it is Aidan can do, yes. With whatever it is *you* can do. They compromised with me, Ember. They did a deal. They never do a deal. They want you badly – and that would be a good reason why.'

Silence descended for a few moments as she turned away, as she stared at the window. She turned to face him again. 'If I get to Midtown, they won't be able to find me. They won't be able to touch me.'

'You think they don't have ways and means, even across the border? You think they don't have contacts there? That device has a good radius.'

'You have wards here. I could have wards. There must be a way of using these symbols outside of this room. If I can wear a symbol somehow ... there would be ways to stop them finding me. Ways to block that device.'

'And brand yourself before you leave? You think you'd get across the border with a witch symbol blazened on you? And how long do you think it would be before someone discovered it? What then if they send you back? Are you going to spend your life in hiding?'

Those scared brown eyes were back. 'So you're telling me I'm not leaving here? Is *that* what you're saying?'

His gaze was steady, cold.

Of course that was what he was saying. Of course that was why she was there. That was why she was there where she was powerless to do anything about it. He was screwed either way.

Of course he wasn't going to let her go to Midtown and risk being found. He certainly wasn't going to risk her coming back to Lowtown as he could only assume she invariably would.

'It's not just about that, is it? You won't let me go because you don't trust me to stay in Midtown. What if I gave you my word?'

'If I let you go, I screw myself and I screw this district.'

'Because you don't trust me. You don't trust a witch, do you, Nate?' She closed the gap between them a little. 'Jonah has already seen me. He knows my links to the café so will have leverage over me in that place for whatever it is they want me to do. Do you really think I'd do something reckless enough to risk my friends? Do you think after what I witnessed, I would give the Hordas clan one more iota of power? Get me to Midtown and I will stay there. If that's what it takes, that's what I'll do.'

'I need to know what your abilities are, Ember,' he said, seemingly dismissing her claim.

'I don't know what they are, Nate. I didn't even know what I was until three years ago. How do you think I got through all the rigorous scrutiny? The lie detector tests? Why do you think my aunt never told me until she was on her deathbed? I'm not sure she would have told me ever if it hadn't been for that.'

'What are your abilities, Ember?'

'I don't know, Nate!' She sighed with frustration. 'Listen to me. I have spent a *decade* working towards this. It is quite obvious that my mother died protecting me and my brother so we would have this opportunity some day – an opportunity snatched from Aidan. You cannot prevent me from seeing it through. I am telling you the truth: I don't know why they want me. I don't know what it is they think I can do.

'My aunt didn't tell me what I was until it was too late for her, despite what my abilities might have been able to do to help her. She pleaded with me not to find out more about what I am, even banned me from using my skills to try and find a way to save her, or even just to take the pain away for a while. She went through all of that to give me a chance to get out of here. She spent her last weeks in agony in order for me to be able to get myself out of this district, so do you know what that means if I don't make it? It would have been for nothing. It all would have been for nothing.'

Ember's defiant, belligerent composure dissipated after her outburst. She leaned back against the windowsill again as a minor whipping of a breeze echoed down the chimney beside him.

He'd observed her enough over the months to know this was no act. The race of her pulse, the shock in her eyes, the things she said were all enough to tell him she had no idea. She was clueless. Completely clueless. She had no answers for him.

The silence was a dominating backdrop, to the point he could hear her every shallow breath as she fought to compose herself again. She turned to the windows despite the lack of view beyond the opaque glass. He could see her hands were cupped over her mouth.

Eventually both her arms fell lax to her sides.

'Is my brother still with them?' she asked.

'I don't know.'

Riddled with disappointment at getting nowhere – at knowing he was going to get nowhere – he stood. He headed over to the kitchen. He spread his hands on the counter and lowered his head.

She leaned back against the windowsill again, her gaze pensively fixed to the floor as she rubbed her thumb back and forth across her opposing palm.

'Why now?' she asked. 'Why, after all this time, are they only coming for me now?'

'I don't know.'

She frowned again. 'Aidan's never told them about me, has he? It's the only answer or they could have used that locator years ago.' Her frown deepened. 'Is this why didn't you tell me any of this yesterday? You knew I'd try to find them and, by doing so, I'd drop you in it? I know why I'm still alive now, but why let me live when you first recognised who I was? Why risk me ever exposing your secret? Why didn't you let those thugs in the alley end it that night? They would have given you the perfect alibi.'

Because he'd made it personal. The only time he ever had – and the last time he ever would.

'Because I screwed up. I was negligent. And this is the result when that happens. And that's why I'm not going to make the mistake again. *That's* why you're here. Up until that device, I didn't know you were a witch. I didn't know your brother was. I didn't know your father was. Why would I? Except now I do. So, yeah, I'd rather have you gone, Ember. I'd have you as far away from here as possible. You *are* my dirty little secret and I need you to stay buried. But now with that device, I can no longer guarantee it like I thought I could.'

'You can't hand me over and you can't not. You're going to take them on, aren't you, Nate? That's why I'm here. That's why you want to know my abilities and why they want me. You want to know what you're up against. You're going after them before they come for you. You're planning to take on the Hordas clan.'

CHAPTER THIRTY-ONE

——◆——

Ember had taken residence on the edge of the bed, her folded arms resting on her knees as she bent forward at the waist.

She knew she had to give herself time to process everything, Nate's silence subsequently a welcome relief as he sat at the breakfast bar, neither of them having uttered a word in the past couple of hours.

He hadn't confirmed or denied that was his intention, giving her nothing to work with.

She crushed her nails into her palms as her mind was flooded again and again with the sounds and images of Jasper being beaten to death, of Stirling's hand slithering up Casey's thigh, of Jonah's smugness as he cornered Harry into a business deal, forcing him to compromise on his principles, on everything he believed in despite what that would be doing to him inside. How everything was being ripped away from Harry and for no reason other than the unnecessary greed of the Hordas clan.

The prospect that her family, her heritage, had anything to do with increasing that power twisted her gut. It made sense now why her mother had never spoke of their father. Why she had struggled so much that night to stop Aidan from being taken. The kind of life he had been taken to.

'What was he like?' she asked.

Nate didn't flinch. For a while, he said nothing.

'My father,' Ember said, to be more specific even though she knew she didn't need to be. Anything to fill the void that had followed her question.

'He was arrogant. Selfish. Overindulged by the Hordas clan. He was close to Jonah and Antonia's father – they're the son and daughter in case you didn't know – real close. From what I heard, they'd grown up together.'

'So they really were friends?'

'Very much so.' Nate had barely looked over his shoulder. 'Like most practising witches, especially in these times, he'd learned to sell his skills to the highest bidder and turn it to a profit, whatever the consequences.'

'You don't approve of the power the Hordas clan have,' she said.

'I'm indifferent to it.'

'You're far from indifferent to it. Which is why if my brother really is something to do with their increased power, you're holding yourself partially responsible for what has happened since.'

'I'm not responsible for the choices other people make. I'm not responsible for their decisions.'

'How many times have you told yourself that since that night, Nate? This isn't only about the Hordas clan, or me, this is about you too. Deny it or not, you've carried the weight of what you did that night every day since. The trouble is, you've got used to it. You've even got to prefer it. It's safer for you, isn't it? Not to feel anything. Not to care. To be indifferent.'

'It's almost as if you're scared of who, of what, you'll be without it. Because it makes it easier for you to do what you do. And without doing what you do, what do you have left? Because you don't have anything else, do you? Even this haven that you claim gives you freedom stops you from being a part of things. It keeps you detached from the outside world. You might feel free in it, but it's still a cage.'

When he said nothing to the contrary, she closed the gap between them a little.

'But there's only one right outcome to all of this,' she added. 'And that's stopping the Hordas clan from doing more damage. Damage to people who do not deserve this. We can't let them cause any more by them getting their hands on me. Let me help you, Nate. Let me work with you on this. We still have just over a day, right? Let's see if we can come up with a way out of this.'

'In the next thirty hours or so before they're expecting me to deliver?'

'So tell them you found me dead. They need never know the truth.'

'They would never have set me on this task if they didn't already know you were alive. That device wouldn't work unless you were alive.'

'Then there must be someone we can talk to. Someone who can help me discover whatever this ability of mine is.'

'I can't risk anyone but me knowing about you.'

'A bigger risk than us knowing nothing at all?'

'I'd have to take you out of here, Ember – and you know why I can't do that.'

'Because I might be found by them first? Or because you don't trust me to use some undisclosed power on you.'

'Both. And I'm sure as hell not bringing anyone back here.'

His definitiveness, his silence, told her the discussion was over.

'Fine, so let's go back full circle to where it all started. What else did my father say to you that night? Did he give you any other clues?'

'No. All I know is that in the twenty-six years since that night, the Hordas clan have become the most powerful cohort in this district and it's showing no sign of letting up.'

'So clearly whatever my brother and I can do, it somehow gives them an advantage.'

'We already know that.'

She sighed with impatience. 'You're not helping, Nate. At this rate, either you're going to keep me in here for the next fifty years where no one can find me or you're going to kill me, because they're your only other options. *Talk* to me. Please. When I came to you for help, you said the Hordas clan were untouchable. You seemed to know that for a fact. Is that the core of their power? Do you know why? Or how? Has anyone ever even tried to kill them before?'

His gaze snapped to hers, lingered on hers. His frown deepened.

'What?' she asked.

He got up. He marched across the room. He grabbed his jacket from the bed. 'The shower's over there. There's food in the fridge,' he said on his way across to the door. 'The holdall's full of your stuff. I packed it while I was waiting for you to get home.'

She hurried behind him. 'Where are you going? What did I say? Have you thought of something?'

He unlocked the door. Without another word, he stepped through it, closing and locking it behind him.

CHAPTER THIRTY-TWO

Mack lived just off Rougemont Street. The street looked like a terraced row of houses but comprised of ground and first-floor apartments.

Nate stepped through the gap where a small iron gate would have once hung, and strolled up to the paint-peeling, racing-car-green door.

There was no knocker, no doorbell, and even the letterbox had been sealed over with a plinth of wood.

Nate used his fist instead. Once and then twice.

Mack didn't answer straight away but, then again, Nate didn't really expect him to. He took a step back and looked up to the window where he knew Mack would be watching.

Nate leaned back against the stone pillar, a clear statement he was going nowhere.

A few minutes later, the door opened.

Mack kept it on the chain. He remained hidden behind the door. 'Whatever it is, Nate, I'm not interested.'

Their paths had only crossed once despite them moving in similar circles, but one meeting was all it took to figure each other out. They'd both been on the same job, albeit for very different reasons.

Nate stepped up to the door but kept back from the step. 'I need to talk to you about what happened to you and your brother, Mack.'

Mack instantly attempted to slam the door but Nate pressed his foot down over the threshold, blocking him from doing so, the flat of his hand on the door. He could already smell the alcohol on his breath.

'I'm not doing this, Nate. And you know why. So get the *fuck* away from my door.'

'You're going to want to have this conversation with me, Mack. I'm risking more than you by being here. Keep that gun on me the entire time if it makes you feel better –' because he knew it was there, hidden behind the door out of sight '– but at least hear me out. If you don't like what I'm saying, I'll leave. I think you're going to want to have this conversation though.'

There was a lingering pause.

'Step back,' Mack said. 'You don't come in until I tell you.'

'Sure.'

He heard the chain being slid off, the subtle sound of footsteps ascending the stairs.

'In,' Mack directed firmly.

Nate stepped into the shadows of the vestibule, only to have Mack switch on the bulb above Nate's head, flooding him with light.

'Close the door behind you,' Mack instructed. 'And put your palms flat to the walls either side of you.'

He didn't know which smell hit him harder – that of booze or the musty, rotting smell of a damp apartment that hadn't been aired in years.

Mack sat a few steps down from the top, square on to Nate, his gun firmly pointed in his direction. Inebriated or not, Nate was willing to bet Mack was still the best shot out there. At close range with nowhere for Nate to hide, far enough away that Mack could pull the trigger before Nate moved an inch, it was the only reason he knew Mack had agreed to his entry.

Nate did as he asked.

'Do you know how fucking long it's taken me to find somewhere I can keep my head down?' Mack asked. 'How did you find me?'

'You're asking me that knowing what I do for a living?'

He'd known where he was for a long time. He'd come across him by accident, but had intentionally followed him home. He'd had no need to other than he never knew when it would come in useful – like now.

'So talk.'

'What happened that night, Mack?'

Mack and Hugh Cordell had been the best independent underground hit men on the circuit, made all the more so by working as an infallible team. They didn't hit often but when they did they had a hundred per cent success rate. The Voys would have paid a fortune to hire them that night.

It had been the Voys' biggest attempt at a turning point in the power struggle between them and the Hordas clan. Instead, the Cordells' failure to kill Antonia and Jonah Hordas had been the start of the Voys' demise.

Nate had no doubt that was a big part of why Mack had been allowed to live. The Hordas clan had wanted someone to tell that tale: of how even the infamous Cordells had failed to kill them. A tale that had subsequently granted the Hordas clan an even more infallible shroud.

Mack exhaled tersely. 'If that's why you're here, you can turn back around. I know you're working for them again. I'm not an idiot, Nate.'

'I'm not here for you. And I'm not here for them, not in that way. You don't make mistakes, Mack. So what happened?'

'I know your links to them,' Mack said. 'I know you sell your services to the highest bidder no matter what. How do I know you're not here for them? How do I know you're not here for the Hordas clan?'

'Because I'm telling you I'm not. I'm taking a risk myself being here asking these questions, but I think we're on the same side. I know you want vengeance for them killing your brother that night. And we all know the Hordas clan are getting too powerful. They've barely begun stretching their wings and already most of Lowtown is in shadow.'

Mack's eyes narrowed warily. 'Are you saying what I think you are?'

'I'm not saying anything,' Nate declared. 'You know better than anyone how this works. What happened, Mack?'

Mack screwed up his mouth amidst his indecision, but Nate knew any mention of his brother would have evoked him to at least reveal something. 'We were set up. That's the only explanation.'

'By who?'

'We don't talk to anyone, Nate. No one knew what we were doing except for the Voys. They must have been the ones to set us up. Or they screwed up somehow and let it slip. Maybe they even had an informant. I don't know. Whatever, *they* fucked up – not us.'

'That makes no sense. If they put the hit out on the Hordas clan, why allow themselves to fail? They would have been as tight as you were over that information.'

'I'm telling you: someone gave the Hordas clan the tip-off. There was no other way.'

'Why are you so adamant?'

'What the fuck has any of this got to do with you anyway? You're a collector, Nate. Why does something that happened ten years ago matter?'

'Because I'm trying to piece things together.'

'For what?'

Nate held his gaze, sending Mack the silent but clear signal that he had his own information to protect.

Mack studied him intently for what felt like minutes before eventually lowering his gun. 'It was planned to perfection. We weren't going to take any risks. A clean shot. We were even in the warehouse before they arrived. There was only three of them there: Antonia and Jonah Hordas and Stirling. And just before we took the shot, all three of them looked up at us. And Antonia had this look on her face, this smile. It was like they were expecting us. Like they were there waiting for us to take the shot. They killed Hugh outright. They left me alive to tell the tale.' He exhaled tersely as he shook his head. 'I should have fucking done myself in just to screw it to them. I owe Hugh more than that though, you know?'

'Yeah, I get it.'

'All I know is no one's dared go up against them since. That's why it felt like a set-up. If the best can't take them down, who can? But what I don't get is why let it get to that point. Why sit down and wait like that. Why even risk going in the building if they knew? Why sit in the firing line? Their guys came from behind. Why not take us out first? We're the quickest there is. They had no guarantee their guys would get to us before we took the shot, or that they'd be able to get back out again. That was one hell of a risk. Why take it at all? Why leave it until the last second?' He stood. 'And that's it. That's all there is.'

'Tell him about the dream.'

The female voice came from behind the wall to Mack's left. A female who stayed out of sight.

Mack backed up a few steps. 'Get back in the lounge. I told you to stay out of the way.'

'What dream?' Nate asked, dropping his hands to his sides.

Mack's gun was instantly back on him, prompting Nate to reluctantly lift his palms to the walls again.

'Tell him, Mack!' she insisted, her profile coming into view. She was maybe in her late thirties. Slim. Dressed in nothing but a pair of socks and an oversized sweater that skimmed mid-thigh. 'Just tell him.'

Mack's hand locked onto her upper arm but she knocked it away.

'He has a recurring dream,' she said, addressing Nate. '*Tell* him, Mack.'

'He's not a fucking dream analyst.'

'Tell him or *I* will.'

'Go!' Mack demanded, his gun directed at Nate again. 'We're done.'

'What dream?' Nate persisted, his attention locked on the woman.

Mack took a few steps down towards him. 'I told you to go, Nate. Don't think I won't use this.'

'She thinks it's important.'

'It's not. You've got five seconds. Four. Three . . .'

Nate opened the door behind him. He backed onto the outside step.

'Just tell him, Mack! Tell him whatever you know,' he heard from the scuffle inside. 'Do it for Hugh. Don't be stupid. Tell him!'

Nate reached into the back of his jeans for his tranquilliser gun. He'd have to take him down. He'd have to do it the hard way.

'He dreamt he'd shot them!' the woman called out. 'He always dreams it. He wakes up thinking it's real.'

Mack was at the door seconds later.

'He's adamant he shot them,' she called out again. 'He can remember every single detail of the aftermath!'

They held their guns aloft simultaneously, Nate's flat to Mack's forehead and Mack's flat to Nate's heart.

The woman fell silent.

Nate stared Mack square in the eye, Mack doing the same. The latter's pulse picked up a notch but it was still impressively calm – as calm and as steady as his hand. The calmness of someone used to firing a gun.

'It's a fucking dream,' Mack said. 'That's all. The mind does odd things after a trauma like that. Lives out preferred outcomes rather than face the truth.'

'How vivid?' Nate asked.

'That I feel the bullet release,' he said. 'The kickback of my gun. The sound of it hitting Antonia clean in the forehead. The look in my brother's eyes when he knew he'd taken down Jonah. As vivid as a memory, not a dream.' He held his gaze only a second longer before dropping his gun, before knocking Nate's gun from his head with it.

Before closing the door in his face.

CHAPTER THIRTY-THREE

'Twice in a week. I'm going to start believing you're crushing on me, Nate.'

'I need to ask you a question, Tamara.'

Nate looked through the windscreen out onto the rain-soaked street. The downpour had come an hour after he'd left Mack's place, as he'd be sat in the driver's seat mulling. Because Mack had been right: it made no sense why Antonia and Jonah would turn up and put themselves on the line if they'd already known in advance that they were going to be ambushed – and especially if they knew *who* they were being ambushed by. It would have been one hell of a risk. A risk that would have made them more than negligent; it would have made them stupid. And Antonia and Jonah were anything but stupid. The clue was in there somewhere. The clue was staring him back in the face.

'If it involves a bended knee and a ring, you should know firstly that I'm not that kind of girl,' Tamara quipped on the other end of the phone.

'Good, because I'm anything but that kind of guy.'

'Anyway, I thought we were done.'

'We will be after this.'

'Then ask.'

'Are you out of earshot?'

'Sounds serious. Is this to do with what you came in here about the other day?'

'I don't know. That's what I *want* to know.'

'No one's around, Nate. I'm on my own.'

'I know there are witches out there who have precognition, but have you ever heard of a spell that can transfer that ability to a non-witch?'

'Not only are witches with foresight almost as rare as serryns, witch gifts are about transferable as catching freckles from a handshake. I've never heard of a skill being acquired from a witch, any more than I've heard of a human being turned into a vampire. First species are first species, second species are second species, third . . .'

'Yeah, I get it,' he said. He rubbed his thumb across his forehead, his elbow resting on the driver's seat window. 'I have a collection to make, but I think they can predict what's going to happen. I get the feeling they're going to be able to outrun me.'

'The witch you're pursuing?'

'No.' He knew he wouldn't be able to get her to talk by admitting that. Besides, it was only a partial lie. 'But I think the one I'm pursuing has gained that ability from the witch.'

'Why do you think it's foresight?'

'Because they have a reputation for dodging bullets, especially when it's in situations where it should be impossible for them to do so. I need to know what I'm up against. I need to know how I'm going to get my hands on them. I need you to make a call for me, Tamara.'

There was a moment of silence on the end of the phone. 'No. No way, Nate.'

'You were happy enough to hire me to find that book for him.'

'That was different.'

'Why?'

'Nate, if he finds out I got you involved let alone that you have me asking questions on your behalf he's going to cut all ties with me. After you screwed around with his sister . . . '

'He doesn't need to know I'm involved. Just ask the question.' He paused. 'I'll suspend all debts, Tamara. If you do this, you'll owe me nothing. Ask him the question and you're free of me. And he'll never know my links to that book; I give you my word.'

Her silence resonated down the phone again.

'I don't know when I'll be able to get hold of him,' she said. 'If I can get hold of him. You know how elusive he is. I'll leave him a message. That's the best I can do.'

'I need to know sooner rather than later.'

'I'll do my best, Nate, but this is Kane Malloy we're talking about. And if he suspects something, he's not going to be happy. You'd better stay away from now on. I'll call you as soon as I hear. Whatever the outcome.'

CHAPTER THIRTY-FOUR

Ember sat perched on the edge of the bed, the best view of the open-plan apartment. She'd made the most of the shower whilst he was gone to get rid of the grime of the day. She'd been grateful for the fresh clothes too, relieved to be out of the uniform she'd been in since early that morning.

She'd helped herself to a glass of water but had no appetite.

Mother: dead.

Aunt: dead.

Ex-fiancé: dead.

Father she'd never met: dead.

Brother who was out there somewhere: could be alive or dead.

And linked to all of them in one way or another: Nate.

When she'd struggled to understand how he'd become such a big part of her life from his visits to the café, she'd truly had no idea.

And now she was his latest collection. Just like he'd collected her brother, he'd collected her now too. Except she had to maintain her determination to do whatever she could to make sure he didn't just cut his losses and deliver her – or kill her and face the aftermath.

She wrapped her arms around herself as she paced the loft again. She'd already circled it several times.

She stopped at the fireplace for the fourth time, her hands on her hips as she scanned the piles of books.

Even the prospect of leaving Lowtown, something that had been so significant a week ago, now seemed like a dim and distant memory. She'd be lucky to even make it to the border, let alone get through it. Right then, she couldn't be sure if she'd make it out alive at all. And yet she was numbed to the fear of it, as if it was an everyday trauma, an everyday occurrence.

She didn't even recognise herself from a week ago – except for the fact that, as with her application to Midtown, she was not going down without a fight. She'd work something out. From the way Nate had rushed out, maybe he already had. Whether that was going to be to her advantage though was another matter.

Whatever the outcome, as she stared at the ashes in the fireplace, she needed to find a way for Nate to work with her and not against her. And that started with finding a way for him to trust her.

Whatever front he put up, he was not inhumane even if not human. He could deny the guilt all he wanted, but he felt it. All his decisions from the moment he didn't take the ring from her told her he felt it. And someone who felt guilt had a conscience. And someone who had a conscience could be reasoned with. And to be able to reason with him, Ember needed something to negotiate with.

But right then, she had nothing.

She crouched down and tilted her head to the side to read the spines of the rows of books.

In many ways it felt hard to imagine him curled up with a book in front of the fire alone. In other ways, it was almost too clear and natural a vision in her head.

She reached out to run her fingers down the well-worn spines, various thicknesses, textures and states of wear and tear caressing the pads of her fingers. She stopped at one near the bottom of the third pile along to the right of the fireplace: a book without title or author on the spine.

At first she tried to ease it out whilst avoiding toppling the twenty or so books above it, but as the piles either side swayed precariously, she removed all the books on top.

She sat back onto the sofa, her find in her lap. There were no markings on the cover either, just the knot of the cord that bound the book shut.

She unravelled it and opened it to the first page. The book was hand-written onto parchment. The pages were dominated primarily by symbols aside from small sections of writing alongside them. Some pages were well worn, others smudged, some of the inked words dissipating into faded blotches.

It didn't take long, despite the hundred pages or so, for her to start spotting the various symbols around the room matching those contained in the book. This was the collection he had referred to. This was the one he had spent twenty years trying to locate.

And *this* was part of her heritage. These symbols were born out of what she was. The heritage she had chosen to ignore. The heritage that played no place in her life up to that point; up to the point three years ago when her aunt had told her on her deathbed what she was. The heritage she now knew had torn her family apart. The heritage that had since caught up with her.

Now the Hordas clan were the instigators of wanting to turn her life upside down again. They wanted to take away everything she had worked for. Worse, they wanted to use her somehow to grow in the power she despised.

Nate was the only one who could prevent that from happening – *if* he could choose her over everything *he* had worked for.

Nate who was still so much of a mystery to her. If she could understand more about him . . .

She found herself searching for it without even thinking about it. In the hour that passed, she examined every page for the symbol over his heart.

Eventually, she found it.

As she read, her heart skipped a beat as so much fell into place. With it, tendrils of dread squeezed.

She rose from the sofa and turned to face the door as she heard it open behind her. She knew it was pointless to try and conceal the book.

Nate closed the door and locked it before hanging the keys next to it along with his jacket. Thankfully, he'd returned alone.

'Where have you been?' she asked as he drew level.

His attention dropped to the book in her hand and the disrupted piles behind her.

He reached to take it from her grasp, Ember not objecting.

'Have you eaten?' he asked as he stepped past her to put it back in its rightful place, reconstructing the piles in the process. She wondered if he was avoiding her gaze on purpose. If he suspected she now knew.

'Oddly enough, I don't have much of an appetite.'

'You need to eat,' he said with his usual a heavy-laden frown as he headed across to the kitchen.

The vampire with a curse on his heart. The cruellest curse there could be on it. And one of *her* kind had done it to him. It was no wonder he was wary around her. It was no wonder he didn't trust her.

Tentatively, she watched him step behind the kitchen counter. 'And you need to tell me why you rushed out of here,' she said.

'I had a thought.'

She headed over to join him. 'I guessed that much.'

He gathered up ingredients from the fridge and cupboard, and laid them out on the countertop between them.

Ember placed her palms on the surface, her thumbs clutching the underside. 'Nate, talk to me.'

'As yet, there's nothing to talk about,' he declared, his full attention on preparing sandwiches for them both. 'I'm waiting to hear back from someone.'

'About what?'

His gaze was steady as it met hers, but he didn't respond. Instead, he slid the plate across to her as he took a bite out of his own sandwich.

She slid the plate directly back at him.

He held her gaze in the persistent silence, his burning into hers until he pulled away, sandwich in hand as he wandered over to the sofa.

Ember let out a curt sigh, rubbed her fingers up and down her forehead as she closed her eyes to ease her frustration. Nate was a loner. Nate had been a loner for a very long time. He sorted problems out for himself. He didn't rely on anyone. They were traits that were hard to break. They were traits that were even harder to break when you were already deemed the potential enemy as she was.

She turned to face him again. Turned to see him sat on the sofa, eating the sandwich in one hand, phone in the other. He scrolled before casting the latter onto the table in front of him and focused on the second half of his sandwich.

She headed over. She perched side-on in the corner nearest to her, facing him. 'Nate, we don't have to be enemies in this.'

'We don't have to be anything in this. I'm a collector and you're my collection. That's all there is to it.'

'We're more than that and we both know it. We slept together.'

'No, I fucked you,' he said, his tone as harsh, as cold, as his glare.

It was a hard reminder. An abrupt reminder. His clear attempt to push her away.

He finished the remains of his sandwich before wiping the corner of his mouth with his thumb, his gaze lost from hers again.

She studied his profile in the shadows of the room. In the virtual darkness, she saw him clearer than she ever had. Understood exactly why he needed to convince himself that was all it had been between them – except now she knew better. Saw his choice of word as the barrier it was.

'I know what the curse is, Nate. I saw the symbol in the book: the one branded on your heart. I know she made sure that if you didn't love her, you couldn't love anyone else – that no one else could ever love you back. Because, if you try to be with them, it'll kill you.'

Without meeting her gaze, he stood.

He carried his plate back across to the kitchen.

For once, he didn't know how he felt: angry at her finding the book; embarrassed that she knew the truth; worried that she knew the truth.

He'd never told anyone. He'd never felt the need to tell anyone. There was never any point in anyone knowing. And, right then, she was the last one he wanted or needed to know.

But then maybe it was better that she did. Maybe it was better that she was under no illusion, especially as there was no way she could be hidden from the Hordas clan outside of that room, not unless she ruined her chances of ever crossing that border by branding herself like he'd had to brand himself. The Hordas clan who now felt even more infallible than ever. And without the answer he needed from Kane as yet – if it would come at all – they would remain that way. And if there was no answer, if that was how it had to be, if that meant ending her life, then so be it. He had no choice. He could do nothing more. He'd spend the next thirty years looking over his shoulder for failing on his mission – or however long the Hordas clan had left without any offspring – but he'd try to do what he always did: he'd move on. Move on to things that didn't necessitate agonising over his decision.

'You flinched at one point when we were together,' Ember remarked. 'Right towards the end. It was as though you were in pain. It was around the time I noticed your contact lenses, so I forgot about it in the wake of everything else. But looking at that book, it came back to me.'

He didn't need reminding of it: the reason why he'd had to abandon her so soon after. Why he couldn't risk holding her or her holding him in return. He hadn't seen it coming. He hadn't detected her feelings beyond lust. He should have known better. He should never have risked letting it get to that point. And now having her there was increasing the risk. For now, it was only the stirring of feelings. He could never allow it to become anything more – for both their sakes. All the more reason why he needed her as far away from him as possible.

'It made sense,' she added. There was a lengthy pause. 'You feel something for me. But it's not pity.'

'And it'll make absolutely no difference to my decision,' he said, finally turning to face her.

But he didn't deny his feelings.

He heard her heart rate pick up a notch. She stood from the

sofa. She took a step towards him. 'I know when you feel some-thing for someone and it's reciprocated, you can't touch them. Not like that. Not unless you're in here. You can only ever have that experience in here, can't you, Nate? That's what she did to you.' She paused. 'If you touch someone you love out there, someone who loves you, your heart will stop. That pain you felt was because you were starting to feel something for me as I was for you.'

'Something that doesn't stand a hope in hell of going any-where,' he said. 'Something that is irrelevant to any of this.'

'Are they still alive?' she asked.

'Who?'

'The witch who did this to you?'

He felt his insides tense at the mention of her. He pulled away. 'I doubt it.'

'How long ago was it?'

'A little before the regulations.'

'You've lived with it for that long?'

'Yes.'

'Can it be undone?'

'No.'

'You've tried?'

'No, Ember. I decided it was more preferable to be a martyr.'

She folded her arms. 'Sarcasm. That's a new one.'

'Then clearly you bring it out in me,' he remarked, his gaze meeting hers briefly.

'How long have you felt something for me?'

'I'm not having this conversation with you, Ember.'

'Why not?'

'Because as I said, it's pointless.'

'No, Nate, it's pivotal. You hanging around me has been about more than pity *and* guilt.'

'Ember, I know what you're trying to do. I get that you're trying to connect with me. I get that you're trying to persuade me to confide in you ...'

'I'm trying to get you to talk, Nate, because I know there's something between us. To me, that's all the more reason why we should be working together.'

'The only thing between us is a past that I'm trying to mop up. Whatever else you see between us is flawed, born out of nothing more than misplaced familiarity. Fascination breeds false judgements. I don't know you and you certainly don't know me.'

'Does anyone?'

'No. And I prefer that way. Now more than ever. Because I've learned one thing out of this, Ember: that complications always ensue when I don't do my job properly the first time. And this situation we're both in now is walking evidence of that.'

'Or you not doing your job properly could be the one thing to bring the Hordas clan down. It could bring it all full circle. It started with my brother and it can end with me. This could be your absolution, Nate.'

He exhaled tersely at the prospect.

'I know you're not sure if I'm telling you the truth, but I am,' she persisted. 'If I knew more about what I was, I would tell you. My aunt told me only about my bloodline. She knew nothing more. And not only did she not want what I was ruining my chances, when I found out what I was, I didn't want what I was to ruin my chances either. I wanted to pretend it didn't exist. You're not the only one with a curse. You're not the only one who needs a haven. You've spent all this time trying to get me to mine. Don't let that change now. You'll never forgive yourself.'

Refusing to continue the discussion, he stepped out from behind the countertop. 'While I wait on this call, I'm going to get some sleep. You need to do the same. It might be our only opportunity. You look like you haven't slept properly for days.'

She folded her arms. 'I wonder why.'

As he kicked off his boots and socks, he glanced over his shoulder to see the frustration emanating from her eyes that he wouldn't engage with her.

He didn't need to sleep. He'd stand no chance of sleeping. But he did need to take some time out – from her persistent questions to which he couldn't give her answers.

And she most certainly *did* need sleep. Her eyes were red-rimmed and turning bloodshot, the pallor of her skin a growing concern, her whole composure flagging. She was reaching the point where she wasn't going to be able to think straight, where her body certainly wasn't going to be able to keep up for much longer, all the emotional stress of those last couple of days no doubt a huge part of that.

He took a step towards her, wanting her to know what he was about to say was a directive and not a request. A directive he hoped would lead to acquiescence rather than a struggle. 'I need you in bed with me. Where I can keep an eye on you.'

Her frown deepened. 'What do you think I'm going to do, Nate? Try and kill you in your sleep? And trap myself in here forever? Unless that's how I can escape?'

'Sorry to disappoint but the barrier still applies whether I'm dead or alive, unless you've got a miracle cure for my curse?'

Ember didn't budge, seemingly far from amused at his glibness.

'I'm not planning to kill you in your sleep either, Ember, if that's what you're thinking. I hardly need you unconscious. I certainly don't need to take you to my bed for it. I want us both to get some rest, that's all.'

'And I'd rather stay conscious for what could be my final hours, if that's OK with you. Live life to the full.'

His heart ached under the intensity of her gaze, the uncertainty in her eyes. She knew as well as he did that he didn't need her permission to get her there, her deliberation merely exerting her last sense of control.

He closed the gap between. 'I want you to know what happens after this is about what I *need* to do, not what I *want* to do. Because of that, I won't promise you a happily-ever-after when I can't guarantee it. I'm doing what I can though, Ember. That's all I can offer right now.'

'And this is more my battle than yours, Nate. My mother died because of them. My brother was stolen from me because of them. The only people I have left to care about were threatened by them. A good man has died because of them. If I'm somehow linked to their success, I can also be linked to their downfall. You need me alive for that downfall.'

The conversation was over. For now, the conversation needed to be over.

He backed off. He slipped under the covers still clothed to assure her he had no ulterior motive.

After a few minutes of further defiance, she eventually joined him, taking the space he had left for her on the window side of the bed.

She lay on her side with her back to him – her last protest.

Physical contact was the last thing he needed, even if she was as fully clothed as him. But there was always a chance, a minor chance, that he could drift off to sleep waiting for her to do so, despite the weight of his thoughts. And a witch was a witch, even if his witch was Ember.

Spooning her, he wrapped his arm around her waist, keeping her close enough that he would feel it if she tried to get out of bed.

She tensed a little at the intimacy of his proximity, no doubt partially because he'd spent every moment since they'd slept together pushing her away. She didn't recoil though. She certainly didn't pull away. But she said nothing either. It seemed, for now, Ember had said all she wanted to say. Because every word she had said had been true: he'd only felt the pain because she'd reciprocated his feelings.

Ember liked him. She genuinely liked him. Or she *had*, before she'd found out who he really was.

He flattened his palm on the mattress at her stomach, creating as little a sense of togetherness as the position would allow. But it was hard not to feel it. It was tough not to linger on the subtle aroma of her skin, to be enticed by her warmth, tempted by the pulse alive and throbbing in her neck. To not recall how her skin felt under his touch; how right her body had felt beneath his; how right it had felt being inside her. Because once she had relaxed, he had clearly become more absorbed in her than he had realised. He'd clearly crossed a boundary he never crossed or he wouldn't have felt anything at all.

Felt something for a witch – the very species that had killed his heart dead in the first place.

And he couldn't let that happen again; he couldn't let any of it happen again, as tempting as it was there in his haven where he was at no risk of feeling pain. Where he could get as up close and personal as he wanted physically as well as emotionally. Ultimately, it would achieve nothing but temporarily sate the frustration and tension though.

He detected her subtle sigh. She wriggled into a comfortable position, moved one forearm under her head as an added pillow, she jutted her behind back a little and bumped his erection in the process. Because that was one thing he certainly had no control over, not lying next to her like that.

He felt her still. But she said nothing.

And neither did he.

Instead, he lay in the silence just like she did, listening to the melody of her pre-sleep breathing. Because without conviction as to what he was going to do, whilst he was waiting on *that* call to determine his next course of action, he wasn't willing to utter another word.

He closed his eyes to the gentle patter of rain on the windows beyond the opaque arches, his entire loft surrounded by an outer corridor, his haven nestled within. Now *their* haven.

He couldn't remember the last time he lay with his arm around someone – not in his bed. Not like that, listening to the subtle tick of the clock echoing around the space, counting down the time they had left together. Counting down the time to the point he would be forced to make a decision.

The first half an hour continued to be the toughest – especially knowing she was still conscious. But it worsened as she drifted to sleep. As her body relaxed and melded against his. As she lay unconscious and vulnerable.

It felt as if part of her had been absorbed into him, invigorating parts of him, warming his cold blood and pushing it through his veins with more vigour, heating his entire body, arousing his entire body, inciting his most basic instincts. Her rich, warm, metallic blood pumping through her veins inches from his mouth. The softness of her feminine curves. The smoothness of her fragile skin. He could have taken it all: her body, her blood, even her life if he so chose.

The temptation to bite, to keep her there, to make her his, trapped in that haven, had him teetering on the question of his own selfishness.

It intensified as he tuned in to her deep and steady human breaths, her pulse ticking away like the clock in front of him, counting down her limited years – another reason he couldn't afford to fall for her any more than he already had.

And that was why, if he found a solution, a way to bring down the Hordas clan, he had to let her go.

He withdrew his arm from around her. He rolled onto his back and turned his head to gaze at the windows, at the first signs of morning backlighting the opaque glass.

He looked back at her again to where she now slept soundly. Thoughts were too vivid: tasting her, touching her, making her gasp and tremble and shudder as he had. Holding her down. Fucking her hard and deep. Feeling her tight around him. Feeling her skin break under the piercing of his incisors. Feeling the heat of her blood fill his mouth.

He forced himself to pull away.

As soon as he did, so did she, turning to face the direction of where he had been, her delicate hand sliding up through the sheet where he had lay, her hips adjusting, emphasising the curve of her behind as the rest of her body realigned in his direction. But she was still asleep, her breathing still deep, with no idea how much the predator in him could have changed everything for her in a matter of minutes.

He grabbed his phone where he'd left it on the covers behind him. He poured himself a glass of water and made his way over to the sofas.

He placed his phone on the table and crouched at his piles of books. He carefully removed the book of symbols – the one Ember had come across, and the one that had exposed his secret.

He nestled into the corner of the sofa, semi-reclining as he flicked through the pages.

'You will never fucking love again. Do you hear me, Nate?' Elissa had all but screamed at him.

Her large blue eyes had flared in fury, more so in indignation. Beautiful eyes, at least aesthetically. Everything about her was beautiful, from her delicate features, to her waist-length dark hair, to her curvaceous body. Everybody wanted her, and yet she chose him. And, for a while, he had indulged in her beauty. He had repressed his own uncertainties about the person beneath. But that person hadn't taken long to rise to the surface – in her attempt to control him, her tantrums, her self-obsession, her foul temper, her arrogance.

She had wanted to own him, and no one owned him. Not even the most beautiful woman he had come across. Not even a witch who had charmed and captivated him with her playful magic, with her ability to bend the rules of nature. A witch proficient in her multiple abilities due to being from a pure bloodline of both elementals and casters. A witch who, little by little, had used her enhanced skills against him: a flying cup when he defied her; a bout of sickness limiting to his bed when he wanted to go somewhere without her; a fallen branch on an attractive girl he had taken a few moments to give directions to.

'I don't love you, Elissa,' he had told her. 'I can't love you.'

There had been no hurt in her eyes, only indignation at him daring not to worship at her feet; to be grateful for her attention.

'I'll never love you,' he'd said.

As he'd left, he hadn't been entirely convinced he would leave with his life – or what had been left of it after three years by her side. Three years without tenderness, emotional intimacy, compassion and, most of all, his view of what love should be. And it had nothing at all to do with external beauty, any more than a delicate and vibrant flower with poisonous pollen did.

But Elissa wasn't going to kill him. Elissa had no plans to free him of any kind of burden.

One moment he'd been ploughing through the field's long grass, away from the home they shared, a home shrouded by nightfall. The next moment he had been flat on his back in their bed, waking to the sense of his blood freezing in his veins, his heart aching, the brand scorching his skin above it.

She'd loomed over him, those blue eyes putrid with resentment. 'You will *never* love again. And you will never feel being loved again. You will never know what it's like to be with someone. I take that from you today. As of today, I make your life barren. I curse that weak heart of yours. A heart that will stop at the touch of your hand on anyone you dare to love and who loves you back. Admire from afar and suffer for it. Act upon it, and leave this world behind. Your only salvation from this curse is death.'

Her smile of triumph had been as cruel as her curse.

'Will you ever love anyone enough to die for them, Nate? When, over time, that heart turns cold and defunct, when you can't even remember what love is, will you sacrifice yourself for someone you can't be with anyway? I think not.'

He rested the back of his hand against his mouth as he turned page after page, studying each in the shadows of the room.

He'd been told by many that protecting himself from the curse was impossible. In many ways, it had been. But that haven was his loophole. There was always a loophole. He just needed to find Ember's now too. Find it, or it was better she was dead. Better than a life with the Hordas clan. A better alternative than what that would do to her. Better than being unable to live with knowing the power she gave them. Whatever that power was.

CHAPTER THIRTY-FIVE

Ember opened her eyes, struggling at first to remember where she was. But as she surveyed the brickwork, the opaque windows behind her, she remembered. But his cool, hard body was no longer pressed against her, his arm no longer wrapped around her as it had been when she'd fallen asleep. She turned her head to see if he was still behind her, but the bed was bare.

She sat upright and drew her knees to her chest. Seeing him pace the room, his back to her, she combed her fingers through her tangled hair to push it from her face.

He was on the phone to someone, Ember then realising that it had no doubt been the sound of his voice – however hushed – that had stirred her from her sleep. It was gone eleven, meaning they – or maybe just she – had managed to get at least a few hours of sleep.

His responses were short, cryptic and left it impossible for her to read between the lines. He paced as he listened, scratching the back of his head as he wandered from the kitchen to the fireplace and back again.

Snagging his attention as she pushed back the sheets, she cast him a fleeting glance as she wandered into the bathroom.

Worse, he exited the room to finish the conversation, taking himself out through the vestibule.

Once she'd finished in the bathroom, Ember stood to face the door, her arms tightly folded. Her heart pounded. The room swayed off kilter a little. The walls appeared to throb.

Nate stepped back inside a few moments later. He met her gaze, but only briefly before locking the door behind him. He cast his phone aside on the bed with a despondency that told her it hadn't been good news. Her stomach flipped, a cold perspiration flooding her skin.

She instinctively took a step back, her arms dropping to her sides.

He wandered past her to the kitchen. He poured himself a glass of water. He knocked it back as he remained turned away from her.

When he indicated the space beside him, she joined him on the sofa, reached for a blanket for comfort as much as to fend off the chill in the air.

'There's a story,' he said, 'a couple of centuries old, about a witch who fell for a regular human. You'll maybe already know for yourself that witches aren't supposed to fall in love with non-witches, any procreation weakening the bloodline and thus the strength of the cohort. Usually it would be enough to banish them, but this witch who fell for a regular human was their leader. So, instead, they turned their attentions to the one he loved. He knew of their plans to kill her and, so, in order to protect her, he devised a spell. If someone murdered her or caused her accidental death, she would be given another chance. She would see it coming, giving her the opportunity to avoid it.'

'Precognition?'

'In a sense. But only triggered by death. Only after it had actually happened. You asked where I went yesterday. Ten years ago, the best assassins known to this locale were paid by the Voys to take out the Hordas clan. And when I say "the best", I mean it. But they failed. One was killed, the other left alive to tell the tale, basically so the Hordas clan could get word out there that no one could touch them. And, as they'd hoped, the rumour spread.'

'Which is why you told me they're untouchable. You think the Hordas clan are accessing that same magic. That spell.'

'And I think there's a connection between that and why they want you, yes.' He paused, his gaze steady on hers. 'I think they're untouchable because they can predict their own deaths. And in the context of that story, I can see why. It also makes sense why your father said what he did about your brother making them even more powerful once they got their hands on him.'

She stared at him in the darkness of the apartment, Nate perfectly still as he assessed her. And the fact he was telling her this, the fact he was confiding the information in her told her that she may have had the breakthrough she'd needed.

Or he'd already made up his mind of the outcome, and what he told her was now not going to make any difference anyway. Dead people didn't disclose secrets.

'What I do know for sure after talking to one of the assassins,' he added, 'is that whatever the Hordas clan are doing, however they're doing it, just like with that story, it's triggered only after someone succeeds in killing them. They can then see it coming and can prevent it from happening. The biggest clue Cordell gave me was that he dreamt he'd succeeded. The Hordas clan might be able to go back in time but, technically, as it had to have happened for the precognition to have been triggered, it makes sense why a fragment would be impinged on the memory of those involved.'

'And they made a mistake by letting Cordell live or you would never have known.' Ember dropped her gaze to the table. 'So now we have something to work with.' She wasn't going to question why he decided to tell her as she looked back at him. 'They failed. We need to learn from that.'

His frown deepened. 'Ember, you can't kill someone who can see it coming. Not least when they can go back in time to prevent it from happening. We could take down as many of their henchmen as we wanted but if they're always at the helm with this kind of power, nothing will ever change.'

'But what we know *has* to be an advantage. Their greatest power is that no one will dare go up against them. It's a self-fulfilling prophecy. And everyone who has tried to bring them down has probably followed the same track despite it being a dead end. We need to find a new path *off* the beaten track. We need to come at it from a different angle. No one's invincible, Nate. They're just cheating – and we need to out-cheat them.'

'How?'

'By somehow using their power against them. I don't know. We need more answers, like how the spell works. Someone has to know more. Just imagine if there *is* a way to beat them. If somehow we can work it out. You've had dealings with them before. You clearly got to meet with Jonah or how else did you get to do a deal with them? We need to get our hands on an insider, Nate. Someone who's likely to know more. Someone close to them. You know them. You know their team. Who are they closest to? More to the point, who can you get your hands on?'

CHAPTER THIRTY-SIX

———◆———

Nate sat behind the wheel, his elbow resting against the closed window, the front of his index and middle finger resting against his lips.

He checked his watch.

Sure enough, like the professional she was, Cordy stumbled across the street bang on time, laughing and swinging her bag, ignoring the downpour, her long, bare legs shimmering from the glow of the street lamps dampened by the dark grey sky.

Stirling followed behind her – or, more to the point, stumbled. She'd ploughed him with enough drink to lower his guard, to get him away from public view with whatever she had offered on a platter to him. And, Stirling, being the letch that he was, had bitten.

'Stirling is their right-hand man,' Nate had said. 'If anyone knows anything it's him. He was with them the night the Cordell brothers tried to take the Hordas clan out. He knows what happened.'

'So it's him we need.'

'The question is how we get our hands on him without rais-ing his suspicion or the suspicion of Antonia and Jonah. He's nobody's fool. Neither are they. I can't be linked in any way. If he tells them where he's gone and that it's me he's seeing, it's going to put them on alert when he doesn't show up again.' He'd paused for a moment. 'He's got a thing for your friend Casey.'

'No,' she'd said firmly. 'You're not using Casey as a honey trap.'

'But he gave her his number. His personal number. I know he did because he told me about it when I met him in the café. If she texts him, he's going to respond. My deal with the Hordas clan is that they back off everyone there. And I can guarantee he's not going to want them to know he's going back on that. He's going to do this on the quiet.'

'And I told you, I'm not risking Casey.'

'All we need is for her to give you his number. I have someone else in mind for the rest. Someone equally persuasive. I don't think he's going to mind being stood up.'

As soon as Cordy and Stirling disappeared through the door-way at the top of the steps, Nate reversed into the alley, tucking his car out of sight, before stepping out into the drizzle of the cool night air.

His holdall over his shoulder, his free hand in his jacket pocket, Nate kept to a steady pace, keeping to the exact time he had agreed with Cordy.

She'd left the door on the latch as he'd told her to. She'd got straight down to business with Stirling like he'd told her to, making sure his defences were down, that Stirling wouldn't see him coming.

It took Nate a matter of seconds to knock him out cold.

And that was it: the decisive move. The no going back. Ember had called it the path to absolution. Like the night he'd left her behind in the apartment, he was far from convinced. And like the night he'd left her behind in the apartment, he chose to ignore the nagging doubt. Chose to ignore it for her.

CHAPTER THIRTY-SEVEN

———◆———

Stirling woke up cold. Icy cold. Knowing he was lying down, he prised open his eyes to figure out where he was.

Head throbbing, recollections of the smack against the back of it hitting him as hard as the implement had, he blinked away his blurred vision to try to absorb the unfamiliar surroundings. Simultaneously, he reached for something, anything, to protect him against the chill.

Because he was stark bollock naked. As he looked down, all he could see were familiar mounds of pale white flesh in the shadows of the room; he quickly ascertained that his arms and legs were spread and secured to the bed.

As he moved, as he fought against the restraints, the crumple of plastic below him told him this was more than a sex game devised by the woman he had gone there with. The woman who, as was now more than clear, had set him up.

Bitch.

'You're awake. Good.'

He instantly knew the voice though it took him a moment to place it. And a moment longer to realise where it was coming from.

He stretched his neck to see Nate sat behind him.

Stirling glanced back around the room before fixing his attention back on Nate. 'What is this?' he demanded, not knowing whether to feel infuriated or panicked.

'Chat time,' Nate declared.

Stirling laughed. It was a deep and uncomfortable laugh from a place that failed to see any humour in the situation.

Because there was nothing funny about Nate's clinical expression, or the sobriety in his eyes. There was never anything funny when Nate looked at anyone like that.

'Seriously, Nate. What the fuck *is* this?'

'I have some questions I'm going to ask you. We're not going to play any games. Your reluctance will do nothing but draw this out. I will get the answers I want. All you have to do is decide just how slow and painful you want your death to be before then.'

'I don't know what the fuck you think you're doing, Nate, but Antonia and Jonah will kill you for this. You know they will kill you for this. Whatever your issue, you need to rethink.'

'Frank Newton had a son. He was called Aidan. Where is he?'

Of anything Nate could have asked, he wasn't expecting that one. 'Aidan? What's he got to do with anything?'

'Where is he, Stirling?'

'Why?'

'Get the gist of this. *I'm* the one asking the questions. I want to know where Aidan is.'

'What do you want with him?'

'The gist, Stirling.'

Stirling shook his head; turned away, flipped both his middle fingers up. But his head soon rolled back as he heard the chair scrape behind him, as he felt movement in the air as Nate stood up. He watched him head around to his left side.

Nate held something in both hands – a small rock hammer in one, and something out of sight in the other. He prised Stirling's hand open, specifically the middle finger of his left hand.

Stirling's stomach coiled in horror as he watched Nate place the needle under his exposed fingernail. He jolted, wrenched and squealed as Nate hammered the needle in deep – once, twice and then three times.

The pain shot through him, causing him to clench his teeth, to squeeze his eyes shut, to arch his back with the agony of such a tiny implement in such a sensitive place.

'What the *fuck*?' Stirling hissed, staring back up at him through watery eyes.

Nate didn't answer, he merely straightened out Stirling's ring finger.

Stirling wanted to believe it just a threat this time. The second needle to be drummed into his hand begged to differ.

'He's dead!' Stirling said. 'What the fuck are you doing, Nate? Aidan's dead. He was killed three weeks ago.'

Nate's gaze locked on his. 'Killed by who?'

Stirling swallowed hard, already knowing he had said too much.

Nate extended Stirling's thumb, the needles already embedded beneath his fingernails preventing Stirling from clenching his fist to stop him. He placed the needle beneath his thumbnail.

'The Voys,' Stirling said. 'The Voys did him in. They'd had an insider in with us for over two years. They were in it for the long game. They poisoned him. Three weeks ago. They poisoned him. Right under our noses.'

'Why?'

'Nate, this is a mistake. Do you hear me? This is a huge fucking mistake.'

'Antonia and Jonah Hordas have a special skill. A skill they used the night Mack and Hugh Cordell tried to assassinate them. Did they get that skill from Aidan?'

Stirling stared up into Nate's uncompromising eyes. How the fuck he knew any of that was anyone's guess. 'You're deep, Nate. Too deep. You hear me?'

'Did they get it from Aidan?'

'No more, Nate. I'm not uttering another word until you tell me what the fuck you're playing at. Is someone paying you, huh? Is it them? Is it the Voys? It's got to be the Voys.'

'Did they get their skill from Aidan?' Nate asked. 'And if so, how?'

Stirling laughed. It was another deep, embedded, uncomfortable laugh. 'You're getting nothing more from me. Do what you like. You're going to kill me anyway. Have a blast with it. And fuck you, Nate. That's all I've got to say.'

Nate's fingers brushed Stirling's left eye a moment later, forced his upper and lower lids open.

Stirling's breath snagged. His whole body stiffened in horror. But he told himself there was no way. Nate could be a clinical bastard. Everyone who had contact with him knew that. But he *knew* him. They'd known each other for years. They'd known each other right back when he'd gone with Frank to collect the kid. The kid who would make up for Frank's deficit those past few years. The kid they so desperately needed. The kid that they thought Frank couldn't reproduce.

Nate kept Stirling's lids open at the same time as he placed the needle down over his pupil. It all happened so quick that he didn't even get another second to protest.

Nate wasn't just a clinical bastard. It was confirmed: Nate was fucking psychotic.

Stirling gasped with pain, his entire body jolting as the needle entered his eye. He wrenched and squirmed, barely able to breathe, the room spinning, his entire body breaking out in a cold sweat as it entered a state of shock.

He looked up to see Nate resting his palms either side of his head, gazing down into his now single functioning eye.

'You want to do the rest of this in the dark, that's up to you,' Nate said. 'I have several hours until I need to be out of here, a fuck load of needles to go and a fuck load more places in you to secure them. The longest I've needed to sustain this practice is five hours, and that was in the very early days. If you want to try and break that record, be my guest.' He leaned close to his ear. 'Because I know what you did to Jasper,' he whispered. 'And I'm not OK with that. I'm not at all OK with that. So, *please*, take as long as you want.'

CHAPTER THIRTY-EIGHT

By the time he got back late that evening, she was asleep again, curled up under a blanket on the sofa. A sleep that was deep enough, evidently needed enough, that his presence didn't wake her even as he stood over her.

The exhaustion had finally caught up with her, her body being given no choice but to relent again. And, for now, he'd let her sleep.

Nate rinsed off quickly under the gentlest spray of the shower so as to keep noise to a minimum; rinsed off any remaining trace of Stirling's blood from his face and body. He'd been meticulous in cleaning up. Had actually been done with Stirling in a couple of hours but had given himself plenty of time to dispose of his body – of any evidence – properly.

Pulling on a fresh pair of jeans and a clean hoody, he poured himself a glass of water and headed over to the coffee table. He perched amongst the books, took a mouthful from his glass.

Absolution. That was what she had called it. Absolution from his past. And, in part, it had felt like some form of absolution getting Stirling back for what he'd done to Jasper. The rest was debatable, especially now having learned what he had.

They needed her. Whatever it was that they did, they needed a replacement for Aidan.

There was no way out for her. They would tear Lowtown apart to find her – further afield if that's what it took. For all he knew, they'd have someone at the border. The Hordas clan had connections. Too many connections. The risk was too great.

There was only one logical option left.

Though how the fuck he was going to bring himself to do it, he had no idea. Already she was more to him than she should have been. There had been something about coming home to her that told him that. Something about walking through the door and the comfort of feeling her presence. That was the most alien feeling of all: comfort. A feeling he had long forgotten. A feeling he'd detected she'd been lacking too.

Ember flinched. Her eyes opened. She sat up abruptly, her gaze locked on his. 'What did he say? Did you get anything out of him?'

He couldn't help but admire her being instantly back on the clock, even though she could clearly barely even see him yet, could barely hold herself up on her elbow.

'No,' he said. 'Not that was of any use.'

To the cause he set out for at least.

He headed over to the kitchen to make them both a coffee.

'But he said *something*?' she said, wrapping the blanket around herself that she seemed to have adopted.

'There are only two people who know the full story: Antonia and Jonah,' he said. 'Even Stirling was kept in the dark.'

Certainly in the dark enough not to be able to give him the information they so desperately needed to be able to do anything about it. It had been a dead end. A literal dead end. And it would no doubt remain a dead end, just as his options were.

She wiped each eye with the heel of her hand, still trying to blink herself awake as she followed him over to the kitchen where he had discarded his glass. She raked her hand back through her hair in a way that had him forcing himself to break away.

'So what did he say?' she asked, resting her folded arms on the countertop.

'That we're right. That they *can* predict when they're going to die from unnatural causes.'

'What kind of timeframe do they have? How far back can they go?'

'Stirling reckons it's anything up to ten minutes. I think that's why Antonia and Jonah entered the warehouse that night they were shot. I don't think they knew until they were inside the building. It would make sense.'

'Did he tell you *how* they do it?'

'No. He doesn't know. And I can believe that. What I do know is that, as they were the only three there, Antonia and Jonah have the skill themselves.'

'Back to that story again.' She sighed with impatience. 'But he told you nothing else?'

'Only that they go to a specific place every few months. That's where whatever it is they do happens. But no one has ever entered except the family. Them and your brother and your father before him.'

'Where is it?'

'It doesn't matter.'

'But Stirling did tell you where it is?'

'And I've been there, and found nothing. Nothing I could get to. It's all barred off. Set right into the rock. There was no budging any of it. I tried everything I could.'

She checked her watch. 'It must have been in Lowtown. Or thereabouts. You wouldn't have had time to deal with Stirling and get to wherever this place is *and* back again if it was too far away.'

'Like I said, it doesn't matter.'

'Take me there.'

'Ember, we can't risk you being out of this place – and you know why.'

'Even for this? Possibly for the answer we desperately need? We can be quick. We need to know what's beyond that gateway. If we know what we're up against, we might be able to work out what it is I can do and how they're using it. And the quicker we get there before they work out Stirling is missing, the better. They're not going to expect us to know where it is, are they? That's our biggest advantage at the moment. We need to act now.'

'I said no, Ember.'

'So what's our alternative?'

He hoped his silence and steady gaze were enough confirmation.

Her breathing snagged. She exhaled tersely. Her eyes flared in disbelief. 'You're giving up. You're giving up on me. You're giving up on us.'

'I keep telling you: there is no "us".'

'Tell your heart that!' she exclaimed, her otherwise steady tone cracking slightly. 'You're not capable of this. You're not capable of spending all these months working towards keeping me alive only to kill me.'

'As I keep trying to tell you, Ember: you don't know me.'

'I think I know you better than you want me to. I think you're stronger than this. I think you can fight harder than this.'

'I can't fight the invisible, Ember,' he said, uncharacteristically raising his voice; irritated that he had felt the need to do so. 'Neither of us can fight the invisible.'

'And I'm not just any target for you, Nate. You care about me. You couldn't hide the evidence of that. You can't deny it.'

'How I feel makes no difference.'

'Bullshit! It makes *every* difference. You have lived with what you did to me every day. This *is* your path to absolution. If you go back on it, it will destroy you and you know it.'

'Caring about you will also destroy me, Ember. I'm fucked either way. I was fucked from the moment I didn't drag you out of that wardrobe and hand you over. All I've been doing these past few weeks is putting off the inevitable. The Hordas clan are impossible to beat and that's only been confirmed now. You're only going to increase that infallibility.'

'Unless I'm just as much the key to changing that.'

'We don't have time to deliberate and find solutions. We don't have the resources or the information.'

'How long have we got?'

'Not long enough.'

If he'd made his mind up – truly made his mind up – she would have been dead already. She had to cling on to the hope of that.

He still didn't trust that if they caught her, she wouldn't drop him in it. And why wouldn't she? He'd seen that vengeful side to her. He'd seen her try to hire him to kill the Hordas clan. He knew she had it in her. He had no reason not to believe she wouldn't turn that on him if she didn't get what she wanted.

But her focus needed to remain on getting out of there and across that border, and the only way she could do that was to find the answer he was seeking. Somehow she had to persuade him to trust her. To trust the kind who had already betrayed him and cursed him with the life he now led.

'I have no intention of telling the Hordas clan about you,' she said. 'I wouldn't do that. You gave me a chance that day. You gave me a fair shot of getting out of this district instead of already being with *them*. Amidst all of this, I owe you for that. And if you help me get across the border, I will owe you even more. And what about you? What are the consequences for you if you don't see through on this deal?'

'I'm more than capable of looking after myself.'

'But you're going through all this because, either way, you've already made up your mind they're not getting me.'

He sat on the edge of the sofa, his knees spread, his elbows resting on them.

She stepped over to join him. She perched side-saddle on the sofa beside him.

'So let us put our heads together on this. As much for you as for me, you want a way out, so let's find it. Together.'

'Working together requires trust, Ember. I might feel something for you, I can't deny that, but trust is a different game.'

'I know you claim I don't know you and maybe you're right. But I know about your actions, your decisions and your choices up to this point. I know that they're more telling than maybe you intended them to be. Just by getting close to me, you let me in without even knowing it. And I guess that's why I started to care back. That's why I'm sat here now, trying to reason with you. We both have history with our respective kinds, with each other, but we can move on from that.

'Take me to that place. I am swearing to you right now that if something goes wrong, if we're found, I will say nothing of what has happened between us. You said yourself they have no connection to work on, that they don't even know I was there that night, let alone that you ever saw me.

'Is it not worth trusting me, taking this one risk to see if the answer is right there? Surely it's got to be worth a try. It *has* to be. Or if you truly have no hope, if you categorically don't believe there is any way out, end this right now.'

He could see in her eyes, in her composure, that she knew it was a reckless challenge she had laid in front of him, but she was not going to keep arguing with him. She was not going to agonise for hours to come over the decision he may or may not make.

Her curt breathing told him she was bracing herself, told him she remained smart enough to be prepared for the worse despite her convictions, despite her greater faith in him than he had in himself.

Ember who he now knew was totally alone. More alone than she knew yet.

Fuck, he cursed in his own head.

CHAPTER THIRTY-NINE

———◦◉◦———

Stood in the weak, morning light, Ember stared down the length of the tunnel ahead. It felt like the entrance to another world, the eerie light in the distance some hundred feet beyond looking as though it could lead to another plain.

It was nestled in an embankment, the barren trees the latter housed fighting for survival amidst the dry shrubbery and pollution-filled skies, fallen branches a testament to their struggle.

'How far in is it?' she asked, focusing her attention back on the way ahead.

'About a hundred feet in.'

The view was obscured from beyond half of that distance. Unease chilled the base of her spine as she felt as though eyes were staring back at her from behind their mask of darkness.

'It's pretty dark in there, Nate.'

'I can see far enough to tell you the coast is clear if that makes it easier?'

She met his gaze fleetingly. 'Maybe a little.'

'You wanted to do this, Ember.'

'I know. And I will.'

She glanced anxiously over her shoulder before looking back down the tunnel again. She *would* do it. For the sake of the lack of an alternative, she *would* go in there.

'Right,' she muttered, albeit with fervency. She switched on the torch Nate had given her. 'Let's get in there and take a look.'

She could feel the density of the atmosphere change, the acoustics of the tunnel making it feel as though it was instantly closing in on her. She walked closer to Nate than she intended, her eyes wide and wary beyond where the torchlight reached. Dankness and the underlying scent of mildew lingered in the air, the silence deafening beyond their footsteps.

'There,' Nate said, indicating to her left.

Ember shone the torch to where he was pointing, igniting a dark recess behind bars set within the stone tunnel wall.

Ember followed him over. 'That's it?'

'Based on Stirling's description,' he confirmed as he reached for one of the bars. He tugged on it but the barrier remained motionless. As if to further prove his point, he lifted his foot and booted it once and then twice, but it didn't so much as budge. He took a step back, his hands resting low on his hips. 'And as I said, it's impenetrable.'

Ember stepped up to it. She reached for one of the bars to give it a tug of her own.

And her hand went straight through it.

She jolted backwards, her startled gaze meeting Nate's.

His frown switched from her to the bars.

She reached for a different one, but her hand went straight through it again as if it wasn't there.

Nate grabbed hold of her upper arm a split-second later,

holding her back. He reached for the same two bars to check for himself but was instantly met with the concrete evidence that it was one rule for him and another for her.

'Clever,' she remarked, meeting his gaze again. 'A spell maybe?'

'Can you see what's beyond it?'

She looked back into the darkness. She shook her head as she reverted her attention to him. 'No. But it seems we've confirmed we're definitely in the right place though.' She glanced down at where he still held a tight grip on her arm. 'And you can let me go now. I'm not planning on diving in there if that's what you're thinking.'

But he didn't relinquish his hold as he stepped close to the bars again. He stuck his hand through the gaps, the correct laws of physics at least seeming to apply to that. He withdrew his hand and, with a pensive frown, he scanned the gateway again.

'Nate,' she said, trying to regain his attention. 'Maybe if you hold on to me, that'll work. Maybe I can take you through with me.'

He gave her a nod.

As he kept hold of her arm, avoiding skin-on-skin contact, she stepped forward, clearing the bars as if she'd done nothing more than step through a waterfall, a rush sweeping over her. But she jolted back before she had time to immerse herself in it, her gaze dropping to where Nate remained trapped on the other side.

She took a step back into the tunnel beside him. 'So what now? I need to take a look in there, Nate.'

'I don't like this. Not without knowing what's beyond.'

'Yeah, well, neither do I. But we can't just stand here.' She turned to face him fully. 'If you're worried I'm going to do a runner, I'm not. We're in this together.'

He held his gaze on hers for what felt like a lifetime.

'You need to trust me,' she said. 'We're here now. We might

not get another chance. Let's at least get something out of it or what was the point? The answer could be a matter of feet away.'

He glanced back ahead into the darkness before meeting her gaze again. 'If you get even the slightest uneasy feeling, you get your arse back here. Understood?'

'Anyone would think you were worried about me.'

He didn't respond. He didn't need to.

With a steadying breath, she stepped forward again. After the initial rush, the silence beyond the gate was even more overwhelming than it had been in the tunnel.

Ember glanced over her shoulder to where Nate gripped one of the bars, his other hand resting above his head against them. The unease etched on his face did nothing to appease her anxiety.

She shone her torch into the darkness ahead, the walls a collaboration of brick and rock. What looked like steps veered down to the left. There was nothing else.

'Shit,' she muttered under her breath, despite not meaning for it to come out loud.

'Hey,' Nate said, catching her arm again through the gap in the bars.

She flinched, her breath snagging, her attention snapping over her shoulder. 'For fuck's sake. I could really do without the surprises right now, Nate.'

He passed her phone through. 'The camera on this might be useful.' He handed her a flick knife as well. 'This too.'

She raised her eyebrows slightly. 'You're trusting me with those?'

'*And* trusting you to come back to me.'

She held his gaze; forgot the darkness behind her for a moment. 'I'll do my best.'

'You'd better.'

She broke a smile before turning away again.

'Ember,' he said.

She looked back over her shoulder.

Grabbing the edge of her coat, he tugged her towards him. His free hand was locked on the nape of her neck a second later. And, a second after that, she felt his lips against hers.

The kiss was lingering, warm, surprisingly tender.

And it was impossible for her not to reciprocate before remembering; before pulling back.

'I'm fine,' he reassured her as she searched his gaze, looking for any sign of pain. 'Go,' he said, releasing her before he stepped back from the bars into the shadows.

And she turned to face the darkness alone.

CHAPTER FORTY

———◦◦◦———

Nate pressed the heel of his hand against his chest as he watched Ember disappear into the darkness.

He fell back against the wall out of sight as the heart pangs intensified enough to restrict his breathing, the sensation of his chest being crushed making him light-headed enough to have to slide down the wall to the floor.

He clenched his right hand over his heart, slammed his left hand to the ground to stabilise himself. But the pain struck again, sending agonising pins and needles all down his left arm.

He lost balance.

His temple hit the ground.

The ceiling above him swayed and contracted as he rolled onto his back.

He gasped for air as it felt as though every artery was clogging.

The dark bubble around him faded in and out.

'*No,*' he said through gritted teeth, his frustration at his weakness doing nothing to appease the growing discomfort.

It was happening sooner than he thought: the intensity greater than he thought. He cared about her far more than he thought – and she about him.

Now more than ever, he *had* to last long enough to see it through.

CHAPTER FORTY-ONE

Ember kept the torchlight ahead, it wavering slightly as her hand trembled. Left hand plastered to the wall, she was mindful of her footing on the deep, narrow and uneven steps that tapered to her left.

But it was the feel of that wall that, more than the looming darkness beyond, had her halting for a moment. A wall that, with her increasing descent, should have felt cold to the touch. Even the air itself should have cooled but, instead, there was a subtle humidity that had become apparent over the course of the last few steps.

She glanced up over her shoulder to the blackened silence behind her, to where Nate lay some distance beyond. But if she retreated now, she knew she wouldn't find the courage to retrace her steps.

Finally reaching level ground, she shone her torch rapidly around the domed room, her breathing terse as she desperately searched for confirmation that she was alone. Within the confines of the space, no more than twenty feet in diameter, nothing but rock stared back at her. Nothing but rock and what looked like a tunnel, set a little to the right, directly ahead.

She cursed under her breath, the prospect of heading even deeper underground as unwanted as the chill at the base of her spine that was pulling her backwards again. But she crossed towards the tunnel regardless, the pounding of her heart painful, the thrum in her ears switching to tinnitus amidst the intensity of the silence.

As she faced the tunnel opening, her grip on her torch tightened.

Instead of dense darkness ahead, there was movement, the whole wall fifteen feet ahead rippling. She instinctively took a step back, until her eyes and brain connected, telling her they were flickers from somewhere beyond where the wall curved to the left, indicating the tunnel took another turning out of sight.

And amidst the subtle ripples, black markings were etched on the rock. If she'd had any doubt they'd made an error about the location, it dissipated. And if she'd had any conviction she'd made a mistake being there, it escalated.

It confirmed something was beyond that turning; something she needed to see. Something that could be the answer they were seeking.

She forced her sluggish feet to move forward despite their reluctance, the grip on her knife tightening. She veered left, following the path, the flickers then licking both sides of the tunnel and coating the rock with a warm amber glow.

Fire.

The breath snagged in the back of her throat, every instinct recognising the danger of fire in an enclosed space; an enclosed space with only one escape route.

She pressed forward, knowing she'd come too far to turn

back now – and emerged into another room built into the rock, this one shaped like a pentagram star. Markings dominated the walls amidst sporadic metal hoops that were embedded in the rock. But even the disturbing dungeon vibe was overpowered by what lay ahead. At the top point, a narrow and low archway led into what looked like a room of fire. Led into what looked like a furnace.

CHAPTER FORTY-TWO

Nate sensed her coming before he heard her. He pulled himself to his feet having shrugged off the pain that had since subsided in her absence, the relief of seeing her return in one piece over-riding anything else.

She stepped through the gate, her heart pounding audibly, her breathing ragged from running.

He gave her a moment to catch her breath whilst keeping a watchful eye on the darkness across his shoulder.

'It's something to do with fire,' she said. 'There's nothing but a furnace down there. That and a load of markings on the wall. She handed him her phone. 'Take a look.'

He swiftly skimmed through the images she had photo-graphed. Images he hoped he could work with.

He glanced into the depths of the tunnel again then back at her. 'Let's get out of here. We've been out here long enough.'

It would have made more sense to take the car, but he didn't want to risk it being seen parked up near the tunnel. Instead, he'd opted for them to walk it. He remained vigilant on the journey back, mindful of Ember but retaining his primary focus on any danger that might be closing in on them. It was less than a thirty-minute walk back to the loft but it felt more like two hours, not helped by the cold pang in the air that was exacerbated by the drizzle that lingered on their exposed skin.

Ember's arms were tightly folded across her chest but she still shivered beside him, her eyes lost in thought somewhere as they marched in silence. Her mind was no doubt working overtime as much as his was.

This time she willingly entered the doorway into the loft first.

'Why don't you take a shower,' he suggested. 'And warm yourself up. Then we can talk.'

She showed no resistance to the idea. Instead she handed him the knife he had loaned her. 'You might want this back.'

He hadn't forgotten he'd given it to her. He hadn't been negligent to the fact she could have tried to use it on him at any point during the return journey. As futile as she would have known it would have been, he'd had every confidence that wasn't why she hadn't made the attempt. Him letting her enter the tunnels without him had confirmed one thing: they *were* a team now. A team that had been sealed the second he'd not let her leave him without that kiss. Because he couldn't have let her go without doing it. If that had been the last time he saw her, he needed her to know he cared more than he'd allowed himself to express to her. Before he let her disappear, he'd needed to reassure her that they were on the same side. That he had accepted, in the face of her challenge to him, that he would fight to find an alternative outcome. He owed it to her. And she'd been right: he owed it to himself. He wasn't going to lose her because of them. They would have to rip her from his dead arms if that's what they wanted.

He accepted the knife without a word, Ember then making her way through to the bathroom.

Hearing the shower run, he headed behind the kitchen counter to make them both a coffee. As the percolator brewed, he started a fire in the grate. Taking the two coffees over to the table, he flicked through the images on her phone again and picked up the book of symbols.

He thumbed through the worn and blotched pages of archaic paper until he got to the section he was looking for. Reigniting the screen on the phone, he searched for any similarities.

Ember emerged wrapped in a towel, her skin a healthier shade of pink. She grabbed a clean sweater from the holdall he had packed for her and pulled it down over herself one-handed, covering herself in it to mid-thigh before relinquishing her towel. She returned the latter to the bathroom before joining him. Grabbing the blanket she'd adopted, she draped it over her bare legs.

Her eyes meeting his swiftly told him she'd noticed his admiring glances, his gaze having lingered a moment longer than it should have on her exposed skin before she'd covered up.

Sat there, her hair still damp from the shower, her skin scrubbed free of make-up as per usual, she couldn't have looked more at home. Her presence there had never made it *feel* more like home.

He handed her the coffee he'd made her, Ember accepting it with a small, grateful smile. 'Any luck?'

'Nothing beyond the obvious,' he said, placing the phone down on the book and sliding both towards her. 'The only symbol that matches one in here is that one. It refers to fire that can exist without oxygen, that keeps burning: everlasting fire. It's part of whatever the magic is but how, I don't know. Whatever the other symbols mean is a well-concealed secret.'

'When you say "everlasting", we can't put it out? So that isn't the answer?'

'Everlasting means everlasting.'

She sighed heavily as she lifted the cup to her lips, her gaze distant and pensive. 'What are we missing?' she muttered to herself. 'What questions are we not asking?'

A minute or so later, she met his gaze again.

'Nate, if they can *already* do whatever it is that they're doing, and if no one has ever told them I exist, why are they looking for me now? Why do they need me at all?'

It was the question he'd hoped she wouldn't ask – the one thing Stirling had revealed that Nate didn't want her to know. He shouldn't have hesitated over telling her, the fact it was difficult to do so reinforcing that he was already in too deep.

Her eyes were laced with expectation, as if she already sensed he was holding something valuable back.

'In order for the locator to work, the deceased blood they used had to be recent, Ember. That's why they couldn't have tracked you up to now, even if they had wanted to – not without sacrificing what they already had.'

Her jaw slackened. Her brow furrowed.

'Stirling told me your brother was killed three weeks ago, Ember.'

Despite the shock and despair in her eyes, he knew it was important that he kept going – that he gave her as many facts as he could as quickly as he could so she had the whole story.

'After the Cordell brothers failed to assassinate Antonia and Jonah, the Voys knew something underhanded was happening. They sent someone in to infiltrate the Hordas clan. They'd spent months building up to it to get a girl on the inside who could get through all the security. And once she was in, she worked it out – that their power was something to do with your brother.

So she spent months more getting close to him, gaining trust to build up to the point of being alone with him. And when she finally was, she killed him.'

He gave her a moment to process it before continuing.

'Soon after, the Hordas clan put a call out for me which is why I think the Voys tried to get to me first. It wouldn't have taken a genius to work out I was being hired to do something about it. There was no way the Voys could know what that was, but neither were they willing to take any chances.'

Her frown deepened. 'The spell needs to be renewed, doesn't it? That's why they're trying to find me.'

'Yes.'

'That's why they wanted the best on this job. Because if they *don't* get their hands on me, they're going to lose their ability.'

He didn't need to say anything to confirm.

'Do you know how long will it take for their ability to fade?'

'No.'

Her gaze dropped. When she looked back at him, the wariness behind her eyes was intense. 'But when it does fade, you can go after them. You just need to make sure they don't find me in the meantime. That's why you've been considering taking me out of the equation. You can't keep me here because being close to me is bad news for you. I put you at risk more than they do. The way you kissed me down in that tunnel ... this is more than feelings between us – you're falling for me, aren't you? Like I'm falling for you.'

It was another question he hoped she wouldn't ask, but he shouldn't have expected anything less. It was the most pertinent question of all. The most pertinent statement of all. A statement on her part that stirred a sensation he hadn't felt in decades. That just by saying it, by recognising and accepting her own feelings even after all he had done, being able to feel anything for him at all after all he had done, was maybe the most significant absolution of all.

'I've tried not to,' he said. 'But it's not easy. It's never been easy. And it has become less easy.'

Her eyes searched his. 'Even if we find a way out of this, we can't be together, can we? Not outside of here?'

'If we fell for each other? *Truly* fell for each other? One mistake, one single touch of mutual affection outside of these walls, and I'd be dead. I wouldn't even be able to protect you out there any more.' He held her gaze in the silence. 'I'm going to get you to Midtown. We'll take the chance. But you cannot return, is that clear?'

'But if you fail to deliver, they'll come for you.'

'It's better that I only have myself to look after instead of having to look out for you too.'

'Give me some time. I'll think of something.'

'Ember, an hour ago all you wanted was out of here. I'm offering you that.'

'And leave you behind no further ahead? There is a solution to this. I know there is. We're still missing something.'

'Once that border closes to you, the situation worsens for us both. You'd be trapped in here for good. There would be no other alternative. We have to get you out of this district. That's the only thing to do.'

Nate moved to stand.

Ember caught his arm in a silent request for him to stay next to her. She held his gaze as the flames danced on the side of his face. 'If it wasn't for any of this, would you want to be with me?'

'That's irrelevant, Ember.'

'No, it's not.'

'*She* made it irrelevant, Ember. I choose not to think about what might have been.'

'There has to be a way to lift that curse on you, Nate. There has to be something we can do about that too.'

'And I told you there's not. You'll leave and I'll move on. That's all there is. That's all there can ever be.'

'But you didn't answer my question.'

'I have spent six months gazing across a room at you. I have spent a significant amount of that time trying to keep you safe to ensure you'll get out of this district and to make sure no one ruins that for you like I once nearly did. I brought you here to buy us some time when it would have been easier to hand you over to them and walk away, whatever the consequences.

'But that's the problem, Ember: I walked away from you that first night and I haven't been able to walk away from you since. So, yes, I'm falling for you. But loving you would mean giving up my life for you only to lose you in the end anyway. I'm not that selfless. That bitch who cursed me might want me living in a constant loop of loss until I die, but I'm not giving her the satisfaction of leaving this world just yet.'

As he pulled away, Ember glanced at the flames. Like the spark that had first ignited them, she felt a warm glow of an idea inspired by Nate's words.

'Nate,' she said, pulling herself to her feet. 'I have an idea.'

CHAPTER FORTY-THREE

———◆———

'No,' Nate said, walking away. 'No way.'

'At least hear me out fully,' she said, following behind him.

He turned to face her. 'Hours, Ember. We have a matter of hours until you have to get to that border. If you go to them, you'll be kissing goodbye to all of that – to any chance of getting out.'

She could barely believe she was saying it. 'Then I won't leave Lowtown.'

His eyebrows lifted a fraction. '*What?*'

'I'm staying. I'm staying in Lowtown if it means I'll finish what they started.'

His frown was deep, his eyes laced with disapproval. 'Tell me I'm not hearing this. That, after *everything*, I'm not hearing this from you.'

'My plan will work, Nate.'

'A reckless plan, full of flaws.'

'But maybe the only chance we have. They will never see it

coming. And if you hand me over to them it might just lower their guard enough for us to pull this off.'

'And if we fail?'

'We won't.'

'Unless they join the dots the second they see you – see us together. One suspicion that I was working with you that time I went to them to do the deal and it'll be over.'

'They have no reason to suspect that was anything to do with me.'

'I said no, Ember.'

She watched him walk away. She stared at the back of him as he stood in front of the opaque glass windows, his hands low on his hips.

'You can't *force* me to cross that border, Nate. I go into that building alone. I sign those papers alone.'

He turned around, dropped his hands to his sides. His glare was intense enough for her instincts to force her to take an involuntarily step backwards, despite him being at least ten feet away.

'You're fucking crossing that border, Ember.'

She couldn't relent. Back down now and she knew any further argument would be negated.

'Or what?' She stared him down. 'I already told you, Nate: this is as much my battle, if not *more* my battle, than yours. I'm going to take them down. For what they did to me, to my family, for what they've put my friends through, for what they've put this entire district through, for what they did to Jasper, I'm going to destroy them. And I think this is how I can do it. Admit it – it's a good plan.'

He closed the gap between them. 'And what about what you said about your aunt? What about you crossing that border for her? What about it all being for nothing if you don't?'

'As opposed to bringing the Hordas clan down? As opposed

to giving this district what might be their only chance of getting back to what it once was? About trying to make things fair again?'

'Which will happen anyway if I take them down.'

'*If*. And only *if* they don't find me first. I'm not spending the next decade or two of my life, or however long it takes those bastards to die of natural causes, looking over my shoulder. I've spent my entire life doing that because of them. I'm fighting for my peace of mind here, Nate, as much as anything. I'm taking it back. I'm opting for the only guarantee we have of ending this. But I *need* your help. I can't pull this off without you. I need you to believe I can do this. That *we* can do this.' She reached for the hem of his T-shirt, scrunching it in her hand. 'Help me, Nate,' she said, gazing deep into his eyes. 'Help me destroy them. Help me bring the Hordas clan down. For good.'

CHAPTER FORTY-FOUR

Ember heard the displacement of gravel beneath the tyres, felt Nate's car slow down, and then everything became still and silent as he turned off the engine. The driver's door slammed, followed by a further crunch of gravel beneath footsteps approaching the boot where she lay contained.

Security light flooded the chasm, Nate's eyes immediately meeting hers. He held her gaze a moment longer than they both knew he should have, but she nodded to let him know she still wanted to proceed, even if her shallow breathing behind her gag betrayed to the contrary.

Nate swiftly lifted her out of the boot, her hands tied behind her back.

He slammed the boot shut before shoving her towards the steps that led up to the entrance of the house.

There was no need for him to knock. She stared down at the black and white checked tiled floor of the vestibule they passed through in silence, the dominating mustiness of the hallway filling her senses as the inner door was promptly closed behind them.

Ember glanced right at the blond guy who had closed the door before stepping back against the wall, his eyes scrutinising her.

'You know the rules, Nate,' a dark-haired guy said, closing in on them.

Nate handed over his gun before cupping his hands on the back of his head to allow the guy to frisk him.

'She's clean,' Nate said as the guy moved on to her. 'Obviously.'

She heard the minor snort before the guy frisked her too, her stomach curdling at the feel of his hands on her.

Finding them both clean of weapons, he backed up against the wall next to the door and folded his arms as he gave his second companion the nod. A companion she recognised: the curly-haired guy who had held a gun to Harry's head in the café. And from the telling look of surprise and suspicion in his eyes, he recognised her too.

He glanced at Nate. His gaze raked him warily. 'Wait here,' he said, before disappearing through the double-doors to her right.

It had to work. The plan *had* to work. They only had one shot at it.

For a few minutes, nothing happened. Whatever was being discussed behind the closed doors, they were taking their time over it.

Ember's heart leapt as the door eventually opened. The curly-haired guy stepped out first, before a woman followed behind him: tall, slender, elegantly dressed in a dark pencil skirt and cream blouse, her blonde hair tied in a chignon on the side of her temple. Last to exit the room was Jonah.

A knot tightened in the pit of her stomach. She clenched her jaw – an accumulation of fear at seeing him again, of not knowing what to expect, as well as abject disgust.

She glared squarely into his eyes as he stepped alongside his sister, the fleck of surprise in his eyes telling her he hadn't seen it coming either. The uncertainty that followed a second later confirmed what she had suspected: they needed her compliance. But his smirk established the biggest risk she was taking: his awareness that they had leverage over her.

She dragged her gaze back to Antonia who scrutinised her silently. She knew why: she was looking for physical similarities to Aidan. Maybe even to her father. Whether she would see any, she had no idea – but clearly Jonah had seen some resemblance back in the café, even if he couldn't place it out of context.

Antonia didn't say anything. Her expression gave nothing away. Instead she crouched side-saddle, her skirt sliding a few inches up her thighs with the motion. She poured something onto the floor before standing again.

Ember stared down at the red droplet that instantly beaded – not only beaded, but rolled. Rolled directly at her as if on a slope.

Despite the temptation to back away from it, Ember stayed rooted, knowing from Nate that this was the ultimate proof they'd be seeking that she was the one they wanted. She watched as the red bead rolled up her shoe before disappearing up under the leg of her jeans, the sensation it left in its wake like nothing more than a droplet of water.

Nothing else happened. Nothing but Antonia's smile. Nothing but Jonah's curt exhale before he folded his arms.

Placing one high-heeled foot in front of the other, Antonia strode towards Nate to stop at eye level with him. 'You took your time,' she said. 'But came good in the end as always, I see.'

'Like you said: as always, Antonia.'

'Untie her,' she said, addressing the blond guy, before clicking her fingers at the curly-haired guy. 'Let's not be uncivilised about this. We need to start as we mean to go on.'

Under any other circumstances, Ember would have already been lashing out the second she was free, but she remained as compliant as she could force herself to be. As soon as her hands were free though, she pulled down the gag and took her first uninterrupted breath in the past forty-five minutes.

'Antonia Hordas,' the woman said, her immaculately manicured hand outheld. 'It's a pleasure to meet you.'

Ember kept her hands to herself and responded only by holding Antonia's gaze.

'No need to look so anxious,' Antonia said with a smile that attempted to be warm. 'No harm is going to come to you. That's not what this is about.'

The curly-haired guy stepped in alongside her and opened the holdall for Nate to see the contents.

'Payment in full,' Antonia said, reverting her attention back to Nate. 'As agreed.'

'I'll refrain from checking.'

'I'd prefer it that way,' Antonia said. 'Less insulting.'

'And I'd prefer it if I could be extended the same courtesy next time,' he declared.

Antonia broke another smile, albeit less sincere. 'Thank you for your usual efficiency, Nate. I believe we're done now.'

Ember's stomach flipped. This was it. This was the point from which she'd be totally alone. This could potentially be the last time she ever saw him. This was the point where he could let her down. Or they would pursue him, as they anticipated, and succeed. They'd be watching him exit. They'd be watching him leave the grounds. They'd be watching him get far away from there. And then they'd make sure he didn't return.

The sudden pain in her chest wasn't eased as Nate avoided meeting her gaze – her last chance to connect with him for maybe the final time. The subtlest spark of paranoia raked through her but she knew she couldn't let it take its hold. Nate was doing exactly what they planned for him to do: leave without quibble.

And Ember didn't look over her shoulder, despite the overpowering need to do so. Instead she maintained the illusion.

'Please,' Antonia said, indicating the room she had emerged from. 'Let's take a seat.'

The Georgian room was grand and immaculately decorated. The pale lemon walls contrasting with the white ornate ceiling gave it a sense of freshness, of warmth even – of relaxed summer days long lost to Lowtown for decades now. The irony was far from lost on her.

Antonia swept her hand towards the low-backed, oversized armchair flanked by adjacent matching sofas. 'Make yourself comfortable.'

Jonah Hordas immediately took the seat to the left of the chair, his composure in her presence grating on every nerve.

Antonia took her seat opposite her brother as a tray of fine china was simultaneously placed on the coffee table between them.

Silence lingered as hot drinks were poured before the guy exited the room, the doors closed behind him by the curly-haired guy who now flanked the door, his hands cupped in front of his groin, his gaze averted and fixed ahead. There was no doubt in her mind that Stirling would have filled the space to his left if he'd still been alive.

Ember opted to retain her silence as she perched on the very edge of the chair.

'Ember, isn't it?' Jonah said, breaking the silence. 'I'm afraid my memory didn't quite serve me correctly but, fortunately, Charlie is better with names than me.'

Ember glanced over her shoulder at the curly-haired guy

whose name she now knew – as irrelevant as it was. As clearly irrelevant as she had been to Jonah at the time he'd turned her life upside down, so as not to even remember what she was called.

Jonah smiled – the same kind of smile he'd given Harry before he'd made him a deal he'd had no option but to accept. 'See, I knew there was something familiar about you. Now I can see why. This is certainly quite the unexpected eventuality. And not the best of introductions the first time we met, I'm sure we can agree.'

Ember remained resolute to keep playing along. Her success depended on her playing along. 'What do you mean you can see why?'

'I can only apologise for my brother's behaviour, Ember,' Antonia interjected. 'He filled me in briefly on what happened at Harry's. He can be somewhat *over-zealous* sometimes.'

'Over-zealous?' It took all her inner strength to refrain from letting the full force of her feelings explode. She glared directly at Antonia. 'He threatened my friends. He beat an old man to death in front of me. An old man who was simply trying to defend me from being exposed and mauled by a complete stranger who viewed me as nothing more than an expendable piece of meat. You refer to that as "over-zealous"?'

Antonia's eyes flared under the intensity of Ember's glare, clearly not used to being challenged so directly.

'*Why* am I here?' Ember demanded – again needing to maintain the illusion that she was clueless as to their intent. She transferred her glare to Jonah. 'To polish your floors?'

Based on his previous behaviour, she had no doubt that, had he not needed her, she would have already received a sharp backhand for her insolence.

But it was abundantly clear as to who was in charge between

the two siblings, who had laid down the code of conduct prior to greeting her in the foyer. And Ember was going to make the most of it.

'Nothing is sexier than a woman on all fours apparently, Antonia. Did you know that?' Ember remarked.

Jonah's attention darted to his sister who reciprocated with a burning glare.

'I can assure you there will be no polishing of our floors here,' Antonia said, reverting her attention back to Ember, seemingly keen to bridge the gap.

They needed her compliance. Just as Ember had suspected, they needed her on board – at least until the point they decided threats were a better option. She needed to avoid the latter.

'So why *am* I here?' she asked. 'Harry told us all you wanted nothing more to do with the café. He said you were going to leave us alone.'

Antonia crossed her legs and interlaced her hands before resting them on the sofa arm nearest to Ember. Turning her body towards Ember, her feet remained pointing in her brother's direction, betraying that he was an equal part of this conversation despite Antonia's attempt to convey a very different message to her. 'This is nothing to do with the café, Ember. This is about something entirely different. This is about you being a part of our family.'

Nate drove away from the house. He knew they'd be watching. He knew they would follow.

He'd told Ember how much time he would need. He'd told her she'd need to keep them talking for a fair while. Fortunately, by the appearance of it, Antonia and Jonah had been in no particular hurry – the only thing that had reassured him enough to leave Ember behind. Because despite having known it would be tough, not even he had anticipated just how hard it would be walking away. If either of them failed, that would very likely be the last he'd ever see of her.

If either of them failed, the weight on his shoulders would be even greater – that his feelings for Ember would have brought about even greater power for the Hordas clan, and even greater devastation for Lowtown as a result. The Hordas clan would be unstoppable.

'I'll agree to this on one condition,' he'd said to her. 'If we pull this off, and if we pull it off in time, you're going to cross that border.'

She'd been hesitant, holding his gaze for far longer than he'd been happy with.

'I mean it, Ember. I want your word on this. If I have the slightest doubt that you won't, then my answer is no.'

She'd dropped her gaze.

He'd pulled away. 'Fine.'

'OK,' she'd said. 'If we pull this off in time, I'll leave. I promise you.'

Now he headed to the one place he knew he could lose his pursuers.

He pulled up not far from The Hive. He parked his car and headed to the discreet outer door. Even if they talked their way inside, they'd never find him in the warren – and they'd know it. Instead, logic dictated they'd wait outside, watching his car, awaiting his return. Further logic dictated he could be quite some time.

Once inside, he headed through the maze. He emerged out in a small side lane known only to the regulars – to the *real* insiders.

He pulled up his hood, took a right and headed out onto the rain-soaked street.

As their attention remained on waiting for him, he needed to turn his attention to making sure he didn't fail on his side of the deal.

That he didn't let Ember down.

CHAPTER FORTY-FIVE

Silence descended on the room as Antonia's words echoed repeatedly in Ember's ears despite her only having said it once. She was speaking figuratively – there was no other explanation.

'I'm *nothing* to do with you,' Ember finally said, looking her directly in the eyes.

'But you are,' Antonia said. There was a slight pause. 'Jonah, give us a few minutes, will you?' The tone betrayed that it was more a directive than a request.

Ember couldn't even bear to look at him again, her attention fixed on Antonia instead. She didn't even check over her shoulder once she heard the door close behind her, Charlie following suit.

It was a risk, but clearly one Antonia was willing to take. Clearly one she was willing to take to try and create some semblance of trust. And one Ember now knew she could afford to take considering the ability that had somehow been bestowed upon her.

'By a distant bloodline, you are,' Antonia said, leaning forward to pour them both a hot drink. She glanced sideways to study Ember's gaze as if calculating every response. She sat upright again. Her frown of confusion could almost be mistaken as genuine. 'You truly know nothing about this, do you?'

Ember shook her head, refusing to believe anything that fell out of Antonia's mouth regardless of what it was.

'You're a witch, Ember. You must at least know that much.'

'Non-practising.'

'Nonetheless, our families span way back – back to a time when a witch and a regular human fell in love, against his coven's wishes. He bestowed a gift on her: the gift of ultimate protection. They went on to have two children and, sure enough, one had the gift and one did not.'

The gift of precognition. A gift that Ember knew she didn't possess, practising or not.

'And so it began,' Antonia continued. 'From then on, those with the gift would protect those without it. A pact within an ever-expanding family, with those who carried the gift recompensing those who did not. Your father understood this and he helped us willingly, Ember, as did your brother.'

Her father, yes. She'd got her head around that. But Aidan too? He would never have known any different though. Would have never known any better.

Antonia waited for Ember to absorb all she had been told as she finished pouring them both a drink before placing the cup and saucer in front of Ember with a hand that was as steady as her gaze.

'My brother was stolen as a child,' Ember stated.

'Not stolen, Ember. He was brought home. By your father. By your family.'

She couldn't respond too quickly. She needed to remember

that she was hearing it all for the first time. Unconvinced she was that good an actress, she dropped her gaze, she lowered her head.

'Of course, we knew nothing of *your* existence, Ember. I can't believe you've been here in Lowtown all this time. Living that kind of life when you could have been with us.'

Ember stared back at her. 'There's nothing wrong with my life.'

'Compared with what you could have with us? There is little we can't offer you: just as we offered your father and your brother. It might not be Summerton or Midtown, but we can offer you as close as it gets: freedom, protection, no need to slog in that café every day; the best food, the best clothes, whatever male companionship you desire. We can offer you sanctuary here. You'll never have to worry again. You are very precious to us and we will treat you as such.'

'By being kept a prisoner here?'

'Not a prisoner. Anything but a prisoner. Frank came and went as he chose, with security for his own benefit of course. Aidan was exactly the same.'

'And what is this best of the best to be built on?' Ember asked. 'The misery of other people? People such as those I care about? Profiteering from keeping them in their place? Are you telling me my family was willing advocates of that? That my father was? That my brother was?'

It had been hard enough when Nate had alluded to it, but now she was hearing the evidence direct from the source. Worse, there was nothing contrite behind Antonia's eyes.

'If we don't manage Lowtown, if we don't stay on top, someone else will. It's human nature.'

'Not all human nature,' Ember counter-argued. 'Not everybody wants to be in charge. Not everybody wants to control others. Not everyone is willing to go to the lengths I saw that night your brother murdered an elderly man in order to get his own way.'

'I can assure you, that's not my brother's usual practice.'

'It looked pretty usual to me. And now I find out it has all been nothing but cheating. That you're using magic to maintain this level of power.'

'Succeeding always requires a little bit of cheating, Ember. As I said, if we don't succeed, someone else will. All we're doing is safeguarding our interests.'

'Whilst trampling on everyone else's? And you expect me to help you with that? Help you use magic to monopolise this district to the point of crushing it?'

'We are looking after this district's interests as much as our own.'

'Rather than people being able to stand up for themselves if there was an equal footing in this?'

'Freedom is not always a blessing.'

'But it should at least be a choice.'

'Shall I tell you why you're here now, Ember? Shall I tell you how we found you? You're here because your brother is dead. Assassinated three weeks ago by the second biggest cohort in this district: the Voys. They spent two years planning it. Two years getting a girl in here worming her way into your brother's affections so as to drop his guard enough to be alone with him. And then she murdered him. All of that so *they* could be in charge.'

Ember did her best to look shocked at her brother's death, still numb from the grief of hearing of it less than a few hours before; the brother she never knew, but she felt the missing piece regardless.

'Don't you worry though,' Antonia declared with a smile. 'She suffered for it. She suffered for days for it. Indignities, humiliation, more than any woman could bear. Sufficient that, in the end, she opted to take her own life – just like she'd taken Aidan's.'

There was no remorse in Antonia's eyes, only triumph – amusement almost.

'The brother who never told you about me. If this is such a paradise, why not? If this is such a great set-up, why did he keep me a secret?'

'I can only believe he never remembered you,' Antonia said. 'He never spoke of you.'

Too traumatised by what he'd seen, it was a possibility. But so was him being smart enough, even as a young child, to keep the secret to himself.

'And my mother? If the set-up is so great here, why was she in hiding? Why was she hiding me and my brother from you? Why did my father have to wrench my brother from her?'

'Because she knew how committed Frank was to us and she never understood it. They split over her disagreement that any children they would have would live under our protection. For a long time, we thought Frank was incapable of conceiving children. He tried for so long. And then, one day, he stumbled on your mother out with your brother. He would never have known the child was his if she hadn't run.'

She frowned. 'Has my brother had children? Do I have a niece or a nephew here?'

'I wish I could tell you yes.'

Her heart pounded harder as the true extent of their plan unfolded before her. 'You need to keep the generation going. You need *me* to keep it going.'

Antonia's silence did nothing to appease Ember's disgust at their intention for her.

'The deal is simple,' Antonia eventually said. 'We need you

to sustain our way of living; the level of *protection* that sustains our way of living.'

'How?'

'By granting us the same skill that your family has for generations, that's all. By granting us the ability to foresee the actions of those who would otherwise have already destroyed us. By using what you have inherited for the very purpose for which it was intended.'

'Whatever it is, I'm certain it was not intended for you to use it to bully, oppress and control. How could you possibly expect me to agree to any of this? I'm assuming you do need my consent or we wouldn't even be having this discussion.'

Antonia was trying to stay calm, to remain compromising, but Ember could see the tension in her hands, the frustration etched on her face. Frustration that was escalating. 'I know what my brother did. He behaved badly. Inexcusably. He *will* make it up to those he has hurt.'

'He's going to bring Jasper back from the dead, is he?'

'No, but he will do whatever else it takes. Work with us and you can turn this into an advantage for your friends. You could do a lot to improve their way of life. We're always looking for sponsorship opportunities. It could get them out of a lot of difficult situations. And, in time, just like your father used to do, you could assist us in the running of our businesses. If you don't like the way we operate, you can help with our decision-making. Help us shape how we manage things from here on. Maybe you could do some amazing things for this district if you have better ideas than ours. We would have a vested interest in listening, of course.'

'Until I reproduce for you and then you can brainwash my child instead. Just like you brainwashed Aidan.'

Antonia reached for her cup and saucer. She took a gentle sip before placing the cup back on the saucer. 'I understand your reticence,' she said. 'Truly I do. This must all be a terrible shock to you. What you need to know though, Ember, is that other than your particular gift, you are quite helpless. You're not a caster. There are no spells that can leak from your lips or your fingertips. You are actually quite harmless. But the power you can bring about with your co-operation is immense. Think about your friends. Think about Harry. Think of the premises he could get – the support, the resources, and the protection. And think about his daughters: bright, attractive young women. How much longer are they going to survive under this remit compared with what they could have if they had the financial backing to move elsewhere?'

She placed the cup and saucer back on the table.

'And then there's Casey,' Antonia added.

Ember's stomach flipped at the mention of her name.

Antonia rested her elbow on the arm of the sofa, her gaze direct. 'You could have so much influence over what happens with Casey. She's a stunning girl. Young. Fit. Healthy. Fertile, hopefully. I understand that my brother has taken quite the shine to her.'

And there it was: their awareness of her weakness. Ember's heart thudded faster at Antonia's clear intent. Worse, at Jonah's clear intent. An intent they had already discussed.

Antonia's lips curled into a slight smile that didn't resonate in her eyes. 'You might like the thought of your young building the next generation with Casey's young – our families reunited. Maybe you will go on to choose a different path for us to take when the time comes. Or maybe you'll come to see why we do what we do and how we do it.' She paused. 'Or maybe you'd rather Casey not be involved at all. Maybe you'd like to see her still working with Harry but under better conditions. Maybe for her to be in prime position to help her mother access what she needs. That's all under your control, Ember. If you're a part of this family, that's the kind of power you will have: to change or to safeguard the lives of those you care about. Are you going to tell me that's wrong? Is it wrong for me to offer you the best possible life you could get in this district? To offer a better life for your friends? To offer you a stake in the business that you so clearly currently disagree with the practices of?'

Ember knew that, under any other circumstances, Antonia was making her an offer she would be unable to refuse. And she knew, above all else, that if she failed in what she needed to do, it *would* be her friends who paid the price. Antonia didn't need to say it. Antonia didn't need to say anything more.

But Antonia continued regardless.

'Let's keep it blunt between us girls. I think what I'm offering, what I'm willing to negotiate on, is more than fair.' She held Ember's gaze for what felt like minutes. 'And I think it would be extremely unfair of *you* to turn my offer down. In fact, I will be offended. Offended enough that you will learn why *I'm* in charge of this operation and not my brother.'

'How do I know you would keep to your word on any of what you've said?'

'Why would I not? Ember . . . ' She leaned closer. 'I want to work *with* you, not against you. I know it will take time to build the trust between us. I'm not unreasonable.'

And that was the point Ember had needed to get her to. That was her way in.

'I want to know exactly what's involved,' Ember said. 'I want to know what it is that I'm supposed to do. If you want us to start working together, I want transparency from the outset.'

Antonia's eyes narrowed a little as she studied her pensively.

'If you want to build the trust between us,' Ember added. 'Let's start now.'

CHAPTER FORTY-SIX

———◦———

'I like you, Ember,' Antonia declared, sat next to her in the back of the car. 'You're a woman after my own heart.'

Ember glanced at Jonah in the front passenger seat. In the distance, she could see the first signs of the tunnel.

Antonia smiled across at her. 'A hard negotiator. But a smart one. Both attributes I appreciate. I think I'm going to like having you around.'

She caught a glimpse of Jonah and Antonia subtly exchanging glances in the passenger mirror, the smirk on Jonah's face betraying how much they were humouring her.

Ember looked through the windscreen as the car came to a standstill.

'I'm not so stupid as to not consider making this advantageous for my friends, Antonia. As long as you know that's the only reason I'm willing to be a part of this. Not that I had any option to the contrary from the way you put it.'

'My job is to protect what my family have spent decades in

this district securing. To put *us* first. The Hordas clan will *always* come first. That's what families do: they look after their own. Blood above water – every time. And in time, you'll come to understand that. You'll see why we need to do this. That this really is the only way to survive.'

The car pulled over. The driver opened the door for Antonia, Jonah promptly following by doing the same for Ember.

She met his gaze as she stepped out, her skin crawling at his proximity despite the door being a barrier between them. His sustained gaze echoed his arrogance, that sense of him believing himself to be untouchable.

She would do everything she could to prove him wrong. To prove them both wrong.

She broke away first, unable to look at him any more. The prospect of him having his intentions towards Casey, of what he planned to do, curdled her stomach.

Just like the last time she'd been there, Ember looked down the mouth of the tunnel, deep into the darkness beyond. Except, this time, she could only hope there *were* eyes looking back at her: Nate's eyes as he kept himself concealed out of sight.

Easily three hours had passed since he'd left her. It should have granted him enough time. And, so far, Antonia and Jonah had bitten her request. They'd gone exactly where she needed them to go, aided by their attention being on making sure no one was following them, not on the prospect of Nate getting there ahead of them.

'Here?' she asked, feigning ignorance. 'There's nothing here.'

'There's always been something here,' Antonia said. 'For as long as can be remembered.'

She indicated the way ahead; indicated for Ember to join her and Jonah.

Antonia and Jonah flanked Ember as they all headed into the darkness of the tunnel, Jonah carrying a small metal case that he'd brought with him. Two others marched ahead of them, their torches on full beam. The two behind followed suit.

As Antonia and Jonah stopped outside the barred opening in the rock, one of the front-running bodyguards headed deeper into the darkness ahead, the other flanking to the right of the gateway. Of those bringing up the rear, one marked the left of the gateway whilst the other turned his attention back to the tunnel opening. This was well-practised protocol. This was routine.

'This is a gateway reserved only for us,' Antonia said. 'No one outside of our bloodlines can pass through. You don't need to let your eyes deceive you.'

Antonia stepped forward, walking straight through the bars as if they weren't there – just like Ember herself had done the night before.

Jonah held his palm out in his sister's direction as a directive for Ember to follow next. 'Walk ahead as though nothing is there.'

She knew she had to show at least some hesitancy – some wariness and apprehension. 'What's in there?'

'Absolutely nothing you need to be scared of,' Jonah reassured her.

As if she would accept any reassurance from him.

Ember scanned the gateway, only too aware that Antonia was watching her from the darkness on the other side. After giving a few plausible seconds of further hesitation, Ember stepped through.

The same breeze whipped through her hair as last time. Her stomach flipped again as if an elevator had suddenly dropped two floors. She stabilised quickly though, in time for Jonah to follow behind her.

'No doubting who you are now,' Antonia remarked, flashing her a smile. And no doubt the final confirmation they had wanted, hence them complying so easily with her request to go there. 'Come this way.'

She followed behind Antonia whose torchlight led the way.

'After you,' Antonia said, indicating the top step that Ember knew led the way to a spiralling descent to the cavern below.

If she hadn't known where they led, if she hadn't been so convinced Antonia and Jonah needed her alive, she would have had to have been dragged down there. Instead, she took the lead as Antonia had requested – neither her nor Jonah seemingly willing to risk going ahead of her.

As they crossed the first cavern, the familiar flicker appeared on the wall at the end of the tunnel that lay directly ahead. A flicker Ember now understood. A flicker that intensified as they turned left again down the narrow stone corridor.

Instantly, exactly as it had last time, the warmth of the roaring furnace gave the room the humidity of a hothouse, amber flames dancing around her feet as they reflected on the rock. Perspiration coated her forehead and the back of her neck already, though she had no doubt the heat couldn't be held solely responsible.

Antonia stepped up to within two feet of the archway. 'It never goes out,' she said. 'Not for as long as one of your bloodline is still alive. That's how we discovered you existed; that you were out there somewhere. We came here expecting to find this fire dead when Aidan was murdered, yet it still raged. That's when we set out on a mission to discover a way to find you.'

And had found the existence of the locator.

'That's what this is? Some kind of beacon?'

'No, that's only the bonus. The furnace exists to protect what's inside.'

'Which is?'

'Green prehnite, Ember. The crystal responsible for the gift of prophecy. The crystal that enhances precognition. An extremely rare version of it. That's why this fire exists: to make sure no one can get their hands on it except for a very particular type of elemental. A very particular descendant.'

Ember's chest tightened as she looked into the flames. Her attention snapped back to Antonia, to Jonah.

That was the reason they needed her. It was nothing to do with her ability to predict what was going to happen – it was her ability to get her hands on what they needed in order for them to be able to do so.

'What is it you expect me to do?'

'We expect you to go in and collect it for us,' Antonia said.

Fire: *that* was her element. Fire was what they expected her to be able to control.

'How exactly? By somehow extinguishing the furnace? By clearing a path?'

Antonia and Jonah exchanged glances, the meaning unclear.

'You don't need to clear a path, Ember,' Antonia added, looking back at her.

'You expect me to go *in* there?' she exclaimed, pointing back at the archway. 'You expect me to walk into a blazing furnace?'

Both looked at her as if they were merely suggesting she step out of the front door to be greeted with a warm, sunny day.

'It's completely harmless to you,' Antonia declared. She frowned pensively. 'You didn't know that?'

'I've never been compelled to shove my hand in a hot flame to test a theory I didn't even know existed,' Ember remarked. 'Oddly enough.'

'But you were never told about your affinity?'

'No. And even if you're right, even if I do have the ability to control it, I'm not a practising witch. I've never practised. It takes years for elements to be able to hone their skills. I won't be able to control anything of that intensity.'

'You don't need to control it. As I said, you merely need to walk through it. That's all that's required. That's all we've ever required. Simple. Painless. And quick,' Antonia remarked. A smile swiftly followed. 'I keep telling you: none of this is intended to bring you harm. In less than a minute, you can change your life for the better, as well as the lives of those you care about. All you have to do is go in there.'

Nate waited against the wall in the darkest depths of the tunnel.

Amidst the silence, he did what all his kind could do: he slowed his heart rate and slowed his breathing with it, making him impossible to detect.

In the distance, he saw Ember enter with Antonia and Jonah, two bodyguards in front of them, two behind.

An alarm call from any one of them and it was over. Antonia and Jonah would suspect foul play and his and Ember's only chance would be gone. Worse, Ember would be trapped behind the gateway with them – with Antonia *and* with Jonah – and he'd have no way of getting to her.

He couldn't fuck up. There was no way he was going to fuck up.

Two of the guards flanked the gateway. The other two manoeuvred away, one heading back towards the tunnel opening, the other heading in his direction.

He watched Antonia pass through the gateway first. There was a pause, some hesitation from Ember, before she followed. Jonah entered last.

And she was gone. Gone from his reach. Too far gone for him to be able to do anything to help her now, other than what they had planned.

'You don't like working with other people, do you, Nate?' Ember's father had said to him, clumping into the passenger seat of the car, his gaze scrutinising.

'I'm glad it shows,' Nate had remarked, hoping they'd keep conversation to a minimum.

'The Hordas clan tell me you're the best.'

'I am.' He'd paused. He'd met Frank's gaze in the dim interior. '*Because* I don't work with anyone else.'

Frank had laughed, his nonchalance considering what they were about to do grating more than he'd liked.

'And why not, Nate?'

'Because I don't trust anyone enough to put my life in their hands,' he'd said, meeting Frank's gaze once more, before driving away.

Driving to end up meeting the very girl who he now depended on being able to pull this off – for both their sakes.

Because however successful he was, he still needed her to succeed on the inside. If they stepped back outside the gateway to find their guards dead, it was game over. He wouldn't be able to take a shot at them even if he wanted to. The logistics, the timeframe, were too greatly in their favour. They could get all the backup there that they wanted. One call, and it was over.

One call, and he knew he'd never see Ember again.

'If you screw this up, Ember,' he'd said.

'I won't,' she'd promised him. 'You do your part and I'll do mine.'

'How long?'

'We worked it out that it took me roughly five minutes to get down there, right?'

'Going slow, yes.'

'So we can expect it will be approximately the same this time around. I can get back up in half that time. I don't know how long it will take once I'm down there but, to be safe, I think you're going to need to have your part done within twenty minutes maximum of us passing through that gateway. Can you do that?'

He'd sighed heavily before folding his arms. 'Twenty?'

She nodded.

'We need to make sure we get you to that border in time, Ember. That's the deal. So I'll get it done in fifteen.'

CHAPTER FORTY-SEVEN

Ember stood in front of the furnace.

'Try it,' Antonia said. 'See for yourself. It truly is quite harmless to you. I promise you.'

She glanced over her shoulder at them both, their eyes silently willing her on.

'See how close you can get,' Antonia added. 'Feel it.'

It was their final test. That was why they had agreed to taking her there. Antonia wasn't one to be held to ransom – it had been their intention from the moment she had arrived. And, for her, that made it all so much easier. *If* she could find the courage to do as they asked.

Ten minutes had to have already passed. In the time they took to explain, in the time she took to deliberate, at least that much time must have passed. The clock was ticking down.

But there was one more thing she needed to understand.

'I don't get it,' she said. 'Surely it would have been good news if the furnace had gone out. If that's the only thing blocking you from getting to the prehnite for yourselves.'

'Ember, that fire is the only thing that keeps the gateway open. If that fire goes out, the prehnite will be locked within the rock forever.'

Unable to lose any more time, Ember stepped up to the archway.

She'd had no idea what to expect: whether for the flames to dissipate, the fire to go out, or the flames to part around her. What she hadn't expected was to feel a chill instead of heat the second she reached inside, as though she'd put her hand in a fountain of cold water. She'd known at the time that it could have been her brain playing tricks on her to counteract the pain, like feeling cold when running a hand under a scalding tap. But as she'd stared at her hand, there was no sign of blistering or melting or peeling of skin. There was no sickening scent of burning human flesh. She hadn't burned at all. Instead, the flames that encompassed her hand ignited in violet before becoming ethereal wisps that felt like a cool breeze against her skin, caressing her hand instead of scorching her.

If she'd ever doubted what she was, that doubt had melted away in those moments.

As she'd caught her breath, as she withdrew her hand again, she felt Antonia and Jonah's tension ease behind her.

She'd looked back across her shoulder at them. Their exchange of smiles, their smile at her, told her she had further passed their test.

She turned to face them. She needed to find a moment of opportunity. She needed to make her move when they least expected it. She needed that moment of distraction. She needed their guards down completely.

'I go in there and then what?' she asked.

'You want to try it?' Antonia asked.

'Yes.'

Jonah placed the case he'd brought with him on the floor. He clicked it open. He removed a wooden goblet from within.

'Made of ash,' he said, handing it to her. 'The most magical of all the woods: the channel between our world and the next. Inside, central to the furnace, is a pool of water. That's where the prehnite is. You place the goblet in the pool and you bring the water to us.'

Ember glanced from one to the other. 'That's it?'

'That's all it takes,' Antonia said. 'As I said: quick, painless, simple.'

She accepted the goblet from him, took a moment to study the greed and eagerness behind his eyes.

'In time, you'll come to understand all of this,' Antonia said. 'You'll have time to learn, to practise. And once you start, it *will* take hold of you. You will become at one with your ability. Thirsty for it, just as all your kind become once it begins. You'll want to become the best you can be, just as your father and your brother did. And, one day, you'll become as powerful as them. As proficient as them. It all takes time, but you'll get there.'

She gripped the stem of the goblet. It was perfect. It would give her the best chance, the opportunity, she needed.

Ember turned to face the edge of the furnace. As the heat swamped her, she held her hand forward, just as had last time. And, again, the amber flames felt cool to the touch as opposed to scalding her skin. As hues of violet burst around her hand and then her arm, she took a steadying breath and stepped fully into the flames.

The silence that consumed her was like one she'd never known, like stepping into a vacuum. Violet flames licked and curled around her, ethereal wisps caressing her skin, the sensation of a refreshing shower encompassing her fully.

She glanced over her shoulder to see two figures in the distance, nothing more than shadows now, as if belonging to another world.

The threat of them seemed a lifetime away, her surroundings as soothing as the comfort of her own warm duvet. The shimmering violet hues were mesmerising, the smoke-like wisps dancing languidly around her. Like teetering on the edge of pre-sleep, she knew she could have easily lost herself in there; could have dropped to the ground and rested, slept even, everything beyond the cocoon suddenly feeling irrelevant.

But it wasn't irrelevant. And time was slipping away.

She jolted herself back to reality, back to her task.

Ahead of her, a few feet away, deep in the core of the furnace, was the pool Jonah had mentioned. A pool that glowed a vibrant, luminescent green against the violet hues of the flames.

Stepping up to the edge, she gazed down into the never-ending tunnel of translucent green crystals, extending deep into the earth, the water that encompassed them so still as to be like staring down through a sheet of glass.

Crouching down, she lowered the goblet into the water, and scooped enough to almost fill it to the brim. The water she removed had that same vibrant glow, as if the essence of the crystals had leaked into the water itself.

But *half*-full. That's what she needed. If her plan was to work, she needed to take it out there half-full. She poured some of it out before standing again.

Ember turned and made her way back through the flames, back out, ironically, into the humidity of the room beyond.

Like maniacal twins in perfect synchronisation, Antonia and Jonah beamed as she emerged.

'It's incredible in there,' she said, sharing a smile with them. 'Like nothing I've ever experienced.'

Antonia stepped up to her. She rubbed Ember's upper arm. She smiled again. 'I told you it was nothing to worry about. Your magic is nothing to fear, Ember. And, in time, you will come to embrace it. You're going to help us do incredible things. *Wonderful* things,' she added, removing the goblet from her hand.

Antonia closed her eyes. She lifted the goblet to her lips, captivating Jonah's full attention. And, just as Ember hoped, only having the goblet half-full necessitated Antonia to tilt her head back a little as she took her first mouthful.

And that was her chance. Maybe her only chance. And she took it.

CHAPTER FORTY-EIGHT

———◦◉◦———

They hadn't seen it coming. That had been her greatest advantage.

'Ember, what you're suggesting is a massive risk,' Nate had said. 'Lowering their guard will be tough enough, but then acting quickly enough and strongly enough to take each down in succession is extremely skilled.'

'But not impossible. Don't tell me you've never managed it.'

'Aside from the fact I'm quicker and stronger than you by the very nature of what I am, I've had decades of practice. One slip-up, Ember, and you're screwed. It's not like in the movies. Knocking someone out isn't easy. Let alone knocking someone out hard enough for long enough for what you're proposing doing. And if you kill them in the process, just one of them, which is exactly what could happen if you don't know what you're doing, this is over. We're both fucked. It's an idea, it's clever idea, but not a workable one.'

'Then what else do you suggest, Nate? We need to get them

alone to be able to do this. *I* need to get them alone. And the only place we can get them away from their guards is down there.'

'And what if we're wrong about the gateway? What if maybe it's just third species who can't pass through?'

'You told me that Stirling said he never went down there. Why not? I'm willing to take the risk.'

He'd remained unconvinced, his gaze studying hers.

'I'm not starting from scratch, Nate. I *have* had training in the past. I'm used to looking after myself. I have got myself out of numerous scrapes over the years, not least an hour before I saved your life. We need to come up with a strategy of what I'm going to do, and then you can teach it to me. You can teach me what you would do. I want to at least try. I *need* to try. I promise you, I *can* do this.'

She'd dealt with Jonah first – *always* take the biggest down first, that's what Nate had taught her.

As soon as his attention was fully on his sister, Ember slammed the heel of her hand hard against his forehead, striking the flat of it with a powerful enough blow to guarantee to rock his brain, causing instant concussion – however short-lived.

Jonah instantly fell to his knees, Ember's second blow – a side-kick to his forehead – sealing his unconsciousness.

As Antonia's startled gaze snapped to her brother, Ember punched her hard in the nose, not unlike she had done to her attacker in the alley less than a week before.

Antonia's confusion, her watering eyes, gave Ember time to get her arm around Antonia's throat a moment later, Antonia too stunned to counteract Ember's attack in time.

'It's all in your forearm,' Nate had told her when he'd been practising with her. 'That's what you need to use to apply the right amount of pressure. You're applying pressure to the external carotid artery, just below the neck where you can feel a pulse.'

'I've spent five years self-studying human and vampire physiology for my entrance exams, Nate. I think I know where the carotid artery is.'

She'd felt him smile against her ear. 'Lower them to the ground as you increase the pressure from your forearm,' he'd said, demonstrating on her as he went. 'The secret is breathing in as you do so and puffing out your chest to add to pressure. Don't let go until you feel her weaken but, for fuck's sake, don't apply too much pressure so as to kill her. And do *not* hang around for a split-second once she's lost consciousness. You are going to have a very short window – maybe only a handful of minutes – before she comes around again.'

And that was the most integral thing of all: executing the manoeuvres without killing them but having them unconscious, or at least disorientated, long enough to do what she needed to do next. Not getting back to them in time meant she was screwed. But accidently killing either of them meant she was screwed even more. It would be game over – for her *and* Nate too.

As such, he'd made her practise over and over again, giving her numerous scenarios. Preparation was everything, he had told her. Cutting down processing time and acting with immediacy was essential. And there was no way he was following through with her plan unless he was convinced.

Despite trying to sustain her concentration, on too many occasions her gaze had wandered from where his vest top clung to his flat stomach, up to his pecs, and across to his biceps. Biceps that had wrapped around her so firmly, yet so gently as he'd demonstrated, explained, talked her through each move, his voice having tauntingly caressed her ear.

And there were moments when she could have believed him capable of straying off task too – something about the way he'd held her, or spoken to her, or when he'd hesitated, or had lingered longer in a position than he'd needed to. But nothing had come of her suspicions, of her hopes. Instead he'd remained focused throughout.

'I know what it's taking for you to trust me to do this, Nate,' she'd said, wiping the perspiration from the back of her neck as she'd caught her breath.

'It works both ways, Ember. You're having to trust me to come good for you just as much. Maybe even more so.'

'Which I do,' she'd said.

Because she did. Unequivocally, she trusted him. She trusted him in a way she didn't think she'd ever be able to trust anyone – let alone one of his kind.

But that wasn't how she saw him any more. She barely even paid heed to those lethal extra incisors that she had once so greatly feared could steal everything from her. Instead, she had more moments of gazing at them with fascination, her mind, at times, wandering into wondering what it would feel like to be bitten by him. Because, beyond those incisors, was Nate. Nate who, right then, was doing everything he could do to prepare her for success. Nate who had listened to her, had trusted her enough to listen.

For what she didn't know would be the final time, she'd taken a last swoop to his leg, knocking him to ground in the manoeuvre he'd taught her should she fail to knock Jonah unconscious with her first blow. She'd placed her bare foot to his forehead a moment later, in a non-contact demonstration of showing him just how efficient she had become.

But instead of pulling away, she'd placed her foot to the left of his waist, promptly followed with her right foot on the other side of him. And she'd lowered herself to sit astride him.

He'd gazed up at her with those beautifully unique eyes that were now those of her friend and not her enemy. Eyes that spoke so strongly now of how he was trying to undo that night – empowering her to avenge what had happened.

Eyes that now spoke of so much more than that.

'Have you never been tempted?' she'd asked.

'Tempted to what?'

'To bite me.'

'Many times.'

She'd held his gaze, her pulse racing, as he'd declared it without hesitation. 'This might be our last time together, Nate.'

'This *will* be our last time together, Ember. I'm taking you at your word. If we do this in time, you *are* going to cross that border.'

'And then what?'

'And then you start a new life,' he'd said. 'The life you should have had.'

'And what if I'm not sure I want that life any more? If we succeed, if we destroy the Hordas clan, things can move forward in this district. Or at least start to.'

'And that can happen without you. But this is your only chance and you're going to take it. Absolution, Ember. That's my payment for this. If you don't cross that border, I've failed.'

'I can come back.' She'd broken a smile. 'I know where you live.'

But her smile hadn't been reciprocated. He'd reached up with both hands, and brushed her hair behind her ears, coiling it at the nape of her neck before holding it there with one hand, slid the back of his other hand down her cheek with a tenderness that had made her heart jolt, her stomach clench.

'We can make it work, Nate,' she'd said. 'I know we can.'

'You're human, Ember. I'm a vampire. I've outlived you by

decades already and will outlive you by decades more. And that means one day, one that will feel like a lifetime away to you but a mere breath to me, I will lose you. And I'll be alone again. I'd rather face that now and have given you something in return than face it in the future knowing I took everything away. I can't give you what you want. I can't give you what you need. And I can't give you what you deserve. And being inside these walls, constantly holding back, never truly being able to be who I am with you, I can't do that to myself either. We would never be complete until what I am became something I could share with you – and I'm not going to give you the choice. Sometimes caring about someone is about walking away. It's about letting go. It's about moving on. *We* need to move on.'

Hand clutching her neck, he'd used his thumb to wipe the tear that had leaked down her cheek.

Using the strength in his abs, he had curled up, his hands not flinching from where he held her hair, her neck. His lips had hovered less than a couple of inches from her, their breath mingling – hers rapid and shallow, his calm, slow and deep – as he'd held her gaze.

Her heart had skipped a beat at his furrowed brow, at the intensity of his non-relinquishing gaze.

She didn't have anything more to say – nothing she could put into words, anyway. Just that she hated that sense of walking away. That sense that, whatever it was between them, too much had been left unfinished. That being there, inside those four walls, was the only place she wanted to be.

Lowering her gaze, she'd raked her hands down his chest. Scrunched the fabric she'd fisted her hands.

She'd met his gaze again a few seconds later. 'Let us be together just once more. Let me get as close to you as I can be just once.'

His gaze had lingered a moment longer. When his lips had

finally met hers, she'd snatched back a breath, her stomach somersaulting at the gentleness amidst the firmness, the hand that had held her hair coiled releasing it to clutch the nape of her neck. He'd slid the other down her chest, his fingertips snagging the neckline of her vest top, dragging it down with the cup of her bra to expose her breast, her nipple stiffening in response.

His lips, his mouth, his tongue on their caressing journey down her neck had made her shudder, her still-clenched fists bunching his vest tighter.

And when his cool lips, his damp mouth, his firm tongue had swept across her clavicle before lowering to reach her breast, her lips had parted with pleasure.

She'd released his vest to clutch his neck as he tore open the front of hers. His touch a dichotomy of feral and controlled as he'd taken both her breasts in his hands simultaneously, squeezing firmly before licking and nipping, his tongue having rolled over each nipple in turn before sucking with a pressure that had had her gripping his hair.

His mouth had been on hers again minutes later, his eyes open, staring deep into hers as he'd snagged her bottom lip between his teeth, tugging it between his as he'd grasped the back of her neck again. He'd licked the underside of her upper teeth, the roof of her mouth, coiling his tongue around hers before lowering her to her back beneath him.

He'd removed her lower clothing seconds later with a swift ease that had made her abdomen clench, locking her in the haze that had already been fast consuming her.

He'd interlaced his fingers with hers, pressed his palms to hers, lowered her hands to either side of her shoulders.

His mouth's journey down her cleavage, down to her belly button, had had her tensing in anticipation. But nothing had prepared her for when his mouth, his tongue, had eventually reached her sex.

Her groans had resonated around the room. She'd clenched her hands. She'd shuddered with ecstasy. His thumb on her clit had been torturous as he'd licked and teased before pushing his tongue deep inside her.

She'd bucked but he'd snagged her hips, pinning and holding her in position, her thighs kept apart by his shoulders, giving her no escape, pushing her even faster her towards her climax with a speed she'd never experienced. And as he'd taken her to the cusp, to the very edge of her free-fall, he'd withdrawn, her whole body shuddering at the agony of.

Snagging her hands again, interlacing their fingers again, pinning them either side of her, he'd met her gaze. He'd held her there for just that second longer, her sex throbbing, her thighs trembling, her breasts aching, her vision blurred to anything but him.

She'd held her breath as his rigidness met her sex. She'd gasped as he'd entered her just a little. And she'd groaned again, louder, sated, as she'd felt his solid girth penetrate her inch by inch, the sensation exacerbated by the painful sensitivity of her pending orgasm in a way she'd never known.

And, with a final push, he'd filled her completely.

His chest was hard, cool against hers as he'd lowered himself, buried her beneath him. Restrained, her thighs held apart by his, she'd felt encompassed in his power, in his strength, in his control in a way that didn't panic her as it so easily could have, but which had only escalated her arousal. Pleasure that had escalated even more as his body had found rhythm with hers until the point she'd lost all sense of anything but him inside her, above her, all around her.

As her orgasm had consumed her body, as she'd felt him

simultaneously come, she'd cried out in their haven, wrapped her arms tightly around him, held him against her, kept him inside her, right up to that bitter moment when she'd had no other option but to let him go.

CHAPTER FORTY-NINE

It was all she could think: that she could not fail.

Antonia fought. Antonia struggled. It became more of a battle than Ember had anticipated trying to contain her, trying to apply the right amount of pressure to knock her unconscious for a few minutes as opposed to outright killing her.

Because the temptation for the latter was there. As Antonia tried to scratch her, tried to kick at her, yanked her hair and writhed in her arms, Ember pulled on every reserve she had not to budge, not to relinquish her grip for a moment – but not to break her neck either; to let all that resentment, that anger, that hatred of everything she stood for flow out in one satisfying wrench.

For destroying her family.

For trying to destroy the lives of the only people she had left to care about.

For the threat she would pose to Nate if Ember failed and Antonia succeeded.

She glanced anxiously at Jonah, lying unconscious beside them.

For every second it took Antonia to pass out was a second closer to Jonah stirring.

Her heart pounded, her grip tightened, her resolve and focus strengthened.

And eventually, *eventually*, Antonia sagged in her arms.

Ember clambered back away from her, cast another anxious glance at Jonah.

She forced herself to her feet, and she ran. She hightailed it back along the corridor and back up the winding steps.

Nate waited for him to edge closer.

The bodyguard had the languid stroll of a security guard wandering an empty building, going through the motions, knowing no one was there. Out of the two flanking the gateway, one of them yawned. The only one who seemed particularly vigilant was the one at the opening of the tunnel. They'd clearly been through it several times before: an uneventful occurrence out of sight in a place few ever ventured.

He waited until the guard was close enough. The second he'd got his hands on him, he'd have to be quick. The torch was the biggest giveaway of all. They'd all see the slightest fluctuation in that.

Nate calculated precisely where he'd need to be stood to give him the best shot, needing to fire off three bullets in succession, unable to afford missing a single one.

He waited.

And he waited, the guard's monotonous footsteps edging closer.

The guard spun the torch to the wall where Nate stood. Nate didn't give him a second to respond. He locked his arm around his neck, spun him in front of him as a human shield.

Nate let off two shots. With silent precision, he hit both guards flanking the gateway, them dropping instantly to the floor.

Lining up the third, he aimed at the guard at the far end of the tunnel. The guard somehow sensed it coming and moved out of the way, taking a shot back at Nate.

'Shit,' Nate hissed under his breath, managing to dodge it but losing sight of the guard.

The guard that could warn Antonia and Jonah.

Nate put a bullet in the side of the head of the bodyguard he held and then ran down to the gateway. He threw the rope and the knife inside as per their plan, before hightailing it towards the mouth of the tunnel.

Ember skidded as she reached the top of the steps, using the wall for leverage and momentum, only hoping Nate had timed it as well as she'd hoped he had.

Sure enough, the rope was there, the knife too.

But no Nate. No Nate beyond the gateway.

She couldn't afford to hesitate. At best they were going to be unconscious for a matter of a couple more minutes, and that meant every second counted.

Ember snatched the rope and knife from the ground before hurrying back down the steps, back to Jonah and Antonia.

Back to finish the job.

CHAPTER FIFTY

———◦◦◦———

'We're not going to kill them,' Ember had said to Nate. 'That's the loophole. We're going to use their ability not to be killed *against* them.'

'I don't get it.'

'They can only predict our move if they actually die, right? That's the trigger. That's what the spell dictates. That's what enables them to travel back those ten minutes or so they have in order to prevent it. But what if we put them in a position where they *can't* do anything to prevent it? That's the key.'

His brow furrowed at first before, finally, he raised his eyebrows slightly.

'The loophole is to create a long enough timeframe between them dying and being able to do anything about it,' she continued. 'A bullet, a stab wound, strangulation, that's all too quick. But a death that takes days to come into fruition, a death that, even when they see it coming, they're in a position preventing them from doing anything about it ... that's *way* outside of their parameters.'

'You're going to starve them,' he said. 'You're going to make them die of thirst.'

'Worse-case scenario, if the spell constitutes it as natural causes, they die within a few days – no bounce back.'

'Best-case scenario?'

'My interference will dictate to the contrary of it being natural causes. They'll die, they'll jump back those few minutes, only to find themselves already bound as it would have taken anything up to a few days to get to that point. They die again, they jump back, they die again, they jump back. And each time, they'll know it's coming. They'll have to face that fate, those days of agony, over and over again. Until, eventually, their body will deteriorate. It's bound to. And that cavern is perfect for it, Nate. We can secure them in a place where no one else can get to them.'

'You think you can do that? Leave them down there? Simply walk away?'

'Give them long enough to think? To let them know what it feels like to be trapped with no way out? To face the same agony day after day? To feel helpless, weak? To feel that level of fear of being at someone else's mercy. To feel all the things they have thrived on inflicting on others? I think it's the least I can do,' Ember had said. 'I think it's the very least they deserve.'

Jonah stirred first as Ember finished securing his sister to the hoops melded into the rock on the opposite side of the room from him.

Perspiration trickled down Ember's neck and chest from the exertion, from the heat of the furnace, her hands damp as she tightened the knots making sure there was no hope of Antonia escaping.

As soon as Jonah realised what was happening, he bucked violently in his restraints, the gag tight around his mouth – removal of his freedom of speech the final indignity Ember had bestowed on him. An indignity he had inflicted on many.

His face reddened, his cheeks puffing with fury, his eyes blazing with hatred and resentment as he glowered at Ember.

It was a matter of moments before Antonia stirred too, coming around more languidly than her brother had, giving Ember time to stand equidistant between them, her back to the furnace.

She'd left Antonia ungagged, hoping that, as a result, Jonah would suffocate first, so she would have those few moments over and over again of watching him die first. That small, ever so small payback for that night Ember had stood by and watched her brother being snatched from her life forever too.

The darkness around her pulsed, not helped by the flicker of the furnace, as Antonia finally came around fully, and finally understood the situation.

Because she knew without doubt that Antonia would understand – a brilliant mind used for most of her life to inflict injustice on others.

'You clever, manipulative, sneaky little bitch,' Antonia hissed under her breath, her narrowed eyes fixed on Ember.

The jury was still out as to whether she would beg for her life. The woman who had never had to beg for anything.

Ember offered her a simple shrug. 'I'll take that. I'll own it.'

Antonia glanced back over at her brother still furiously trying to free himself. She exhaled tersely as she looked away before chuckling to herself – a slightly maniacal chuckle laced with the realisation of her own helplessness.

'I must admit,' Antonia said, glaring back at her. 'I can appreciate the irony of it.'

'Me too,' Ember said.

'See,' Antonia added. 'I knew we'd understand each other.'

'I think the evidence in front of us shows I understand you more than you understand me.'

'Turning so soon into a true witch? Capable of this kind of cruelty to get your own way within an hour of your initiation? I think I know your kind well enough. I knew your father, your brother, well enough. Excuse the cliché, but the apple never falls far from the tree, Ember.'

'And not all apples that fall are rotten, Antonia. Whatever my family did, whatever those links to the past, it ends today.' She glanced at the furnace. She glanced back at Antonia. 'This is not what this spell was intended for. The problem was you. The problem was your brother. By the sounds of it, your father before you. My family may have started this, but I'm ending it. Now.'

Antonia's eyes flared a little, the first glimpse of genuine uncertainty behind them. There was a minor tremble to her upper lip as she twisted her wrists warily in her binds.

'You can't do this, Ember,' she said. 'Murder is not as easy as you think.'

'No?'

'No. You're not the type. You'll come back here. I know you will.'

'Will I?' Ember asked, keeping her gaze steady. She wandered over towards her. She crouched in front of her. 'Well, let me make you this promise. If I get tempted, I'll remember how your brother allowed – sorry, incited – the beating of a kind, helpless, innocent old man to death. And then maybe, *maybe* I might come back to my senses and leave you both down here to rot in this hell.' She stood. Glared down into Antonia's eyes. 'But if you believe differently, if that's what gives you hope over the next few days, you cling on to it.' Ember sent her a fleeting smile, before losing it again. 'You'll realise soon enough. Because all I

see is countless more people going the same way as Jasper did if
I let you out of here.'

She stepped away. She headed towards the steps.

'So what do you want, huh? An apology? A deal? You want
me to beg?'

'Are you even capable of begging, Antonia?'

Antonia exhaled tersely again.

'No,' Ember said. 'I didn't think so.'

Her foot reached the bottom step.

'Don't do this,' Antonia pleaded. 'I will give you whatever you
want. Everything you want.'

Ember headed back over to her. She crouched in front of her
as they were at eye level. 'You already are,' she said.

'*Please*,' Antonia said.

Ember held her gaze, watched the flames flickering behind
her eyes again, held her on a knife-blade of anticipation. Held
her on a thread.

Satisfied, she stood.

'No,' Ember said. 'I don't think so. Instead, I'd rather you
know what it's like to have *your* fate in someone else's hands for
a change. You reap what you sow, Antonia. I told you, tonight
this ends – right where it all began.'

CHAPTER FIFTY-ONE

Ember ascended the steps, the flick knife still in her hand just in case.

'Ember!' Antonia's voice screamed up the stairwell behind her. 'You can't do this! You *can't* do this!'

But she was. She actually was.

She shocked herself with how numb she felt towards their plight; how walking away from them gave her more satisfaction than she would have believed possible. The scuff of her boots on stone soon overrode the sound of the protests, what was left of the Hordas clan becoming nothing more than an increasingly distant echo.

With the gateway in sight, she stopped to absorb the darkness that surrounded her; the darkness of what she was doing. But she kept her attention on the light ahead, no matter how dim it was. The light where she could only hope Nate would be waiting for her. Where he would be OK.

Driven by eagerness to see him, Ember hurried towards the

gateway. She stopped just short of the bars to listen out for any voices or movement beyond, knowing that there was no guarantee Nate had succeeded. That there was no telling what situation lay waiting for her beyond.

Met with silence, she took the last few steps forward. After another brief, tentative pause, she stepped through the bars and out into the tunnel.

She instantly clenched her knife at seeing the three bodies lying in the darkness. Remaining watchful of any sign of movement anywhere, her heart pounded as she quickly assessed one after the other.

Confirming that none of the dead men were Nate, she searched the shadows for him. Pulse racing, she was on the brink of calling out for him, held back only by the prospect of drawing attention to herself. When, beyond the tunnel opening, she saw a figure perched on the bonnet of one of the cars.

Her heart skipped a beat. Her already shallow breathing snagged. Until she could be sure it was Nate, she used the cloak of darkness to head closer.

Finally convinced, Ember picked up pace, each footstep nonetheless feeling sluggish in her eagerness.

The distant onset of dawn softened his backdrop as he sat with his knees partially drawn to his chest, his gaze locked in the distance.

The refreshing breeze skimming her hair after the claustrophobic heat of the cavern, Ember came to a standstill a few feet away.

'All sorted?' he asked as he looked across his shoulder at her. It was almost as if he was as numb to the reality as she was, other than no doubt sharing that same deep sense of satisfaction, of completion. Because that was it: the Hordas clan were finished.

'Left to rot,' she confirmed.

He glanced down at the knife still in her hand before looking ahead again.

'It's going to haunt you, Ember.' He looked back at her again. 'For a long time it will haunt you.'

'I still think I'll manage to sleep easier rather than knowing they're out there.'

'So we're done,' he said, lowering himself down from the bonnet.

As he stopped in front of her, her heart pounded amidst the finality of it all.

'That's it then,' she said with a shrug.

'That's it,' he echoed, his gaze steady on hers.

'So what are you going to do now?' she asked.

Ask me to stay, she said to herself. *Tell me we'll find a way. Because there's always a way. Tell me you want me to stay.*

'Get closure,' he said. 'It's been a long wait.'

'Absolution,' she added.

As he broke a smile, a sense of warmth flooded her.

'Yeah,' he said, glancing away before his gaze lingered on hers again. 'Absolution.'

He paused, the ambient pending dawn light already consuming his backdrop even in those passing minutes.

'The same goes for you, Ember.' He checked his watch. 'You've got three hours. You don't want to be late.'

She glanced up the dirt track behind him. She wrapped her arms around herself as she met his gaze again. 'Lowtown can be a different place now, Nate. I know there's still some of the Voys left to contend with but if enough of us stand together . . .'

'That's not your problem now, Ember. You've done your bit.'

The fact he still wanted her to go hurt more than she wanted to accept. They had a deal. A deal he clearly intended to keep to.

'I'll be back for visits,' she said. 'I'll want to check in on Harry and Casey. Maybe try the café as a customer for a change.' She shrugged. 'You know – for old times' sake.'

'I won't be there,' he said.

It was like a blow to her stomach. As much as she tried not to, she dropped her gaze to the floor before daring to look back into his eyes, to face the rejection behind them. 'There's a solution out there somewhere, Nate. Look what we've achieved tonight,' she declared, indicating the tunnel behind her. 'That seemed impossible forty-eight hours ago. Being a witch, I might be able to get others to open up to me, to find a way around the curse . . .'

Because she would not let it end there. She would get into Midtown to fulfil her promise, would settle in Midtown, and then she'd be back for him. She'd be back with a solution. She wouldn't rest until she could give him total absolution. Until she could free him completely; free him to be with her.

'We had a deal,' he reminded her. 'You gave me your word. Your focus now needs to be on moving on. I've been a part of you for too long now, Ember. You need to start your life afresh without me in it. What is it you said to me: too scared to be without the familiar, even when it causes you pain?'

'This isn't about familiarity or about being scared to let go. You care about me and I care about you. Until we find the answer, we can spend time in your haven. Even if we can't be together out here, we can be together in there. That would be enough for me if it could be enough for you.'

'Potentially for the rest of your life?'

'For as long as it takes to find an answer. Because I *will* find one. I'm not going to give up on you. I'm not going to give up on what we might be.'

It was his turn to drop his gaze. His sigh was heavy. 'I knew you'd do this,' he said, his eyes locking on hers again. 'You never know when to quit, do you?'

'Not when I want something this badly.'

'Your life is not here with me, Ember. You have no future with me. All of this you have done to secure your freedom would have been for nothing.'

'You're not nothing, Nate. You're *far* from nothing. You could become everything to me. You deserve to be everything to someone.'

'So do you, Ember. Someone you can sustain a life with. Someone you can *live* a life with. I don't want you giving up your life in Midtown for me. I don't want you spending however many more years wearing another ring that will come to nothing.'

'So why wait here, Nate? To tell me *this*? Why not be gone already?'

He closed the gap between them. Using the very tip of his forefinger, he brushed a strand of hair from her eyes. The agony of not being able to touch him, not being able to hold him, ripped through her.

All she could offer him for now was compliance; to make him think she had acquiesced. In time, he would know differently. In time, he wouldn't be able to say no when she held the answer in her hands. Because she was not letting him go. There was no way she was moving on because he *did* care. And she was not giving that up.

As she studied his gaze, she realised he knew that. Tendrils of ice coiled around and through her. The second she worked out what he was about to do, she knew it was already too late.

'Nate,' she said, barely able to breathe, taking a step back to create some distance between them.

'You say you care about me,' he said.

She shook her head slowly, warily. 'Nate, don't you dare go there.'

'You asked why I hung around. This *is* about closure. For both of us. There's only one way I can be freed of this.'

'You don't know that.'

'Yes, I do. Do you think I'd be doing this to you, to myself, if I believed for one moment that there was any other way?'

'No,' she said, shaking her head adamantly. 'Fuck you, Nate. Fuck you for even suggesting it.'

She stepped away, her hands trembling, the approaching dawn suddenly feeling cold, almost hostile.

'You're one of the bravest people I know,' he said.

'No,' she said, fighting back her tears of anger. 'Don't use that.'

'You can break free and, finally, so can I. You talk about absolution, then grant me the ultimate.'

'Selfish, selfish bastard,' she snapped, unable to hold back her building tears as she turned to march away.

His arms were around her a moment later. He carried her across to the bank.

She could feel from the tension in his body, from his curt breathing, that it was already causing him pain to be holding her so close, but he wouldn't let her go. Even as she kicked and flayed, he remained steadfast on his journey up the bank and down into the dip on the other side.

Broken twigs snapped beneath them both as she struggled against him.

'I'm begging you,' she said. '*Don't* do this. Don't make me fight you.'

But despite using every iota of strength to pull herself free, he didn't let her go.

'Nate. *Please.*'

'I need you to understand,' he said against her ear. 'I need you to get why I'm doing this.'

'I will stay away. If that's what you want, if that's what it takes, I promise I will stay away. I will never try to find you.'

'You're the only one who can do this for me. What I feel

for you, what you feel for me, that doesn't come easy. I could spend another century waiting for this chance, and I know I'll never find anyone I feel this way about. No one I'll love like I love you.'

The pain emanating from the tension in his body fractured her heart. She knew he wasn't going to let her go. She knew he'd made up his mind.

'If you kiss me, it'll be over quicker,' he said. 'You wanted to free me. You can do that. If you love me enough too, you can do that. Do you love me enough, Ember?'

'That's not fair!'

'And it's fair that one day I would have to lose you?'

'I know you're doing this for me,' she said. 'To make sure I go. You're not doing this for you.'

'I'm doing it for both of us.'

She shook her head.

He turned her around, his grip on her wrists unrelenting.

She stared into his eyes – eyes that were resolute, at peace.

'Harry's on his way,' he said. 'I called him. He's going to get you to the border.'

'No,' she said, shaking her head again.

'Ember, listen to me. Please.'

As he fell to his knees still gripping her wrists, she fell to her knees in front of him, the pain in his expression, in his eyes, breaking her heart.

The tears trickled down her cheeks as she fought the urge to touch him, to comfort him.

He moved his hand from his chest to clutch the back of her neck, his grip on her wrist unrelenting.

She could do nothing to stop him forcing her down onto her back. Nothing to prevent the increased contact it created.

He gently clasped her jaw, forcing her to look into his eyes.

She could feel him weakening. Could feel the heat of her tear trickle down her cold cheek.

Dappled with the weak light making it through the bare, dense branches above, he gazed down at her.

'It hurts, Ember,' he said. 'It's too late now anyway. Please. Please end this for me.'

She shook with the force of her tears. She freed her wrist to cup his jaw, to rub her thumb across his lips.

Unable to bear seeing him in pain any more, she kissed him.

His smile shattered her heart as his cool lips lingered on hers for the last time. The lips of the vampire she had once saved only to now let him die.

The vampire who fell away from her.

He lay on his back, his arms lax either side of his head.

She scrambled onto her hands and knees beside him. 'Nate?'

She grabbed his wrist. There was no sign of a pulse. She lowered her ear to his mouth. And no sign of breathing.

She clutched the side of his head with her trembling hand. He was cold. Colder than she'd ever known him. Colder than when he'd been dying in her stairwell.

In *their* stairwell.

She sat astride him. She clutched his head in both hands. 'Nate?' she said again, despite knowing it was futile.

And she stopped breathing as her world fell apart.

CHAPTER FIFTY-TWO

——◦◦◦——

Ember sat perched on the edge of the sofa, wrapped in his blanket, staring into the dead, cold fireplace. The only thing that remained was the epitaph of the charred embers from the night before.

She'd said her final goodbye too many times. Could only go back to the bed so many times before accepting she had to walk away; that nothing miraculous was going to happen as she'd hoped. That he wasn't going to wake up.

She'd been unable to contain her trembling as she'd knelt shivering in the rain beside Nate's cold body.

'Ember?'

To her frustration, she'd broken into sobs at the sound of Harry's familiar voice. Heel of her hand pressed to her head, she'd rocked as she'd tried to find the strength to speak.

She'd remembered him placing his coat around her shoulders. Remembered him trying to get her to her feet; to guide her away.

She'd fought against him, insisting they needed to take Nate with them. That there was no way she was leaving him there alone; that they needed to get him back home.

It had taken every ounce of her persuasive skills to convince Harry, and every ounce of their strength to get Nate into the car, let alone up the stairs to his loft apartment. To get him back to his haven.

She'd known in time that she'd been kidding herself. That it had made not the slightest bit of difference. Nate was gone. All she had done was extend him the courtesy of not being left alone in the dirt, eventually to be embroiled with the remains on the Hordas clan's fallen empire.

But at least she'd taken him to the one place he'd ever felt safe. Done the only thing she could do for him.

Amidst fragmented pieces of information, Ember had eventually told Harry the full story. And Harry, being Harry, had listened in silence. Eventually, he had understood.

Now, draped in the blanket, she didn't look over her shoulder as the door was unlocked behind her. Harry had returned – and that meant time was up. Numbness consumed her. Consumed her everywhere except for the sickness she felt in the very pit of her stomach and the emptiness in her chest.

He perched on the sofa beside her. He waited a moment before speaking. He tenderly rubbed the back of her head. 'All your bags are in the car. And I packed the other bits and pieces you wanted too. I've brought you some clean clothes. You won't be able to turn up caked in dirt.'

She'd not been able to bring herself to go back to the apartment – not only because it would lessen the last of her time with Nate, but because she couldn't face it. She couldn't face the memories that would be so vivid there.

'We've got half an hour to get there if you're going to make it in time, Ember. You need to do this as much for him.'

When she met Harry's gaze again, she was worried it would set her off once more. But she soon realised she had no more tears left – just dry, itchy eyes and an arid throat that made it painful to swallow.

'I don't know if I can,' she said.

'Ember, you *need* to do this.' He brushed her head once more. 'He's gone. He's not going to come back.'

She stood but kept the blanket with her, hugging it tight to her chest.

As Harry left her alone for a few minutes, she swapped her jeans and sweater for the smart dress he had brought her.

She walked towards the door. Stopped in the middle of the room. She looked towards the bed where Nate lay; where Harry had now covered him in a blanket.

As compelling as it felt to lie beside him for a lifetime, she knew if she went back over again, she'd never be able to leave him.

She scanned the room once more. She glanced around at the array of symbols and then forced herself, one footstep at a time, to reach the door. To leave their haven. To leave Nate behind.

CHAPTER FIFTY-THREE

'That's it,' the woman said as she busied herself slotting all the relevant paperwork into various sections of the folder that was rapidly filling up.

It had taken three hours in the end. The final medical assessment had at least been swift – a strip down and a check over for bite or syringe marks. She'd explained the cut on her hand. By that point, she wasn't even sure she cared if they questioned it further. But common sense had prevailed on their part that she wasn't going to do anything stupid days before she got out. And, at the end of the day, they still needed their quota filled.

The rest of the time had been spent on filling in forms and going through checklists of protocols and systems. She'd spent most of the time merely nodding her head, most of it going over the top of it, her mind still fixed on the events of the night.

Harry had got her there with ten minutes to spare. Ten minutes for her to find the strength of resolve to continue.

'You'll be OK,' Harry had said, reaching for her hand and squeezing.

She'd met his gaze and squeezed back. She hadn't been so sure. The numbness was still rife – not just at losing Nate but the prospect of moving on from everyone else she cared about too.

'I know it feels strange,' he'd added. 'But you know where we are. It's not the other side of the world although I know it feels like it at the moment.'

'I'm not sure I want to go,' she'd said. 'It doesn't feel right. Why do I feel like he's not gone, Harry? Why do I feel like he's still alive?'

Harry's eyes had been laden with empathy as he squeezed her hand again. 'Ember, I know this is tough but we both saw him.' He'd turned his body more towards her in the confines of the car. 'You know I understand what it feels like to wish that you didn't have to lose someone, but once they're gone, they're gone.'

'I need to go back there. I need to be sure.'

'If you go back there now, you will miss your slot. You will lose your chance to get to Midtown.'

'Maybe that's for the best.'

Harry had sighed with impatience. 'Ember, this is not the time to be making rash decisions. You've been through a shock. One hell of a week. You're clinging on to the familiar, that's all. It's perfectly natural, especially after a loss.'

'Everything's different now though, Harry. The Hordas clan are gone. We can all find ways to band together, to make sure no one gets that level of power again. We're on the right track now.'

'And think everything you've worked for. Everything you've saved for.'

'Which I can plough back in to ventures here.' She paused. 'Maybe make an investment?' she said, her eyebrows raised as she captured and held his gaze.

'No,' Harry said with a shake of his head.

'Harry, nothing is ever going to get better in this district if the people who can help do something about it keep running away. All I know is that my gut is telling me that this isn't the right thing to do.'

'Get across the border,' Harry said. 'You can always change your mind after. But if you don't cross, that chance will be lost. Do it for your aunt. Do it for Nate.'

'Fully processed,' the woman finally stated with a smile, bringing her back to the present.

Ember wanted to smile back, but she couldn't. She knew she should have been elated. It should have been one of the happiest days in the past decade. Instead, she felt nothing but the burning sense of loss.

She glanced over her shoulder, back towards the doors. Back to where she'd said goodbye to Harry – at least for now. She'd promised him to give it a few days before she came back. A few days to settle in and overcome the homesickness.

The woman slid a piece of paper towards her. 'All you have to do now is sign on the dotted line and then you're officially a Midtown resident.'

Ember accepted the pen. Her hand hovered over the paper for a few moments.

'Miss Challice?' the woman said expectantly, snagging Ember's attention from however long she had been staring at the piece of paper.

Ember nodded. She scribbled her signature and placed the pen down. Her gaze dropped to her dress as she brushed away an imaginary crease.

In the distance she heard the further ruffle of paper. The sliding of a metal filing cabinet drawer.

'Whenever you're ready,' the woman said. 'You're free to cross the threshold.' She smiled. 'I almost feel like we should have a fanfare every time we do this.'

Ember stared across her shoulder at the doors. Something niggled. Something small. Something she couldn't quite reach. She looked back at the woman. 'What did you say?'

'A fanfare. It's such an achievement when someone gets through here. A bit like a graduation, I suppose. A bit like . . .'

But it wasn't that.

You're free to cross the threshold.

Ember's heart pounded. She instantly stood.

She didn't remember her journey back through the doors, back through the way she came. The concerned and confused pursuit of the woman following behind her became a distant echo as she ploughed through the external doors out into the car park.

She rang his number. She rang for Harry.

'Ember?'

'Harry, I need you to come back and get me. I need you to take me back there.'

'Back where?'

'To Nate's.'

'Ember, seriously–'

'*Please*,' Ember said, clutching the back of her head. 'I think I missed the most obvious thing of all. I *need* to go back there. *Now*.'

CHAPTER FIFTY-FOUR

His head throbbed. His chest ached. Nate brushed the blanket away from his face and squinted at the glow beyond the opaque windows. He forced himself up onto his elbows and stared through the streams of daylight falling across the room, igniting the dust motes in the air.

'Ember?'

He could still smell her in the room – on the sheets, in the atmosphere, her scent mingling with the aroma of the burnt wood in the fireplace.

She'd brought him back there. She hadn't left him amidst the dirt – she'd brought him home.

He pushed himself to his feet and squinted again, this time with pain as the blood rushed to his head.

She was nowhere visible. The bathroom beyond was silent. He headed over to be sure.

Finding it empty, he checked his watch.

He stared back at the bed. He registered how he'd woken

with the blanket over his head. He had died, just as the spell had dictated he would. For over five hours, he had been dead. More accurately, he had slipped into a coma whilst the spell had unravelled before he awoke anew. Had awoken curse-free.

Not even he had known how long it would take before he recovered: minutes, hours, maybe even days.

What mattered was that she'd believed he was gone, just as it had been essential for him to lead her to believe – not only for the sake of the curse, but also because he couldn't be entirely sure he *would* come back.

But he had.

And Ember had left, exactly as he'd wanted her to. Just as she had promised him she would.

Her time to get across the border was now overdue. He could only hope she was either already in Midtown or her processing was well underway.

He needed to get to the café. He needed to find out from Harry if she'd gone through with it. Because if she'd changed her mind, that was the only other place she would have been – there or back at the apartment. Besides, Harry was a safe bet to talk to. He'd seen the way Harry had looked at him in the café on more than one occasion. Harry wasn't going to blurt the details to Ember about him still being alive.

He grabbed his jacket and his spare keys. It would take him a while to walk there, his car still back at The Hive.

He stepped through the panel and made his way down the stairs, his hand sliding down the balustrade that doubled back on itself as he turned the corner.

He'd be at that café every day until she came back. Because she *would* come back. Now that the Hordas clan were gone, he had no doubt at all that she'd be back to see her friends. And then any further decisions she made could come *after* she had crossed the border. After she had fulfilled her promise and had done what she'd needed to do. After she'd done what he'd long set out for her to achieve.

He stepped out onto the shale, his eyes narrowed against the morning light again despite it struggling to filter through the matted grey clouds. He lifted the collar on his coat, already planning his primarily undercover route to avoid too much exhaustion from the UV by the time he got to his destination.

He halted mid-courtyard.

The car pulled up twenty feet away.

Ember stared at him through the windscreen, Harry looking just as shocked in the driver's seat beside her.

For a few moments, none of them flinched.

Ember pushed open the passenger door. She stepped outside. She clutched the top of the door, a barrier between them, the light breeze whipping through her hair as she stared across at him.

She'd either crossed the border and come back, or she hadn't left at all.

His chest knotted. She'd better have done the former. After everything, she'd better have stepped across the threshold.

She cupped her hands over her mouth as she fought back the tears. Hands dropping back to her sides, she closed the gap between them. Her gaze wandered the full length of him as if not yet fully believing he was there.

She reached out to touch him. He let her, as much to have it confirmed for himself as confirmation for her that it was now safe to do so.

The warmth of her fingers against his cheek had him uncharacteristically closing his eyes for a second as he relished in her touch.

Seconds later, her arms locked around him in a hold that could have squeezed the life breath out of him.

'I knew it,' she said. 'There was no way you were going to give up like that. I can't believe I didn't see it. I can't believe I missed that I'd crossed the threshold without your permission.'

As she trembled against him, her face buried in his neck, her ragged breaths warm against his skin, it was impossible for him not to wrap his arm around her too, his other hand clasping the back of her head.

'I remembered you telling me it made no difference if you were dead or alive,' she said, 'that the barrier would still be active. So either you'd lied or there was only one explanation as to why I was able to cross.' She pulled back, her eyes glossy. 'The barrier had dropped because the curse had lifted, hadn't it? You had to be willing to die for me for the curse to be lifted, didn't you? That was why you did it. *That* was the loophole.'

As she searched his gaze, despite them both knowing she didn't need his confirmation, he nodded.

Her punch came from nowhere, smacking him hard on the side of the jaw.

He turned his head away. He rotated his jaw to make sure it was still functional.

'You'd better have a fucking good explanation for not letting me in on this!' she said, her eyes scorching him with a concoction of fury and relief.

'You had to believe it, Ember, or it wouldn't have worked.'

'Believe I had *killed* you?'

'You had to be willing to make that sacrifice for me too. You needed to love me enough to let me go.'

Her frown was deep and pensive as she waited silently for him to continue.

'Every spell has a loophole,' he explained. 'Elissa – the one who cursed me – wasn't willing for me to find one, so she created her own. The only way the curse could be undone was for me to love someone enough to die for them and for them to love me enough to be the one to kill me. It was Elissa's guarantee that even if I did find love again, there would never a happy-ever-after.'

Ember shook her head slightly, her horrified gaze remaining fixed on his. 'Just how evil was she?'

He knew he didn't need to answer.

'But clearly you knew this all along?' she said.

'Yes.'

'You told me there was no loophole.'

'I told you it was impossible, Ember. I'd believed at the time that it was.'

'So when did you change your mind?'

'I'm not sure I ever really did. Not completely. But I wanted this for you strongly enough to try.'

She cupped her hand over her mouth again. She took a step back. She raked her fingers through her hair. She closed the gap between them. She punched him again, this time in the arm, before shoving him in the chest. 'You fucking risked your life on a possibility?'

He didn't flinch, despite the power behind her push.

'And exactly how long had you been planning this, huh?' she demanded.

'Since you said you wouldn't go to Midtown. Since you came up with the plan.'

She exhaled tersely. She shook her head again. She walked away.

'If I'd been a hundred per cent sure it would work, maybe it wouldn't have. There had to be that element of doubt that I wouldn't make it or where was the sacrifice?' He paused as she turned to face him. 'Either way, you would have left for Midtown. You did cross the border before coming back here? Tell me you did. Tell me you secured your place.'

She heaved a heavy sigh. 'Yes, Nate. I signed on the dotted line.'

He nodded. 'Broken promises are hard to live with. You needed to do what your aunt wanted. I owed it to her to make sure you did what you needed to do.'

He turned his attention to the car, to where Harry was still watching them from within its confines. Harry who, by now, would have pieced together what he had done. Harry who no longer looked at him the way he usually did. Instead of greeting him with a frown laden with suspicion and caution, there was almost a smile in his eyes.

'I'm guessing you told him everything?' Nate said, looking back at her.

'It was the only way to get him to bring me back here.'

She looked over her shoulder. She raised her hand to her friend.

Turning to face Nate again, Ember folded her arms. She dropped her gaze. She looked back up into his eyes. 'You could have left me a note, Nate. Anything to let me know you were going to be OK.'

'You wouldn't have left if I had. Knowing you, if it hadn't worked, you would have sat by me until I'd rotted.'

She broke a smile, an almost-laugh.

He'd needed to see it. He hadn't realised just how much he'd needed to see it.

'I'm guessing you didn't know how long it would be before you woke up?'

'No.'

'Which is why you led me to the shrubbery out of sight. Did you really think I'd leave you there? And if I had, what if it had taken days? Anything could have happened to you.'

Another risk he no doubt had been willing to take.

She broke from his gaze only to pensively scan the courtyard.

'So what were you going to do after this?' she asked. 'Were you ever going to tell me?'

'I would have found you. And I would have told you. After you'd settled in Midtown. After you'd been away from the situation long enough to get your head straight.'

She raised her eyebrows slightly. 'To get my head straight? Did you seriously just say that?'

'I can't offer you what you want, Ember.'

'How do you know what I want?'

'And you can't give me what I need.'

Her brow furrowed. Her eyes glazed momentarily with uncertainty. The breeze whipped through her hair with a little more fervency. 'Meaning?'

'You know what I mean.'

'Feeding.'

'Yes,' he said. 'Feeding. Syringe, connected, whatever. That's not something we can change.'

'Not with my life in Midtown, right?'

'This isn't just about the here and now. As I told you before, our relationship will never be complete if I can't truly be myself with you. I will always have to hold something back. And I will not have you giving everything up for me. This will only get harder.'

She wrapped her arms around herself. 'Let's go inside, shall we?'

'What about Harry?'

'I asked him to give me a little bit of time.'

But as she stepped past him, he placed his arm across in front of her, catching her hip.

As her eyes locked on his, his pulse picked up alongside hers.

'That's not the best idea,' he said.

She caught hold of his hand, peeled it from her before choosing to ignore his advice. 'You're not going to leave me out here to freeze, are you? We need to discuss this – unless you want to draw a line under everything right now.'

When he didn't confirm the latter, she continued past him, her shoes crunching lightly on shale.

She made her way inside and up the stairs without once looking over her shoulder – the first time she had ever truly had her guard down around him.

But despite her composure, she was not completely at ease. Her pulse was still racing enough to add to the enticement, to the thrill, of her acknowledging there was still a risk involved in where it was leading, however calm she wanted to appear.

She pushed her way through the panel. Waited inside for him to unlock the door.

He did so without lingering in the darkness with her for too long; to spare himself from the proximity for too long.

He let her enter first, before closing the door behind them.

She strolled around the room, her arms still wrapped around herself.

'I need to know what you want out of this,' she eventually said. Her gaze met his again. 'And maybe you need to know what I want before writing us off as too complicated. As us being in such a hopeless place.'

'I want you to be happy. I can't make that happen.'

'You say that with such certainty.'

It was his turn to walk away. He scratched the back of his head as he made his way over to face the fireplace.

'Because of the feeding?'

'I primarily use regular feeders – one in particular.'

He turned to see her waiting on a knife's edge to find out where the confession was leading.

'For syringe feeds, as well as contact feeds. And sometimes for more too. Her name's Cordy.'

Her lips parted. He could hear her heart pounding. She nodded. 'OK,' she said with a pensive lilt. 'What are you trying to tell me, Nate?'

'I can't be doing that with her when I'm with you.'

Her eyes flared a little. 'There's more to you both?'

'No. Not like that. Not on either side. But I can't be with you both. And I need to feed, Ember.'

'Which I understand.'

'Now you do. In time, that will most likely change.'

'You don't know that. You don't know how I'll feel.'

'And neither do you.'

She pressed her lips together. Her gaze didn't waver from his. 'Then don't have Cordy, have me. All of me. And let me have all of you. If you think I'm going to return to Midtown anyway after all of this, you've learned nothing about me.'

He didn't need her looking at him the way she was when she said it. He didn't need to be tempted by the resolution in her eyes. Her recklessness coupled with the being alone with her stirred him in the most instinctive ways – both as a male and a vampire.

'What you're suggesting is easy to say, Ember. It's not so easy to do.'

'It's who you are, Nate. It's what you are. And I'm not afraid of either.' Her gaze didn't flinch. 'I can deal with both.'

'Ember, what you're talking about is permanent – at least for you. This is not something you can take back once it has started. We've still got a lot to learn about each other. It's a commitment. You'll be closing doors.'

'To open one with you. You say you want me to be happy, I think this is it.'

'Ember, you've been through one hell of a fucking week, I—'

'*Don't* patronise me, Nate. *Please.*' She closed the gap between them again. 'Just like you, all my aunt ever wanted for me was to be happy and to be able to make choices. That's what Midtown represented. But that's exactly what I can have here now. Here where my friends are, where the people I care about are. Where *you* are.

'I should have felt elated getting to that border, but I felt nothing. Nothing but what I was losing. I already knew what I wanted. I'd already made choices. I've known for the last six months, ever since you walked through that door, what I wanted. The feelings I would get when you'd take a seat, when I'd watch you, those rare moments when you'd look me in the eye. I knew all along.

'I've had my life on hold all for a place that offers me no more than what I can have here. A place that will never be able to offer what really matters to me. You talk about a new life and a fresh start, but there's just as much to be said for history, Nate – and we've got a *lot* of history. History that I think joins us more than it separates us. After all we've been through, I think that says a lot.' She paused for a moment. 'I want to stay in Lowtown. I'm going to stay in Lowtown. And it's up to you what you do about that.'

She held his gaze expectantly. Her breathing was terse, her hands clenched, even if she wasn't fully aware of either.

His heart pounded to an almost human rate as he rocked between the two decisions: to let her go and to stand by what he always intended; or to take her there and then. To bind her to him. To not think too far into the future – of what would inevitably lie ahead, forced on them by the very nature of what they both were. To instead focus only on having her as his for all that time would allow, the prospect of the latter making him feel more complete than he had in decades. A time before Elissa. A time when he was who *he* was.

'I'll give you time to think about it,' she said, whether out of impatience or losing her confidence, he couldn't be sure.

One thing he did know for sure though was that she had said her piece. She was not going to stand there begging.

She headed back over to the door. Despite her composure, he could sense the disappointment, the anticipation, emanating from her. He half-expected her to turn back around.

She didn't.

He retained his ground. Because it was about more than what she was sacrificing, it was about what he was sacrificing too. Because if she did change her mind, even a month or a year down the line, he wasn't going to be able to let her go. Once they'd sealed it, that would be it.

Nonetheless, he didn't expect to be able to let her cross the threshold.

But he did.

CHAPTER FIFTY-FIVE

⎯⎯⎯◉⎯⎯⎯

Ember sat on the top step in the chill of the stairwell, their respective apartments her backdrop.

'How long are you going to wait?' Harry had asked when he'd dropped her off in the alley, outside what she would now make her home again.

'The rest of the day. All night. Don't worry though, I'll be at work on time in the morning.'

'Who said I'm giving you your job back?'

'Harry, that place will crumble without me. Just admit it.'

He'd smiled. He'd laughed. A laugh that promptly faded. 'Are you *sure* you're doing the right thing?'

'This is my home, Harry. This district is where I want my life to be. And it'll be better now. I know it will.'

'But the research. All those things that matter to you. Making big changes for the better.'

'I've decided to start small. It can be just as impactful. Besides, maybe I'll just find more inventive ways of trying to find the answers to the bigger picture. Maybe the answer doesn't lie in a lab at all. Maybe that's where they've all been going wrong.'

'And Nate. You're sure he's the one you want?'

'He was willing to die for me, Harry. That's got to earn a bonus point, even with you.'

He'd laughed again, but his eyes had just as quickly glazed over with sobriety. 'If he doesn't show up?'

'He will,' she'd said, trying to sound convincing, even to herself.

But now that was waning. Three hours later, her confidence was wavering. Even Casey's text message had only raised a minor smile, the celebratory cheers at having received the news she was staying brashly dominating the screen in a splurge of excitement.

If nothing else, she'd see to it that her and her mum were OK now. As soon as she got her money back, she'd see they were all okay.

A key turned in the lock at the foot of the stairwell.

Her heart skipped a beat before pounding.

Despite the shadows of the recess below, she'd recognise him anywhere.

Nate stepped onto the bottom step, fully in view, and gazed up at her.

Her pulse raced. She remained rooted to the spot. She couldn't take her eyes off him. He'd never looked more handsome, dressed in an open-necked black shirt and dark jeans. There was something about his stance too, his composure – something authoritative, controlled, decisive. But there was nothing sexier or more entrancing than the look in his eyes as they remained locked on hers.

His ascension up the steps was relaxed but focused as Ember promptly rose to her feet to greet him.

She wasn't going to say anything. It was time he did the talking. It was time he let her know how he felt.

But seemingly Nate wasn't in the mood for talking either.

Rarely had she backed away from him, but she retreated a little then – not only to give him space to join her, but also in anticipation of what he would do next.

He reached for both her hands simultaneously. She knew he would feel them trembling, but it didn't put him off. Instead, there was the subtlest, almost undetectable, upwards curve of his lips as if he was not deterred in the slightest by her anxiety.

Palm-to-palm, he interlaced their fingers. He pressed her back against the wall, caused her breath to snag as he did the same with her hands, pinning them either side of her shoulders.

Behind slightly parted lips, he dabbed one of his extra incisors with the tip of his tongue, reminding her of exactly what he was.

And she felt not an iota of fear. Even as she gazed into his mix-matched irises that had terrified her as a child, she felt nothing but her pounding heart, the heat burning in the pit of her abdomen, his cool hands firmly holding hers, the wall against her back.

And as his lips finally closed over hers, her heart stopped. Damp heat rushed to the apex of her thighs, thighs that he parted with his own.

He slid her hands together above her head, holding them there with one of his as he freed his other to gently clasp her jaw.

The tenderness and depth of his kiss, his cool, firm, adept tongue, made her lose sense of the space around her; made her momentarily forget where she was, what she was doing.

'Last chance,' he said, almost in a whisper, as he pulled his lips back from hers just a little.

'You're not getting away from me that easily,' she replied.

He smiled – a playful, dark, lethally masculine smile. 'I could say exactly the same about you.'

Her stomach flipped.

Seconds later, he'd snapped the fragile band of her knickers, had unfastened his jeans and lowered his shorts.

Still holding her wrists pinned above her head, his free hand clasped the back of her thigh, lifting it outside of his.

He was neither tender nor brutal as he entered her – just enticingly forceful, deftly balancing his desire with her ability to take him. And she gasped at every inch of his slow but unrelenting penetration until he filled her to the hilt, his lips as breathless against hers as hers were against his.

His playful nip of her lower lip followed by another enticing hint of a smile in his eyes was the final push for her to relax.

He released her hands only to lower her onto her back on the floor beneath him, one hand clasped to the nape of her neck in the process, the other still holding the back of her thigh to keep hers parted around his.

The cool air of the stairwell caressed her bare breasts as he ripped the front of her dress open, tore the fragile band between the cups of her bra.

His hands were even cooler as he slid them both simultaneously down her neck, her shoulders, both her breasts, his thumbs sweeping across her hardened nipples on his way down to clutch her hips to move her into the position he wanted her in.

He pinned her hands to the floor either side of her shoulders again. He lowered his head to look to where he was still buried inside her.

He gazed back into her eyes, deep into her eyes as he withdrew only to enter her again and again, causing her breath to snag repeatedly at the sensation.

He found his rhythm alongside finding hers, her abdomen

clenching in response, her wet heat that now coated him allowing him inside her with increasing ease so that her discomfort subsided amidst her growing pleasure.

And as his tongue, as his mouth, found each breast, each nipple in turn on his journey to her collarbone, to her neck, she couldn't stop looking at him. Couldn't stop taking in the hunger behind his kisses and licks and nips, the escalating need behind his deeper, harder thrusts.

If she wanted to change her mind, she knew it was then. If she wanted him to stop, she knew that was her last chance to ask.

But the moment escaped her no sooner had she thought it.

He licked her first, right along her artery, as if she was coated in something sweet.

She felt her breath shudder. She clenched her hands in his.

'I'd like to be able to reassure you it's not going to hurt,' he said softly against her ear, his cool breath caressing her lobe.

She instantly tensed.

Nate didn't linger.

His bite was controlled, steady, but deep and unrelenting as if he was savouring every moment of it. But the intensity of the pain of it was like one she had never known.

She jolted. He didn't suppress her from crying out, her voice echoing around the shadows of the solitary stairwell. Neither response put him off.

As he fed, she could feel the blood being drawn backwards through her veins, her heart aching a little, her extremities feeling numb. But she could focus only on him inside her – buried deep in her sex, his rhythm increasing along with his feed.

Sensations like none she had ever felt consumed her body. Her mind emptied. The tiniest of prickles danced over her skin, caressing every inch of her. She felt the tension hit. She felt her abdomen clench. Her orgasm made her cry out again, created sparks behind her eyes as she squeezed them shut; as she felt him come into her as he drew her blood into him.

Never had she felt more complete. Had never felt more sated as her body fell lax in his arms.

The sensation of his incisors leaving her skin again was just as painful, even in her languidness, appeased only by the look in his eyes as they locked on hers again.

As he subtly licked the remains of her blood from his lips, it was anything but repulsion she felt. And as he lowered his lips to hers again, the metallic taste was anything but disconcerting too.

His kiss was tender, reassuring, before he gently withdrew, rolled onto his back beside her.

She closed her dress over her. Pressed her knees together. Lay staring up at the ceiling as the minutes crept past.

He reached for her hand. He held it against the floor between them. He interlaced their fingers again.

It was an affection that made her smile. A connection that reassured her everything was going to be just fine.

'What are you thinking about?' he asked a few minutes later.

She turned her head to look at him. 'Where we go from here. You?'

That pensive frown was back. 'How easy it'll be to knock through our bedroom walls and make it one apartment.'

She lifted herself onto her elbow as she turned on her side to face him. She couldn't help but smile as warmth flooded her. 'You don't waste any time, do you? Anyway, it's a bit presumptuous. I don't even know your surname yet.'

He brushed a few loose strands of hair away from her eyes, his gleaming in a way she had never seen as he gazed deep into hers. 'It's Haven,' he said. 'Nate Haven.'